Island Experience

Experiences: Book 7

Kink and Pink in a Tropical Paradise

Simone Freier

OTK Publications
www.OTKPublications.com

Island Experience

EXPERIENCES: BOOK 7

By Simone Freier

Published by OTK Publications
http://otkpublications.com

ISBN: 978-1-942054-18-4
v1.5

Manufactured in the United States of America

COVER DESIGN BY OTK PUBLICATIONS

This is a work of fiction. All names, characters, and incidents in this work are fictitious. Any resemblance to actual events, or to real persons is purely coincidental. No humans or animals were harmed during the creation of this work.

Caution: This work contains mature content, including graphic sexual descriptions and scenes, and is provided for adults only. Neither the author nor the publisher intend to encourage or promote any of the activities depicted in this work. Many of the specific activities and scenarios described in this work can potentially be dangerous, and should not be attempted without special knowledge or training and, as appropriate, use of sterile single-use supplies. No information contained herein is intended to constitute advice or serve as instructional material, and this work should not be relied upon to ensure safe practices in real life.

Table of Contents

CHAPTER 1: TRIPPING OUT

The flowers were in full bloom and the sky clear, a gentle breeze caressing my body, as I sat on the side of the pool, my legs dangling in the sparkling water. Sam's backyard – *our* backyard – was beautiful, the black-bottomed pool framed by an aggregate walkway and some huge boulders, surrounded by the bright green lawn, and bordered by more boulders and flower beds.

Huge trees created a park-like feel and, as I gazed up into the branches, I realized that tiny lights were still strung around them. Tiki torches created an island feeling, and I chuckled as I gazed across the lawn at a large flat-topped boulder that had been the scene for some of our recent play with my friends.

Sam had pushed them once again, and Julie, Linda and Kathy had responded with enthusiasm and surprising openness. But my friends had experienced a lot, since we'd had my birthday party eleven months ago. The backyard looked the same now as it had then, but we'd all changed – not just my friends and I, but Sam, also: And, not just growing much closer – even intimate – but becoming more open, more trusting, and more loving.

It was hard to believe that I'd lived with Sam for six months, now. We were still deeply in love with each other. Sam was a unique guy; well, that was a real euphemism! Although he was twice my age, he was in great shape, quite handsome in fact, with only a few silver-tinged hairs above his ears revealing his chronological age. Sam had incredible enthusiasm and amazing stamina – in the bedroom, and out.

I shook my head, as I remembered a few of our sexual experiences with each other – from our first lovemaking down in the playroom, with the rose petal path and a multitude of candles flickering; to our attempts at achieving some of the Kama Sutra positions; to some very romantic lovemaking in Europe.

But our relationship was about much more than sex; we had challenged each other with an unbelievable array of kinks and fetishes, including spankings – often climaxing in some of the most incredible orgasms I'd experienced.

And then there was Sam's obsession with medical exams and devices: From rectal insertions and enemas to injecting saline into each other's butts. I shook my head again, thinking how open and adventurous my friends had been just a week ago.

It had gone far beyond being good sports: Sam had pushed them to their limits. I couldn't help but chuckle again, as I remembered thinking after my birthday party that there must be nothing more that Sam could do to challenge my friends – putting them in embarrassing situations, and seeing how they responded.

I couldn't have imagined how my perspective would change; *all* of our perspectives! And, I also couldn't have imagined the friends I had thought I'd known well for more than a decade 'playing' with us as they had. We'd found that Linda was turned on by spanking scenes, and I'd discovered that I was turned on by other women; at least a few other women, like Julie and Fiona.

We'd met Fiona, and her aunt – Sam's neighbor – Alex, at the pond that first long weekend I'd stayed with Sam. Fiona, with her ginger hair and petite body, had proven to be a really hot woman! We'd had a steamy scene in the playroom bed. That was after I'd had my first girl-on-girl sex experience with Julie.

Sam and I had been incredibly turned-on by watching Julie masturbate, as she lay across Sam's lap after he'd given her a sample spanking ... just after he'd given Linda a birthday spanking! That had also been during the first long weekend I'd spent with Sam.

Linda, the usually conservative one in our group, had demonstrated her sexual side, and her openness to new adventures, many times, over the past ten months. She was probably twenty pounds overweight, but had a unique personality – not quite 'vivacious', but always slinging barbed comments that had kept us in stitches.

I had never laughed so much as over the past year with Sam and my friends. Things were going well – my relationship with Sam, the research project for my Ph.D., and my newfound interest in domination and submission. The amazing thing was that we'd all submitted to each other.

Sam had always had fantasies of being the 'top' – the dominant in a relationship; but he had also submitted to me, both when he'd screwed-up a few times and I'd punished him, and when I'd wanted to take the dominant role. Sam got turned on either way: He was a 'switch'.

When we had visited the dominatrix in London, it became clear that I was truly the dominant one 'in the family'. Elena had invited me back for a month-long training session that I'd thought would be this summer. But she had recently informed me that she would not be available, and I'd decided to focus on my research project, and leave the domme course for another time.

I wondered whether that would ever happen – because I was both finishing my education and embarking on a career in biotech. Sam and I had formed a company to develop and commercialize the technology that was the subject of my dissertation, and the inventions that I'd come up with during our Europe trip. I probably wouldn't have time for anything else ... for several years.

And Sam had been hurt when Elena had selected me for more attention; he certainly wasn't a 'macho' man, but his fantasies were rooted in his self-image as a 'dom'. Perhaps it would be better for our relationship, if I didn't go to London to be trained?

But Sam had never stood in the way of my own desires. In fact, he had supported me fully in my education, my career goals, and our personal exploration of D/s. As my friends had recently agreed, Sam was a 'sweet' guy, even though he had spanked us, 'played doctor' with us, and pushed us to our limits.

My friend Julie had thought that *she* was the 'wild' one, shocking everyone around her with her outrageous pranks, her openness, and her outgoing personality. But Sam had brought Julie to her knees – which she may have enjoyed, but which showed her that she was not the most shocking or open among us.

Kathy, who we all had thought was the most open person – having been raised by 'hippie' parents, going often to nude beaches, and having some serious boyfriends, had been least interested in Sam's fetishes. Her background precluded seeing spanking as a sensual or sexual experience, and her fear of needles had limited her appreciation of Sam's medical fetishes.

Despite this, Kathy had been a trooper, participating in our 'submission training' ... up to a point. The nice massage that Sam had given Kathy – and his offer of taking us all to Hawaii – had softened the experience we'd recently had together.

Sam's concept of BDSM had nothing to do with sadism or masochism, and we'd done no bondage – such as shibari or kinbaku (the subject of a book Kathy had given Sam for his birthday). And, it wasn't really even about domination. Sam was turned-on by submission: A female voluntarily submitting to something embarrassing or painful, just because he wanted her to.

And Sam was willing to take the submissive role, if not to get turned on, then to make me happy. We'd given Sam a wild birthday party. Well, it hadn't been quite as wild as the one he'd given me nearly a year ago; but Sam had submitted to many things, demonstrating his own openness with my friends.

However, as I'd found, Sam had his own hang-ups. With all his sensual fetish play – and his talent at masturbating women to incredible orgasms – he had been hung-up about having actual sex, which he defined as the sharing of body fluids. During my first experience with Sam, he hadn't even wanted us to eat or drink after each other!

It was the morning after my birthday 'slumber party', when my friends had gone down on Sam, that he'd begun to accept intimate contact with other people. He had seen the worst of the AIDS problem in the 1980's, and had pointed out numerous times that there were still incurable sexually-transmitted diseases, such as herpes and hepatitis.

Sam had insisted that my friends and I get HPV and hepatitis vaccinations, and had enjoyed watching us take our shots – something that definitely turned him on.

Since then, we'd had a ménage with Julie, Sam had had sex with Linda after her schoolgirl spanking scene, and we'd had oral sex with Henk and Zöe – his friends in The

11

Netherlands, and with Fiona and her fiancé Justin. Sam had come a long way over the past year!

We had become incredibly close with my three friends, almost a relationship of polyamory. But we saw them as 'intimate friends' more than 'lovers', and they knew that although Sam and I might share ourselves with them, occasionally, our relationship with each other was strong and resilient.

Sam sometimes joked that he might lose me to a woman, but he knew that my love for him would surpass any short-term infatuation I might have with Julie, Fiona, or anyone else. Despite our age difference.

My parents had finally begun to accept Sam as my partner, and our families had enjoyed a friendly, more than cordial, Christmas dinner together. Although the dinner had been strained by my parents' (mostly, my father's) shock by – and disdain for – one of Sam's sons, who happened to be gay.

I smiled, thinking that it would be unlikely that I'd ever move back in with my parents, as my father had converted the apartment over the garage into his 'man cave'. Well, I didn't plan on living with my parents any longer. Sam had shown me a lifestyle of high standards and an appreciation for fine things – from relationships, to wine and food, to travel. Not to mention openness and trust.

It was late afternoon, and my stomach growled, so I decided to go downstairs to the playroom to check with Sam on our dinner plans; and, to see how he was doing with the arrangements for our trip to Toronto, to attend Fiona and Justin's wedding. I wondered how I would ever finish my research and write my dissertation, with all the travel Sam was planning for us.

Kelly came down the stairs, bounding into the playroom and over to my desk. Her long auburn hair – falling below her waist – swung behind her, but her firm breasts barely bounced. We had both lost the weight we'd gained in Europe and over the holidays, and Kelly looked again like an athlete, the taut muscles of her long legs outlined clearly, and her stomach firm – with no visible flab or fat.

It had been more than a year since we'd re-met at her parents' party, but I still could not get over her beauty – my heart palpitating, and my breath catching, as she sat down on one of the two chairs facing the desk.

Kelly's hazel eyes sparkled, and the smooth skin of her face shone, as she smiled at me. "How are you doing with the travel planning?" She settled into the chair, and looked into my eyes, once again melting me, and scattering my thoughts.

I took a deep breath, and finally responded, "Well, we have a few decisions to make." Kelly cocked her head, and I explained, "I feel like I'm going to be doing travel planning for the next week or two. We have our trip to Toronto in a few weeks ... and our trip to Hawaii. And I'm finding both of them challenging."

Kelly nodded, and I continued, "I haven't planned much for the Hawaii trip, yet – other than making a rough itinerary listing all the things I'd like to share with you and your friends. As I had suspected, it should really be a two-week trip, if you guys can take off that much time."

Now for the difficult part: "And after checking with the airlines and looking at the condo and house rentals, it would be much better if we could schedule the trip for the first two weeks of September, rather than the last two of August." I held my breath, knowing that Kelly had to get back to school around that time.

Kelly smiled, "Well, that sounds OK. I'm finished with all my seminar classes, so only have to complete the research project." Then, she frowned, "But I don't know how I'm going to get it done, with everything we have planned." I had told her that it would probably take at least another year, but she was anxious to get her degree and focus on the biotech business we had started.

"That's great, Kelly. Maybe you could check with Julie, Linda and Kathy and make sure they're also available. Then, I can firm up the dates and make some reservations." Kelly nodded.

As I looked at the itinerary that was now on the computer screen, I realized that we would all have to get into condition for some of the 'challenges' of the trip; the physical challenges. Looking up at Kelly, I said, "I really would like us to spend two or three days camping, but we'll have to hike a world-class trail."

Kelly nodded and smiled, but she had no idea what that entailed. "It's only a 12-mile hike, but there's about 3,000 feet of elevation gain and loss, and I'm not sure we're all in shape to make it. Especially Linda." I chuckled, "I'm not even sure *I* can make it, without getting into better shape."

Looking at me skeptically, Kelly asked, "Can't we get there another way – for example, by car, or horse?"

I laughed, "No, Kelly. The Kalalau coast of Kauai is very rugged, and has a narrow, winding trail that's only accessible by foot. It *is* possible to get there by boat, but it can't land – so we would all have to swim ashore. I was thinking of having a boat pick us up at the end, so we would only have to hike the trail once."

It did make more sense to just go there and back by boat, but Kelly and her friends would miss out on an incredible hiking experience. Well, that could always be a backup plan. We would be hiking the first two miles of the trail to Hanakapiai beach, and then another two miles to the waterfall, so that would be a good test, before we attempted to conquer the full hike to Kalalau.

I knew several people with boats that could potentially drop us off, and decided it would be prudent to schedule a boat; if we hiked the trail, then the boat could drop off some supplies – and much better food than we could bring by backpacking. And, if necessary, the boat could drop us off, avoiding the trail altogether.

"I'll make backup plans, but we should all get in shape, anyway. Maybe you can suggest that to your friends?" I gave Kelly a smirk, "And, perhaps you and I should start doing some jogging? We could run in the morning, before you go to the lab."

Kelly nodded slowly, "That sounds OK ... but it will take even more time away from my research."

I countered, "Well, you might have more time than you thought." Kelly looked at me inquisitively, and I explained, "I know you had your heart set on taking the domme class in London this summer, and I thought we might fly there after Fiona and Justin's wedding, in early July. But all the flights seem to be packed, and even the better hotels are already booked."

Giving Kelly a sheepish look, I apologized, "It's only a month away. I guess we should have started planning our summer travel earlier." Being an elite member of several airline clubs, I was pretty sure I could get flights, especially if our schedule was flexible. But early July would be a challenge.

Kelly's mouth dropped open, and it seemed that she was stunned. I was sorry to disappoint her; perhaps the domme course could be rescheduled for later in the summer? But now I realized that Kelly was not upset; she gave me a smile that melted my heart, again.

I was amazed that Sam had tried to book flights to London for the domme training. He had been upset that Elena had chosen me, and had implied that Sam was not dom material. I also knew that Sam was bothered by the fact that the course would be sponsored by a wealthy benefactor, with whom I would have an 'experience' at the end of the training.

But we both understood that I would be the dominant one, and that there would be no sex involved. I had already 'dominated' one man – Max – when we'd visited the sex club in Amsterdam. So Sam's concern wasn't valid, and I suspected that he was mainly upset by the prospect of me becoming a domme, and making *him* submit.

Of course, that was silly – we both submitted to each other, and our relationship would not change, just because I'd taken a course. In fact, our 'play' would probably be safer, and get even more interesting ... although it was hard to imagine how much more 'interesting' it could be: Sam and I had done more things than imaginable.

Well, at least more things than *I* could ever have imagined. Sam had a very fertile imagination, and seemed able to come up with a continuous string of new challenges for me and my friends.

"Sam, I haven't told you ..." Now Sam cocked *his* head, as I continued, "I e-mailed Elena, and she won't be able to teach the course this summer. She suggested that next spring would be more feasible."

It now dawned on me: With the domme training on hold, and the Hawaii trip delayed until September, I would have nearly the entire summer to work on my research project! I knew that I could get a lot done – with no classes or other interruptions ... except a short run every morning.

"I think this might work out very well: I can be in the lab nearly all of July and August. I don't feel so guilty, anymore." Of course, I would need to check with Raj, my advisor; but it seemed like a good plan. I would throw myself into my research, and begin writing my dissertation. If the lab work went smoothly, I could imagine finishing by the end of the year.

I knew Sam would consider that very optimistic, and decided to move on to the next subject. "So how are the plans coming for our Toronto trip?"

Sam nodded, and sat back in his executive chair, "I had originally hoped that we could go to Fiona's wedding, and then drive to Montreal and Quebec, then down through Maine and New Hampshire, ending in Boston, and flying home from there." I nodded, remembering Sam's rough description of the trip.

He continued, "But that would be a lot of driving, and I wanted to keep the trip to a week; that was so that you could get to London in time for the course. But, as I looked at all the things we could do near Toronto, I decided that it would be much easier – and probably more fun – to make a week trip just in the area."

I asked, "Would we still be going to Niagra Falls?" Sam had originally wanted to start with that, and then drive to Toronto for the wedding.

Sam responded, "Yes. Actually, I think it will work out better if we fly into Toronto, go to the wedding, and then go to Niagra Falls. There was only one challenge, but with my clout with some of the big hotel chains, I think I've solved it."

There were *always* challenges; not just the external ones, but many that Sam created for himself. But he was usually victorious ... like getting a hotel room within walking distance of the Oktoberfest, when everything was sold out anywhere near Munich. "So, tell me." I awaited the explanation of the problem Sam had faced and solved.

Sam smiled broadly, "Well, the timing – going to Fiona's wedding, then doing our exploring – will put us in Niagra Falls on July fourth, Independence Day: There is a huge fireworks display over the falls! And I guess everyone's traveling this summer, because all the hotels are fully booked."

Sam leaned forward, putting his arms on the desk, and I saw a twinkle in his eye. He grinned, "Somehow, I managed to get us a suite overlooking the falls!" Then, he gave me a curious look, and continued, "But part of the deal was that we would stay for at least four nights."

"I thought we would just be there for a day, looking at the falls. Is there enough to do, if we stay there that long?"

Sam was nodding, "I've found some neat things for us to do – pretty adventurous." That surprised me, as Sam was an adventurous person, and I couldn't imagine anything at a tourist site that would be exciting enough for him. But I trusted Sam; he had put together an incredible trip through Europe, and I was sure he would surprise me on our upcoming 'wedding' trip.

Sam concluded, "So we can fly back on July 5, and you can work the rest of the summer in the lab. If you want to."

Now, I was nodding, "Yes, Sam. I'm looking forward to finishing my research; so we'll have a product for KS Biotech to develop and sell."

I chuckled, "And you have plenty of time for travel planning. The only thing we have coming up – in a week – is Linda's birthday."

Sam nodded, "Shall we take her to the French restaurant? That's where she ate last year, with Julie."

Yes, that had been during our long weekend together; and the French restaurant is where Sam had first met Linda and Julie. "That sounds like a good idea," I said. "I'll talk to Linda. Maybe she would like to come over for a little skinny-dipping and lying around the pool, first?"

Then, I gave Sam a mock-serious look, "And we'll have to work on our all-over tans before we go on our island vacation!" Sam smiled and nodded, but I continued before he could comment, "Kathy's in Mexico again, with her parents; she's *already* working on her tan."

Sam reached into his pants, and I wondered what he was thinking that was obviously getting him turned on. Perhaps our recent weekend of submission challenges for my friends? Or our upcoming trip to a tropical island with them? Or, possibly just Linda's birthday.

I smiled, "And, Sam ... you *don't* have to plan a big party for Linda! No games or challenges, OK?"

Sam grinned, and looked sheepish again, "OK, Kelly. I wasn't planning anything." Then, he admitted, "I was just thinking about our schoolgirl roleplay with Linda ..."

So *that's* what he was getting turned on about! But I couldn't blame him: It had been an incredible day for all of us. I'd played the roles of student, school nurse, and headmistress. And, Sam and Linda had had their spanking fun, with a surprising 'happy ending' that I'd orchestrated.

My stomach growled again. "Shall we do some dinner planning now? I'm getting hungry."

Sam smiled at me, and shut down his computer. Then, he asked, "Shouldn't we get cleaned up, first? I'd sure like to bathe that beautiful body of yours!" I glanced down, and realized that I was still topless, and somewhat sweaty from sitting out by the pool.

I gave Sam a lascivious smile, knowing full well that our shower together would result in more than just getting us clean!

CHAPTER 2: BIRTHDAY GIRL

I had e-mailed my friends, asking them whether the first two weeks of September would work for the Hawaii trip, and also gently letting them know that they should get themselves into shape. I didn't know whether Kathy would get the e-mail during her trip, but she was very 'in shape', already.

Julie also kept herself trim, but I didn't know how active she was; we had to take Sam's word that the hiking could get difficult. But Sam was a man of his word, and we all trusted him.

Fortunately, he would be booking a 'backup' boat; it was Linda who we all knew would struggle on the trail, as she was carrying an extra twenty pounds of weight, and wasn't prone to doing heavy exercise.

But Linda had surprised me: When I called to invite her out on her birthday, she said that she had already planned to go on a diet … starting the day after her birthday. I wondered how far she would get with her weight loss, but this was the first time that I'd ever heard her seriously discuss dieting.

Linda was a very good-looking woman, with shoulder-length dark hair, and a beautiful face graced by fair skin, big lips, and penetrating brown eyes. She was big on top, her breasts shapely, and had wide hips and a large butt; if it were not for the extra pounds around her middle, she would be a very sexy lady.

I chuckled, realizing that she was *already* a very sexy lady, even with her plumpish figure. Linda had a great sense of humor, and had repeatedly demonstrated that she appreciated sensuality. She had few boyfriends, her most reliable date being a guy she called 'the shlub'.

Linda surprised me further by asking whether Sam would cook her birthday dinner, rather than going out to the French restaurant. She requested Italian, which was one of Sam's specialties, although Linda had only tasted his pizza. Sam was an excellent chef, and I was sure that he would enjoy the opportunity to cook for Linda.

When I offered to have her over for a pre-dinner pool party, Linda said she would be delighted to spend the day with us. Then came still another surprise when she said that she would make a list of her 'special requests' for the day.

Linda knew that Sam would want to give her a birthday spanking – this would be her second one; but she also knew that Sam might get carried away with other challenges for her. I assured her that I would keep Sam under control, the best I could, and Linda laughed, saying that her list would probably keep Sam both excited and subdued.

I wasn't sure what that meant, as Sam was seldom 'subdued' by anyone. Although, at Sam's recent birthday party, my friends and I had subjugated, if not subdued, him. I couldn't help but smile, remembering our 'pet play', turning Sam into the puppy 'Samo'; and then putting him into a diaper, as he became the baby 'Sammy'.

Linda said that she would come over around 1PM, and suggested that we also invite Julie, but have her come over a couple of hours later. I wondered what Linda had planned for her own birthday party ...

We had marketed, and I had completed all the preparations for making an Italian feast for Linda. The antipasto salad was ready to mix, the thick marinara sauce with sweet Italian sausage was already simmering on the stove, and the mushrooms were sliced for the veal marsala. A glass baking dish was in the fridge with what was to become roasted Brussels sprouts with fresh garlic.

Serving a five-course meal was a bit over-the-top – we probably didn't need the cheese plate that would be served before the dessert. I had originally planned on buying cannolis, but finally decided on some beautiful Napoleons, which I picked up at the pastry shop.

I hoped that Linda would not be disappointed that I hadn't bought a birthday cake, but we were all trying to get into shape, and didn't need leftover cake tempting us.

I went down to the playroom and entered the wine cellar, selecting a Pinot Grigio for our antipasto course, and an Amarone for the pasta and veal courses. I had some nice bottles of Brunello di Montalcino, but preferred them with steak.

Then, I decided to give the girls a wine tasting experience, so I also selected a Barolo that would go great with the pasta; it seemed too heavy for the veal, but would pair well with the fine Parmesano-Reggiano cheese. If anyone wanted white wine with the veal, the Pinot Grigio would work.

Then, I selected an Asti sparkling wine which would be an alternate for the cheese plate, and would go nicely with dessert. Once again, it seemed over-the-top ... but that was my style. There were five of us, after all, and I didn't want anyone to be thirsty. I just hoped we could all stay up for the presents and Linda's birthday spanking!

As I was putting the white wines in the fridge, the doorbell rang; Linda had already arrived.

Kelly and I greeted Linda with a big hug. Linda hugged Kelly, and gave me a quick peck on the lips. She handed me her overnight bag, and I ran up to the guest bedroom with it. As I came down the stairs, I heard Kelly laughing; she was holding a piece of paper, evidently still reading it, as Linda stood there smugly.

Looking at me, holding the paper up, and still laughing, Kelly announced, "Linda has made a list of some activities she would like during her birthday party." That's interesting! I had no idea what she would request, other than relaxing by the pool, having an Italian dinner, and – of course – taking her birthday spanking.

I smiled and nodded. Then, Kelly elaborated, "There are a few 'submission challenges' for you on the list." Kelly and Linda chuckled, and I raised my eyebrows theatrically. I ushered Linda into the kitchen, and offered her a drink, as we sat at the breakfast table.

As I poured Diet Cokes for each of us, Linda looked up at me with her big brown eyes, and said, "Thank you, Sam, for letting me celebrate my birthday here. And, for offering to make dinner for us." I nodded again, and she smiled, "There are really just a couple of things on the list that I thought would be fun (for me, that is), if you're willing to demonstrate your openness."

I couldn't imagine what Linda had in mind, except perhaps having another schoolgirl spanking experience. "Linda, you guys have been open with me ... especially the last time you came over. If there's something special that I can do to make you happy today, that would be fine."

Linda, smiling sweetly at me, said "Thank you, Sam. Actually, the challenges are based on some of the things we did last time ... and during the schoolgirl role-play we did together." Linda glanced at Kelly, and added, "I suggest that we start the party with those, before Julie arrives."

Linda smiled at Kelly, and Kelly smiled back at Linda, then rose, "I'll start getting things ready ..." Kelly bent down and gave me a kiss on the cheek, then went down the stairs towards the playroom. Now, I wondered whether Linda wanted me to 'take her' over the desk, as we'd done as a climax to the schoolgirl role-play.

"What else is on your list for the party?" I didn't see the paper, but wanted to be prepared for whatever Linda had planned.

"Oh, not much," Linda began, "other than the dinner, and my birthday spanking." We both laughed, then Linda added, "But Sam, if you wouldn't mind, I'd love to get a massage today. Kathy couldn't stop raving about the one you gave her the last time we were all here."

I nodded, "Of course, Linda! I'd love to give you a massage." I really enjoyed giving massages, probably as much as those receiving them, although it did require a concentrated effort, and quite a bit of energy. It would be good exercise.

Linda leaned over and kissed me on the other cheek, then batted her eyelashes, "And, you can give me a 'happy ending', if you're up for it." Linda knew that I was *always* 'up' for it. I sat back and smiled, realizing that today would be another interesting experience with Kelly's friends.

Just as I was beginning to relax and enjoy the prospect of Linda's birthday party, Linda stood, took my hand, and pulled me out of my seat. "Well, then I guess we should get started!" I still didn't know exactly what we would be starting, but I was ready.

We walked down the stairs and my stomach flip-flopped, as I saw the open door, and light coming from the exam room. I guess I had stopped on the stairs, as Linda was now pulling me toward my fate, whatever it might be.

We stepped just inside the exam room, where Kelly was obviously making preparations. Linda said, "Get undressed, Sam, and onto the table."

As I slowly removed my Hawaiian shirt, shorts, and underwear, I wondered what Linda had planned. I didn't have to wait long: I sat on the edge of the exam table, and Linda explained, "As I said, there are only a couple of things I'd like to do ... or have you do; things that were surprising, or shocking, to me."

Linda turned to Kelly, and chuckled, "Although I guess nothing should surprise me anymore. Sam really is perverted, you know!" Kelly was nodding, a huge smile on her face. My mind was a blur, trying to think of what might have shocked Linda, as we had done so much. I would have thought she wasn't shocked by much we did, anymore.

"The first shock was when I came over for the schoolgirl role-play ... and suddenly was sitting on this exam table, being told that I would be getting a shot." I closed my eyes, now knowing where this would lead.

"But, Linda, it was *Kelly* who gave you the shot, not me." I realized I had said this in a whining tone.

Linda shook her head, "I know who came up with all this stuff." Then, she smiled, "And the second thing will require some preparation ... so why don't you get in a knee-chest position for me?" Uh oh ... 'preparation'? I hoped it wasn't what I thought it would be.

I got into the knee-chest position, and felt one of the large butt plugs against my anus. Linda moved it around slowly, gradually inserting its length into me, as its width dilated my sphincter. Once again, I had to pause to wonder how our relationship with Kelly's friends had progressed to this point. Of course, I realized, it had been mostly due to my own pushing.

But now, Linda was pushing – hard – and the butt plug entered me fully.

Linda said, "OK, Sam, you can lie down, now. You're going to get a nice, big shot." I glanced over at Kelly, who was handing the syringe to Linda, and could immediately discern that she had prepared a 6cc shot, with a large needle. I put my head into the pillow and closed my eyes.

Linda was swabbing me, and then the now-familiar feeling of cold steel penetrating my butt. I had agreed not to ask Kelly's friends to take any more shots, but I guess Linda didn't feel that applied to me. I tried to relax, as I felt the pinching of the saline being injected.

It was obvious that Linda was taking her time, drawing out this procedure; but I took it like a man – without whimpering or groaning (as Kelly would point out I was prone to doing). Linda pulled the needle out, and commented, "That was fun. And good practice. Maybe, I should give you one on the other side?"

Now, I felt like groaning, but before I could respond, Kelly said, jauntily, "Maybe he'll let you give him a second shot, if you'll let him give you one?"

Linda closed her eyes, and shook her head, "I'm not particularly interested in getting a shot on my birthday." Then, seeing me look up at her from the exam table, she said, "But, if Sam really wants, I guess I could do that."

Suddenly, it was up to me. As much as I like to 'play doctor', I wasn't anxious to take another shot. It was tempting to call Linda's bluff, and make her take a shot. But, I finally decided to let us both off the hook. "Linda, seeing as it's your birthday, and all, maybe we should just quit now?"

Linda chuckled, "Thanks, Sam, for not pushing too hard." Then, she added, "And you were right – it was Kelly who gave me the shot, so maybe *she* should be the one to get her comeuppance now?" Kelly smiled at Linda, but the discussion ended there. My thoughts were now focused on what else Linda would ask of me, today.

Kelly said, "Sam, why don't you turn over onto your back, and scoot down, so we can put your legs in the stirrups? That will make it easier." Make *what* easier?!??

As I got myself into position, Linda said, "I guess he'll only need one enema. But it should be a big one." Once again, my stomach did a flip-flop. So *that's* what Linda wanted: To see me take a big enema, as I'd made her (and Julie and Kathy) do, during their last experience here.

Kelly prepared the solution, hanging the large bag from one of the IV poles. Then, she rummaged around in the drawers opposite the exam table. When she turned around, she was holding up the *Bardex* – the same enema system I had used on her friends. Now, I groaned.

Linda stepped between my legs, and took the device from Kelly, as Kelly explained the procedure. First, the tip, along with the deflated balloon, had to be inserted into my rear; then, Linda would pump up the balloon to retain the device in my rectum.

It took her some time to insert the device, and I let out a loud 'Ow!' when she pumped the bulb to inflate the balloon. Then, she pumped the other bulb, and the exterior balloon inflated, locking the device in place. Kelly explained how to connect the tubing from the bag, and open the valve. Warm saltwater was now flowing slowly into me.

Kelly whispered to Linda, and Linda nodded; it sounded like Kelly would be going out to Linda's car to 'get things ready'. I closed my eyes again, now realizing that my ordeal might not be over, yet.

My eyes flew open, and I looked down my body, as Linda began stroking my manhood with the flat of her hand. "I'm not turned on, Linda ... and I'm not sure I *can* get turned on with the water flowing into me."

Linda chuckled, and said, "Why don't you try?" She continued to stroke me, and despite my brain saying no, my other head was cooperating with Linda. Soon, her fingers were curled around my growing length, and I let my head sink into the pillow and closed my eyes again.

As I fantasized about Linda giving Kelly a shot, and then taking a shot from me, I forgot about the enema. Linda's 'manual labor' was working, and I realized I was on the brink of an orgasm. I briefly wondered whether Linda would finish me with her mouth, but she continued stroking, now making spiraling motions with both hands.

My eruption burst forth, spewing hot liquid up my stomach and onto my chest. My mind was a blur, but I had the fleeting thought that neither Linda, nor Kelly's other friends, had watched me come before. Maybe they had, but I couldn't concentrate enough to remember when.

Linda was now cleaning me with a moistened paper towel, and I glanced at the enema bag, happily surprised to see that it was nearly empty. Thankfully, Linda closed the valve and disconnected the tubing, then deflated the balloons and carefully pulled the *Bardex* out of me, putting it into the exam room sink.

She helped me up, and walked me into the bathroom. I had assumed that she would want to watch, but she walked to the door, turned, and announced, "Please come up to the backyard when you're finished, Sam. Then, you'll have your last challenge." She pulled the door shut, as the first flood issued from my rear.

I was now pretty sure I knew what Linda had planned – something that would probably be embarrassing, even after all that we'd done. I groaned again. But I had made Linda, Julie and Kathy 'perform' for me, and it was only fair that Linda ask me to reciprocate. The girls hadn't complained, and I was determined not to, either.

Linda came out to the backyard, just as I was finishing the preparations. That included bringing a gallon of milk from her car, putting a towel on the flat-topped boulder, and setting a flower on the lawn each foot from the boulder.

Linda was wearing a summer shift, her figure thick and straight, and I wondered again whether she would actually lose weight before our Hawaii trip. Then, I wondered how difficult the trail on Kauai would really be; it was twelve miles long, but Sam had also said there were a lot of ups and downs along the way.

I smiled at Linda, and she shook her head. "If you had told me a year ago that I would be sticking Sam with needles and giving him an enema, I would have thought you were crazy. But with everything he's put us through, I wanted to see him take some of his own medicine."

Nodding, I said, "He likes to give more than receive. He doesn't like taking enemas, and I *know* he's not going to be comfortable on that boulder. If it weren't your birthday, he probably would have refused. At least it's only you and I here; that should make it somewhat easier for him."

The sliding door to the pool room slid open, and Sam came out, carrying a stack of towels that he dropped onto the glass-topped patio table. As he walked toward us, he was shaking his head. "Linda, do I really have to do this? Wasn't the enema enough?"

Linda said nothing, but led him to the boulder, and – trooper that he is – Sam got into a knee-chest position, his feet over the edge of the boulder, and his butt high in the air. Linda filled one of the huge syringes with milk from the bucket, and put the tip against Sam's rear. Then, she pushed the plunger, and the white liquid column shortened, until all the milk had disappeared inside Sam.

As Linda repeated the process, she said, "You should be able to squirt the milk farther than any of us. Maybe I should take the paddle to your rear, if you don't 'measure up' to our standards?" Sam groaned, but knew not to complain any more, lest Linda expand his challenge.

When four syringes of milk (about 24 ounces) had been injected into Sam's rear, Linda brought the bucket and syringe across the lawn to where I was sitting on the bench at the edge of the narrow, free-form, aggregate pool deck. "OK, Sam. We're going to give you the count down."

Together, Linda and I yelled '3', '2', '1', 'Now!' and, on-cue, Sam squirted the milk across the grass, hitting the sixth flower. I laughed, "Not bad, for your first try, Sam. But it only went about six feet. We know you can do much better than that!"

Linda walked behind Sam, and began filling him with milk again, this time with a couple of syringes of air in-between. And, once again, Sam squirted for us; but rather than a narrow stream, the milk exploded out of his rear in a wide fan, not even reaching four feet.

The third time, Linda filled Sam with eight syringes of milk, and no air. Then, she sat down on the bench next to me, and started chatting about her summer plans. Sam behaved well, only groaning once while he waited. Finally, we counted down, and Sam shot a stream of milk nearly ten feet. A record!

From behind us came a bellowing laugh, and we realized that Julie had arrived and let herself in. She walked out to us, and gave Linda a big birthday hug. Then, she gave me a small hug, and a big kiss. Finally, she walked around the boulder, and knelt so her face was at the level of Sam's. She held his cheeks, and gave him an even bigger kiss than she'd given me.

"That was quite a show, Sam! I had no idea that there would be entertainment at Linda's party."

Sam snarled exaggeratedly, and said, "I guess this is one of my birthday 'presents' to Linda; it's something she specifically requested."

Linda shouted, "And, we're not finished, yet!" As she walked over behind Sam, she instructed, "Let's see how you do lying on your back." Sam groaned again (I would have to get on his case about that), then turned over onto his back, with his legs pulled to his chest. Linda began injecting more milk into Sam's rear – at least six syringes.

Julie offered, "Let me help you, Sam." She pulled Sam's legs back, lifting his rear off the towel-covered boulder. Linda came back to the bench, but Julie continued to hold Sam's legs, as we counted down. This time, Sam squirted more than eight feet.

Julie asked, "Do I get a turn?" Linda chuckled and nodded, and she and Julie exchanged positions, Linda now holding Sam's legs, and Julie injecting the milk. I didn't see how many syringes Sam took, but it seemed like a lot. Julie came over to the bench, and the three of us counted down. Sam squirted a narrow stream that went at least ten feet, and seemed to never end.

He gave a final groan, and Linda let go of his legs. "Wasn't that fun?" Both Linda and Julie were hysterical, and I had to admit that it was a funny scene. I thought again about taking the domme class in eight or nine months, and coming home to Sam, my 'sex slave'.

We walked into the pool room, and the three of us got undressed, as I told Julie and Linda about our upcoming trip to Toronto and Niagra Falls. Sam related some of the activities that he'd already scheduled, and my friends were again impressed at the adventures we would be having.

While Julie, Linda and I were lying on the chaises, Sam went into the kitchen to continue his preparations for dinner.

I turned to my friends, more serious now, and informed them that Sam and I planned to start jogging together every morning, in preparation for the Kauai trail experience. I also told them that Sam wanted to be sure they were comfortable in the water, and knew the basics of snorkeling, including how to do a surface dive.

Both Julie and Linda had snorkeled before, but neither had been taught the fine points; neither had I. When Sam could finally take a break from cooking, he brought a huge duffel bag of masks, snorkels, and fins out to the pool.

He demonstrated how the snorkel is attached to the mask with a 'snorkel-keeper', and how the mask should fit – being able to stay on your face without using any straps. He also demonstrated some surface dives, jack-knifing until he was diving straight down to the bottom of the pool.

We all tried-on the equipment: Masks and snorkels, neoprene booties, and large fins – none of it fitting very well. Sam explained the difference between diving fins and body-boarding fins, and demonstrated 'clearing his ears' – which he said was an advanced technique that we might need if we tried to dive deeper than the water in the pool.

After we all had tried snorkeling and making some not-so-pretty surface dives, we sat on the chaises, as Sam provided more details about the trip.

"I've decided to bring you to Kauai in style, and have booked first class seats for all of us." Julie and Linda 'Oooh'ed' and 'Aaah'ed'. "And, before we leave, I'm going to take you guys to the only dive shop in town, and outfit you properly." Sam smiled, adding, "And, when we get to

Kauai, I'm going to buy you each an island-style dress at a small boutique on the north shore." More tittering from my friends; this was the first time I'd heard most of these things, also.

Sam continued, "And I have a special birthday present for Linda – which you," pointing to Julie, "and Kathy will also get for your birthdays." We all looked at each other, having no idea what the 'special' present would be. Sam concluded, "And, I'm going to take you guys to the camping store and buy each of you a pack that you can use on the trail." There were big smiles all around.

Sam had mentioned that the trip would be expensive – I recalled hearing the ridiculous figure of $15,000. I couldn't understand how a simple trip to Hawaii could cost so much ... until hearing everything that Sam planned to buy for us. And, I knew that he had booked a nice two-bedroom plus loft condo for the first week, and a private house for the second week.

Sam looked at Linda, "We can get started in about ten minutes, if you like." Linda nodded. When Sam went back into the kitchen to stir the pots, Linda explained that she had requested that Sam give her a massage. Now *that* was going to be a nice birthday present!

———————————

After making sure that nothing was burning, I went into the pool room, and got set-up for Linda's massage: Draping the table, getting a clean sheet to drape Linda, and putting the oils on the rolling metal stand. I went upstairs and put on a pair of running shorts and a tank top, then went out to the patio, and escorted Linda into the pool room.

The sliding doors were open, the massage table open to the fresh outside air. It was another beautiful summer day, not as warm as usual for June. Linda made a stop in the half-bath, and then got up onto the table. I began to drape her with the sheet, wondering whether she would prefer going *au naturel*. But she didn't say anything, so I decided to cover her with the sheet, as would any professional masseur.

Linda put her face into the hole in the table, and I turned down the sheet so that her back was exposed down to her waist. I squirted some oil into my hands, rubbed them together to warm them, then laid them on Linda's back, and leaned forward, pressing down, as my hands slid toward her waist. Linda moaned.

I gave Linda a full-body massage, taking my time and using all the techniques that Liz had taught me. After covering her legs, feet, and toes, I moved up to Linda's hips and large bottom. Using my thumbs, I pressed deeply into her flesh, stroking until each muscle relaxed.

I almost felt bad having to ask Linda to turn over onto her back, she was so relaxed. As she turned over, she smiled at me, then closed her eyes again as I re-draped her and began working on her ears, forehead, and neck, then moved down between and around her large breasts. Once again, my oily hands traveled down her body, massaging her legs and feet, then back up to her thighs.

Leaning over her, I gently kissed her forehead, and then her cheeks. Linda opened her eyes, and I asked, "Are you ready for your 'happy ending', now? Any special requests?" Linda nodded yes to the first question and shook her head to the second, closing her eyes again, as I moved to the foot of the table.

Putting my hands under her hips and bottom, I helped her scoot down the table, then took my position between her legs, draping them over my shoulders as I leaned forward and did one last 'massage' with my open hand over her genitals. Then, I went down on her in earnest, applying all of my oral skills: Sucking and lapping, nibbling and licking, exploring Linda's sensitive tissues with my tongue.

Linda responded nicely, gyrating her hips, and squeezing her legs rhythmically against my neck. As my mouth did it's magic, my hands clasped her hips, my fingers massaging deep into her tissues. Linda let out a couple of grunts, and then emitted a continuous soft moan, as her middle rose up to meet my ministrations.

I must have continued the attention on her clit too long, as she grabbed my hair, pulling my head up. Her motions abated, and I lifted her legs off my shoulders, and came around the massage table, running my hands along her sides, until they were holding her head. I bent down and gave Linda a lingering kiss, which she returned fully.

"Happy birthday, Linda." I lightly massaged her temples, my thumbs moving in opposing circles, as I rubbed her nose with mine, Eskimo style.

Her eyes opened, and she smiled up at me. "Thank you, Sam." Then, she chuckled softly, "It took a year to get a massage from you ... but it was worth the wait."

I said, seriously, "Linda, if you had told me you wanted a massage, I would have gladly offered you one anytime." Then, I laughed, "That reminds me of the old joke ..." Linda was smiling, and looked into my eyes questioningly.

"The couple was making out in his car, finally having sex for the first time. Afterward, the guy says, 'If I'd known you were a virgin, I would have taken more time.' The girl responds, 'If I knew you had more time, I would have taken off my panty hose!'" Linda laughed easily, and I helped her sit up on the table.

We walked out to the patio, where Kelly and Julie were lying on chaises, talking quietly. Linda beamed, "Sam really does give a good massage. What a nice birthday present!" Then, she frowned, "But, I guess I'll have to get showered before I join you guys out here."

I offered, "Now that I'm sweated up, I should get a shower, too. Maybe Linda will allow me to bathe her?"

As Linda nodded, Kelly and Julie sat up, and Kelly said, "I think we've had enough sun. Maybe Linda would allow all of us to bathe her?" Julie smiled, and Linda nodded again. We all made our way to the downstairs bathroom, and I got the shower going.

Despite the number of showers I'd taken with Kelly's friends, it was still fun for me – and, apparently, for the girls, too. We gave Linda a six-handed birthday shower, and then bathed each other, all of our bodies now squeaky clean.

The girls wrapped themselves in towels, and dispersed – Linda going up to the guest bedroom, Julie to the pool room, and Kelly and I up to the master bedroom – to get dressed. Back in the kitchen, I took the Pinot Grigio out of the refrigerator and opened it, put the Brussels sprouts into the oven, and started sautéing the mushrooms.

When Kelly came down, she set the dining room table and lit the candles. I mixed the antipasto salad and served it onto small plates, then poured the wine. I wouldn't be cooking the veal until the last minute, so we all sat down to enjoy our candlelight Italian dinner.

After the antipasto, I opened and poured the rich, dark Barolo, one of Italy's classic wines. The bottle was ten years old, and had a relatively high alcohol content. I explained the 'flight' of wines that we would be tasting, as I served the pasta.

"This wine, considered by some to be Italy's greatest, is made from Nebbiolo grapes, and grown on hillsides in the northwest of Italy." Everyone sipped a taste, and there were nods and smiles around the table.

Linda's eyes went to the ceiling, as she tasted the thick pasta sauce. "Sam, you can come over and cook for me, anytime!" Turning to Julie and Kelly, she added, "Sam's Italian flavors are better than you can get at any restaurant we have around here."

I laughed, "It might be easier if I were to teach you. Next time, you can come earlier, and we'll cook together." Then, a second thought popped into my head, "But only if you agree not to give me any more submission challenges."

We were all laughing, and Linda retorted, "Only if you don't give *us* any more challenges!" I just shook my head, knowing full well that I was already thinking of some 'challenges' for our island adventure.

As the girls talked about how they would pack for the trip to Kauai, I cleaned up the salad plates, and finished cooking the veal. Linda's eyes were wide, as I carried plates of veal and Brussels sprouts to the table. Then, there were a few groans, as I poured the Amarone into clean crystal glasses, setting them next to the Barolo glasses. We now each had three wines lined up in front of us.

I offered, "Actually, clothes for the trip should be easy: A couple of bathing suits, two or three pairs of shorts and tops, and maybe one dress. I'll be buying you special t-shirts and an island-style dress while we're there." Then, as an afterthought, "And, you should probably bring the pareos, also."

I visualized the four girls topless, with only a pareo around their waists, walking along a remote beach on the Na Pali coast. Most of the planning for the trip was done, and it was sure to be an epic experience for all of us.

Kelly and I brought the dirty plates and silver back to the kitchen, and put them into the dishwasher. Then, I walked into the dining room, opening the fourth bottle of wine. "Sam! Are you trying to get us drunk?" Julie's mouth was hanging open, her head shaking.

Chuckling, I answered, "I hope you guys *don't* get drunk or fall asleep! But I thought you might like to taste a variety of Italian wines. This one," holding up the bottle of sparkling white wine, "comes from the Piemonte region, just like the Barolo, but is made from white Muscat grapes. It's sweet – perfect for desserts – and low in alcohol. It's a sparkling wine, but made using a different method than that used to make Champagne."

I disappeared into the kitchen again, and prepared the cheese plates – a small sampling of a half-dozen of the more than 300 varieties of cheese made in Italy. Including Burrata, Gorgonzola, Pecorino, Parmigiano-Reggiano, Taleggio, and Provolone. There were more groans when I started setting the small cheese plates in front of the girls.

"Well, maybe we can have the dessert course later, out on the patio," I glanced at Linda, "along with the Asti ... unless Linda would prefer Champagne?" Linda just shook her head.

With everyone helping, the table and kitchen were cleaned up quickly, and we all retired downstairs to the playroom. Julie asked, "Are you going to show us some pictures of Kauai? The last time we were here, you showed us all the other islands." I remembered how emotional I had become, thinking about the many trips Sarah and I had taken to Kauai.

I used the remote to lower the large screen, found a set of pictures on the computer, and began projecting them. "Kauai is an almost-circular island, around 30 miles in diameter. In the center is Mount Wai'ale'ale, an extinct volcano, and the wettest spot on Earth. As I mentioned last time, it gets about a foot *per week* of rain."

I flipped through the slides, giving a tour of the island counterclockwise from the southwest side. "Here is Waimea Canyon, which Mark Twain called 'the Grand Canyon of the pacific'. From here, you can look down into Kalalau Valley – which is the destination of our long hike."

More pictures. "The west side is dry, but there's some good diving." I showed a few of my underwater shots of eels, sea turtles, and sharks. "The south side has some nice hotels, and is less rainy than the north shore, so is a popular vacation spot for people coming from the snow."

Flipping quickly, I showed some snapshots of Lihue, the biggest town, and Na'wili'wili harbor; then, up the east side, with the Wailua River and fern grotto. Around to the northeast shore, with Kapaa, Anahola and Aliomanu; then the north shore tour, starting at the Kilauea Lighthouse, and showing Secret Beach, Princeville, and Hanalei.

"Hanalei Bay is spectacular." I showed some pictures of sailboats anchored in the summer, and some beautiful sunsets. "That is where the movie '*South Pacific*' was filmed." It occurred to me that the girls may not have seen it, and that was confirmed when I asked them. "Well, maybe we should watch the movie tonight?"

Continuing on with the tour, I flipped through more images. "As you drive toward the end of the road at Kee (pronounced 'Kay-ay') Beach, you cross seven one-lane bridges, and it looks more and more lush. There are some great beaches on the north shore, and we'll visit quite a few of them." I showed pictures of Lumahai, Ha'ena, and Kee.

The last few pictures were of the Kalalau trail – Hanakapiai Beach and waterfall, and Kalalau Beach, where we would be camping. There were a lot of 'Oooh's and 'Aaah's' from the girls. The scenery was gorgeous.

It was still early, so we decided to watch '*South Pacific*' before opening the presents ... and giving Linda her birthday spanking. Kelly put on her 'birthday' tee, Linda donned the 'Paris' tee that we had brought back from Europe for her, both of them just wearing panties underneath. Julie took off her shorts, her tee barely long enough to cover her bikini underwear when she was standing.

The movie seemed funny to the girls, with its simple style and story; but they enjoyed the music. I couldn't help but get emotional a few times, but I didn't think anyone noticed.

I pointed out Mount Ha'ena, now called the 'Bali Hai Ridge', as it was used to create the fictional island in the movie; and, Black Pot Park and the pier on Hanalei Bay. Then, Lumahai Beach – of 'I'm gonna wash that man right outa my hair' fame. And the plantation house on the hill in what is now Princeville.

Next, came the birthday presents, although there were only two of them. Julie gave Linda a cute bracelet. And Kelly and I gave her a waterproof digital camera – one that she could use on the Kauai trip, both above and below the water. Linda thanked us with kisses. Then, she stood. "I guess I'm ready for my birthday spanking, now."

I had already read Linda's birthday party activity list, and knew that she wanted to preempt Sam from coming up with one of his bizarre challenges. She explained that she would take 100 spanks from Julie and from me, then go over Sam's lap for 26 swats with the paddle. Sam suggested that he use a leather paddle, which would sting, but was less serious than the Ping-Pong paddle.

Then, Linda blushed, and announced that, for the three final spanks, she would take hard swats with the school paddle, and she hoped that Sam would take her from behind, as he had done at the end of their schoolgirl role-play experience. Although Linda had envisioned bending over the desk, Sam suggested that she bend over the corner of the bed for the finale, to which Linda readily agreed.

Sam and I sat on the couch, while Julie took her place in the center of the loveseat. I noticed that Linda's hand was already under her tee. Julie patted her lap, and Linda took off her powder blue bikini underwear, pulled up her tee, and positioned herself across Julie's lap.

Linda turned her head to Julie, and whispered, "You may spank me hard, Julie. Please don't hold back." Julie shrugged, and smiled at us, then focused on Linda's large bottom. The first few spanks were tentative, but then Julie really got into it, spanking Linda hard, one spank every couple of seconds.

Before Julie had reached 50 spanks, Linda's right hand went under her. By the time Julie finished, Linda was panting loudly and rocking her hips, both her hands moving under her. Julie rubbed Linda's bum, then her hand slipped down, and she let two fingers slide into Linda.

It had been a year since Julie and Linda had first come over and met Sam, Linda taking a simple birthday spanking, and then Julie masturbating, as she lay across Sam's lap, having received a sample spanking herself. Now, Linda was masturbating, and she was every bit as sensual as Julie had been; perhaps even more so, as she bucked, and her head flipped from right to left and back again, her hair now a black blur.

There was no scream when she climaxed, but Linda's motions slowed, and she finally collapsed onto Julie's lap, still panting. I nearly started clapping, but realized it wasn't meant to be a show, just a very open demonstration of Linda's sexuality, as she satisfied herself.

We were all silent, as Linda's breathing slowed. Finally, she pushed off of Julie's lap, and stood in the narrow space between the loveseat and the coffee table. Then, she bent down, took Julie's head in her hands, and gave her an open-mouth kiss. "Thank you, Julie."

I glanced at Sam, his mouth hanging open and his own hand inside his shorts. Julie's mouth was also open, and she was shaking her head, apparently bewildered by Linda's performance. Both of my friends had now masturbated in front of Sam and I on that loveseat.

Julie stood, and we switched places. As I sat down on the loveseat, I noticed that Julie's hand was now in Sam's shorts. I wondered whether Sam's orgasm could wait until he put Linda over the corner of the bed. Or, whether he would 'blow it' ... in a manner of speaking.

Linda chuckled, and said softly to Sam and Julie, "I don't have to ask Kelly – I *know* she's going to give me a hard spanking." Then, she put herself across my lap, her hands encircling the pillow at the end of the loveseat. I rubbed Linda's bum, which was already reddened by her first spanking.

I decided to fulfill Linda's expectations, and give her a hard and fast spanking. My left hand held Linda's right hip, pulling her to me, and I began her spanking without warning. Linda grunted a few times, but held herself in position, as the spanks rained down on her rosy bottom. I knew that it had to hurt, as my hand was smarting by the time the hundred spanks were done.

Linda stood, bent down, and kissed me – open mouthed, but it didn't seem quite as passionate as the one she'd given Julie. Turning to Sam, Linda announced, "Well, I guess that's enough spanking for one night!"

Sam stood, shaking his head, "Oh, no. You had a plan, and I'm not going to disappoint you." He sat on the loveseat, and patted his lap. "Over my knee. Now, young lady!" Then he chuckled, "Well, maybe not so young anymore, now that you're *more* than a quarter century old."

Linda shook her head, but took her position over Sam's knee. Sam put his right leg over Linda's legs, probably unnecessary, but sure to keep her in position for her spanking. He picked up the leather paddle, and bounced it lightly off Linda's butt. Then, he leaned over and whispered, "We don't have to do this, if you've already had enough spanking."

Linda chortled, "I was kidding, Sam. You *know* that I can take a lot more than what Julie and Kelly gave me!"

Sam nodded, patted Linda's bum again with the paddle, and then said, "OK ... here we go!" With that, he began paddling Linda, alternating sides, one swat every few seconds. They were hard swats, but Linda barely moved, and didn't make a sound.

When 26 swats had been administered, Sam rubbed Linda's bottom. After another couple of minutes, Linda got off Sam's lap, and stood, once again bending down to kiss her punisher. This time, it was definitely a long, wet, open-mouth kiss.

Sam asked, "Do you still want your 'finale'? The 'happy ending'? You've already had a couple of orgasms today."

Linda smiled and nodded, "Yes, Sam. As you said, I had a plan, and we should stick to it. I think three swats with the school paddle might just get me turned on again."

Sam shrugged, and got up. Julie offered, "Linda, if you'd like some privacy, Kelly and I could go upstairs, and get the dessert ready." Then, she smiled, and added, "Or, maybe you could let Kelly and I participate?"

We all looked at Julie, wondering what she had in mind. She looked at me, and said, "I wouldn't mind trying that strap-on again, and doing Sam, while he does Linda."

Linda looked shocked, and Sam winced, but I laughed, "That might be fun. Then, I could use the other strap-on, and do *you*." Julie gave me a small nod, and I got up to get the strap-ons and some lube.

When I brought them out, Julie and I put them on, as Linda howled with laughter. "Those are hilarious!"

Julie explained, "We tried them during our ménage, and they worked pretty well."

Now, Sam was shaking his head, "But you guys and Linda should really have something in your butts, also." He got up and went to his desk, bringing back a couple of butt plugs: The bumpy one for me, and the small black ones for Linda and Julie. We lubed everything, and put a large towel over the corner of the bed.

Sam had the school paddle in his hand. It was the wooden one with the holes, a serious implement – about 18" long, and a half-inch thick. He helped Linda get into position, her legs straddling the corner of the bed, and her head on a large pillow. Sam asked, "Linda, are you ready for your last three swats?"

Linda gulped, and answered hoarsely, "Yes, Sir. I'm ready." Her arms tightened around the pillow, and she relaxed her bottom.

Julie and I watched, as Sam put the large paddle across Linda's bum, then brought it back. I nodded, and we called out, together, "One for good health!" The paddle came down with a loud 'SMACK!' on Linda's now-quivering buttocks, and she let out a little yelp.

Sam brought the paddle back again, and we shouted, "One for good wealth!" Again, the paddle impacted Linda's now bright red bottom with a huge 'CRACK!!' Linda couldn't help but cry out, but she remained in position.

Finally, we yelled, "And one for long life!" Sam swung the paddle, now coming up from below, and striking Linda's lower bum with a 'THWAP!!!'

Linda drew in a deep breath, and whimpered into the pillow. Then, she collected herself, turned her head back to Sam, and said, "Thank you, Sir."

Sam smiled, and rubbed her bottom. "You're very welcome, Linda. I hope this satisfied your birthday spanking 'needs'."

Linda nodded into the pillow, "Oh, yes Sir!"

Sam crooked his finger, indicating that Julie and I should come help. We held Linda's buttocks apart, as Sam slowly inserted the butt plug. Then, he had Julie and I bend over the bed, as he inserted the large glass plugs into our rears. I turned around, and took Sam in my hands, stroking him in preparation for Linda.

Positioning himself behind Linda, Sam entered her, and Linda drew in a large breath, then moaned softly. Without delay, Julie stood behind Sam, and Sam briefly stopped his motion, allowing her to insert the dildo into his rear. Then I stood behind Julie, and inserted the phallus of my strap-on into Julie's already-dripping cunt.

It wasn't entirely synchronized, but Sam made long strokes into Linda, as Julie and I made our own motions, all four of us now being stimulated. I was using the strap-on that had a double-ended dildo, one end moving in me, as the other end moved inside Julie. I put my hand under Julie, stroking her clit, as Sam did the same with Linda.

There was a lot of heavy breathing in the otherwise-quiet room, as we all got it on with each other. It didn't take long for Julie to come, her head facing the ceiling and her eyes closed. And shortly after, Sam's motions quickened, and he came, letting out a loud 'Ah!', 'Ah!', 'Ah!', as Julie's strap-on dildo plunged into Sam's rear every time he pulled back for another forceful stroke into Linda.

Linda came with a loud cry, having obviously been well satisfied by Sam. Sam relaxed forward onto her, as Julie leaned onto him, and I bent forward, holding Julie's breasts. Our breathing slowed, and finally we extracted ourselves from each other.

While Sam, Julie and I had had a similar experience during our ménage, this four-way coupling had been really unique and interesting ... and I was again amazed that we had found something 'new' to do, after all the experiences we'd had together.

Julie and I took off the strap-ons, and we all went into the bathroom to clean up. Sam put on his shorts and Hawaiian shirt, and went upstairs to prepare the desserts.

When Julie, Linda and I walked into the kitchen, Sam was decorating the plates of Napoleons with blackberries and a sprig of mint. He had already set the patio table, and turned on the patio light, pool light, and the strings of tiny lights in the branches of the trees, which had been up for nearly a year, since my birthday. A crescent moon was up, and the backyard was again a wonderland.

Julie, Linda and I sat at the patio table, and Sam came out and poured the rest of the Asti sparkling wine. Then, he brought out Linda's Napoleon, with one candle on it, and we all sang 'Happy Birthday' to her. She had no trouble blowing out the single candle, and we all laughed.

Sam brought out the rest of the desserts, and then toasted Linda. There may not have been a birthday cake, but the Napoleons were incredible, and it was obvious that Linda was enjoying hers.

Julie was joining her parents for Sunday brunch in the morning, and decided not to stay over. She kissed Linda, and kissed us, then took her leave. The thought again popped into my head of how open Sam had become – to share bodily fluids with others, something that he had been very up-tight about just a year ago.

Sam cleaned up the dessert dishes, and again offered to open a bottle of Champagne for Linda, but she declined. There were still three unfinished bottles of wine in the kitchen. Sam had made an incredible dinner, as usual, and Linda thanked him for all his effort.

We decided to go into the pool – our first night swim with Linda. Sam turned off the patio light, and we floated in the sparkling water, blue flecks of light bouncing around the walls and eaves of the house.

Sam swam over to Linda and I, and shared something else he planned for us to do in Kauai: A night snorkel. That sounded pretty adventurous, but then I realized that Sam had plenty more adventures in mind for the trip.

But before Kauai, Sam and I would be going to Fiona and Justin's wedding in Toronto, in just a couple of weeks, and then I would be putting in a full two months of effort on the research for my dissertation. And, Sam and I would begin our daily jogging on Monday morning.

Linda, Sam and I took a shower together downstairs, then we all went upstairs. Sam tucked Linda into her bed in the guest room, giving her a last birthday kiss. Then, he tucked me into our bed, giving me a passionate kiss. I hadn't expected Sam to be 'up' for another lovemaking session tonight, but I was proud of him for being open enough to satisfy Linda on her birthday.

CHAPTER 3: WEDDING TAKES THE CAKE

The Toronto trip would take only a week from my research schedule. Although Sam had wanted to leave a couple of days earlier, to tour Toronto before the wedding, we would be flying there on a Saturday, going to the wedding on Sunday, then touring the city on Monday and part of Tuesday, before going to Niagra Falls, where we would spend the rest of the week, culminating in the Fourth of July celebration on Friday, and flying back home on Saturday.

We had been surprised to receive *two* wedding invitations – one for the ceremony and small reception in the early afternoon, and the other for the main 'party' that would be held at Justin's sex club that evening. I spoke with Fiona on the phone, and she explained that the more sedate reception would be for family – mainly Justin's, and the evening party would be for their friends.

I decided to pack a black dress, as well as both of the sexy black fishnet dresses I had bought at the sex shop in Amsterdam. Sam wanted me to also pack the 'gummi suit', the bright red full-body latex outfit that I had been given in Zurich, but I refused.

I didn't mind wearing the nearly see-through fishnet, at the sex club, as Fiona said most people would be dressed in wild outfits ... but I wasn't planning to perform, and the latex body suit would be too uncomfortable to wear for more than a few minutes.

Sam and I had been jogging for two weeks, starting with round-trips to the stream, which was about four miles, and – this past week – running all the way to the skinny-dipping pond. The first couple of times, we took a break and went for a short swim, but this morning we'd run the entire round-trip without stopping, which was nearly six miles, a third of it on a narrow trail.

Sam had researched jogging trails in Toronto and Niagra Falls, and we had decided to bring our running shoes and outfits. I finished packing my roll-aboard, and set out my outfit for tomorrow's flights. Sam had managed to get first class upgrades on all the flights, two going and two returning. This would only be our second trip together, but I was already getting spoiled.

I had managed to secure bulkhead seats, and Kelly sat by the window. We settled in, Kelly preparing for the flight like a seasoned traveler: First class socks on, her Bluetooth noise-cancelling headphones over her head, and her iPad in her lap. We were served Mimosas, and toasted to the trip.

Both flights were on Super 80s, and I knew that we wouldn't be having a 'mile-high' experience today; Kelly had already decided that. But we would be in Toronto soon, and I hoped that Kelly and I would have a little 'fun time', before we went to dinner.

We stopped at the airline lounge between flights, but only had time to use the bathrooms. On the flight into Toronto, we both had a Bloody Mary – with a splash of beer, at the suggestion of the male flight attendant. I had never thought of doing that, but it turned out surprisingly good – especially with the Tabasco I had brought.

We took a taxi to the hotel, which was on the waterfront. The Toronto weather was spectacular, with a blue sky, and a gusty breeze. There were sailboats heeled over on Lake Ontario, and I considered re-scheduling the tour boat for this afternoon, rather than on Monday, as planned.

Our hotel suite was exquisite, and had a sweeping view of the lake. After our clothes were hung, I held Kelly, and we kissed. This was only the second trip we'd taken together, but – with the length and variety of the Europe trip – it seemed like we'd been traveling with each other forever.

I put my hand down the back of Kelly's slacks, and held her bottom, pulling her to me. Kelly smiled, but then pushed me back, and said, brightly, "I thought we could go for a run? Get some fresh air, after all that time on the plane. We didn't get our run in, this morning."

I pulled my hand out of Kelly's pants, and nodded dejectedly. Kelly laughed, and said, "Don't worry, Sam. I'll take care of you when we get back from the run," she dipped her shoulder and batted her eyelashes at me, "if you're still interested."

My tongue came out, and I panted, putting my forearms up with my hands down, like the paws of a dog. I nodded my head vigorously, and barked. Kelly said, "OK Sammy, I'll take you for a walk ... and a run." Then, she bent over, raucously laughing.

When she looked up and saw my questioning expression, she said, "Maybe, if you're going to act like a dog, I should hold you to it ... walking you. As Linda did on your birthday?" I dropped my paws, shook my head, and took my running shorts and tank out of my suitcase.

It turned out to be a great run, four miles to the outlet of the Humber River, along the waterfront, past small marinas, through narrow parks, with the whitecapped waters of the lake to our left. We walked nearly another mile, to the point at Humber Bay park, and quickly cooled down, as we surveyed the boats on the lake.

"You know, Kelly," now I batted my eyelashes at her, "we've never had sex in a public place, before." For the year I'd known her, she always thought that we had done just about everything, in terms of sensual and sexual play. And then, I'd come up with even more new experiences.

Kelly smiled and shook her head. It was a Saturday, and there were quite a few people walking the paths of the park, as well as a few children riding their bikes. I guess it wouldn't be the best choice for our first time with public sex.

I kissed Kelly, a modest lips-only kiss, but she returned it with passion. Then, she jumped back from me, and teased, "Five miles back ... and I don't think you'll be able to catch me. If I win, I'll have sex with you ..." I looked at Kelly like she was crazy, but she clarified, "and if *you* win, I'll be your slave for an hour."

Kelly smiled sweetly, "And, you just might have to punish me for not submitting to public sex, and taunting you ..." With that, before I knew it, Kelly had turned around and was running down the path, having to run on the grass to get around a few people.

I chuckled, not knowing whether I could beat Kelly back to the hotel; I have a lot of stamina, but Kelly has the speed of youth, and I could only hope she tired, letting me catch up with her. I glanced at my watch, and ran after Kelly.

She was definitely faster than me. But, by the fourth mile, Kelly was slowing, and I was slowly catching up, now only a hundred feet behind her. Kelly looked back, and slowed to a walk. I quickly caught up with her, and she smiled devilishly at me.

"I guess I'll be your slave." She was almost laughing.

"Did you just do that to get us going faster on the way back." Kelly was nodding slowly, as she laughed. Then, she took off again, down the path. I trailed behind her, almost catching up again by the time we had reached our hotel.

For the last half mile, I had been thinking about what I would do with slave Kelly. And I had to make a concerted effort to get those thoughts out of my mind before walking through the hotel lobby and into the elevator. I pulled my tank out of my shorts, and let it drop in front of me.

Back in the suite, I opened the drapes to the expanse of lake view, then took off my sweaty running outfit. Kelly came into the room nude, and got into the standing position in front of me. "I'm yours, Sir. For the next hour, you may do anything you like to me ... or with me." What a great offer!

We had brought a few 'toys' with us, and I considered the possibilities. "How do you suggest I punish you for 'taunting' me?" I looked at Kelly, hoping for some guidance on what she wanted, or expected.

"You know, Sir, we'll be at the sex club tomorrow night ... and I can imagine at some point that we might be nude. Maybe we should show off our BDSM 'stripes'?" I raised my eyebrows, and Kelly continued, "Maybe a five minute OTK warm-up, and 36 with the belt?" My mouth fell open.

"Kelly, ... do you really want that much?" She didn't need to show off her 'stripes' to make me feel good.

She smiled, "Well, Sir, I think I can take it. And it will be something that will last until tomorrow." Then, she chuckled, "And I'll be thinking about Linda's birthday spanking, and her masturbating ... not Julie's performance a year ago." I nodded. It was amazing how much we – Kelly, and her friends – had done over the past year, and how open we all were with each other.

Then Kelly's eyes widened, and she offered, "It would probably be even more impressive to everybody tomorrow night, if *you* had a matching set of stripes!" She looked at me expectantly, and I involuntarily closed my eyes, and shook my head.

Kelly said, quietly, "You don't have to do that, Sam. I know you will, if I ask you ... and that's enough." I breathed out, and felt my stomach relaxing again.

I nodded, then took Kelly in my arms, and held her tightly. "I love you, Kelly." Our cheeks were together, and we held each other for a long time.

Then, Kelly took the standing position again, and said, "I'm ready for my punishment now, Sir." I quickly got my leather belt, and brought a towel from the bathroom, laying it on the couch. Then, I sat and patted my lap. Kelly took her position quickly and quietly. I glanced at my watch.

"OK. Let's see how you do with a five-minute OTK warm-up." Kelly had given me a very hard over-the-knee spanking when we had visited the domme, and she had done the same with each of her friends. She would need a good warm-up before taking the belt, and I had never given her a really long and hard OTK spanking.

Kelly squeaked, "I'm ready, Sir." I patted her bottom, and then began spanking her with my hand, alternating sides, and not letting up on the intensity. It didn't take long before I realized that I should have worn a glove, as my hand was getting sore before we had even reached the two minute mark.

Kelly held her position, although she started bucking and rolling from side to side on my lap, as we got into the second half of the spanking. She was now whimpering, but hadn't said a word since her spanking had begun. I finished the spanking, and rubbed her bottom, which was now uniformly red.

"You may get up, now, Kelly." Kelly got off my lap and took the standing position, her feet apart, hands on head, and facing into the room. I put the towel on the corner of the bed, and pointed. Without a word, Kelly straddled the bed, lowering herself until her chest was against the spread. I pulled a pillow down, and put it under her head.

Standing close behind Kelly, I took her hips, and pulled her to me; Kelly reached under and put me into her. She was very wet, and I moved inside her with little friction, as I massaged and rubbed her bottom.

"We'll do a dozen strokes each time, and then I'll get back in you, and see how long I can last. And, as this isn't a real punishment, you may end it whenever you like." Kelly was probably right that I wouldn't make a good dom: I enjoyed seeing Kelly – and others – submit ... but didn't really want to hurt her. I certainly was not a sadist.

Kelly replied, "Thank you, Sir. But hopefully, we can both hold out to the end."

I pulled out of her, and picked up the wide leather belt, considering whether I should fold it over. But I decided to coil it and use half its length on Kelly. When I placed the belt across her bottom, Kelly flinched slightly, then took a deep breath and released it.

I pulled the belt back, and let it fly, making a loud 'WHAP!', and immediately leaving a two-inch white stripe on her red butt. Kelly let out a soft 'Aaaah!'. I waited about ten seconds, and gave her a second hard stroke of the belt.

Kelly held herself in position, and kept remarkably quiet, with just a little sniffling, barely audible above the sound of the air conditioning. I kept up the pace, giving Kelly one stroke about every ten seconds, and finishing the first dozen in about two minutes. There were multiple parallel stripes crossing her bottom.

Putting down the belt, I once again slipped into her from behind. Kelly sniffled a couple of times, then moaned, "Oh, Sam. That feels so wonderful!" I assumed that she was referring to our lovemaking, and not the first third of her strapping. I lightly massaged Kelly's bottom, as I continued with different types of strokes.

I managed to last two minutes before needing to pull out, lest I come before Kelly's strapping was finished. Once again, I placed the belt across Kelly's bottom; a moment later, Kelly said, "I'm ready, Sir." As well as I knew Kelly, by now, her fortitude still amazed me.

The second dozen strokes took about five minutes, as I rubbed Kelly's bottom between each stroke. Kelly was again sniveling, but now had her hands underneath her – doing herself, as I made stripes across her rear.

I stepped up behind her, easily sliding into her wetness, as I held her hips, and began thrusting. This time, I only lasted a minute until I was nearly on the brink of an orgasm. I stopped my motion, and leaned over Kelly, lightly stroking her back. "Are you sure you want another dozen strokes, Kelly? We don't have to do this, you know."

Kelly nodded into the pillow, "Yes, Sir, I know. And, yes, Sir ... I'll take the third set." Then, she chuckled, and said, "I'm pretty sure I'll be feeling this during the wedding. And, if anyone sees my bum, I know they'll have something to look at."

Kelly's bottom was 'something to look at', even without stripes from the belt. I wondered whether anybody would actually be seeing her bottom tomorrow night at the sex club. I thought it unlikely, but Kelly was right: She would certainly have her stripes to show off, if there was the opportunity.

"OK, then ... let's do them quickly and get this over with." Kelly's arms hugged the pillow tightly as I laid the belt across her bottom for the last time. I considered, for a moment, giving her lighter strokes for her last dozen, but finally decided to give Kelly exactly what she had requested. This was going to be challenging for both of us.

The belt came down hard on her quivering buttocks, leaving overlapping stripes of red and white, every two seconds, and her ordeal was over in less than half a minute. Kelly was now blubbering, but her hands dove beneath her as soon as she had received the last stroke.

As I entered her, she was already bucking and thrusting back her middle to meet me. Before I had gotten into the rhythm, Kelly came, crying out into the pillow, "Oh, Sam! Oh, Sam!!" I leaned over and kissed her back, then began long, slow movements deep into her, as Kelly's vaginal muscles alternately grabbed and released my shaft.

It didn't take long for me to come, and I collapsed down onto her back, reaching under and holding her breasts in my hands. We stayed that way for several minutes, only the sounds of the air conditioner and our breathing breaking the silence.

Then we took a shower together, and dressed for dinner. I had made reservations at one of Toronto's fine dining establishments, and it was very enjoyable, Kelly even able to sit without too much pain.

We'd had a great dinner last night, and had made love slowly and sensuously when we got back to the room. This morning, we'd slept late, and ordered a small breakfast from room service. My bottom was not noticeably sore, until I pulled on pantyhose as we dressed for the wedding.

The ceremony and family reception would be in another hotel within walking distance, and Fiona suggested that we bring our 'sex club' outfits with us. There would be a bus taking those attending both receptions to the sex club. Sam had brought a foldable, lightweight, ballistic nylon duffel bag, and we packed it with our skimpy outfits – including my fishnet dress and G-string, and a pair of black jeans and lightweight, black leather vest that Sam would wear bare-chested.

In the early afternoon, with me in my black evening dress, and Sam in a bespoke suit and tie, we walked to the wedding venue. A ballroom was set-up for the ceremony on one side, and small round tables filling most of the rest of the room for the reception.

As we walked in, our eyes met Alex's, and we greeted each other warmly. Alex was wearing an elegant evening gown that had to be a designer original. It was a one-shoulder, black chiffon floor-length dress, with an exposed back and peek-a-boo cutout at the hip. Both the shoulder and cutout were finely beaded in silver, and the shoulder portion held an asymmetric black strap that crossed her upper back, above the diagonally-cut waist.

"Hello, Alex!" Sam said, hugging her, and then putting his cheek lightly on hers. Alex and I hugged, and we congratulated her on Fiona's impending marriage. We had only a short time to chat, before an announcement was made for everyone to take their seats.

The ceremony was beautiful, with plenty of flowers, and music by a folk guitarist. Justin appeared in front, under an arch of fabric with flowers woven through it. He wore a double-breasted English heritage suit which appeared to have a green and brown plaid print, along with a cream shirt and thin, dark tie.

The wedding march began, and Alex walked Fiona down the aisle. The two dozen guests took a collective deep breath, Fiona a striking image, her ginger hair complementing an ivory sheath dress in organza and satin. It was almost a period piece, sleeveless, with spaghetti straps, and a brush train that was ruched at the waist.

Fiona smiled at us as she passed, continuing to the front, and stepping up onto the platform under the flowered arch.

Glancing at Sam, I could see that his eyes were wet. I took his hand in mine, and wondered how he'd been at his own son's wedding. Then, I wondered whether Sam's younger, gay son, Mark, and his partner, Greg would ever get married.

The ceremony was amazingly brief, and before we knew it, Justin was kissing Fiona, languorously, his hand cupping her bottom. The guitar music started, and the newlyweds walked back up the short aisle.

As the wedding guests walked into the reception area, a four-piece jazz group started playing, and uniformed hotel staff glided through the room with large plates of hors d'oeuvres.

We were eventually able to make our way over to Fiona and Justin to congratulate them. Fiona was glowing. Sam exclaimed, 'That was quite a ceremony: The most humanely short wedding I've been to in years."

He hugged Fiona and shook Justin's hand, then told us, "Sarah and I wrote most of our own ceremony, but it wasn't that short. We'd had to put our lines on 3x5" cards ... and the stack of cards fell during the ceremony, mixing up the lines." Then, he chuckled, "Maybe that was a bellwether of how things would go later?"

I chided him, "Sam! You and Sarah had a great marriage, as far as I can tell."

He smiled, and kissed me, "Well, all marriages – in fact any relationship between two people – goes through its difficult phases." I didn't pursue this; it had seemed that my relationship with Sam had gone very smoothly, although admittedly it had only been a year, so far.

Justin gave us a devilish look, "If you thought this first part of our wedding was 'different', wait 'till you experience the second part, at my club!"

I gave Justin an inquisitive look, and he explained, "My family is small, and mostly conservative: I'm the rebel among them. My parents didn't react well to our ideas of having a nude wedding, or the live tattooing of our vows on our private parts during the ceremony."

My mouth dropped open, and Sam was cracking up, but Justin continued, "And although the club is a perfect venue for the party, my family didn't want to have to explain to their friends that our wedding had taken place at a sex club." Fiona shrugged, and I nodded.

"So we decided to have a small family affair here in town, and invite most of our friends – and my business colleagues – to the club for the *real* party." Then, Justin turned a little more serious, and offered, "Some of our guests will be providing the entertainment ... but if you guys want to 'perform', that can be easily arranged."

Sam nodded, and I shook my head, but we didn't have a chance to reply, as more of Justin's relatives were now congratulating the newlyweds. Sam looked at me questioningly, and smiled. "Don't get any ideas, Sam. This will already be the first wedding I've attended wearing a see-through dress with virtually nothing underneath."

Sam took an hors d'oeuvre from the passing tray, and gave me his innocent 'What, me?' look.

We drifted over to Alex, and congratulated her again. She smiled, "Well, we got through that part pretty easily. It will be interesting to see what Justin has planned for the evening."

Both Sam and I were a bit surprised that Alex would be coming to the sex club, but perhaps we shouldn't have been: Alex had demonstrated her openness, and desire to connect with her niece and new nephew, despite her normally socially conservative bearing. Alex suggested that we sit together at the club, as she would know no one else there and, of course, we gladly agreed.

Alex said, "I doubt there will really be much 'sex' at the club – I think Justin just wanted to impress his friends, and show off the food and entertainment, which he raves about. I understand the owner offered to throw the entire party at no cost."

In less than two hours, the reception was thinning. Cake had been served, although Fiona and Justin didn't feed each other, as is usually typical. I also realized that Fiona hadn't thrown a bouquet or her garter at the end.

About a dozen of us boarded a 'party bus', which was seen off by Justin's parents and some straggling relatives and friends. Fiona introduced us to Justin's younger sister, Jasmine, and several of the bridesmaids and best men, who were close friends.

We and several others had duffel bags, but we wondered what everyone would be changing into. I glanced at the sexy gown that Alex wore, but couldn't imagine that it would be *de rigueur* at the club; if it was, then Sam and I would certainly be under-dressed!

Justin walked to the back of the bus, and opened a cooler, next to a large box (which we realized, later, held the cake), and pulled out a bottle of Champagne. As he opened it, the cork popped out, and ricocheted around the small bus.

No glasses were offered: The bottle – and then another – was passed around, and we were all pretty relaxed by the time the bus arrived at the club, which was located somewhere about 30 minutes to the southwest of downtown Toronto, in an industrial-looking area.

We all piled out of the bus and into the club, being greeted by twin lines of Justin's colleagues, who threw streamers over everyone. Entering the main party space, we saw that there were about a dozen round tables set in front of a large dance floor and stage. In a small alcove, a DJ was cueing up the music, and colored lights reflected in moving patterns from the mirrored balls on the ceiling.

A 'master of ceremonies' suggested that everyone get more comfortable, and pointed to changing rooms back by the entrance.

As Sam and I left Alex at the table, and made our way back through the room, we saw several of the bridesmaids stripping down at their tables – they had worn sexy things under their dresses. One wore a gold camisole set, and another wore a black corset over a G-string. It was at this point that I realized we would *not* be under-dressed for the party.

We came out of the changing rooms along with several others who wore an amazing variety of outfits: A bright blue stretch metallic dress, a silvery halter dress with V that came down below the navel, a black-banded bodycon dress with see-through mesh, a black jumpsuit with cutouts down the front and along the sides of the legs, a red-sequined miniskirt with matching bra top, and at least three women and a man in latex.

Walking back to the table, I *did* feel under-dressed: Not that I was wearing too little, but my simple fishnet seemed not fancy enough. And, Sam's jeans and leather vest combo was downright shabby, compared to some of the other guests. When Alex saw us, she put her hand over her mouth, and tried to stifle a laugh.

I modeled the fishnet, and explained, "We bought a couple of dresses like this at a sex shop in Amsterdam during our Europe trip. I can see now that it isn't really fancy enough for this party, but it will have to do." Alex looked me up and down, from my bare breasts to the skimpy G-string, and down to the diagonal ruffles of the dress. She nodded, and picked up her drink.

There were waitresses, also wearing skimpy outfits, who poured Champagne at each table, and there was an open bar. Sam made his way through the room, and returned with a couple of margaritas. He leaned over to Alex, about to ask her something, when the MC appeared on the stage. "And here are our newlyweds!"

Fiona and Justin walked out onto the dance floor, to deafening applause and, without delay, the sexy music of a Tango began. Fiona and Justin must have practiced, as they were great dancers, very sensuous. They were still wearing their wedding attire ... but I was sure it wouldn't be for long.

As part of the dance, Justin threw off his jacket, then undid his tie, and used it around Fiona's neck as a dance prop. They were both barefoot, and the continuing dance became a sort-of strip-tease, Fiona unbuttoning Justin's shirt, and Justin unbuttoning Fiona's dress.

Soon, the shirt came off, and the dress dropped to the floor, revealing a garter belt and nylons that Fiona now wore. Rather than a bra, Fiona wore a cream-colored bandeau. Justin wore a pair of satin boxers with a purple and pink paisley pattern.

The tango ended dramatically, with Fiona bending over backwards in Justin's arms. Then, the music changed to the old rock classic, '*Light My Fire*'. Justin dropped his shorts, and swung them in circles over his head, and signaled for other guests to join in the dancing.

Now, Fiona took off her bandeau and twirled it, then finished the strip tease with her garter, stockings, and thong.

Soon, the dance floor was a jumble of bodies – plenty of skin showing, along with lace, leather, and shiny fabrics. Sam and I joined in, and I realized that it might be the first time we had ever danced together.

When we returned to the table, Alex was still drinking Champagne. Sam offered to dance with her, but she declined, making some comment about fast and loud music. But when the DJ moved to the next song, a slow ballad, Justin and Fiona came to our table, Justin asking Alex to dance with him, and Fiona asking Sam.

Alex pointed to me, but Justin wouldn't take no for an answer. Finally, Alex stood, and kicked off her shoes; she glanced at Sam and I, shrugged, then pulled the beaded strap of the dress off her shoulder, and pushed the dress down to the floor, surprising all of us.

Alex took a swallow of Champagne and stood back up, proud and elegant, wearing only a black lace bra and panty set, no nylons. Both Sam's and Justin's mouths had dropped open, but Alex pretended not to notice. She gave Justin a sweet look, and took his hand, as they headed for the dance floor.

Sam shook his head, still looking at the seat where Alex had been sitting a moment ago. Fiona took Sam's hand, and pulled him up; then they walked onto the dance floor together.

———————————

As I held Fiona, and we began to dance to the slow music, I bent down and kissed her on the cheek. "You guys are really great; what a neat way to have a wedding." I had to chuckle, before I could add, "Your aunt is really something, too!"

Fiona laughed, "She insisted on coming tonight, and we really wanted her here. I would have been happy to go shopping with her, and pick out a sexy outfit ... but Alex thought her dress would suffice for both parts of the party. She looks hot in her underwear, but I really wouldn't have believed that she would take her dress off."

I nodded, "It's pretty surprising. But she went skinny-dipping with us in the pool, and I guess she doesn't know anybody else here ..."

Fiona was shaking her head, "Only Jasmine. I wonder what stories *she'll* bring back to her parents about 'auntie Alex'?"

"Well, that might make them loosen up, a little."

Fiona shook her head again, "I don't think so. Justin's father is in banking, and they are the model of 'prim and proper'. But that's what I had thought about Alex, also."

I saw a tear in Fiona's eye. "Are you OK, Fiona?"

She nodded, "Just thinking about how I much I would have liked my parents to be here." She put her head onto my chest and sighed. Now, my eyes were wet: The last wedding I'd attended had been my son's, and that had been the last time I'd danced with Sarah.

The music segued into another slow song, and we switched partners. I held Alex close, and whispered, "You're beautiful." When she looked at me, I added, "And I don't just mean your body. You're a beautiful person." Now, Alex's head was against my chest.

When we got back to the table, Kelly applauded, then pointed, "I think the buffet is open." There was a vast array of food, arranged on several round tables, spaced around the perimeter of the upper level, so as to minimize lines.

Many people were still on the dance floor, the music now back to classic rock.

There were a lot of cute people here, of both genders, mainly in their late twenties to late thirties. But I had to chuckle, watching Alex (who was pushing fifty) serve herself, as she stood confidently in her bra and panties.

And Kelly, always the model of self-confidence, chatted with the guests, totally unfazed that her body was on display through the fishnet. Of course, Kelly had a great body – nothing to be ashamed of.

By the time most people were eating, the DJ took a break, and the jazz quartet that had played at the hotel took the stage. The music was quiet enough to allow conversation, and we had a chance to talk to Jasmine, Justin's sister, who sat next to Alex in a satin camisole.

Jasmine was a stunner: Long, straight blond hair and deep blue eyes. She was younger than Kelly, the image of youth and innocence. She smiled at Alex, "Maybe we shouldn't say too much about this party to my parents?" Alex nearly choked on her food, but nodded vigorously, as she grabbed for her glass of Champagne.

I noticed that the music had stopped, and the stage was transformed, the jazz group gone, and three gleaming metallic poles now rising toward the colored stage lights. Soft music played as three beautiful and graceful young women, wearing only thongs, performed a synchronous and sensuous pole dance.

At the end, the curtain came down, and then went back up, leaving a screen illuminated by circles of colored light. Shadows of a man and woman appeared, walking from either of side of the stage, then spinning around each other. The two shadows undressed each other, flinging clothing aside. Then, they coupled romantically, merging into a single shadow.

The female knelt, and took the man in her mouth, head nodding back and forth. Soon, the couple rose, and their shadows got smaller as they moved from the screen. Then, words were projected onto the screen: Consternation, Convocation, Computation, Connotation, Conflagration, Confirmation, Concentration, Conjugation, CONSUMMATION!

Suddenly, the screen rose, and the couple was on a huge bed in the center of the stage. It was Fiona and Justin!

The entire back wall of the stage was a projection screen, and now images of their coupling – from many different angles – were projected. Being a techie, I located the remote-controlled video cameras high above the stage, panning and zooming, as an unseen technician mixed the images artistically, and projected them behind the live lovemaking.

It was obvious that the live sex show was real, and it didn't take long for the couple to reach their climax. The stage lights went off, and the curtain fell. There was a stunned silence for a few moments, and then tremendous applause, everyone standing. I glanced at Alex, and her face was flushed, head slowly shaking.

Then, the curtain rose, and the lights came back on. Fiona and Justin were sitting on the edge of the bed, waving for people to join them. A technician gave Justin the microphone, and he said, "We invite our friends to get sexy and come up here for a hug fest!"

It only took a moment before several people stood, and stripped down from their already-skimpy clothes, then ran across the dance floor and up the stairs to the stage. The video began again, with a collage of images of Justin and Fiona hugging, kissing, and rolling around the bed with their friends.

Then, more people joined the hug fest – a few completely nude, but most men wore underwear, and most women were in a thong and topless. Kelly looked at me, and I shook my head, "I'm not going to 'get sexy', no matter how much clothes I take off." Kelly rolled her eyes, and pulled her dress over her head, wadding it up and putting it on the table.

I looked across the table, and saw that Jasmine already had her camisole top off, and was heading toward the stage in only her satin bottoms. Alex was looking up at the ceiling. Kelly pulled me up, and began undoing my black jeans. My vest came off, and we headed onto the stage, me wearing my black European string bikini underwear, and Kelly wearing her black G-string.

We had barely left the table, when I heard Alex gasp, and I glanced back: Alex's eyes were glued to Kelly's bottom which, I now realized, showed off the stripes from her strapping. I smiled at Alex and shrugged, and we proceeded onto the stage, and onto the bed – sort of, as there must have been a couple of dozen people trying to hug Fiona and Justin, and each other. And us.

It was an interesting feeling, being hugged by total strangers, not to mention being dressed – or undressed – as we were. I finally got to Fiona, and she smiled broadly when she saw Kelly and I. Her arms went around me, and we hugged and kissed, then I rolled off the bed, into someone else's arms.

It was Jasmine, who was running her hands around my body, kissing my chest, and then looking into my eyes and kissing me lightly on the lips. I held her briefly, running my hands through her hair, and cupping her bottom.

She smiled at me, then turned and put her arms around another guy, and I turned toward the bed to see

Kelly rolling on the bed with Justin. Several people who had just come up to the stage dived in – literally – creating a mass of contorted, mostly-nude bodies on the bed.

When Kelly came up for air, she slipped off the bed, and hugged a few other people – both men and women – before taking me by the hand, smiling, and leading me back down the steps to the dance floor. The DJ was now playing rap music, modifying the sound with his scratch technique.

I had thought we would go back to the table, but Kelly had other ideas, and we were now dancing – nearly nude – along with a mash-up of other couples, similarly undressed.

Then, Jasmine joined us – although I really couldn't tell whether she was dancing with either of us or both of us. She had medium-sized breasts, pointy, and – like Kelly – firm enough to dance without hurting herself.

When the music ended, I took Kelly's hand, and pulled her toward the table, Jasmine trailing behind. Then, we heard her yell "Kelly!"

Kelly turned, and Jasmine pointed to Kelly's striped bottom. Kelly crooked her finger, and the three of us returned to the table, where Alex sat nearly catatonic, staring into the crowd of people on the dance floor. Jasmine sat between us, and as Kelly explained that we were into BDSM, Jasmine's eyes grew larger and larger.

"Yesterday, we ran along the lakeshore, and I bet Sam that I could beat him back to the hotel." Kelly glanced up at me with a mischievous smile, "But he beat me ... and then beat me." I was shaking my head, but Kelly corrected herself, "I told him that I would submit to a spanking and a strapping, and Sam did a good job satisfying me ... during and after the spanking."

Jasmine's eyes were wide, and she shook her head slowly, her mouth open. Alex was looking our way, evidently having heard part of the conversation, and laughed, "You should have seen her bottom after Sam caned her!" Jasmine shook her head faster.

Kelly laughed, "But it's all in fun ... and Sam lets me spank him, also, sometimes."

Jasmine squealed, "Really!?!?" Kelly nodded. Then, I saw a look in Kelly's eyes that I didn't like; because I knew what it meant.

"No, Kelly. Don't even think about it!" I groaned.

Kelly smiled brightly, "But, Sam, Fiona and Justin were asking for volunteers to perform tonight. Your bottom is ready for a good strapping ..." She reached for my pants, which were folded on the table, and pulled out the wide leather belt. "And, we have the perfect implement, here!" All I could do was close my eyes and shake my head.

Kelly was now cackling. She contained herself long enough to whisper something to Jasmine, who went running off. I realized that almost everyone was dancing now, and it appeared that Fiona and Justin had finished their 'hug fest', as the bed on the stage was empty. Kelly leaned to me, and whispered loudly enough to be heard above the sounds of the music, "I'm really turned on, now, Sam."

I *wasn't* turned on – and it was a good thing. I wasn't hung up about people seeing my body, but it would be very embarrassing to get a hard-on in front of a hundred people. I was ready to plead with Kelly, and didn't think that BDSM would be appropriate at a wedding party, anyway.

But before I could think anything else, the music faded, and Justin was on stage with the microphone in his hand. "I want to thank all of you for your love." There was applause. "And I want to thank one special couple for offering to perform tonight – this *is* a sex club, after all. And we promote all kinds of sensual and sexual experiences."

Now, Kelly was hysterical, and Alex was shaking her head, as she stared at us. I shrugged, and pointed repeatedly, accusingly, at Kelly. Justin continued, "So our friends Kelly and Sam are going to give a demonstration of light BDSM for our enjoyment ... and hopefully theirs!"

Oh my God! It was actually going to happen. As Kelly pulled me up, and we headed to the stage, a blur of thoughts ran through my head: How could this be happening? Why had I strapped Kelly, yesterday? And what would happen if this monster I had created actually took the domme class?

This wasn't funny anymore ... although I realized inside that we would probably laugh about it afterward. My stomach flip-flopped, and I was glad I hadn't eaten any more. There was laughter and applause as we stepped onto the stage, but my mind was blank, and my throat dry. Kelly was still holding my hand, and suddenly she was talking into the microphone.

"Hi, everybody! Let's all give another round of applause to congratulate Fiona and Justin ... and for their on-stage consummation of their marriage!" There was thunderous applause.

Then, Kelly spoke softly, her voice echoing around the room, "Sam and I are a little into BDSM – submitting to each other as a turn-on. Yesterday, we ran along the lake, and I bet Sam that he couldn't beat me back to the hotel, but if he did, he could give me a good spanking." There was nervous laughter, but the room was amazingly quiet.

"Well, he *did* beat me ... and then he *really* beat me. I went over his lap for a spanking, and then I bent over the corner of the bed for a strapping." There were a few gasps, as Kelly turned her bottom to the room, and a spotlight illuminated the stripes that still decorated it.

Kelly chuckled, "Of course, he was also having sex with me at the same time." There was nervous laughter.

"Now, I'm going to ask Sam to submit to *me*. It will only be a demonstration, but I know that this isn't what Sam planned – or expected – at tonight's party: Getting spanked and strapped at a wedding, on stage, in front of a hundred people.

"But I think he will do it because he loves me, and knows that it's something that I want. Something that will turn me on." My eyes were closed, and I realized that I was still shaking my head. I was suddenly getting hot and cold flashes.

"So, Sam ... will you show me your openness, and your love, and consideration? Will you submit to me?"

I couldn't help it – I put my hands over my face. This was really too much. But I didn't want to disappoint Kelly ... and the crowd of people awaiting my response. I gulped a couple of times, and in a hoarse voice, answered, very softly, "Yes, Kelly. I'll submit to you."

There was more deafening applause, as Kelly sat on the edge of the bed, and pulled me across her lap. Then, she lowered my skimpy underwear, and put her hand on my bottom. She had put down the microphone, and now whispered to me, "Just relax, Sam. You'll do fine." Then, with a grin in her voice, "I love you."

With that, she began a very hard hand spanking. I don't know where the microphone was, but the sounds of the spanks were amplified around the room. I couldn't hear anything else.

I tried to relax, but Kelly was really spanking me hard, and fast. My bottom stung, but that didn't really bother me much; it was the thought of a hundred people watching my bottom being reddened that was psychologically difficult for me. I wasn't *that* open; and I guess Kelly was demonstrating that to me; while she 'demonstrated' my bottom to 200 staring eyes.

About the time I was wondering how many spanks Kelly would give me, she stopped, the sound of the last spank still echoing – at least in my ears, if not throughout the room. Kelly rubbed my bottom and pulled up my underwear. Then she patted my bottom, and we stood up.

Taking me by the hand, she led me to the corner of the bed, and put me into position, straddling the corner, my chest flat on the bed, and my fingers locked together. Once again, she lowered my underwear – this time, to mid-thigh – and I felt the strap being laid across my rear. I tightly closed my eyes.

The strap was gone, and then there was an incredibly loud sound, and I felt a line of searing heat cross from my left hip to my right. I let out an involuntary yelp. Then, a second searing line, slightly below the last one. There were already tears in my eyes.

The otherwise silent room was filled with the sound of the belt impacting my butt, a loud 'CRACK!!!' each time, with a corresponding line of pain. My bottom was on fire. I'd received six strokes, and wasn't sure I could take any more.

I waited, and thankfully there wasn't another stroke. Then, I heard – more from the audio system than the voice directly above me – "Too bad I didn't have my strap-on!" Laughter and applause. Then, Kelly's voice again, "Sam will now count out the last six, with a 'Thank you, Miss' after each one." I sobbed, and Kelly asked, "Won't you, young man?"

My eyes still closed, I tried to halt my sobbing, and said, "Yes, Miss." I thought I heard some rustling in the audience, or perhaps it was just the blood pumping through the arteries in my head. Then, I felt the belt across my bottom again.

I heard a 'CRACK!' and felt the pain, my head lifting, and an 'Arggggh' coming unbidden from my mouth. Then, I said, quietly, "One, thank you, Miss!" The next five strokes repeated the process, but I realized – afterward – that I had shrieked after the last two strokes.

Now, I was sobbing, my breath catching, as Kelly rubbed my bottom. There was silence, and I opened my eyes, as Kelly put the microphone in front of me. I knew what she wanted. "Thank you for the spanking, Miss."

Now, there was cheering and applause. The stage lights mercifully went off, and the curtain came down. Kelly switched off the microphone, and rubbed my bottom again, as I wept. Then, I lifted my middle, as she pulled up my underwear, and she sat next to me, stroking my back.

"Thank you, Sam. That was very brave of you – both taking the spanking, and doing it on stage in front of all those people." She bent down and kissed my back. "I'm proud of you."

It took several more minutes, but I finally wiped my tears in the sheets, and got up. Kelly hugged me, and walked me to a backstage bathroom, where I peed, and then washed my face. When we came down the stairs to the dance floor, everyone applauded again, and the music started. Kelly smiled, "Do you want to dance?"

That wasn't even funny. I walked slowly to our table, and sat down. Alex rose, and came around the table to kiss me on the cheek. I was glad I had washed the salt of the tears off my face. Then, Jasmine sat down next to me. She had put on her camisole top. "That was really impressive!"

I nodded, "Yes, it really made an impression on my butt!" We all laughed, and Kelly poured more Champagne for everyone at the table.

When the music ended, the MC asked everyone to sit down, as the cake was rolled out. The cake in the hotel had been three layers, but only the middle layer had been served. The lowest layer would be served to the guests at the club, and Fiona and Justin would be taking the top layer home.

The cake was cut, and the newly married couple fed each other, Fiona managing to smash most of the cake against Justin's face, in the process. The lights were turned down, and the DJ changed to softer music, as everyone was served. Cake and Champagne! The thought of Linda flashed through my head – it was her favorite combination.

Then, I wondered whether Linda would lose weight, and if we would all be in shape for our island adventure. Images of Kauai flitted through my head, until Kelly leaned over and hand-fed me a large piece of cake. 'It was a piece of cake' was the expression.

Kelly put her dress back on, and I put on my pants and vest, although at least half of the guests were still semi-nude. It hadn't been the 'sex club' experience that we'd expected, but it had been an interesting experience. And it was certainly the most unusual wedding I'd ever attended.

Sam had really been a good sport. Actually he'd been more than that: He had truly shown his love for me, and his ability and willingness to submit to me. It had been a submission not only to pain, but to something that I knew had to be embarrassing for him – getting spanked on stage in front of all the wedding guests.

I fed him my cake, and we drank Champagne, as the party raged on around us. At some point, Fiona and Justin came over, and congratulated us on our performance. Sam meekly responded, "I hadn't *planned* to perform at your wedding. It was all Kelly's fault!"

They laughed, and Fiona bent down and gave Sam an extended, open-mouth kiss. "Thank you, Sam. It will be something we'll all remember!" Sam started to make a joke, but Fiona put her finger across Sam's lips, and added, "... as a very loving gesture."

Then, Justin laughed, "And you guys aren't even married!" I glanced at Sam, who was smiling, noncommittal. I had wondered what effect, if any, going to a wedding would have on Sam. And I now wondered whether being married would change our relationship in any way. Fiona and Justin had shown us that marriage doesn't need to follow the usual rules. But, of course, we already knew that.

It was after midnight when the bus took us back to downtown Toronto. Fiona and Justin, Jasmine and Alex, Sam and I, and a half dozen other members of the wedding party rode mostly in silence. Most were staying at the hotel where the wedding ceremony had taken place, except Sam and I; we would have a short walk back to our hotel.

As Fiona and I hugged again, Sam took Justin aside, and spoke with him, Justin nodding excitedly. Then, we switched, and I hugged Justin. "Congratulations, again. That was really an awesome wedding!"

Justin chuckled, "Well, that wasn't our *usual* evening at the club. I guess we'll owe you a rain check for visiting the club another time, on a more normal night."

"We'd love to come back and visit again, Justin."

We hugged again, and Justin nodded, "As we told you before ... you guys are really hot!"

Sam and I walked back to our hotel, and undressed for bed. We had partially dressed for the ride back to Toronto – Sam leaving off his jacket and tie, and me leaving off the pantyhose. It had been an incredible evening, something that I never could have imagined when we'd gone to Alex's house for the engagement party. And something I never would forget.

I rubbed Sam's bum, and then we made love silently, both of us turned-on by the experiences we'd had over the past few hours. We held each other as we drifted off to sleep, and I thought again about spending my life with Sam. My Sam.

CHAPTER 4: FALLING FOR NIAGRA

We slept in on Monday morning, then began our tour of Toronto. The weather was still beautiful, and we had skipped our morning run, so we walked through the Discovery District – where the University of Toronto and several hospitals were located, and where much of the region's biotechnology developments were taking place. We then walked through Queen's Park to the Royal Ontario Museum.

The museum was interesting, with a lot of galleries and special exhibits, including one of Pompeian art that included an X-rated room that showed some of the sexual art from the town that was covered by ashes during the 79AD eruption of Mount Vesuvius.

Sam promised that he would take me to Italy and, on the walk back to the waterfront, he described places we could go in northern Italy, including the small village of Sirmione on a peninsula on the southern tip of Lake Garda; Cortine d'Ampezzo in the Dolomite mountains with their beautiful wildflowers in the Spring, or skiing in the winter; the tiny town of Portofino on the Italian Riviera; the sights of Venice, Florence and Rome; and the beautiful Amalfi coast, with the island of Capri.

By the time Sam had finished talking about the foods of Italy, we were hungry, so decided to eat at the '360' rotating restaurant which is more than 1150 feet up in the CN tower. We ordered the three-course *prix fixe* lunch, which was superb, and then finished our tour of the tower on the Lookout level, and the Glass Floor. Sam did fine looking down through the floor, his fear of heights apparently limited to unenclosed spaces, like the Sky Fall ride at the Oktoberfest, and the Eiffel Tower.

We were stuffed from the big lunch, so took it easy in the afternoon with a boat tour of Toronto harbor and offshore islands. As we cruised by the skyline, I asked Sam how his bottom was feeling from last night's spanking performance.

He gave me a dirty look, "I still feel it. That was really pushing me to the limit, to do that in front of a hundred people."

Sam grumbled, and then looked at me seriously, "Kelly, you may recall the night I cooked an Italian dinner for you the first time ... when I wore the apron with nothing else?" I nodded. "You said you were concerned that you wouldn't satisfy my desire for a submissive." I remembered the discussion well.

Sam continued, "Well, I'm not sure that I'll be able to satisfy *your* desire for a submissive! You know that I'm usually willing to submit to you ... but that experience last night was well out of my comfort zone. And, if you take that domme training from mistress Elena, I just don't know whether I'll be able to satisfy you."

I hugged Sam, and consoled him, "You satisfy me just as you are, Sam. And you *could* have refused last night. I would have understood." Then, I chuckled, "And don't you think it was difficult for *me* ... showing everyone my bum, not to mention standing in front of everyone topless?" Sam nodded slowly.

Thinking a bit more about the experience, I added, "It's different than being on a nude beach, where hundreds of people might see you; in this case, we were in the spotlight, performing for the audience." Sam was nodding more forcefully, but still looked disturbed.

I laughed, "But you know ... after everything we've done, that was another new experience for both of us." Once again, I wondered how many *more* 'new' experiences there would be for us.

We rented a car on Tuesday morning, and drove the short distance to Niagra Falls. It had become much more commercial than the last time I'd been here; then I realized that had been nearly two decades ago. Things had changed everywhere.

It was still mid-morning when we checked in to our hotel, but fortunately our room was available. Kelly gasped when I opened the door to the luxury suite that had a jacuzzi and fireplace, and she ran to the window and marveled at the spectacular view of the falls. "This is incredible!" she exclaimed.

I nodded, "We're in a central location, and can walk to many of the attractions. But before we leave ..." I rummaged in my suitcase and smiled at Kelly. "Your birthday is at the end of the week, but I'd like to give you one of your presents today. It might come in useful during parts of our tour."

Kelly cocked her head, as I handed her the wrapped box. Her eyes went wide, as she realized that it was one of the waterproof digital cameras. "These were mainly for our trip to Hawaii, but I have a feeling that you can get some use of it right here in Niagra Falls." I quickly added, "And you can practice on this trip, so you'll be an expert on Kauai."

Kelly hugged me, "Thank you, Sam." We kissed, and I briefly considered taking a 30-minute time-out for a little nooky; but then, I decided that we should get going.

"Shall we start our tour?" I had already bought an 'adventure' package online, and printed out the tickets. We unpacked our rolling cases, took a quick bathroom break, and left the room.

After barely a five minute walk from the hotel, we arrived at the funicular, which took us down to our first experience: the 'Journey behind the falls'. I chuckled, "I hope you don't mind getting a little wet, today?" Kelly shook her head, smiling. Then, I said, "Actually, we might be getting wet every day that we're here!"

We were given lightweight yellow ponchos, then took the elevator 170 feet down, and walked through a long tunnel out to a deck that was right next to the Horseshoe Falls. We couldn't help being impressed by the power of the 100,000 cubic feet of water *per second* falling next to us. I told Kelly, "That's about 600,000 gallons per second! Really amazing."

Kelly nodded, as we walked to the railing at the edge of the falls. She took a few snapshots of the falls, trying out her new camera. Our ponchos were soaked, and any non-waterproof camera would have been trashed.

We then walked through another, even longer, tunnel to the Cataract Portal, behind the falls. There was a sheet of water, and blowing mist, but a fence prevented people from getting dangerously close.

Then, we went through more tunnels to the Great Falls Portal, behind another sheet of water. It was impressive, but there wasn't much to see – the noise, wind and spray giving us an idea of what we weren't seeing.

As we headed through Queen Victoria park on our way to the tour boats, I asked Kelly, "Are you hungry? We didn't have breakfast this morning." Kelly raised her eyebrows at me, and I raised mine at her.

"Now that you mention it, I guess I haven't eaten much, since our lunch, yesterday." She smiled at me.

We took a quick detour to the Skylon tower, that rises 775 feet above the falls. It was still early, and we were able to get a window table in their rotating restaurant. Kelly exclaimed, "But we just ate in the rotating restaurant of a tower yesterday!"

I shrugged, thinking how easy it was to get spoiled – and how everyone wants more, regardless of what they already have.

The lunch was nice – both the food and the view. We continued our walk through the park to the embarkation point for the Canadian boat tours. I had thought about taking the 'Maid of the Mist' tour from the American side, but the Canadian cruise was included in our package; and I had read good reviews of their modern boats.

As we boarded the boat, I became more aware of the crowds of people. We had seen plenty on our behind-the-falls tour, but now I remembered why I didn't like traveling during the summer. We were given another disposable poncho.

Being adventurous, we took seats near the bow on the top deck. The day was getting quite warm, but I hoped that we wouldn't be soaked, as we hadn't brought a change of clothes. Leaning toward each other, Kelly and I kissed, and I put my hand down the back of her shorts.

She smiled, "I don't think we're going to get the chance for an experience like in Paris." A nice memory: Kelly sitting on my lap on the top deck of one of the *bateaux mooches*, while I made her come.

Giving her my most evil smile, I suggested, "When we get going, you can lean forward over the bow rail, like in

Titanic, and I'll stand behind you, my arms around you ... down the front of your pants." I laughed, "And nobody will see anything; they'll be looking at the Falls, anyway."

Kelly didn't think much of that, and just shook her head, as she gave me a peck on the lips.

The tour was fun, the boat getting close enough to the Falls to cover us in spray and wind whipping down along the water. The ponchos did their job, and Kelly got a few nice shots during the cruise with her new camera.

As we walked onto *terra firma* again, I informed Kelly, "So this was just our warm-up cruise." Another cocked head, and more raised eyebrows. "Tomorrow we're booked on the jet boat tour of the whirlpool."

Kelly rolled her eyes. It *did* sound fanciful, and I wondered whether she didn't believe me. But she should have learned by now ...

I had no doubt that Sam was planning to take us on a jet boat. He was always over-the-top. Sam hadn't told me what *else* we would be doing on this trip; it was only Tuesday, and I had no idea what would keep us busy here until our flight back on Saturday.

We walked along the river, and crossed the Rainbow Bridge – standing halfway across (along with all the other tourists) with one foot in the U.S. and one foot in Canada.

Continuing on, we entered Niagra Falls State Park. We decided to forego the Discovery Center and Aquarium, but did watch a movie about Niagra Falls in the Visitor Center.

We walked out to the end of the observation deck, enjoying the view of all three of the main waterfalls. It was spectacular! Then, we took the elevator down to the water level, and climbed up to the 'Crow's Nest', an observation deck near the north side of the American Falls.

Back on the park level, we walked across the pedestrian bridge onto Goat Island. We passed the Nikola Tesla Memorial, and headed for the Cave of the Winds complex. There were a lot of people, and we waited in line for ten minutes. But Sam bought ice cream for us to eat, and the wait didn't seem that long.

We donned blue ponchos, and descended 175 feet, coming out near the base of the Niagra Gorge. The view of the river downstream of the Falls was beautiful. We climbed steps and crossed rust-colored wooden walkways, eventually standing on a small deck below Bridal Veil Falls.

Our feet were awash in the water coming down from the upper Falls across huge boulders, then crossing over parts of the viewing platform. The new waterproof camera that Sam had given me was really coming in handy! I took some videos of the waterfall, and of Sam getting a face-full of water when the wind shifted slightly.

Once more we continued up the wooden steps, finally arriving at the 'Hurricane Deck' – which was positioned literally under the edge of the Falls. Everyone up here was soaked, despite the ponchos, blasts of water blowing over the deck by the gusty winds coming down the waterfall.

As we stood at the railing, only a few feet from Bridal Veil Falls, getting hit by gusts of wind and water, Sam turned to me, and we kissed. The hoods of our yellow ponchos almost made a private 'tent', as our faces came together.

My mind whirled, and I suddenly felt this was symbolic of my relationship with Sam: Being blasted by a storm, Sam at the middle of it also being blasted, and we were standing up to the storm, being blasted together. We were both willing and enthusiastic to do adventurous things, even ones that pushed our usual limits.

We made our way back along the wooden walkways, and took the elevator back to the top. As we had eaten a big lunch, Sam suggested that we have a light supper at the 'Top of the Falls' restaurant that has views of the Horseshoe Falls. It was still a bit early, so we stopped by the restaurant, and the *maître d'* told us he could have a window table for us in about an hour.

We strolled to Terrapin Point, at the edge of the Horseshoe Falls, and then on a path that led to a footbridge that crossed to Three Sisters Islands. Once again, it was spectacular, and I took a few more snapshots.

We seemed to be the only ones on the farthest island. I saw Sam looking around; then, he gave me the evil grin, and I knew what he was thinking. "But, Sam, this place is overrun with tourists. People will see us!"

Sam chuckled, then scrambled through the plants, and over a small boulder. I waited for him to return, then took one more look across the footbridge, before following him. We were on the rocks, at the edge of the water. Sam bowed, and pointed to a relatively flat rock surface.

As I looked out at the rapids, I shook my head, "Sam, do you realize that if we went into the water, we would be going over the falls in less than a minute?"

Sam laughed, "Probably more like thirty seconds! But we're not going into the water." He lowered his pants and sat back on a rock. Were we *really* going to do this? It would be our first time trying 'public sex'. Although there really weren't that many people around here right now, it was about as public as I wanted to get.

I shook my head, and Sam smiled. Then, I knelt on the rock below Sam, and went down on him. It didn't take long: I was sure this was something that really turned Sam on. I wasn't so sure about its effect on me: I was just nervous.

Sam patted his lap, and I straddled him, putting him in me, and rocking forward and back, his arms around me – hopefully not letting me fall backwards into the water.

I had to admit, it was a beautiful place, the only sound being the rushing of water. I put my arms around Sam, and closed my eyes, continuing my rocking motion. There didn't seem to be much motion for Sam, but he was 'hitting the right spot' for me.

Within a few minutes, my rocking had increased, and Sam was thrusting his hips into me, as our twin orgasms exploded. As we slowed, I relaxed forward onto Sam, my head on his shoulder. Images flew through my brain of standing next to the Horseshoe Falls, being soaked by the Bridal Veil Falls; and the scenes from the bow of the boat.

Sam stroked my back, and then lifted my head to his, and we began a romantic, passionate kiss ... that was rudely curtailed when we heard voices from behind us. I giggled, but Sam put his finger to his lips in a stern warning not to make a sound.

I wasn't sure what anyone would see – perhaps just the two of us sitting together ... Sam, with a bare butt. There was some talking in a language I didn't recognize, and then footsteps, as they walked back over the footbridge. "That was a pretty close one!"

Sam shook his head, "Nah, just enough to be exciting." Well, that was enough excitement for one day, for me! Then I flashed on the fact that just about *anything* new we did, at least sexually, would probably be pretty exciting.

Sam had managed to get us a prime view table at the Top of the Falls restaurant, and we decided to 'graze', and just enjoy the view. Sam ordered the charcuterie plate to start, along with a bottle of chardonnay.

After a few swallows of wine, my body and my mind relaxed. I thought how nice it was that Sam and I were traveling together again. Sam really knew how to enjoy a place – not skimping on the experiences ... or the food. We savored the food, and the wine, and the view ... and each other.

The third time the waiter came back to ask if we would be ordering anything else, we placed our order: A cobb salad for me, and a 'beef on Weck' for Sam; with chicken wings on the side. Well, I guess Sam's appetite had returned!

Sam had thought we would have front-row seats for the illumination of the falls, but there was no way that we could stretch our dinner to 9PM. We took the trolley to the main entrance of the park, and walked back across Rainbow Bridge to the Canadian side.

We had just entered our suite when we saw, through the sheer drapes, the falls suddenly being illuminated in a rainbow of colors. From our room, we could see both the American Falls and the Horseshoe Falls. As I stood at the window looking at the sight, Sam came up from behind, and put his arms around me, kissing my neck.

I turned around, "Again?" Sam's sexual energy was never-ending. Sam turned me around and smiled, then we kissed. Of course, I enjoyed sex – especially with Sam – but I was also enjoying the incredible light show out our window. "OK, Sam. But only if we can watch the light show at the same time."

The colors had morphed, the entire Horseshoe Falls now a boiling cauldron of red, with billows of red mist rising to the top of the cliff. I smiled at Sam, "Well, it *is* romantic." We turned off the room lights and opened the drapes; one entire wall of our suite was glass, and it was like watching a widescreen 3D show.

We undressed, and I pulled one of the armchairs next to the window, the back of the chair only inches away from the glass. Getting into the chair position, my arms folded on the back of the chair, I arched my back, and thrust my bum into the air.

Sam stood behind me, stroking my back, and reaching under to hold my breasts. Now the light was morphing again, the Horseshoe Falls now a deep blue. The American Falls were multihued, and I tried to make out the Cave of the Winds on one edge and the Crow's Nest on the other edge of the Falls, where we had been this afternoon.

I took a passive role, letting Sam get himself ready, while I watched the spectacle. But Sam is nothing, if not gallant, and he got me ready, also. I gasped, as Sam's hand slid under me, his fingers finding their target, my arousal quickly heightening.

Sam entered me slowly, both of us savoring the feeling of our joined bodies. He moved in slow strokes, as the light show continued. I hadn't been turned on when we started, but between Sam's manual skills and the romance of the evolving colors of the Falls, I came – as they say – 'never looking back'.

Sam's orgasm followed quickly, and we cleaned up and went to bed, the falls still illuminated in changing colors.

On Wednesday, we stashed a change of clothes in Sam's pack and took the WEGO bus to the White Water Walk. Once again, we took an elevator down to the river level, and strolled along the boardwalk next to the Whirlpool Rapids, where trillions of gallons of water rushed by at 30 miles per hour.

Then we took the bus the short distance to the our next adventure: The whirlpool jet boats! After a too-long orientation, and signing our lives away, we took a shuttle to the dock and boarded the boat. We were given another poncho, and I pointed to different-style boat that had a dome. Sam said, "Yeah, we could have taken the old-people's boat, and not gotten wet ... but that wouldn't have been nearly as much fun!"

The boat backed away from the dock, and we were soon traveling at more than 50 miles an hour upstream. The boat bucked the waves, and sheets of water poured over all of us. We were soaked within minutes!

We were shown the famous 'Hamilton turn', where the boat spins around in a 360-degree circle, and I was glad that we hadn't eaten lunch, yet. But the highlight of the trip was entering the whirlpool that occurs naturally in a bend of the river. Now we saw why the boats needed their 1500 horsepower engines.

I glanced up and pointed at the cable car that traversed the gorge, giving tourist a birds-eye view of the whirlpool. Sam shrugged. I remembered his fear of heights; and I would agree that seeing the whirlpool by boat had to be much more exciting.

When we returned to the dock, we put our soaked clothes in a garbage bag that Sam stuffed into his pack. Sam gave me the evil smile. "We could have taken that cable car ride ... but we have something much more exciting scheduled for tomorrow."

I stared at Sam, not able to imagine what could be so exciting, after all that we had done, already; and how that might relate to the aerial tram. Sam put his arm around me, and said, "Fiona and Justin will be joining us." Well, that was surprising! I hadn't thought we would see them again on this trip.

I gave Sam a 'look', and he shrugged, "We're going sky diving tomorrow." Now *that* was really surprising!

"But what about your fear of heights?" If Sam couldn't look over the railing of the Eiffel Tower, I couldn't imagine how he was going to deal with jumping from a plane.

Sam laughed, "Yes, that's the problem. So we're going to experience 'free fall' *without* going up in a plane." I must have given him a crazy look, as Sam cracked up. "We're going sky diving inside a vertical wind tunnel." All I could do is shake my head; what *else* could Sam come up with?

But I should have learned by now: Sam was an endless fount of creative ideas for new adventures and experiences. I was still spinning from our jet boat ride!

Then, Sam surprised me again. "We could go to the casino ... or drive to the safari park ... but I thought we might do something a little quieter this afternoon." I shook my head, not knowing whether Sam was being serious or facetious.

We boarded the WEGO bus again, and rode the short distance to the botanical gardens. I guess Sam was being serious. We walked through the gardens, which included the largest rose garden I'd ever seen. Then, we had a quick lunch and toured the butterfly conservatory.

It was still early when we got back to the hotel, and Sam still had energy, so we went on a short run. Back in our room, we showered together, then took advantage of the jacuzzi tub. Sam confirmed his reservation in one of the restaurants in the hotel for Friday night, and then we walked around the town.

Food-obsessed Sam couldn't decide on where we should go to dinner – the choices were numerous. There was Indian and German, Greek and Italian, Thai and Vietnamese. We had beers in an Irish pub, and then more beers in one of the local brew-pubs. We finally decided on dinner at one of the Brazilian steakhouses.

When we returned to the room, the falls were illuminated again. Sam suggested that we turn on the fireplace, and then ourselves, and we did ... but this time, we made love in the nice big, comfortable bed.

On Thursday morning, Fiona and Justin met us at the hotel, the 'sky diving' experience within walking distance. When we walked into the place, I saw prices on the board behind the counter. "$70 each for only three minutes?"

Sam shrugged, "I thought about doing *real* sky diving. We would have spent a full day of training, done an initial dive from 3,000 feet, and then done a free-fall from 10,000 feet. And it would have cost a few hundred dollars each."

My mouth was hanging open ... but so were the mouths of Fiona and Justin. Then, Sam explained, "But I wasn't sure we would all be up for that (and, yes, I would have been terrified), so I thought this might be a good alternative." We were all nodding.

Sam smiled, "So, as your birthday is only a few days away, I decided to get the 'birthday package' – which gives us some instruction, and about ten minutes each in the wind tunnel." Sam leaned over and whispered, "It's about the same price as the two of us doing a jump from a plane."

He didn't have to convince me: It was a good compromise, and Sam didn't have to face his fear of heights. It was a production, with all the equipment and instruction. We finally entered the wind tunnel, and the instructor demonstrated some incredible acrobatics – spinning, flipping, and flying from one wall of the silo to another.

We stood around the periphery of the padded space, as the instructor helped each of us get started. Amazingly, we all did pretty well, after a few hesitant first tries. Justin, especially, seemed to be a natural at sky diving ... at least, in this controlled environment.

The instructor was impressed, and we did well enough for him to allow Sam and I to 'fly' together. Actually, we weren't 'together' for more than an instant, but I knew that Sam was already considering whether we should take 'real' sky diving lessons – his ultimate goal probably being for us to 'hook up' in the air.

That part was a pipe dream, but I realized that sky diving could also be one more 'challenge' – especially for someone afraid of being a few hundred feet off the ground.

In any case, we all had fun, the experience still too short, once we started getting the feel of flying. As we exited, Sam asked if we wanted to try the 'Lazerball' game, where we would shoot each other with foam balls, similar to paintball. When there were no takers, he suggested the mechanical bull. I had to drag Sam out of there.

We enjoyed a late lunch with Fiona and Justin, all of us reminiscing about their wedding. Fiona laughed, "You guys really put on a good show. Several of my friends have already commented on it."

Sam responded, "Well, maybe we should have let some of them try being on the receiving end?" He looked at me, "We could design an interactive BDSM adventure." Fiona was still laughing, but all I could do was shake my head.

Then, I turned to Justin, "But I really *would* like to visit your club sometime on a more 'normal' night."

Justin nodded, "We'd be happy to have you, anytime. And, maybe Sam's got something there: We could organize a BDSM night, with people demonstrating and offering a small taste to some of the guests." Sam's eyes lit up; I was again shaking my head, but also smiling.

Friday was the fourth of July, and Sam had arranged for the hotel to provide a picnic basket with gourmet fare. After a short run in the morning, we went to Victoria Park, and ate our picnic lunch. Amazingly, Sam had nothing special planned for the day, until dinner in our hotel's best restaurant. But we still found a *few* things to keep us busy!

We had a late dinner reservation, and window seats again, this time enjoying an incredible meal, as we watched the fireworks. As usual, Sam went overboard, not only with the multi-course dinner and bottle of Pinot Noir, but then ordering desserts and a bottle of the local 'ice wine'.

We floated back to our room, both of us fully spent. We didn't take advantage of the jacuzzi, or fireplace, or even lovemaking. But we kissed and held each other until we were both asleep. This had been an incredible trip, even though it had been only a week, and we'd seen only Toronto and Niagra Falls.

Saturday morning, we drove to the airport in Buffalo, and took our first class flights home. I was a bit hung over, and didn't partake of the alcohol on the flights, but it was still nice to be traveling in style.

Sunday was my birthday, and we celebrated – just the two of us – by running to the pond, and relaxing most of the day, clothes-free. We had the pond to ourselves the whole day, nobody showing up, and Sam made love to me in the beautiful setting – the second time in a week that we'd had sex 'in public'.

I now had an Apple watch, Sam having copied my idea for a birthday present. He thought that the health-tracking capabilities would be useful, and he was looking forward to wrist-based communication. It was a nice present, but I'm not as geeky as Sam, which – of course – he knew.

Sam took me to dinner at the French restaurant, which was nice, but didn't seem quite as special, after all the great places we'd eaten in the last few days. But it was nice to be together, alone; no party, and not even a birthday spanking! Actually, we had both forgotten ...

CHAPTER 5: PULLING DOWN MY GENES

I sat on the uncomfortable wooden stool in the lab, watching the flashing lights of the gene sequencer, and the seemingly endless lines of data scrolling on the computer monitor. I had finished writing the first version software, and was now doing a 'real' experiment using the set-up.

Sequencing the genes of the *Borrelia burdorferi* bacterium had already been done, but I hoped that my software would elucidate the specific mechanisms and pathways of Lyme disease.

Although it wouldn't be the most important application of my software, Lyme was reported each year in some 30,000 people in the U.S. alone; and as many as ten times that number of people could be affected. And, this application seemed relatively easy, compared to many other diseases.

Of course, nobody had come up with a real solution, yet. Generally, antibiotics were given to kill the bacteria, and those would undoubtedly still be used; but my goal was to identify and block the specific signaling pathways involved in the disease.

I had wanted to work on identifying the mechanisms and potential drug targets for malaria, but my advisor, Raj, had thought that was overly ambitious, due to the half dozen types of protozoa responsible, and the multiple possible routes of disease.

But malaria was high on the list for development by KS Biotech, the company Sam and I had started, as it affects 500 million people per year, and is the number one cause of death of children, among all infectious diseases.

It was already August, and since returning from Toronto and Niagra Falls, I had kept up a nonstop schedule: Running every morning with Sam, then spending ten hours per day in the lab ... sometimes longer. I was in the lab some weekend days, and on others Sam and I brainstormed new inventions that he would write up, so they could be filed as patents.

I knew it would take many more months of hard work, but I hoped it wouldn't end-up taking years, to complete the project and finish writing my dissertation.

Of course, it was possible that I would *not* be successful in identifying specific drug targets, but I hoped that the development of the hardware and software, along with my novel algorithms, would still be enough for the Ph.D. project. Of course, we would need more than that to put KS Biotech on the map.

Sam had just returned from Oregon, as a grandparent, after attending the birth of Robert and Jessica's baby, who they named John Samuel. Sam had been there for nearly two weeks, and I missed him, but I'd made great progress on my dissertation.

Sam had insisted that we take the coming weekend off, and invite my friends over. He looked forward to taking all of us on a shopping spree, including at least REI for camping supplies, and our local dive shop for snorkeling equipment. And he was now talking about buying swimwear for us from Victoria's Secret.

The lights on the sequencer were still flashing, and data was still scrolling down the screen of the lab computer. I pulled out my laptop, and e-mailed Julie,

Linda and Kathy, asking if they were available, and suggesting that they come to Sam's house at 10AM Saturday morning.

I was looking forward to seeing my friends; I hadn't seen Julie or Linda since Linda's birthday, and hadn't heard from Kathy since the submission challenge and competition at the end of May. There was a lot of news to catch up on, including the trip Sam and I had taken to Toronto and Niagra Falls, and Kathy's trip to Mexico.

I also wondered whether my friends were working out as hard as Sam and I were, to get into shape for our Hawaii trip in less than a month. Sam had voiced his concern several times that we would need to be in good shape to hike the Kalalau trail for our camping experience. I was especially concerned about Linda, and curious whether she had actually lost weight; she had been somewhat 'chunky' ever since I had first met her in high school.

Glancing at my new Apple watch, I was shocked to see that it was already after 5PM. I pushed the 'digital crown'. "Hey, Siri. Send a text message to Sam: 'I'll be home as soon as the experiment finishes ... but it might be close to seven'." Then, I drew a heart on the screen, which I knew would be reproduced on Sam's watch.

I had given him the watch for his birthday, as Sam was such a 'techno-geek', and he'd bought one for my birthday, so that we could more easily keep in touch. It was actually pretty neat. We'd both been keeping track of our running, and were making great progress. I hadn't seen Sam in such good shape since I'd met him. And I was probably in the best shape of my life.

As I read Kelly's text message on my watch, I was glad that I'd decided to make dinner for us tonight. It was only a simple Italian chop salad, but I'd also made my special garlic bread as a treat, since we were both doing so well with our weight. I opened a bottle of reserve chianti, poured a glass for myself, and went out to the patio.

All of the plans for the Hawaii trip were completed, and I looked forward to seeing Kelly's friends, and getting them set-up for backpacking and snorkeling. I had given up on the idea of taking Kelly SCUBA diving, but pondered whether I should organize a 'demo' dive for all of the girls, in one of the condo pools.

As I sat back in the patio chair, I smiled; the trip to Kauai was shaping up to be an epic event.

I closed my eyes, thinking back to the submission challenge we'd had with Kelly and her friends. I wasn't planning on giving the girls any extreme challenges in Kauai, although there would still be a few new 'experiences' which would require openness and trust.

But Julie, Linda and Kathy had already demonstrated their openness, and their trust; and I knew they would enjoy the trip ... and would be fine with the few 'special' events that I had planned.

My continuing thoughts along those lines resulted in a growing bulge in my pants, and I left my wine on the patio table, and went down to the playroom, where I lay on the couch, closed my eyes, and took care of my 'needs'.

Walking into the house, I put my books down on the kitchen table, and looked around: There was no food on the stove, and Sam was nowhere to be seen. I peeked out to the patio, and saw a wine glass, but no Sam. He was probably working on his computer downstairs.

As I stepped into the playroom, still not seeing Sam, I called his name. I heard an 'Oh!', and saw Sam sit up on the couch, then stand, his pants undone, and a wad of tissues in his hand. He looked at me sheepishly, and shrugged his shoulders.

"You couldn't wait for me?" I asked, giving him a knowing smile. Sam was the horniest man I'd ever known; it took very little to get him turned on. I could only try to imagine what he'd been fantasizing about, this time.

Sam fastened his pants, and came over to me, giving me a big hug, the tissues still in his hand. "I was just thinking about you!" I put my hands on my hips, and stared at Sam, until he relented. "OK. I was thinking about the submission challenge for your friends; and our trip to Hawaii."

I shook my head, now wondering what Sam had planned for our island adventure. I hoped that he wouldn't put my friends through too many more 'challenges'. "Are we going out for dinner? I didn't see anything on the stove."

Sam smiled, "I made a salad for us. And garlic bread. And, opened a nice bottle of chianti." He gave me a peck of a kiss, "Why don't you get cleaned up, and I'll toss the salad, put the garlic bread under the broiler, and pour you some wine. I thought we might eat out on the patio, tonight."

That sounded good to me, so I went upstairs, grabbed my notebooks from the kitchen table, and headed up to the master bedroom.

I had made a list of the supplies that Kelly and her friends should have for the hiking and camping experience. I would be bringing the tent and a lightweight fly, as well as a backpacking stove, water pump, first aid kit, and a few more special items, some *not* hiking or camping related.

The girls would also need basic snorkeling equipment, including mask, fins, booties, and snorkel. I would also be giving Kathy and Julie their underwater cameras – early for their birthdays, but in time to practice in the pool before we left on the trip. I hoped that we could get everything done today, so we could relax tomorrow. Kelly had really been putting in long hours in the lab, lately.

Around 10AM, as I was cleaning up things in the kitchen, I heard the doorbell, and Kelly ran to greet her friends. As I took the last dishes out of the dishwasher, I heard a scream. It was Kelly: "Oh my *God*! You look *fabulous!*" I walked past the dining room, and stepped through the living room to the door ... and was dumbfounded!

Linda stood just inside the door, beaming. At least, I *thought* it was Linda. My mouth dropped open, and all I could get out was a sincere, "Wow! You look *great!*" Linda was wearing a sheer coffee-toned blouse tucked in to tan slacks. She looked *incredible* – at least 20 pounds lighter than the last time we'd seen her.

She had let her dark hair grow a couple of inches longer, her face was oval, not round, and her waist had to be as narrow as Kelly's. I wondered whether she was wearing Spanx but, from the rest of her body, I knew that she had lost a major amount of weight.

I stepped up to her, and gave her a big hug. "Well hello, beautiful!" I glanced at Kelly, who was also beaming, and she gave me a small nod.

Linda did a pirouette, and held her arms out, palms up. She gave Kelly a serious look, and said, "Kelly, I know you've been working hard ... but so have I." She smiled demurely, "So what do you think?"

Kelly and I were speechless. We'd seen her only two months ago, but Linda had made a major transformation.

She had always been 'cute', and had a great personality, but she was now beautiful. Once again, all I could get out was another "Wow!!!"

We ushered Linda into the house, and out to the patio. Kelly and Linda sat down, and I offered them drinks; they both chose Diet Coke.

When I got back to the table with their drinks, Linda was explaining, "... so after two weeks on the cabbage soup diet, I started eating healthy – a lot of raw fruits and vegetables, very little meat, and no alcohol. The day after my birthday party, I started walking – three miles a day for the first week, then four, and then five." Kelly nodded.

Linda continued, "In the last couple of weeks, I've been doing a slow jog, and have worked up to five miles a day; every day of the week. And, I've been going to the gym three days a week, and got a trainer." She smiled at Kelly, "He's a cute guy."

Kelly nodded blankly, and Linda continued, "After doing the stair stepper, and weights, I've been swimming. I'm up to 100 laps in the pool."

I glanced at Kelly, and turned to Linda, "I can't believe you could do that in only two months! I'm so proud of you, Linda." I got out of my chair, and bent over to hug Linda, then gave her a very sincere kiss. As I sat down, I couldn't help but shake my head.

Linda looked at Kelly, then at me, and exclaimed, "You guys look great, too!" I realized that my head was still shaking, slowly. Linda said, "Sam, it was really great offering to take us to Hawaii. And, I'm really looking forward to the trip."

I nodded, and she continued, "And I've learned to trust you ... what you say ... and I know you were worried that we wouldn't be in good enough shape for that hike you're planning." Linda looked back and forth to Kelly and I, "So I got motivated."

"It's incredible, Linda. You must have lost at least 25 pounds!"

Linda smiled, "Well, it was only twenty two pounds ... but I've gotten rid of fat, and put on some muscle. My whole body has changed." I could see that.

Laughing, Linda looked at Kelly, and said, "Among other things, my cup size has gone from a double-D to a C." She laughed again, "So I'm in the process of buying a lot of new clothes."

Then she looked at me seriously, "And I plan to keep the weight off. If my new clothes start feeling tight, I'm going to cut down on calorie intake, and exercise even harder." She finished her Diet Coke and sat back in the chair.

This was the *new* Linda. Her hips, and especially her butt, were much smaller – perhaps not as overtly 'spankable' as before, but overall she looked terrific.

The door to the kitchen opened, and Julie and Kathy came out to the patio; we hadn't even heard the doorbell ring. They smiled and waved at us, and then Linda rose and faced them, with her hands on her hips.

Julie and Kathy froze in their tracks, and their mouths simultaneously fell open, their eyes wide. Julie screamed, and ran to Linda, hugging her. Then, Kathy took her turn.

Julie turned to Kelly and I, "I've invited Linda to lunch a couple of times in the past month or so, but she's declined my invitations. I was wondering what the problem was ..." She turned to Linda, "But now I can see it wasn't a 'problem' at all. You look *great!*"

I stood, and gave my chair to Julie, then went into the kitchen and brought out a few cans of Diet Coke and glasses with ice. The girls were chatting animatedly.

Pulling over one of the chaises, I sat between Kelly and Kathy, as the girls updated each other. Kathy related that her Mexico trip had been nice – no men, but a lot of pampering in spas with her mother. And, she had been running on the beach every morning, and working out in the hotel gym.

Kelly briefly described our Toronto and Niagra Falls trip, including our jet boat tour and sky diving adventure ... and telling her friends a little about the wedding party at Justin's sex club.

With the Cokes finished, and the conversation dwindling, I suggested we head out to do some serious shopping. Kelly chuckled, and looked at her friends, "Yeah, when *we* do 'serious' shopping, we buy clothes ... but Sam's idea of 'serious' is buying dive and camping gear."

As Kelly's friends laughed, I stood, and said, "Well, I thought I would take you guys to Victoria's Secret, and buy each of you a couple of nice bathing suits."

Then, I looked at Linda, "And, as a small reward for Linda, I'm going to give Linda a budget of $300 to buy whatever bras and underwear she wants."

Linda's mouth dropped open, "Thanks, Sam. That's a really nice offer." I didn't know how far $300 would go, but hoped that would at least get Linda started with her new wardrobe.

Sam was a very generous person, and I wasn't surprised that he'd made that offer to Linda. He had bought me plenty of clothes over the past year, including the ski jacket from Koblenz, and the satin negligée for my birthday, as well as a lot of more mundane things.

We headed out, first stopping at the dive store. I hadn't even known this place existed, and it was a bit weird, since we were nowhere near the ocean. But they had a large stock – from wetsuits, to dive computers, to buoyancy compensators, to the masks, fins and snorkels that Sam wanted us to try.

Sam explained that we would need neoprene booties, for wearing under the fins; they would also enable us to walk safely over lava rocks. Once we had all found booties that fit, we tried a variety of fins. Kathy picked up a pair of triangular blue and yellow fins, very stiff, which Sam said were for body surfing and boogey boarding.

Sam showed us some nice fins that he said would be appropriate for snorkeling. Then, he helped each of us pick out a mask.

As we began adjusting straps and pulling them behind our head, Sam laughed, and showed us how to try on the mask *without* straps – just pushing them against our faces, and breathing in slightly through the nose. The masks stuck to our faces, and Sam had us breathe through our mouths, while the mask was covering our nose, still held by a slight vacuum to our faces, even without straps.

Finally, Sam selected snorkels for us, and showed us how to hook the snorkel to the mask, using a 'snorkel keeper'. Sam had told us about some of this when he'd demonstrated snorkeling in the pool, but it meant more, now that we were actually buying equipment.

Sam spent a few minutes perusing the latest dive computers, and also spoke quietly with the owner for a few minutes. As we walked back to the car, I asked what he had been whispering about. "Oh, I was just finding out about the dive classes they offer."

I shook my head, "Sam, I really don't have time for something like that … at least, until my research is over and I've earned my doctorate. And then we'll be pretty busy with KS Biotech."

Sam nodded, "I know. But at some point, I would like you to get certified." When I gave him a strange look, he smiled and clarified, "... In SCUBA diving, that is." We laughed. It was something I would like to do, someday, but I couldn't imagine when I would ever have the time.

Next, we went to the camping store, and Sam helped us pick out hiking packs. He would be carrying most of the gear, and food for the first night; he had already arranged a boat drop-off of the rest of our food with a friend he knew on Kauai. Although he already had several of them, he bought a few more waterproof bags.

Sam also bought each of us a light sleeping bag and air mattress, bug spray, hats, and sunglasses. He bought himself a new water purifier pump, and then decided to buy a small one for each of us. He said that the streams and waterfalls could be contaminated with a small parasite (he called it a 'fluke') that can cause 'leptospirosis'.

Although he hoped that the weather would be good, he bought a lightweight rain shell for each of us. Then, we went to the shoe department, and we tried on a variety of hiking boots, but Sam suggested that we try on a pair of trail-running shoes instead.

We were at the store for a couple of hours and, by the time we checked out, we'd run up a bill of well over two thousand dollars. Julie offered to pay her share, but Sam explained that he considered this part of the 'trip expense'.

"I invited you guys to go to Hawaii with Kelly and I, and some of these things are needed for the trip. I don't want you to get stuck with any extra expenses, just because you're coming with us."

Sam smiled, looking at each of my friends, in turn, "And, the trip was supposed to be a thank-you and reward for putting up with the submission challenge."

None of us commented, but I was sure we were all remembering the crazy day we'd had ... and the preparation Sam had insisted on. It was amazing that Julie, Linda and Kathy were not only still friends, but upbeat and enthusiastic to continue 'playing' with Sam and I. I could only hope that Sam didn't push my friends too hard during the 'reward trip' to Hawaii!

It was already mid-afternoon, and we drove to the shopping center, and Victoria's Secret. Linda headed over to look at bras, while Julie and Kathy perused the selection of bikini bathing suits. Sam followed me around, as I looked at a caftan and a knotted cover-up.

I made a selection, and then picked up a monokini, holding it up for Sam's review. He shrugged, and glanced over to the tiny bikinis and thongs that Julie and Kathy were comparing.

Looking back to me, he said, "The only question is whether you want the suntan pattern these will leave. Actually, I like the suits you already have."

Sam had already bought me swimwear, but I could always use another suit. I looked at a few of the bikinis, and held up a couple. Sam smiled, "Those are sexy!"

Linda walked up to us, carrying several bras, a few pairs of bikini underwear, and held up a thong. She would never have been able to wear that before losing weight. She whispered to Sam, "You're welcome to come in with me, while I try these, if you like. You can help me select a few things."

I thought Sam would jump at the chance to go into the dressing room with Linda, but he replied, "That's a nice offer, Linda. If you really want me to come in with you, I will." Then, he said, more seriously, "But I think you should pick things *you* like, that you'll be comfortable in."

Linda was surprised, too, her mouth dropping open for a few seconds. Then she hugged Sam, the underclothes in both her hands. "Thank you, Sam." She chuckled, "Well, I guess you'll get to see me in whatever I pick, anyway." With that, she headed off to the dressing rooms.

Neither Julie nor Kathy consulted with Sam, but each picked a couple of suits. Sam sat on a chair outside the dressing room area, while we all tried on our selections.

When we checked out, and Sam pulled out his credit card, I laughed inside, wondering whether the checker thought that we were all Sam's daughters. But we all looked too different to be in the same family ... unless we had been adopted.

I flashed on the news my mother had given me about my birth parents – my mother being the sister of my adoptive mother, and my father evidently a scoundrel, and in jail.

I had put this out of my mind for the past six months. My adoptive mother was now my mother, but the revelations about my birth parents had hit a nerve. The thought that my father wasn't the caring, loving person I had remembered hurt, and I tried to think of other things.

The bill here was less than $1000, but not by much. The trip was already getting expensive, and we hadn't even left, yet.

We exited Victoria's Secret, and walked past the Apple store, then Sam pointed, "How about an early dinner at the Mexican restaurant?" It was the usual lunch spot for my friends and I, but we had never been there for dinner, and never gone there with Sam. Julie and Kathy were nodding, but Linda was quiet, and looked away.

As soon as we sat down, a waiter brought chips and salsa, and took our drink orders. Sam asked if everyone liked Margaritas, and ordered a pitcher. Then, Linda surprised us by ordering iced tea. As we all reached for the chips, Linda put her hands in her lap and just stared at the basket. Then, she picked up the menu.

We all ordered our favorites – all but Linda, who ordered a shrimp cocktail and albondigas soup. Sam looked at her, "Is that all you're going to have?"

Linda handed the waiter her menu, and said, "OK. I'll also have a small salad, dressing on the side, please."

I leaned over and hugged Linda, "You're really being strong! No wonder you were able to lose so much weight."

Sam looked at her, "I'm sorry, Linda. Maybe we should have gone someplace where you could have ordered more easily."

Linda shook her head, "That's OK, Sam. But I still need to let my weight stabilize, if I expect to be able to enjoy the food in Hawaii ... and still fit in my new clothes."

Lifting the Margarita glass, Sam toasted, "We're proud of you, Linda." Then, he looked around the table, "I'm proud of *all* of you, for getting into shape for the trip." He smiled, "I think it's going to be an epic experience for all of us." And, I knew that it would be.

———————————

We were all in good shape, and I was much less nervous about taking the girls on a twelve mile, world-class hike on the Kalalau trail. I had already arranged an offshore boat pickup, so we only had to make it one way ... but that would be hard enough, doing it in a single day.

When we got back to the house, we went down to the playroom, and I hit the remote to lower the screen, start the projector, and dim the lights. Then we shared pictures from our Toronto and Niagra Falls trip, beamed from Kelly's laptop to the projector.

We only had a few snapshots from the wedding ceremony but, unfortunately, hadn't taken any pictures at Justin's sex club. Then, Kelly surprised me: She fiddled with her computer, and announced to all of us that Fiona had sent the video of our performance on stage. The huge screen was filled with an image of Kelly taking me over her lap, colored lights moving over us as she spanked me.

The girls first gasped, then giggled, seeing me squirm. Then, came the more serious part, where I bent over the bed, and Kelly lowered my underwear, then strapped me. We could hear the audience gasping, then laughing, then cheering, as my poor bottom took the strap, expertly wielded by Kelly.

I really didn't remember that much, except for the pain. I had been a little tipsy by that time, and with the endorphin rush my mind was in a haze. Now that I was watching the video, it did seem pretty impressive. I thought I had been quiet, but by the end of the strapping, I cried out a few times, and could clearly be heard whimpering, even over the cheers from the audience.

Kelly didn't know it, but I was working on a video of my own, to be shown when we were in Kauai. It was a huge compilation of scenes from over the past year, which I'm sure would be both impressive and hilarious for the girls to watch. I would have to add this 'wedding spanking' segment.

After the video, Kelly showed her pictures and a few short videos of our Niagra Falls adventure, including the thundering water coming down on us at the Cave of the Winds, more water splashing over us during our jet boat ride, and some funny videos of each of us trying to 'skydive' in the huge silo.

There were a lot of 'Oooh's' and 'Aaah's' from Kelly's friends. We really had done quite a lot during our week-long trip. The last videos were of the Fourth of July fireworks over the illuminated falls.

I went to my credenza, and pulled out two wrapped packages, bringing them back to the couch. "I already gave one of these to Linda for her birthday, and one to Kelly for the Niagra Falls trip," I looked at Julie and Kathy, "but I also want you guys to have one." I handed the packages to them, and Julie smiled, already knowing what they were.

When Kathy unwrapped the underwater camera, she screamed, then hopped up and hugged me. "This is fantastic, Sam!" Then, she sat down, and gave us a pout, "But this is too much. The trip to Hawaii is enough, without buying all this stuff for us."

I shrugged, "You can consider these early birthday presents ... but I want you to have them for the trip, so that you can capture your own memories." Julie hugged me, and both girls thanked me effusively.

"We can try all the equipment out tomorrow in the pool. I want all of you to be comfortable, when we go snorkeling." Then, I smiled, "Unless you want to do a 'night dive' in the pool? We could try the cameras out tonight. Then we can adjust the fins and masks tomorrow morning, and do a little more snorkel practice."

Julie whispered to Linda and Kathy, and they nodded. "Let's wait until tomorrow to go in the pool, Sam." I must have looked disappointed, because Julie immediately followed-up with, "We'd like to give you a little fashion show of all the things you bought us at Victoria's Secret."

I couldn't help but smile. That was an offer I couldn't refuse. As many times as I'd seen the girls nude, it would still be exciting to see them modeling their bathing suits and, in Linda's case, her new bras and panties.

The girls went upstairs to get their shopping bags, and I poured diet sodas for all of us. I heard a lot of whispering and some giggling. Finally, they all came down the stairs, dressed as they had been, and each carrying a Victoria's Secret bag; except Kelly, who had gone into the exam room.

Kelly brought out a box of items, and ducked behind the screen. I offered sodas to everyone, and they set the bags down in the desk area behind the couch. As Linda took a big swig of her drink, Julie undid her pants and pushed them down.

Kelly sat down next to me, turned my head back toward her, and announced, "Sam, we appreciate all the things you've bought for us. And I've told my friends how hard you've worked to make the Hawaii trip a great experience." She looked into my eyes, "So they would like to thank you."

Leaning forward and giving me a kiss, Kelly added, "We *all* would like to thank you." I had no idea what they were planning, but it sounded good. Then, Kelly blinked her eyes, and added, "*If* you can relax about it."

I shrugged, "I'm always relaxed!" Of course, I knew that wasn't true, and Kelly put her hands on her hips, and gave me a piercing look ... until *she* relaxed, and broke into a smile.

"You'll enjoy it, Sam." Then, I heard, under her breath, 'Whatever we decide to do with you ...'. Kelly reached over to the corner table, and picked up the remote. After a bit of staring, she punched a few buttons, and light jazz music came onto the surround sound system.

Julie came around the love seat, wearing a small, lacy white bikini top, and tiny white thong. She turned, and modeled the sexy outfit, then reached in back, and unhooked her bra. She swung back around, and smiled at Kelly and I over her shoulder. It was obvious that she'd spent some time in the sun, topless.

Julie threw me a kiss, and went back around behind the couch as Linda strutted out, wearing black, cheeky panties, and matching bra. She smiled seductively at me, and twirled around, dropping a fistful of underclothes on the carpet.

I had to applaud: It wasn't the cute underwear, but Linda's remarkable body that compelled me to praise her. She'd shown true strength and willpower, losing so much weight over only a couple of months. She had always been a cute girl, but now I could see real beauty in her body.

Linda pushed the panties down, and shook them off her legs, then picked up a thong – this one with much more material than the one Julie had modeled, with pink between bands of black lace. She turned around, and looked over her shoulder, batting her eyes at me.

She then put on a small black bra that I couldn't believe would contain her. Her breasts *were* smaller, now, but there was still plenty of cleavage she could flaunt, when wearing an open-buttoned blouse. The music and the show continued, Linda changing between several different bras and panties.

I noticed that she had trimmed her formerly square of black pubic hair into a narrow vertical strip. I would need to ask her about her waxing experience ... if that's what she'd done.

Kathy came out, wearing a tiny string bikini, in a rainbow of thin strips, and matching top comprised of a couple of tiny triangles of material connected by a multi-hued string. I applauded again. Kathy looked happier than I'd seen her in a while; she emanated a positive energy that was contagious.

Julie came out, pushing Kathy aside, and modeling her hot pink bikini, with halter top, and small bottom accented by gold clips. Kathy changed into a cute turquoise bikini made out of what appeared to be neoprene, a wetsuit material. It had two thin black strings at the waist, and black strings holding the small top in place.

I wondered how much Kathy's top would be on; but we *would* be going to a few places, where the girls would need to be somewhat covered. I had already suggested that they also bring the pareos that I had given them at Kelly's birthday party.

Linda pushed Julie and Kathy aside, and modeled a very elegant bathing suit, in a black-and-white snakeskin pattern, with a relatively large bikini bottom (after all, her hips were still 'generous'), and crisscross halter top.

Then, Kelly got up and, after her three friends had modeled still another suit for me, came back, wearing another elegant number: A bikini with black bottom trimmed and tied with three thin gold straps, and a top similarly detailed, with white panel hooked around the back.

Kelly glanced at her friends, and they nodded, then all their suits came off, and Kelly stepped up to me, pushed the remote to raise the screen, and pulled me off the couch.

As I approached the bed, the four women undressed me, and then I was lying on the bed, my head on the pillow, as Kathy crawled over to me, and turned around, straddling me.

Kathy lowered her head, and took my already-growing length into her mouth. I relaxed my head into the pillow, and gazed up at the wispy, thin blond hairs gracing Kathy's pubic area. I wasn't too surprised that Kelly's friends were 'thanking' me in this way. I remembered back to the morning after Kelly's birthday party ...

Then, Kelly was leaning over from the side, and kissed my cheek softly. I glanced to her, and she held up one of the longer and thinner of the butt plugs in our collection. "Put it in her, Sam."

I took the butt plug, and reached up to Kathy's rear. She was still sucking me, obviously aware of what was to come. Her anal muscles were entirely relaxed, and it was easy to slip the butt plug into her. As I moved it in and out of her, and her mouth moved on me, I realized that I was getting seriously turned on.

I pushed the plug in all the way in, and Kathy lapped at my engorged member, and then swung herself around, and kissed me on the lips.

Before I realized what was happening, Julie took her place, straddling me, and taking my throbbing organ into her mouth. Kelly handed me another butt plug – the same, but purple, rather than black. I inserted it into Julie's rear, as she continued to mouth my manhood.

Too soon, Julie turned around, and licked my lips, then gave me an open-mouth kiss. It was only recently that I had gotten more comfortable tasting my own juices. But it still was more of a turn-off than a turn-on. That was probably good, in this case, or I would have come before Linda had taken her turn.

But Linda got her chance: She first gave me a penetrating kiss, holding my head, and devouring me, before she turned around, straddling me, and gave me her oral attention. Kelly handed me the third butt plug, and I inserted it into Linda, as she moaned.

By now, my mind was a blur, and I was in another dimension, as I realized that three gorgeous women had just given me fellatio, as I'd invaded their posterior privacy. Although we'd all done these kinds of things together previously, it was suddenly an incredible turn-on, and I nearly blacked-out, as the blood drained from my head.

Linda was off me, and Kelly pulled me up, and handed me another butt plug. When I gave her a questioning look, she lay down and pulled her legs up to her chest, then raised her eyebrows.

I smiled, and raised my eyebrows at her, then inserted the butt plug into her, playing with it a little, as I went down on her. My tongue moved in a circular motion, surrounding her clit with stimulation. She pulled my hair, and I moved up on her, as she took me in her hand, and inserted me into her warm cave.

I am a very controlled person, and have great sexual stamina; but by now, I was using breathing exercises to avoid coming immediately. As soon as I was in Kelly, and beginning to make long, slow strokes, I felt something cold, and rounded pressing against my butt.

Someone – I think it was Linda – was inserting a butt plug – one of the larger ones – as someone else (I assumed it was Kathy) held my balls. Julie lay next to me, and slipped her hand between Kelly and I, and I lifted up my middle when I realized that Julie would be diddling Kelly, even as I moved inside her.

I closed my eyes, and lowered myself onto Kelly, as I tried to extend the excruciatingly ecstatic feeling of being attended by four beautiful women. Kathy was now pushing on my perineum, as Linda moved the butt plug around slowly in me.

Kelly was right: It took a new level of openness and relaxation for me to enjoy this experience, but I was determined to do so. I melted into Kelly, as our three 'assistants' continued their consideration. I don't know how long this continued ... but not long enough.

With several jerking thrusts, I came explosively. In the moment, it was an amalgam, a montage, of feelings – mainly physical, but also the underlying knowledge that my orgasm was due to the efforts of four women; very open women. And women, for whom I had true feelings.

Neither Kelly nor I would be interested in communal living. And we had recently discussed the concept of polyamory. I certainly believed that there were many people that each person could love; and in the best of cases, it is possible to love many people simultaneously.

The problem, both due to our society and training, and due to the innate jealously of *homo sapiens*, is that polyamory can only be successful when all participants are unusually open, sharing people. I can imagine it happening, but didn't think it was something that Kelly and I would accept; even with her friends.

But I had to admit that they were all special. It had been amazing that Julie, Linda and Kathy could have shared so many things with Kelly and I. I continued to thrust, as I thought of some of the experiences we'd had – together, and separately.

I realized that Julie was still 'doing' Kelly, who was undulating rhythmically. I kept moving inside Kelly, as I continued to shrink, having been totally satisfied, physically.

I kissed Kelly and, fortunately, her surging increased, her breath ragged, and she finally climaxed, our bodies one, but with the help of Julie ... and – as I felt the butt plug moving inside me, and my balls being held – Kathy and Linda. Amazing!

We got off the bed, and Kelly handed me a fluff of tissues. The girls smiled at each other, and got into a knee-chest position along the foot of the bed. The view was incredible, and I was very appreciative of how lucky I was to have Kelly, and her friends; to play with, but also to love, to care for, and with whom I could share important experiences.

I pulled the butt plugs out of the girls, holding them in the tissues, and then walked down the line, giving each of them a playful slap on each of their buttocks.

Then, we retired to the downstairs bathroom, where we peed and took a long, hot, and caring shower together. The girls left their new 'Secrets' in the playroom, and we climbed the stairs to the bedrooms. I gave each of the girls a quick peck on the cheek, and headed to the master bedroom, leaving Kelly to say goodnight to her friends.

By the time Kelly climbed into bed, I was nearly asleep. Kelly knew I was finished. She turned off the light and spooned me. My last thought was – again – how lucky I was to have Kelly, and her adventurous friends.

We were all up early, and Sam suggested that we go on a jog, together. It would be the first time my friends had seen the idyllic pond that was only about three miles from the house.

I'd suggested that my friends bring their jogging outfits and shoes, and they all had. And Sam proposed that we try our new packs. He helped us adjust the straps, and suggested we each bring a small towel and our flip-flops. In his own pack, Sam also squeezed the large sheet, his new water pump, some beef jerky, and a first aid kit.

None of us knew how fast the others ran; as Sam and I did trail running, we monitored our time on our Apple Watches; we weren't really focusing on speed; but we were developing some great stamina.

We started out on a slow jog, and everyone kept pace. When we crossed the small stream and turned onto the narrow trail, I glanced back at Sam and took off. We twisted with the trail, ducked under branches, and propelled ourselves off boulders, as we'd gotten to know the trail well.

Somehow, Sam managed to tag me, just as we entered the clearing by the pond. We laughed, and hugged each other. Sam was already laying out the large sheet when Linda arrived, panting, but smiling. She bent over, her hands on her knees, as she recovered from the run.

Kathy was next, and she didn't appear winded; she had kept at a slower pace, and conserved her energy. Finally, Julie walked into the clearing, and plopped down on the sheet. She looked up at me, "Maybe, I should be running a little more?" Then, she glanced at Sam and back to me, "You guys were *flying*!"

I shook my head, "We barely got warmed up by the time we crossed the stream; and we normally wouldn't have stopped here to take a break."

Sam interjected, "We're now running eight miles a couple of times a week, and I think we're ready to do a ten mile run next week." He raised his eyebrows, and I raised mine.

Looking at each of my friends, Sam said, "We don't *have* to stop here ... if you want, we could run right back to the house." Everyone was shaking their head slowly. Julie volunteered, "No, Sam, I think it would be nice to take a short break." She was laughing, but serious.

By this time, my friends were staring at the pond, ringed with boulders, the waterfall, and the overhanging trees. Kathy said, solemnly, "It's beautiful." Now, everyone was nodding.

"This is where we met Alex and Fiona, the first long weekend I stayed with Sam." I smiled at Sam, and said proudly, "And I had the stripes of a cane across my bum!"

Linda was shaking her head. "Well, I can understand it now, but at the time ... when you first told us about Sam, I was afraid he was a psycho."

Sam gave Linda a sour and disappointed look, but before he could comment, Linda added, "But that same weekend, when Sam gave me a 'birthday spanking', he reignited some latent desire in me; all of my fantasies about spanking came back."

Then, she chuckled, looking at Sam, "By the end of Kelly's birthday party, I think we all knew each other pretty well." I knew everyone was remembering the Spank Poker game on the 'Lazy Sam' turntable.

Linda laughed, "And now, we *KNOW* that Sam's a psycho!" Sam started chasing Linda around the sheet, and over to the pond. Kathy was already nude, stepping up onto one of the boulders.

Linda put her hands up, "OK, Sam. I give up." Linda pulled off her top, and pushed down her running shorts, then took off her sports bra.

Sam gave Linda the evil eye, and said, "You know what that means, Linda?" I wasn't sure I knew, but Linda certainly did: She nodded, and said "Yes, sir."

Sam put his left foot up onto a large rock, and Linda bent herself over it. Sam proceeded to give Linda a hard but short hand spanking – probably about two dozen swats on her rear. She was laughing the whole time.

Linda's body really had changed: Her hips were still wide, but her bottom was much firmer than it had been. Sam lifted Linda off his leg, and hugged her. Then, Linda followed Kathy into the pond.

Julie and I quickly undressed and walked to the rocks near the water. I kissed Sam, and let myself fall forward into the water. As I swam over to the waterfall, where

Linda and Kathy were talking, I waved to Sam, "Come in with us!"

Sam shrugged, then took off his tank and running shorts, and got onto a boulder, getting ready to cannonball into the small pond. But then he smiled, sat down, and let himself slide into the cool liquid.

It would be a hot day later, but it was still morning, and the pond was mostly in shade, the air fresh and cool. There were flowers around the pond, but some of them had already surrendered to the summer heat.

The air was very still at ground level, but we could hear the rustling of leaves in the canopy far above. Specks of blue sky peeked between leaves that hung over the verdant foliage.

We didn't stay in the water long, and nobody ate the snacks that Sam offered, but we all drank our water, and prepared for the run home.

As we put on our running shorts and tops, Sam said, "OK. I think it's time for a small challenge."

Oh no! Now, what? There was some groaning from Linda and Kathy ... but then I saw their smiles, and realized it was 'mock' groaning.

Sam smiled, "No, not *that* kind of a challenge! Let's go back in our flip-flops. I'd like to see how comfortable you all are in them. Maybe, we could even jog the narrow part of the trail?" Everyone shrugged. We took out our flip-flops, and packed our shoes and socks in our packs.

I led the way, and Sam took up the rear (in a manner of speaking). Kathy and I were the most comfortable in flip-flops, but we all kept together all the way home.

Kelly and her friends were in pretty good shape. They would have no problem on the trails in Kauai. But, like a marathon run, the Kalalau Trail takes a certain willpower, persistence, and positivity. All of us doing it together would hopefully provide the support they would need.

I got a quick shower upstairs, then went downstairs to make a small breakfast for everyone. I prepared fresh pineapple, papaya, mango, and kiwi, along with a nice selection of fresh berries. Then, I cut diagonals of seeded baguette, lightly buttered them, and stuck them under the broiler.

I put the pink tablecloth on the patio table, and set it for five. By the time I had brought out the coffee and fresh juices, platters of fruit, and the bread, Julie and Linda were coming up from the downstairs bathroom, and Kathy and Kelly from the upstairs bathrooms.

I offered to make oatmeal, or set out jams, but everyone seemed happy with the selection that was on the table. "I wanted to get you into the tropical mood with the breakfast, but we can't get fruit here like we're going to have in Hawaii."

Kathy looked up, "This is delicious, Sam. I never seem to get papaya, unless we're in Mexico. We have it almost every breakfast, with a drizzle of fresh lime."

I hit my hand to my forehead, "*That's* what I forgot!" I ran to the kitchen, and quickly washed a couple of limes, quartered them, and put them onto a small plate. The girls were shaking their heads, as I came back to the table.

Linda smiled, "I guess he's a 'Type A' psycho." They all laughed, knowing that Linda was right; it was semantics, but they knew me very well, by now.

We spent the rest of the morning adjusting the snorkeling equipment, and I gave them tips on how to use the underwater cameras. Fortunately, Kelly and her friends were all very comfortable in the water. At least, the calm pool water.

By the time everyone left in the afternoon, I'd taught them about clearing their ears, clearing water from their mask, and blowing the water out of their snorkel when they surfaced. We took underwater pictures of each other ... and that was the first time I realized that we were all nude.

We were so comfortable with each other by now that we were like family. One that got along well. There was no more I could do: We were ready for our epic tropical adventure.

CHAPTER 6: GARDEN ISLE

We each had our backpack and a rolling case, and I'd had to check a large rolling case with the camping and snorkeling equipment, and a few 'toys'. I'd made a checklist, and Kelly had gone over it with each of her friends by phone a few days before the flight. I'd also completed a big project, the result of which would be seen near the end of the trip.

The flight to LAX was easy, once we got above the late summer weather. Although we were in first class, there was only a small breakfast service, and fairly cramped seating. But Kelly's friends were impressed, already.

Kelly and I sat in the port bulkhead seats, and Kelly was now a veteran of getting her things arranged in the plane. Kathy and Linda were across from us, with Julie one row behind them. It was an early morning flight, and we all slept, read, or listened to music.

At LAX, I brought everyone to the airline club lounge, with its quiet atmosphere, comfortable seating, and clean bathrooms. Being a Sunday morning, it was relatively uncrowded, and we spread out around a couch and chair seating arrangement.

Julie whispered to Linda, "That's the most food I've had on a plane since 9/11!" The lounge had coffee, some juices, and small pastries, but none of us indulged.

We boarded the 757 to Lihue, Kelly and I again taking the port bulkhead seats, with Julie and Linda in the starboard bulkhead (Linda by the window, this time), and Kathy in the window seat one row back. This was still a relatively small plane – only a single aisle – nothing like the triple-7 ... but it was much roomier than the Super 80 in which we'd flown the first leg.

After a smooth takeoff, we were almost instantly over the water, settling back for the five-hour flight. I took out my bottle of Tabasco sauce, and ordered a Bloody Mary, while Kelly ordered white wine, and Linda and Julie ordered Mimosas. It appeared that Kathy was drinking a pink-colored juice – probably guava nectar.

The lunch service was good, and the girls kept smiling at each other and at me. Except for Kathy, who was talking to the guy in the aisle seat, next to her.

He looked every bit the 'island' guy, with jet black hair swept back, deeply tanned skin, and a bracelet of shells. He wore Dockers and an Aloha shirt, giving him a bit more distinguished look than most other passengers who wore tank tops or t-shirts. He appeared to be in his mid-thirties, with a very confident air, and endless smile.

I leaned across the aisle to Julie, and said, "Happy birthday, by the way! I'm sorry that we couldn't make a party of it, but I've arranged a small gathering a week from today." Then, I gave her the evil eye, and added, "And, of course, I'll give you your birthday spanking."

Julie smiled, "I was expecting that." Then, she clarified, "Not the party, but the birthday spanking." We laughed. At least, I'd already given her the underwater camera as her main present.

Throughout the rest of the flight, Julie and Linda watched a movie on the small screen on the bulkhead, while Kathy talked with the guy next to her, and I went through the detailed itinerary for the trip.

Kelly had her laptop out, and earplugs in, and I assumed that she was also watching a movie; until I leaned over, and saw that she was typing something technical. I gave her a quizzical look.

She pulled one of the earplugs out, and explained, "I'm writing the next section of my dissertation, on my experimental set-up and technique." It was incredible: Kelly really had the will to succeed at whatever she did, and the work ethic to actually get it done.

Inside, I was shaking my head, amazed that she would be working on this trip, and not taking the time to relax. But outwardly, I smiled, and nodded to her. It was exemplary of her to use the time on the plane for her project, and she would have plenty of time to relax when we got to Kauai.

Soon, the plane was descending, and I got only a fleeting glimpse of Na'wili'wili Harbor through the port window before we touched down. We taxied to the terminal, a dark brown, low-slung building, passing a hangar filled with helicopters.

While Kelly and her friends stayed in the baggage claim area to get the big case that had been checked, I ran across the street to the car rental offices, and got our car – a Dodge minivan. It wasn't very sexy, but it would be practical.

We drove north, along the east coast of Kauai, passing groves of coconut trees on the left, and beach parks, with scattered hotels and condos on the right.

Julie commented, "That was a really nice flight. Thank you, Sam. Now I know what it's like for those lucky people up in first class."

Linda agreed, "Yeah, that was so nice, compared to the flights I've taken, where you're squished between two people, with a seat back in your face." We all laughed, but

Linda continued seriously, "But I thought that Sam was going to make us members of the 'mile high' club."

Sam glanced back, "Did you *want* me to?" He shook his head, "All you had to do was ask."

As everyone laughed, Sam winked at me. He hadn't anticipated turning this into a sex-oriented trip, but I knew that if Linda had asked, he would have responded.

Crossing the Wailua river, we drove through the small town of Kapaa (pronounced "Kah-pah-ah"), and along windswept Kealia Beach, then gradually turned west, as we passed Anahola, Aliomanu, and Moloaa. I pointed out the expanse of grass and trees, with a backdrop of the mountain ridge, that had been in the *'Jurassic Park'* movies.

Then, we passed through the town of Kilauea, and I pointed down the road to where the Kilauea Lighthouse stood – the northernmost point of the main Hawaiian islands.

I mentioned some of the celebrities and sports figures who owned homes in Kilauea, on the bluff over Secret Beach – probably the best-known clothing optional beach on Kauai. Then, I dropped a few more names, of the people who had houses around Hanalei Bay, and still more with homes in Ha'ena, where we would be touring tomorrow.

There were 'Oooh's' and 'Aaah's', as we passed a waterfall, and crossed over the Kalihiwai Stream. I took a big breath, and then sighed: I was back on Kauai, probably my favorite place on earth.

We passed the tiny Princeville Airport on our left, and I told the girls how Sarah and I used to fly in from

Honolulu on the Twin Otter plane that landed at this airport. I sighed again.

"Are you OK, Sam?" Kelly asked. I snapped out of a funk, realizing that there were tears in my eyes. I wiped them with the back of my hand, as we passed the main entrance to the resort village of Princeville, and turned into a small shopping center.

Pulling into a parking space near the door of the supermarket, I turned off the engine, and looked back at Kelly's friends. "Although we'll be eating out for dinner almost all the time, we should pick up some food and supplies – things you guys would like for breakfast, some snacks to take to the beach, and drinks."

We split up, Kelly and her friends taking a basket to look for the basics, and me to find a few more 'special' items. When we met up at the checkout counters, Linda was exclaiming, "Boy, everything is sure expensive, here!"

I nodded, "Yes – they have to ship everything twice; first to Honolulu, and then to Kauai." I chuckled, "Plus, we're in a tourist resort, and the prices are a little higher here on the north shore." I gave Kelly the car keys and she and her friends exited the market, as I paid for our haul.

We drove down Ka Haku Road, the main drag in Princeville, with the golf courses to our left, and homes to the right. As we turned into a driveway, I pointed down the road, "That's where the Princeville Hotel is ... and another group of nice condos with a Hanalei Bay view."

We found the building of our condo, and parked in front. We went up a few steps, opened the door, and walked in. It was a nice size, with large living area and kitchen, two bedrooms with ensuite baths, and a loft.

But the main attraction was the view. I slid open the glass door, and walked out onto the deck. Kelly and her friends followed me, each of them gasping at the beauty:

There was a wide expanse of ocean, with the 'Bali Hai' ridge and Ha'ena point to our left, the outermost part of Hanalei Bay, a peekaboo view of a tiny beach below the condo, and sailboats in front of us.

It was late afternoon, and we would see some incredible sunsets from here, but probably not tonight, as I was hoping to get everyone out to dinner while it was still light. But we were all enthralled by the view.

We brought all our junk in from the car, and I explained the layout. "Kelly and I will take that bedroom," pointing to the 'master' suite, "and two of you can take that bedroom; one will have to sleep in the loft." I laughed, "But, as you know, I'm hoping that each of you will spend one night with me. Perhaps Kelly could sleep in the loft, then?"

The girls nodded, and Julie said, "Don't sweat it, Sam. We'll work it out." We all disappeared into our respective rooms to unpack and freshen up.

Twenty minutes later, we reconvened in the living room, and I pulled out a large map of Kauai, and spread it on the coffee table. I gave the girls an orientation – where we were in Princeville, and the overall layout of the island, and north shore, specifically.

"Even with two weeks here, we're not going to be able to see and do everything," I grinned at the girls, "but I've got a lot scheduled. Tomorrow, we'll tour the north shore, from here to the end of the road at Kee Beach. It's spelled 'K-E-E', but pronounced 'Kay-ay'; you pronounce every vowel in Hawaiian."

Kathy complained, "I thought we would be going to the beach, snorkeling, and taking it easy."

I had to laugh, "Yes – we're going to go to several beaches tomorrow, and nearly every day of the trip. We'll do a little snorkeling tomorrow, and even more on Tuesday and Wednesday." Then, I looked at Kathy, "And we'll have a *little* time to 'take it easy'.

"Let's take a short walk down the path to the beach, and take a look. You can put on a bathing suit, if you want, or just keep your shorts on. I'd just like to see the conditions, and give you guys a preview."

We walked down a narrow and winding paved path, passing incredible tropical flora, including torch ginger, *laua'e* fern, and the red *lehua ohia* flowers.

I pointed out the hala trees, with their aerial roots, and breadfruit-like pods. "This is the *lauhala* – or just 'hala' – tree, scientific name, *Pandana*. The fruit can be eaten, but it's mainly the leaves that are used, for weaving."

Linda cried 'Ow!', and I chuckled, "Yes, the edges of the leaves are very sharp. I'll show you how to prepare them for weaving in a couple of days. But try not to grab onto them – which will be tempting in some places along the Kalalau trail."

Linda harrumphed, "*Now* you tell me!"

We continued down the path, coming first out onto a grass area with small barbeque, and then walking over some rocks to the beach. Kathy exclaimed, "This is gorgeous!"

Julie whistled, "Sweet!"

There were only a couple of couples on the beach, which was about a hundred yards long, and slightly curved. I pointed out the shallow portion of the reef and the outer reef, and described how the lava flows created ridges under the water.

We'll snorkel here, but on Tuesday, I'm going to bring you to my favorite beach, not far from here; it's very similar to this one, but even more private, more beautiful. It has incredible snorkeling with sea turtles, sea caves and lava tubes and maybe even a monk seal, if we're lucky.

The girls were awestruck, and walked slowly down the narrow beach, a few boulders just at the waterline, and hala trees along the cliff. I picked up a 'key' dropped by the hala, and held it up, "The hala is also called a screw-pine tree by *hau'olis* – or people from the mainland. And it's sometimes called the 'paintbrush tree', because of these."

I scraped the orange pulp of the key with my teeth, until you could see the fibers that looked like a paint brush. We continued down the beach, the water gently lapping up onto a few of the small, black, water-smoothened boulders. It was great timing: Past the busy summer tourist season, but still with calm water. I just hoped there wouldn't be too much rain; this *was* the north shore, after all.

As we walked back toward the path, I informed the girls, "These are looking like pretty good conditions. We'll probably do a 'night snorkel' from this beach." There was a small frenzy of 'tsk'ing' and comments, the girls not really believing me.

We walked over the rocks, and stopped on the grass area. "I think you guys already know this, but it's very important to me that you show trust in me ... and *have* trust in me. We're going to be doing some exciting things, some of which could be dangerous. But please trust that I will take care of you, not let you get harmed."

Kelly just smiled, while her friends objected. Julie said, forcefully, "We *do* trust you, Sam."

Linda chimed in, "Yeah. We wouldn't even *be* here, if we didn't trust you."

I nodded, "OK. I'm just reminding you." Then, as a thought flashed through my head, I smiled, "And I may be testing you, once or twice." There were groans, or 'mock' groans all around, and – on that note – we headed up the path. It seemed a lot steeper going up.

When we returned to the condo, I made a few preparations in the kitchen, and then turned to Kelly, "I think this might be a good time for a 'test'."

She shook her head. "Sam, be nice."

I hugged her, "I'm *always* nice, Kelly! You know that." She continued to shake her head, as she looked at me warily. We went out onto the lanai deck, where Julie, Linda and Kathy were sitting around a small table, chatting quietly, but mostly looking at the view.

"How are you guys doing?"

Julie repeated, "This is just awesome." Linda and Kathy nodded their heads heartily.

"Good. We're going to have a small 'event', and I'd like us all to meet in the living room in ten minutes. And use the bathroom, if you need to!" The girls shrugged, but Kelly was still shaking her head. I hadn't shared with her everything that we would be doing on this trip, but she had some pretty good ideas of the possibilities.

Ten minutes later, the girls came into the living room, and I had them stand next to each other behind the couch. I stood in front of them, and said, seriously, "Please undress down to your bra and underwear." I looked at Kathy, "Or just your underwear."

The four of them didn't groan, but I heard Kelly say – under her breath – 'Here we go ...'. A few moments later, there were four cute twenty-something females standing in a line in front of me, their shorts and tops shed, and dropped onto the couch. They were staring at me, waiting for the next instructions.

"I thought about designing something myself, but finally decided that you guys should have one of these." I stepped up to Kathy, and handed her a small paper-wrapped package. Then, I moved to my right, and handed one to Julie, Linda, and then Kelly.

As they tore the wrapping off, and held up the t-shirts, smiling broadly, I took off my tank and slipped mine over my head. I was still wearing my jogging shorts, but the t-shirt came down far enough to hide them. The girls put on the tees, and each hugged me and thanked me.

"These are the famous 'red dirt t-shirts' of Kauai. As you'll see, the dirt here is red, and after our hikes, you have to expect your clothes to be stained with the mud. About twenty years ago, some enterprising guys decided to wash t-shirts with a load of red dirt, instead of detergent. And *these*, you can get as dirty as you want!"

The girls laughed, and modeled the tees, which looked good on them, almost like a short dress; they would make good beach cover-ups. I grabbed my phone, and took a few quick pictures of the four of them.

Next would be one of their 'trust' challenges. I tried not to laugh, as I thought of how they would respond. I had thought about this in the market, and it would be a bit of an improvisation.

"OK. Now for the event."

Julie mumbled, "I thought that *was* the event?"

"Please line up again, and get into the standing position." They stood next to each other behind the couch, and now I heard Kelly mumble, 'Oh no ...', although she still had no idea what we would be doing.

I tried to stifle the laugh that was erupting from within, and look grim, "It's just a little 'trust' challenge; it won't be a big deal." Then, I let the shoe drop, "I'm just going to give each of you a couple of shots."

Now, the girls exploded. Kathy cried, "But I thought you *promised* not to make us take any more shots!"

Linda was grumbling, and Julie's mouth hung open, but she closed it and smiled, and I saw a twinkling in her eye. There was no twinkle in Kelly's eyes, however, as she put her hands on her hips, and glared at me.

I opened a small bag I had put on the tiled bar counter that separated the living room from the kitchen. "Please turn around put your legs apart, and bend over the couch, with your hands on the cushions."

Despite the grumbling, they did as I had requested, and I handed each of them a blindfold, which they put on. "This is also a test of following instructions. I want you to be silent during this. When I tap you three times on the back, you may take off the blindfold, stand up, and turn around to face me.

"Are you all ready?" I heard a chorus of weak 'Yes, Sir's', and then the girls were quiet. I worked from left to right, raising the t-shirts onto each girl's back, starting with Kathy, then Julie, then Linda, and finally Kelly.

Then, I walked down the line again, lowering each of their panties to mid-thigh. I reached into the bag again, and pulled out several alcohol swabs. I tore one, and rubbed Kathy's left hip, and then her right one. Then, I moved down the line, and did the same with Julie, Linda, and Kelly.

I then walked over to the bar, pretending to get the syringes, but actually picked up my phone, and took another couple of snapshots of the lined-up girls, their butts on display.

Then, I stepped behind Kathy, spread the tissue of her left hip with the thumb and forefinger of my left hand, and suddenly brought my right hand toward her, *pretending* to give her a shot.

I had considered actually inserting a needle, but didn't want to start our tropical vacation that way. I had also thought about simulating the 'shot' with my fingernail, but decided that wasn't required.

Kathy was great, holding her position, and not making a sound, although I was sure she was confused about what was actually happening. I repeated the movements on her right side, pretending to give her a second shot. Then, I pulled up her underwear, smoothing the band, and lowered her new t-shirt.

I tapped her firmly three times on the back, and Kathy took off the blindfold and stood up, turning to me with a bemused expression. I ran to the bar counter, reached over it, and brought Kathy a small shot glass, filled with a well-aged *añejo* tequila. When I handed it to her, she smiled, and brought her hand up to cover her mouth, trying desperately not to laugh.

Then, I stepped behind Julie, spread the skin of her left hip, and jerked my right hand toward her, again pretending to give her a shot. She let out a breath, that I realized was the start of a laugh.

I gave her another pretend shot on the right side, then pulled up her underwear, and lowered her t-shirt, as Kathy watched with a broad smile. I tapped Julie three times and, as she took off the blindfold and stood, I retrieved the next shot glass of tequila and handed it to her.

Julie started a giggle, then stifled it, and took the small glass. She leaned forward, and we briefly kissed. Then, I put my finger to my mouth, and stepped behind Linda. For the third time, I pretended to give a couple of shots. When she stood, she couldn't help but laugh.

"What's going on?" Kelly asked, uneasily.

I chuckled, "It's *your* turn, now." I repeated the process with Kelly, as her friends watched, although I was very tempted to use actual needles on her, due to the poor attitude she'd had. But she was only trying to look out for her friends; and she knew that I liked to push situations.

By the time I was raising Kelly's underwear, she was laughing, and when she stood, turned around, and saw me handing her a shot glass of tequila, she bent over in stitches. She was almost choking by the time she stood again, smiled and nodded at me, and then took my head in her arms and kissed me.

"When we were at the market, I saw a couple of bottles of '*añejo*' – which means 'aged' in Spanish. This one is an añejo tequila, actually an 'extra añejo', which has been aged for more than 3 years." The girls were still holding the glasses. "And, unlike throwing back shots of cheap 'blanco', or even 'reposado', this one should be sipped."

I grabbed my own glass, and we toasted, then sipped the fiery liquid. "And, I didn't choose a Mezcal with a worm in it! That might have been a bit more challenging."

When we had finished the tequila, I lined up the girls' glasses on the bar, and refilled them – this time, with an añejo rum. "I know that people say you shouldn't mix alcohols, but I also wanted you to taste this: It's an añejo rum, aged seven years." We all sipped a little.

"Tequila is made from *agave*, which is a succulent plant (not a cactus) that grows especially around Guadalajara, Mexico. This rum is made from Caribbean sugar cane. Since Hawaii has so much sugar cane, there are a few rums made here, also."

I went around to the kitchen, and held up a pineapple, and a can of coconut syrup. "Over the next few days, I plan to make some classic tropical drinks for you, such as Piña Coladas," I held up a bottle of light rum, and "Mai Tai's," I held up a bottle of dark rum and another bottle of Cointreau, the orange liqueur.

"And, for you health nuts (I looked at Kathy), we have guava juice to make Island Punch – also with rum, and orange juice to make Tequila sunrises."

I opened the refrigerator and pointed, "And, I've stocked up with some good Hawaiian beers, such as Kona Brewing's 'Longboard Lager'," which I knew the girls would like, "and Maui Brewing's 'Bigswell IPA'," which would be my favorite.

Glancing at my watch, I suggested, "Why don't we go down to Hanalei, and I can show you around a little, then we can get some dinner?'"

Everyone was amenable to the plan, so we retired to the bedrooms to change. As I took off the tee, and put on an Aloha shirt, Kelly looked at me, "I'm glad you didn't *really* give my friends shots! You *did* promise, after all. And this trip was supposed to be a reward for the submission challenge you put them through, not another challenge."

I smiled, and kissed Kelly, "I know. There are only going to be a few 'challenges', and I don't think your friends will have a problem with them." I breathed in deeply, "I still think the biggest challenge will be some of the hiking and the swimming we'll be doing."

"Swimming?" Kelly asked.

"Well, mostly snorkeling. But there will be one challenging swim when we go to Kalalau."

"Are you worried about sharks? My period is over, I think; but Julie will have hers for at least another two days. And, Kathy will probably get hers by the end of the trip."

I had to chuckle; I knew someone would ask that question. "No, I'm not worried. We'll be lucky to see a shark or two. There are a lot of white-tip reef sharks here ... but they're nothing to worry about."

I remembered, "Unless you try to dive into a small cave or lava tube with them. They don't like being cornered."

Then, I responded to Kelly's question. "It's a very big ocean, and it's unlikely any dangerous sharks would be close enough to detect a few drops of blood.

Kelly rolled her eyes, "Lucky? Unlikely? That doesn't sound very reassuring."

I held Kelly, and gave her a light kiss on her moist lips. "Kelly, we're on a small island in the middle of the Pacific Ocean. And we're going to be pretty far from civilization when we're in Kalalau. It's an adventurous place! So, of course there will be some dangers."

Kelly shook her head. Then, we held each other tightly; until we heard her friends laughing in the living room.

We drove down the hill, and across the single-lane bridge over the Hanalei River. Driving along the river, I pointed at the trees lining the bank of the river across from the road with the yellow flowers. "Those are *hau* trees, actually a type of hibiscus. The wood is so light, it is used – like balsa wood – to make things like outrigger canoes, and fishing net floats."

We drove through the town as far as the Waioli Mission and the elementary school, then turned back, and parked next to the old school, which now houses several shops and a bar. We walked across the street, and – after a short wait – got a table on the deck of a funky restaurant.

I offered to get a bottle of wine, but everyone wanted to order separately. Kathy had her guava juice and Julie got a Mai Tai, while Linda and Kelly drank white wine, and I had a draft microbrew. Then, we all ordered different kinds of foods, from salads, to burgers, to pasta.

Kelly's friends were very upbeat and talkative ... except for Kathy. When the conversation diminished, I asked Kathy if she was OK.

"I'm fine, Sam. Just thinking." As Kelly, Julie and Linda stared at her, Kathy smiled, "About the guy I met on the plane." Now, Julie and Linda were prodding her for more information.

"His name is Christian. He's actually Tahitian, but has a house on the south shore. He owns a sunglass company." We were all waiting for more, and Kathy didn't disappoint us. "I think I'm in love."

Now, our table was in an uproar. Linda said acerbically, "I thought you had given up men?"

Without giving Kathy a chance to reply, Julie teased, "Kathy! You can't be 'in love' … you just met him." Kathy just shrugged, and looked past us to the old Hanalei school house, and the mountains and waterfalls beyond.

After dinner, we decided to walk the couple of blocks to the beach, and head toward the Hanalei pier. It was near sunset, and the clouds caused by the high humidity changed hue through pinks and oranges and purples.

Reminding the girls of some of the scenes from the movie 'South Pacific', I pointed ahead to Black Pot Park, just past the pier. We walked through the park, and to the outlet of the Hanalei River. There were some 'locals' in the park, but it was relatively quiet and serene.

We walked out onto the pier, and I explained that this was the 'new' concrete pier, after the original one had become weakened and dangerous. Continuing under the corrugated tin roof, we stood at the end of the pier watching the atmospheric sunset.

I described the 'green flash', something I'd seen several times, but there were evidently clouds on the horizon, and there would be no flash this evening.

Looking around at the circular bay, I explained, "This is Hanalei Bay. 'Hana' means bay, and 'lei' means round. As you can see, it's a circular bay. It's only about two miles across, so if you guys would like to do a 'challenging' swim, let me know."

The girls shook their heads, and I laughed, "Well, it *is* more difficult than it looks, as the current flows from the sides of the bay to the middle, and then out to sea." This was a good time for some ocean cautions, so I spoke to the girls seriously.

"As I was telling Kelly earlier, this is an adventurous place, which – to some extent – means it also can be dangerous. You guys are good swimmers, but you should know that about one person *per month* drowns on this island." The girls were all ears, now.

"It mainly happens near the river mouths. People stand on the lava rock, not watching the ocean. Every once in a while, there are large waves that can crash over the rocks, and knock people off them into the water. People try to swim back to the rocks, and get dashed on them."

I looked at each of Kelly's friends, in turn, "And once you're unconscious in the water, you're dead." They nodded. "People playing at the river mouths sometimes get pulled out a ways, and they try to swim against the current, *then* get tired, and knocked into the rocks."

Continuing the lecture, I pointed out, "You should always swim *across* the current, parallel to the beach, and find a sandy place to swim to shore." Of course, there were places that are rocky for miles, like the Na Pali coast; but I wouldn't worry them with that detail.

Pointing to the mountain ridge, I showed the girls the form of a dragon, winding around Hanalei ... perhaps, it was 'Puff', the magic dragon? Who 'lived by the sea' ... in the town of 'Hanalee'?

That got me thinking about procuring some smokes, and being able to expose the girls to a whole different side of Kauai. I still had several friends on the island, but would need to make contact.

As the sky quickly darkened, we walked back along the beach toward the pavilion in the center of the bay. I looked up, and there was no moon; but perhaps we could take a 'moonless' swim, instead of a moonlight swim?

I suggested we sit on the beach for a while, and watch the stars come out. A few other people walked by us on the beach, and then it was dark, and we were alone. The last hues of the sunset came out of the horizon, and clouds over the Bali Hai ridge turned a deep red, the surrounding sky now purple.

"Anybody up for a swim?" I inquired. We had all put our toes in the water, which was around eighty degrees; the air was cooling, but still in the mid-seventies.

Linda replied, "We don't have towels." That was true, but I wasn't going to let a little thing like that stop us from having another experience together.

"OK. If you guys want to go in, you can use my shirt to dry off with." I thought it was a gallant offer.

Kelly and Julie sat on the beach, while Linda, Kathy and I quickly removed our clothes, and waded into the calm water.

Kathy floated on her back, and quietly said, "That's incredible!" Linda and I followed her gaze to the sky, where a billion stars shone brightly, and the Milky Way cut diagonally across the heavens. It was a magical moment. I knew it would be one of many we would experience during our island adventure.

On the short drive back up the hill to Princeville, the girls joked about my 'shots' prank. Kathy said, "Yeah, I wasn't too happy about it." I could hear laughter in her voice, as she continued, "But, of course I expected that Sam would be doing *something* like that on this trip."

Linda said, acidly, "Maybe we should give Sam some of his own medicine?"

I objected, "But it was a joke! A 'punny' joke. I didn't really do anything to you guys."

Julie chimed in, "He should be punny-ished, if for nothing else than his jokes!" I groaned, but Linda and Kathy chuckled, and the car was quiet the rest of the way back to the condo.

When we were sitting in the living room again, I offered, "Well, if you guys really want to 'punish' me, I did get something at the market that might be interesting to try." When everyone gave me a curious look, I said, "It's called 'figging'. I've read about it, but Kelly and I have never tried it."

After more curious stares, I went into the kitchen, and took something from the counter, trimming it with a small knife, and cutting it into tiny cubes, which I brought back and handed to the girls. "Have you guys ever eaten raw ginger?"

Nobody responded until Kelly said, "We've eaten ginger in the Japanese restaurant." I nodded, and popped a cube into my mouth. The girls tasted it, Linda making a sour expression, but Kathy evidently enjoying it.

Then, I explained. "Figging is a punishment, where the ginger is carved into the shape of a butt plug, and it's inserted in the rear. Just as you feel it burning your mouth, you would feel it burning your anus." Kathy groaned, and Julie cackled.

Linda looked at me, "That sounds like it might be fun." When all eyes were on her, she clarified, "Watching Sam suffer a little for putting us through his 'joke'."

I looked at Kelly, "But I think Kelly should take it, also, since she seemed to be the least trusting of what I was going to do, when I told you I'd be giving you 'shots'." Kelly shrugged.

Linda commanded, "OK, then. We want you and Kelly in your tees, and standing behind the couch in ten minutes!" The tables had turned. Kelly and I chuckled, as we went into the bedroom to get undressed.

When we returned to the living room, Linda was in her PJs, Julie wore a short nightgown, and Kathy wore a tank that only came down to her waist, her bikini underwear fully exposed.

I told them, "Just for the record ... I didn't even bring syringes or saline with me." Then, I chuckled, "Just a box of needles, in case we felt like some sharp sensations."

Kelly seemed annoyed, "You brought a whole *box*? A hundred needles?"

I shrugged, "It was the easiest way to pack." Kelly was shaking her head. Again.

I went into the kitchen, and spent some time carving two ginger butt plugs. I had no idea whether the figging would be painful, but was glad that Kelly would be experiencing it with me.

Kathy sat in the chair, while Linda and Julie came around the couch, and told us to bend over. Kelly and I spread our legs, and bent over the couch, turning our heads to face each other.

Standing behind me, Linda raised the tee onto my back, and I saw Julie doing the same with Kelly. I hadn't provided any lube, but I could see Julie putting spit on her finger, and rubbing it around the tip of the phallus of ginger. Then, I felt Linda press the ginger against my anus.

It didn't feel bad, and I relaxed, letting the ginger enter my rear. Kelly and I smiled at each other. Over the next few minutes, we felt the burning sensation ... but it still wasn't that bad.

Kelly's friends went out to the deck, but Linda stuck her head back inside, and announced, "You guys can take those out whenever you think you've had enough." Then, she closed the sliding glass door.

I stood, and stepped behind Kelly, held her hips, and entered her from behind. "Sam!" Her head was up, looking through the glass to the deck. Her friends were looking out to the ocean.

Laughing, I asked, "What? Are you afraid your friends will see us having sex?" Kelly let out an exasperated breath, and lowered her head again, as I began thrusting into her. It didn't take long for me to come.

We walked into our bathroom, and took the ginger out of each other. As I washed my hands, Kelly sat on the toilet. She chuckled, "You're lucky I'd already taken out that last tampon!"

Yes, I was lucky. In many ways. Kelly and her friends were all good sports. Well, Kelly was much more than that, of course. There probably weren't many women who would let their partner get it on with their friends. And, there probably weren't many fivesomes who were as close – as intimate – as we were.

Kelly and I left on our tees, wearing nothing underneath, and went out to the deck to join her friends. Well, not exactly 'join'.

We looked toward the west, at the few lights on Ha'ena point, and I thought about our itinerary again. It was shaping up to be the epic trip that I had planned.

CHAPTER 7: NORTH SHORE

We were up early, and ate our breakfast out on the lanai, the view enthralling. We'd all put on bathing suits already, although Kathy only wore her bottoms. She had gotten a good all-over tan in Mexico, but Sam was still concerned that we would get burned, and reminded us to bring sunscreen. He also suggested to Kathy that she bring her top, as it would be needed at a few of the beaches we would be visiting.

Before heading down the hill to Hanalei, we stopped at the Hanalei Valley lookout, across from the small shopping center where we'd gone to the market.

As we took snapshots of the spectacular view, Sam explained, "Kauai is the only Hawaiian island with navigable rivers – mainly Wailua on the east shore. But it's possible to make it a ways up the Hanalei river, also. If we have time, we might hike through the bamboo forest up to where the river is a shallow stream."

We read the large posters describing the native birds, and Sam continued, "Hanalei Valley is where most of the taro is grown in Hawaii." He chuckled, "Taro chips are not bad – kind of like purple potato chips. But the main use of taro is to make *poi*, which is a thick, pasty, flavorless starch, one of the original staple foods of Hawaii.

"We'll go to a luau in a couple of days, and you guys will be able to taste it. It's often eaten with Kalua pig, which is fatty and salty, so makes the poi a little more palatable."

We hopped back into the car, and Sam drove down the hill, across the one-lane bridge, and into Hanalei town. We ended-up back at Black Pot park and the Hanalei pier, where we'd seen the sunset last night. "Are you guys ready for a morning swim?"

We looked at each other and nodded. Sam smiled, "Then, I'd like to see how everyone does swimming in saltwater. It's as calm as a swimming pool." We walked to the short beach between the pier and the outlet of the Hanalei River, and took off our tanks and cover-ups.

As we waded into the water, Sam said, "I would like us to swim around the end of the pier, and back to the beach. It's not a race – just slow and steady; it's farther than I've seen you guys swim before." Sam stood knee deep in the crystal clear water, then dived in, and began swimming alongside the pier.

We all followed, but as I approached the end of the pier, I glanced back, and realized our group had separated, Linda and Kathy lagging somewhat behind Julie and I. Sam was treading water just past the pier. We all regrouped, and then swam slowly together around to the other side of the pier, and back to the beach.

As we panted, Sam chuckled, "I was going to suggest that we run around the bay and then swim across, but maybe we'll skip that, and I'll drive you to the other side." Sam pointed, and we could see where the beach ended near a small yellow house directly across the bay.

We piled into the car, and Sam drove us past the houses along the beach. "As I said, quite a few of these homes are owned by celebrities." Then, Sam rattled off the names of a half dozen famous people who owned homes along the bay.

Sam parked, and we walked back out onto the beach. There were a few small waves coming in. "This is called 'Pine Trees', for obvious reasons." It was beautiful, this curve of beach lined by pines, a few Hobie Cats pulled up to them. Sam pointed, and named a few other famous people who owned houses around this beach.

Back in the car, we made a couple of turns and were once again on the main road. After passing the picturesque Waioli Mission church, we crossed a small stream, and Sam said, "Next week, we'll be staying in one of these houses across from the beach."

We passed a large garden, and a few horses, on our left, and continued around the bay. Sam pulled over into the pine trees to our right, and we all got out again. There were a few 'Ow!'s, as we walked over some tiny pine cones down to the beach.

Sam pointed directly across the bay, "And that's the Princeville Hotel, now a St. Regis – very luxurious. We'll be going there on Friday for the seafood buffet. And, at some point, we'll have lunch by the pool." We watched, as Sam walked to the water, and swam past the small waves, then floated on his back.

The water didn't look as inviting here, and my friends and I sat on a couple of rocks, waiting for Sam to swim back to shore. I noticed Kathy's eyes staring at the horizon, glazed over. "Are you OK, Kathy?"

She turned her head and smiled at me. "Yeah. I just can't get Christian out of my head." Kathy hadn't moved, but her eyes were suddenly more serious. "He's the sexiest man I've ever known; and we weren't *doing* anything, but sitting in an airplane."

I nodded, "He *was* very handsome."

Kathy shook her head, "No, Kelly, it was more than that. *We connected*." She looked down, thoughtful, then looked into my eyes, "We were really *interested* in each other. There was a *chemistry*..."

It was obvious: A match of pheromones, those chemicals that we secrete that cause a sexual, primal, response in someone we're with. They *were* a biological match-up. But I wondered whether the interest was more one-way; Kathy seemed needy to believe that a man was interested in her.

I nodded to Kathy, then smiled, "It's really nice to connect with someone like that. I don't think it happens very often." Kathy shook her head and looked back out at the horizon.

Sam body-surfed in on a small wave, and walked up to us, his feet suddenly lifting whenever they stepped on a stickery pinecone. "Sorry, I just have to try the water everywhere. Each place brings back certain memories ..."

Then, he brightened, "And next, we have a really neat beach – actually two beaches: Lumahai. Or, as my sons used to call it, 'Luma-Hi-Hi-Hi'. It's an incredibly long beach, and like a desert to walk across. But we'll walk a trail down the cliff to visit 'little Lumahai', and then park at the Lumahai River to see 'big Lumahai'."

My friends nodded, blankly. We got in the car, and drove up a winding, lushly-vegetated hill, and around a few curves, Sam pulling over behind a half dozen other cars. We walked down a steep trail, coming out at a cute little beach.

Sam pointed, "You guys can explore the lava rock tide pools, if you want ... just be SURE to keep an eye on the water, and come back down, if the surf starts to break onto the top of the rocks." We walked onto a beach of fine, white sand, and Sam set out the king-size sheet. We each carried over a couple of rocks to hold down the corners.

Sam pulled off his tank, and said, "I'm going to challenge myself ... and swim around that little island." We looked out at waves, now crashing more than they had been in Hanalei. But they were still small; and so was Sam's 'island', which was just a big boulder sticking out of the water.

As Sam did his swim, I walked with Julie onto the lava rock, and we walked along the cliff; there were no other people. I told Julie, "Kathy seems to have really fallen for that guy on the plane." Julie nodded, "I could see that. You have to admit – he *was* a hunk."

I nodded. "Christian. Julie said he lives on the west side of the island, and commutes to Honolulu to work. He's evidently got a large estate. Kathy can't get him out of her mind."

We stopped and turned around, and Julie looked at me, "I think Kathy's been starved for a man – a 'hunk' – and needs to bounce back from that experience she had in Mexico." We started walking back towards the beach; the water never splashed on the top of the lava, but there were small tide pools.

Julie continued, "And as independent and liberal as she is, Kathy really wants a permanent relationship, a home." Then, she chuckled, "But I don't get the impression that she's ready to have children, yet." That *was* funny: I couldn't picture Kathy with kids.

When we climbed back down to the sand, Sam was lying on the towel, his Speedo now off, and he was wearing a thong. There were only a half dozen other couples on the entire beach, and none of them was paying any attention to Sam or us.

"Are you sleeping?" I asked, facetiously.

Sam turned his head, and opened one eye at me, "No. Just trying to get a little sun at a time, so I don't burn to a crisp on the Kalalau Trail."

I opened a small tube of sunscreen, and put some on my finger. "Let's give you a chance to get through the first few days." Sam didn't argue with me, and I rubbed sunscreen into his entire backside, from ears to toes. Then, he turned over, and I did his front. I could see that he was a little turned on, but was being contained by the front of the thong.

We folded the sheet and grabbed our towels, and climbed the trail back to our car. Another short drive, with more horses grazing in fields to our left, backed by waterfalls, and Sam slowed and turned right into some pine trees. We piled out, this time Sam only wearing his thong, and walked to the slow-moving river.

Sam stepped in, and pushed off into a small pool in the river. We all followed, nobody bothering to take off her tank. When we got out, our wet tanks felt great; it was getting hot out here.

We walked to the river mouth, and turned right along the beach. Sam said, "This is one place where people get in trouble. There are usually crashing waves here, and people get sucked out at the river mouth, and try to get back in, then are crashed on those rocks."

We were all listening, and got the message. Sam was lecturing to us, but we couldn't ignore the fact that he felt responsible for us, not getting us into too much trouble. Life-threatening trouble.

There were small waves, and only Sam and Julie made their way beyond them, and swam for ten minutes, barely making headway up the beach. Then, Sam's head popped up, he looked around, waved, and they turned and swam back along the beach ... which took about a minute. We were all baking by that time, and headed back to the car.

As we crossed the bridge over the Lumahai River, Sam pointed to the left. "That's where one of the first scenes of Indiana Jones was filmed ... where he's running from the natives, and swims to a seaplane."

We wound around another hill, and saw a bay to our right. Then, we came to a stop. Sam explained, "That was Wainiha Bay. And we have to go across two one-lane bridges. A few cars go, then the rest wait for a few in the other direction. It works, but takes some time."

The flora became more and more lush, as we approached the end of the road. Beyond Kee Beach, the only possibility of continuing was on the Kalalau Trail.

Sam pulled over and parked, along with a line of other cars, at the Ha'ena Beach Park. We walked across the street, and explored the dry cave, then Sam bought us shave ice from the food truck. We followed Sam, as he walked quickly across the park, and down to the beach.

"I'm going to show you Tunnels Beach, which is famous for the original Zodiac rides that started there, and also for the young girl, Bethany Hamilton, who's arm was bitten off by a shark, outside the reef." There were a few gasps, and Sam said, "It's known as a snorkeling beach, but we're not going to dive here, just go in for a quick dip."

We walked by about fifty people lying on towels, and many more snorkeling in the shallow water. Sam pointed, "There is an inner reef, which is only a couple of feet deep, and an outer reef, that protects this whole area from the ocean waves. You can see a crystal clear pool in-between the two reefs."

Sam stopped, and pointed to the people snorkeling, and a slightly darker spot on the reef. "There is a huge cave underneath this reef. If you can free dive to at least 30 feet, you can go into it, and come out through that small hole in the shallow part of the reef. Sometimes you see white tip reef sharks in there, and it's beautiful, the way the rays of light shine down through cracks in the shallow reef."

We continued walking, past the people, and around the point. "This is Ha'ena Point, which is unofficially a nude beach. But, as you can feel, it gets pretty windy here. Sam pointed to several houses on the beach, "And there are more celebrities who live in these houses, or at least vacation in them."

Sam said, "And now for one of the most spectacular views on the island ..." We turned around, and looked back toward Tunnels Beach, and the Bali Hai ridge towering above. It was an incredible scene. Linda took some snapshots, and so did I. Kathy and Julie would need to remember to carry their cameras, next time, and not leave them in the car!

We walked back down the beach. Continuing in his role as tour guide, Sam told us about the history of the beach park. "All of this land along here was owned in the late 1960s by Howard Taylor, the brother of Elizabeth Taylor. He was going to build a big house here, but the government wanted him to pay a large tax on the land, and wouldn't give him a building permit."

Taking a deep breath, Sam continued, "There were a lot of hippies living here, Vietnam war protestors and 'flower' people, and the police kept charging them with vagrancy. So Howard gave up on building the house, and allowed all the hippies to live here. It became known as 'Taylor Camp'."

"Over the next five or so years, in the early 1970s, there were tents, and shacks, and tree houses built and lived in ... and very little sanitation. Everyone went nude, and there were a lot of drugs, including acid. But in the late 1970s, the state finally condemned the property, and kicked out everyone living there, turning the land into a beach park."

We walked across the park back to the parked cars, and Sam bought drinks for us at the food truck. "I usually carry a cooler with drinks; we'll have to buy one when we get back to Hanalei, and bring it to the beach tomorrow."

We hopped in the car, and Sam drove the short distance to the end of the road. Despite it being September, and the big tourist season supposedly over, the parking area was full, so Sam dropped us off, along with our snorkeling equipment, and his beach pack. Then, he drove down the road to park.

Kee Beach was cute, but there were quite a few people. By the time we had the sheet laid out, and our snorkeling stuff unpacked, Sam was running breathlessly to us. He bent over, putting his hands on his knees. I asked, "Are you getting in position for the paddle?"

He tried to laugh, but coughed. "I parked pretty far down the road ... but you guys will see the area better, if we walk. Then, we'll have our next adventure." I just nodded, and handed Sam a water bottle.

With all of us sitting on the sheet, Sam pointed to the right, "You can see a shallow reef there – too shallow to snorkel." Then, he pointed ahead, "And you can see the pool here – almost like a swimming pool." My friends nodded; the water was a beautiful blue color.

Sam breathed deeply, "And you see quite a few people snorkeling. This will be a good place for you guys to practice, but it's not the best snorkeling around."

I saw blank expressions on Julie's and Linda's faces, and Sam explained, "The water's clear, and along that wall of the reef you may see some crab, shrimp, sea urchins, and a few more things."

Sam took another breath, "But in deeper areas, you'll probably see pipefish – the narrow, silver, long-thin fish that swim in schools; and the trumpet fish – the much larger, yellow, strange-looking thing, with a head like a horse."

He put on his booties, zipping them as he said, "Just go out and have fun. You may see more by hugging the right side, or maybe along the rocks on the left, next to the cliff. Look for starfish, and sea urchins. And, don't forget to turn your head right and left; don't just look down or ahead."

Sam stood, grabbed his large fins, and mask and snorkel, and walked to the water's edge. Then, he walked in, putting his fins on when his body was mostly underwater. It took us a while longer to get ready, but we were eventually all in the water.

Sam had disappeared, but I kept an eye on my friends. They seemed to be doing well. I tried a surface dive – it wasn't much deeper here than Sam's pool. I swam underwater to Linda, and her eyes went wide for a second, before she realized it was me.

When we surfaced, Linda pulled her mask to her forehead, and treaded water. "You scared me! I thought some huge fish was coming to get me." We laughed, but Linda hit her hand on the water, sending a spray into my eyes. I dived down, Linda following, and headed for the middle of the pool.

Just ahead of us was a school of the pipefish that Sam was describing, and in their midst was one very large, yellow thing – as Sam had said, looking almost like it had a horse head: The 'trumpet fish'. I glanced over to Linda, and saw that her eyes were wide. This really was a new experience for most of us. And another chance to grow together as friends ... and lovers.

When we got back to our sheet, Sam was sitting there, fiddling with the underwater camera. We sat down, and Sam said, "Well, I think I might have gotten some great shots here, of a couple of sea turtles. But we won't be able to see them in this direct sunlight."

He looked up at all of us, and asked, "How did everybody do?" Linda was effervescent, "We saw a pipefish and trumpet fish ... and I saw a huge shark coming my way." Sam raised his eyebrows, a grin forming on his strong face. Then, Linda finished, "But it was only a KellyShark, and it didn't eat me."

I looked at Linda as earnestly as I could, "Did you *want* me to 'eat' you, Linda? I could still do that, you know." We all laughed.

Sam spoke up, "Well, I have the perfect place for it; if you guys are up for a short walk." We all nodded, and got up, leaving all of our stuff on the sheet, and walking with Sam down the beach.

We stopped in the shade of a huge tree, on the dirt several feet above the beach, with aerial roots descending down to the sand. Sam turned on the camera, and shared a few pictures with me: They looked professional!

Julie, Linda, Kathy and I were too busy learning the basics of snorkeling to worry about a camera. But I decided that I would bring it with me everywhere, as I never knew when I would want it.

Sam led us around the curve of the beach and, miraculously, the crowd of people thinned to less than a handful. We continued walking, until we reached a small stream. Sam carefully stepped on rocks going upstream, until we were under a hollow of trees, the atmosphere dark and foreboding.

Sam looked at me, and I looked at Linda. "That's OK, Kelly. I'd rather do more exploring around here." I smiled.

It was OK with me too, not going down on Linda right here. But, if she'd really wanted to ...

We walked back to the main beach, and put our flip-flops on. Sam led us to the beginning of the Kalalau Trail, which we would be hiking in a week or so. Then, he informed us, "This is how we're going to get to Kalalau for our camping experience." He pointed up the rocky trail.

"And, on Friday, we're going to hike this to get to Hanakapi'ai Beach and Falls." Then, he gave us the evil eye, and said, "But since we didn't run this morning, why don't we walk up – *just* to the first viewpoint – and then we'll head back?"

We were all gung ho, and Sam led us steadily up the rocks – some of them boulders – as the trail wound around the hill, higher and higher. Sam finally stopped at the edge of the trail, and waited for us to catch up. There was a lot of panting. Then, Sam pointed back, down the cliff, between the palm trees to the beach. It was beautiful!

Sam said, "I wanted you to see the view of Kee Beach from up here." Then, before we could object, he continued up the trail. Fortunately, Sam only went another hundred yards, and stood at the end, before the trail turned left.

We followed Sam's gaze, and saw the cliffs of the Na Pali coastline. Sam turned to us, "We're going to hike the full length of this trail. And then swim to the next beach." Sam looked down, trying to decide something, then looked up at us and smiled, "And, on Saturday, we're going to take a boat ride all the way down this coast."

My friends clapped, their energy level apparently revived. Sam started back down the trail, then turned around, "I love to 'fly' down this trail, hopping from boulder to boulder. But you're welcome to go down the regular way; and please don't twist your ankle!"

With that, Sam literally flew down to the next boulder, pushed off with one foot, then down to the boulder below, in an incredible demonstration of strength and balance. Then, I realized that – like us – he was wearing flip-flops!

That was my Sam, eccentric but capable, sometimes pedantic, but knowledgeable, and always adventurous and exciting.

When we got down to the trailhead, Sam was looking at his watch. "It's just after noon. If you guys are hungry, we could get something from the food truck ... maybe a 'Hawaiian plate lunch'?"

Sam may have been hungry, but we'd all had breakfast, and at least two of us were still trying to watch our weight, so we declined, and decided to wait for dinner. I had to ask, anyway: What is a 'Hawaiian plate lunch'?

Sam chuckled, "You can choose pork or chicken or ahi poke (raw fish), and it comes with two scoops of white rice and a scoop of macaroni salad." That settled it: We could wait until dinner. Not that it didn't sound good, but Sam had promised us a special dinner tonight.

We walked on the side of the road, next to the towering cliff, ferns and other tropical plants growing out the side of the rock. We passed the main parking lot, and continued, and finally saw the minivan parked with two other cars in a tiny space on the side of the road.

Sam opened the car, and put the heavy beach pack down, then told us to carry our own towels, and he grabbed his underwater flashlight. We hiked up a short trail, then, looking up, we saw an incredible tangle of roots and vines, dropping 20-30 feet from the cliff. As we continued around a couple of turns in the trail, we saw, directly ahead of us, the mouth of a huge cave.

We walked under hanging plants that dripped on us, into the cave, and followed Sam down through the rocks and dirt. The cave had to be at least 200 feet wide, and 100 feet deep; I looked up, and nearly stumbled. The ceiling was at least 50 feet above us. At the bottom of the cave was a black pool of water.

Concentrating on the trail, now, we continued down, two other couples passing us, as they climbed uphill to the cave entrance.

We finally arrived at the edge of the underground lake. Sam took off his tank top, and his bathing suit. "This is one of the wet caves, and we can swim all the way to the back of it." He pointed across the lake, to a black void.

"But the more interesting thing here is the 'Blue Room'. We all shrugged, and looked around, but it was very dark, except for the incredibly bright cave entrance far above us.

Sam pointed to the wall of rock maybe forty feet across the lake. He chuckled, "This is another matter of trust." My friends didn't react, and Sam continued, "That rock wall only comes down to the water, or a few inches above. But, if you duck underneath – you will have to go underwater – you'll come up in a rock chamber. It's big enough for all of us ... I think."

I said, sarcastically, "You *think*?"

Sam nodded, "I've never been here with this many people. And most other people don't know about it. And I've never been here with an underwater light before." I nodded. Sam added, "I don't plan to use the flashlight, except to make sure you're all there."

A bunch of blank faces stared at Sam, trying to understand. He said, "Just follow me. We'll swim across the lake, and then duck under that rock. Hopefully, we'll come up in air." He stepped to the water, knelt down, and propelled himself into the lake, just missing the rocks that lined the edge.

He turned back, and said, "It *is* a bit cold, though." Then, he cackled, similar to how Julie sometimes laughed.

We took off our suits, and stepped into the water. It was freezing. But, one-by-one, we all got in and side-stroked across the water to Sam. He pointed, "Let me try it first. Then, I'll come back out, and lead you guys in."

Sam pushed himself under the water and I saw his body disappearing under the rock. A few moments later, he popped up next to us, and smiled. "I think you're going to like this."

Kathy yelled, "Let's *go*, already. I'm getting cold!"

Sam dived under the rock, and I followed him. I held my hands in front of me, as I couldn't see a thing. But I came up in a chamber, as Sam had described. Sam turned on the flashlight, and shined it around. There would be plenty of room for all of us.

My friends entered the Blue Room, and Sam turned off the light and spoke softly, echoing in the small space. "This is a little like the 'Blue Grotto' in Italy – on the island of Capri, near Sorrento, on the Amalfi Coast.

"You can take a rowboat into the cave, which is just above the water. Then, you're in a much larger cave, and the only light is coming up from under the water at the cave entrance." Sam said, "Look down." We all 'Oooh'ed' and 'Aaah'ed', as we realized that the room was sparkling with blue light coming from under the rock face.

Sam said, "So this is a good example of what I meant by 'trusting' me on this trip. Something that is potentially dangerous, but I've done it, and can make sure you guys are safe."

I couldn't see anything, but could hear the smile in his voice. "It's not trusting me about sex ... but about taking care of you and making sure you're safe while we're here." We all knew that.

Linda blurted, "We trust you about sex, Sam." Now, there was a smile in *her* voice. "We trust that you'll give us a good orgasm, every time!" We all laughed, the laughs resonating, and filling the chamber with echoes and reverberating noise.

We ducked back under the rock wall, and followed Sam, side-stroking, to the back of the cave. It was very dark, but we could feel ledges on the back wall, which allowed us to more-or-less stand. There was still nobody else in the cave, and the atmosphere was eerie.

As we were getting out of the water, a small group of young people were coming down into the cave. We dried off and dressed, then hiked up to the cave entrance and down the trail to the car.

Sam stopped at the Wainiha store to get sodas for all of us, then stopped again at a small clothing store, where he ran in, and came out a few minutes later with a large bag. We drove back to Hanalei, where Sam stopped at a hardware and fishing store to buy a small cooler. Then, we drove back to the condo.

After dropping off our things and taking a bathroom break, we decided to lounge out by the pool for a while. There was nobody else there, and Sam wore his thong, while Kathy went topless. Then, Linda decided to go topless, as well.

Sitting on the chaises, Kathy remarked, "That was more than just a day of 'touring'!"

Sam nodded, "Yes – that's what I call our north shore tour, or beach tour. Tomorrow, we'll have a snorkeling tour, then Wednesday we'll have an aerial tour, Thursday an island tour, Friday a waterfall tour, and Saturday a Zodiac tour."

It was overwhelming, but we all trusted Sam to show us a good time, and he'd done a lot of planning to make this trip memorable. Which it already was.

Back in the condo, Sam made Piña Coladas for us, a frothy, creamy, icy, blended concoction of coconut, fresh pineapple and rum. We sat on the deck, and watched several canoes being paddled seriously along the coast. Dark clouds were gathering, and several times there was a five-minute downpour, before clearing again.

We dressed nicely, Sam in an Aloha shirt, and me in a summer dress. Linda looked especially nice, with her hair done up, and wearing a pale blue polka dot dress with a fitted waist. Kathy wore a white Boheme skirt, with a pink shirt tied at the waist.

And, Julie wore a green dress with bold leaf patterns, and a hem that was down to her ankles in back, and above her knees in front. She looked sexy, and Sam teased her by lifting the front of the dress to see her white bikini panties underneath.

After finishing the second pitcher of drinks, we piled into the car, and Sam drove us down the hill again, to the first restaurant in Hanalei, right on the river. It was a well-known seafood place, and we took a table on the deck, while waiting for the corner window table that Sam had requested.

Sam ordered a bottle of white wine, which we sipped, none of us needing much more alcohol. We were finally seated, and studied the menus. Sam highly recommended the fresh ahi, but there were several other fish available that were caught fresh earlier in the day.

We shared a huge salad bowl, and were waiting for our main courses, when the skies opened and large drops of rain reduced visibility to the point that we could barely see the river only a hundred feet away. The rain pounded on the tin roof, making a racket inside the restaurant. The windows were open – there was no glass – and a thick mist of water blew in on us.

The ahi was unbelievable; neither my friends nor I had ever eaten anything like it. Even the fish I'd had at our local French restaurant couldn't compare. The atmosphere of the restaurant was island-style, even without the rain beating on the roof.

As the sun set, the sky again became multi-hued, large puffs of pink and purple clouds floating by, and the sky a deepening shade of blue. Somehow, we finished the wine, and we were all now floating in a surrealistic tropical haze.

It didn't take much nudging from Sam for us to order dessert. Sam and I shared the ice cream pie, Julie and Linda shared the macadamia nut chocolate brownie, and Kathy had the lychee sorbet.

We climbed into the car, and Sam apologized, as there wasn't any nightlife on the north shore, but none of us was up to it, anyway. It had been a pretty energetic touring day, and we were all happy to get back to the condo.

Julie decided that she would take the first night with Sam, and I took her place in the bedroom with Linda, Kathy still in the loft. We watched a few minutes of television, and then decided to go to bed; after all, it was already after midnight, back home.

Sam asked brightly if we were ready to do a night snorkel, and he got two laughs, one harrumph, and a coughing fit. I chuckled, "Good night, Sam. Good night, Julie." As Sam and Julie headed for the master bedroom, he turned around, and replied, "Goodnight, Moon."

Julie and I went into the bedroom and shut the door. While Julie was in the bathroom, I got undressed, and turned on the television – to a real estate channel showing local properties. For only two or three million, you could find a very nice home here on Kauai. If I had money to burn, and Kelly didn't have a decade or two of a career ahead of her, I would consider it. I loved this island.

Julie came out in her bra and underwear, and leaned over to kiss me before taking off the bra and slipping her nightgown over her head. She lay on top of the covers, and pulled the pillow under her head, as she turned on her side toward me.

"Thank you again, Sam." I gave her a questioning look, and she said, "For everything. Bringing us on this trip, taking care of us, and showing us a great time."

I shrugged, "It's my pleasure, Julie. I'm enjoying it, too." Then I gave her a quick smile, and added, "Especially coming to my favorite island with four beautiful women."

Julie's hand slipped under the cover, and she stroked me lightly. She smiled, "Sam, I'm still having my period, but we can make love, if you want."

It was a good offer, but I hadn't intended our 'sleeping together' to necessarily imply sex. "That's OK, Julie. We can just snuggle a while, then go to sleep." I still had mixed feelings, but Julie and I had already had sex, and Kelly was very comfortable letting us 'play around'.

The stroking continued, and I realized I was already hard. Julie smiled, "Well, let me at least give you head. Or, if you really want, we could do anal." These were even better offers. At this point, I would want to come before going to sleep, even if I had to masturbate.

Julie sat up, grinning broadly, and asked, "Was there any of that coconut syrup leftover from the Piña Coladas?" I nodded; there was at least a third of a can left, in the fridge.

Julie jumped off the bed, and ran to the kitchen, bringing back the can and a spoon. She took the saran off the top, and looked in. "It looks like semen." She smiled at me, "But it tastes a lot better." She took a small spoonful and tasted it.

I assumed that she would spread some on my shaft, and then lick it off, as Kelly had done a few times with jelly.

But, after crawling back onto the bed, and positioning herself, she tilted the can, filling her mouth with the sweet, thick, white liquid. Then, she lowered her head, and took me in her mouth. There was an initial shock of cold, but as she moved her tongue around and swirled the syrup around me, it became an incredible sensation.

Julie continued sucking and licking, and my involuntary motions became more urgent, as I thrust my length into her mouth. It didn't take long, and I whispered a considerate warning, "I'm going to come soon."

Julie's only reaction was an 'Ummm hmmm', as she took my balls in her hand, and pressed her finger into my perineum. I thrust and spasmed, filling Julie's mouth even more, as my hot cum mixed with the cool coconut syrup. It took a minute more for Julie to swallow, then lick most of the sticky mess off me.

She brought a washcloth from the bathroom, that she had soaked in warm water, and finished the job of cleaning me. Then she climbed on top of me, and I held her tightly as we kissed.

When we came up for air, I offered, "May I return the favor, Miss?"

Julie laughed, "No, that's OK, Sam. Maybe we'll get another chance later in the trip?" I nodded. There would be plenty of 'chances' for Julie and I to get it on.

We turned out the lights, and I spooned Julie. The day had caught up with us, and we fell asleep quickly.

I woke early, but Julie was not in bed. After my morning routine, I peeked out the door, and Julie was sitting on the patio, still in her nightgown. She looked up and saw me, then came back into the bedroom. We kissed briefly, and I suggested that we take a shower together.

Julie smiled, and took off her nightgown and underwear, and walked into the bathroom, sitting down on the toilet. I looked at her, and she smiled, "You can come in. I just have to take out my tampon." Her smile broadened, "And then we can have some 'shower sex'." It was another good offer!

But I sat on the bed, as she did her thing, and then joined her in the shower. Julie laughed, "You're not afraid of a little blood, are you?"

"Not unless it's my own." More laughing, and then Julie leaned forward, holding both of us under the spray, as she gave me a deep kiss. She reached down and stroked, my erection uncontrollably increasing.

"I see you decided to go completely 'bare'." Her pubic area was smooth, all her hair waxed off.

"Are you just noticing that now?" She chuckled, as I slid into her.

It was funny: On Sunday, when I gave the girls their 'shots', Julie had been facing the couch. And yesterday, when we'd gone skinny dipping in the wet cave, it was so dark, I hadn't noticed. And last night, she'd worn her underwear. So maybe this *was* the first time I'd noticed.

My hands went behind Julie, and I held her bottom, pulling her toward me. There were no more words, and none were needed. It was a nice experience to have with a friend. Well, she was more than a friend. And she was a turn-on for both Kelly and I.

After the sex, we bathed each other, then washed our own hair. We dried off, and stepped into the bedroom, where Julie collected the outfit she'd worn last night, her underclothes, and her nightgown. Then, she opened the door, strutted across the condo, nude, and went into her 'regular' bedroom.

As I looked out the door, still drying myself, I saw that Kathy was out on the patio, topless again, and Kelly and Linda were sitting on the couch, talking quietly. They both wore bathing suits, and looked ready for the beach. Kelly looked up, smiled at me, and waved.

The girls had their cereal and fresh fruit, and I packed the cooler for our beach outing. I had washed my snorkeling gear in the bathtub, and left it on the deck to dry. Not seeing any other equipment, I wondered whether the girls had washed their snorkeling gear in fresh water.

Kelly and I made sandwiches, and put them in the cooler, then I stuffed my pack with snacks, including some beef jerky, oranges, grapes, chips, nuts, trail mix, and cookies. I didn't want anyone to go hungry, and whatever leftovers we had could come with us to Kalalau.

I smiled at the girls, "Today, we're going to go to my favorite beach, and spend the rest of the day there." Chuckling, I added, "At least until we've all had enough sun." We were all a little pink around the edges, but none of us had gotten sunburned, yet.

CHAPTER 8: BEACH BABES

We piled into the car again, with the cooler and all of our beach stuff. Sam had suggested that we take it in our hiking packs, which were now bulging with snorkeling gear and towels.

It was only a five minute drive – just a few blocks – to the trail that led to Sam's favorite beach. He explained, "It's not that different than the one below our condo, but more difficult to reach, so there are seldom any people there. And it's a great snorkeling beach."

The trail was cute, crossing a small stream, ducking under a canopy of tropical foliage, then walking down improvised muddy steps to the lava rocks that would take us to the beach. It was only a little challenging, the shady parts being wet, and both Linda and Julie slipped at least once in the mud, falling on their rears.

Sam laughed, "Just wait until we hike to Hanakapiai Falls on Friday!"

The beach was tiny, perhaps a couple hundred feet across, backed by hala trees and the cliff. There were some small boulders (or very large rocks) at the waterline, and the water over the shallow reef looked crystal clear. We walked to the far end, set-up our king size sheet, and took out our snorkeling gear.

Sam had worn his pack and carried the cooler. As soon as the sheet went down, so did his shorts. He announced, "No bathing suits required here!"

We all stripped, and started exploring the beach. There was a small cave at the end by the trail, and a lava ledge along the cliff on the far side, near our set-up. The 'paint brushes' from hala trees littered the sand, and tropical ferns grew thickly around the edges of the beach.

Kathy was walking slowly, bending over, then crawled along the sand. I walked over to her, and she smiled up at me, "The 'sand' is actually gazillions of tiny shells!"

Sam came over, and looked into Kathy's hand, where a couple of dozen tiny pink shells, each with a hole in it, sparkled.

"You're finding *Niihau* shells. They can be strung onto a bracelet or necklace." He chuckled, "If you find a real Niihau shell puka necklace in a store, it will be very expensive. But we have all day here, so if you work at it, you might find enough to make some jewelry."

Then, Julie walked up to us, "This beach is fantastic!" She glanced at me, and then at Sam. "It's just too bad I didn't bring any tabs of acid." Sam shook his head. Julie was still the wild one, pushing every situation. Just like Sam.

Sam said, "Actually, I called a friend last night, and we should be getting some smokes soon. Probably by tonight." He looked at Julie, "I'm not so sure about acid ... I've never tried it ... but it *would* be great to be stoned down here."

Now I was shaking my head. I had actually brought a couple of notebooks and pens, so that I could continue drafting my dissertation. I was more excited than ever about the project, and felt certain that I could submit the dissertation by the end of the year.

Sam looked at the water, and back to the beach. "It looks like the tide is coming up. That will make it easier to snorkel the shallow part of the reef." He went back to the sheet, and pulled out his mask, fins, snorkel, and booties. He spit into the mask and walked to the water to rinse it out. Wearing only booties, he looked ridiculous. That was my Sam!

When we got back to the sheet, Sam suggested that we all try snorkeling in the shallow area that went out at least a hundred feet before dropping off to deeper water. "There are lots of holes in the reef, and animals live in those holes. You'll find sea cucumbers, several types of urchins, different kinds of reef fish, and maybe even an octopus."

Sam said, "Let me see how the conditions are off the reef, and I'll come back and show you around the reef. But you guys can also do it on your own – the water's only about two feet deep. The main thing is to stay horizontal – you'll float over any rocks. Please try not to stand on the reef, as it will cause damage to the coral."

With that, Sam carried his mask, snorkel and fins down to the water, put them on, and quickly snorkeled out to the deeper water. Then, he disappeared. It was probably ten minutes later, when we saw him walking along the lava ledge back to the beach. He smiled, "The conditions are *great!*"

Then, he looked at each of us, struggling to get our gear together, "You guys haven't gone out, yet?"

We all went down to the water, which was as calm as a swimming pool. We sat in the sand or on a small boulder, and put on our fins, then our masks. We were a motley group, all nude, but with multi-color gear.

Sam laughed, "I usually wear at least a thong when I snorkel," he was belly laughing now, "because I don't want any dangling appendages to be tempting bites for a sea creature." But he didn't bother putting anything on.

We snorkeled out, following Sam along narrow channels in the reef, and peering into some of the larger holes. Sam carefully held the lava rock and pulled his head down into one hole after another, bringing up samples of the fauna. He tickled a spiny sea urchin, and the spines moved in waves. Then he lifted a rock and pulled out a brittle starfish that scampered across his hand and back into the water.

We made a big circle around the tiny cove, staying in the shallow water. When we were almost back to the beach, we passed several large boulders that had schools of tiny fish swimming around at their bases. We finally pulled ourselves up onto the beach, and sat in the shallow water, taking off our gear.

Kathy was smiling, "That was great! I saw more here than I've ever seen in Mexico."

Linda was effusive, "Yeah, that was really neat. I love snorkeling!"

Sam laughed, "This was just the baby step. Next, if you feel comfortable, I'll take you on a *real* snorkel tour."

We sat on the sheet, and shared some sodas from the cooler. Sam said, "I don't want to come across as lecturing you guys, but there are a few things you need to know – before we go out into deeper water – just to be safe." None of us complained; we were all ears.

Sam explained that we should be sure to look ahead and to the sides, as well as down. And, we should frequently look at him, as he would be signaling when he saw something we should see. He said that we could snorkel alone or in pairs, and if we saw something we should squeeze our partner's hand.

Then, he explained the itinerary for the tour, saying that there should be quite a few sea turtles. He would be diving into some sea caves, and we should stay on the surface and watch. But he also said we should each try some surface dives, so that we would be closer to the reef and rocks, and be able to see more.

Finally, he showed us some hand signals – for OK, not OK, turtle, and shark. Julie asked, "Are there really sharks around here?"

Sam chuckled, "We'll be lucky if we see one today. But right out there," he pointed off the reef to the right, "a guy lost his arm to a shark."

Now, my friends weren't so sure about going off the reef into deeper water. Sam laughed, "But it was later in the fall, the mating season for the sharks, and he was on a boogey board, riding a large wave, and he looked like a sea turtle from below."

Linda couldn't resist, "What happened to him?"

Sam looked at Linda, no longer laughing. "One minute he was coming down the wave, and the next, his board, with his hand still attached, was twenty feet away."

Linda put her hands over her eyes, and Sam continued, "He flipped onto his back, held his stump up, and back-stroked with his other arm until he got to the rocks; then, he ran halfway up the trail before people heard him screaming."

Kathy asked, "Where is he now?"

Sam answered, "I'm not sure. The last time I heard, he was somewhere on the California coast. He still windsurfs, and got pretty good playing the piano with one hand and a stump."

I couldn't believe that Sam would tell us that story right before we would be snorkeling in the deeper water. "Sam!" I was shaking my head.

Sam asked, "What? They were asking." He looked down at the sheet, "And it's a pretty good story."

Julie asked, "Are there waves here often?"

Sam replied, "In the summer, it's like now – very calm. But in the winter, there are giant waves; Hanalei Bay and other places along the north shore are some of the best surfing spots in the Islands. On this beach, the waves roll all the way into the hill in back of us, and there's frothy white water filling this entire cove. That's NOT a good time for snorkeling, or doing anything else in the water; except surfing, if you're an expert."

Then he added, "But in the winter, the south shore is usually pretty calm, so there might be snorkeling down there." Then he looked up and exclaimed, "Oh! And between late November and late April, there are humpback whales cruising the north shore. You can see them from the hill up there."

He pointed to the top of the cliff, which was probably two hundred feet above the beach. Then, he stood, and put on his tiny thong. "Is everyone ready for an epic snorkeling adventure?" We all grabbed our stuff, and went down to the water.

Sam led us down one of the channels again, until we were off the end of the shallow reef. There were places where the water was ten feet deep, and others where the rocks nearly reached the surface.

Sam looked back and, seeing that we were all together, ducked under the surface, and swam underwater between the rocks, and through some deeper channels. We kicked hard, trying to follow him, but couldn't catch up, until he stopped and floated on the surface, waiting for us.

When we were all in an area of deeper water, Sam went vertical, and slowly swished his fins, keeping his head above the surface. We all did the same.

He pulled his mask up to his forehead, and said, "You should only go vertical like this when you're in this deep of water, or deeper. And try to keep your masks on and the snorkel in your mouth. If water gets into your mask, try to clear it, as I taught you in the pool."

We all nodded, and Sam continued the tour. The sandy bottom was now getting deeper and deeper, with huge lava ridges on each side. Sam gave us the 'OK' sign, and we all gave him an 'OK' back. Then, he indicated that we should follow him.

As soon as he turned around, he did a beautiful surface dive, going down, and down further, until he was gliding just above the sandy bottom, probably 30 feet below the surface. He looked up and gave us all the 'OK' sign again, and we replied. Then, he ducked under the lava ledge and disappeared.

We saw a crack in the lava, and bubbles coming out, so followed them, kicking our fins on the surface to keep up. Then, Sam emerged from the other end, and let himself rise to the surface, as he slowly spun around, looking in every direction.

As I approached, I saw his eyes go wide, and he smiled, putting his finger up to his mouth – asking us to keep quiet? – and again giving us a 'come along' signal. As soon as we were moving again, Sam pointed.

It took a few moments, but I heard a loud, underwater scream from one of my friends and, at the same time, saw several sea turtles approaching us from the deeper water. Sam gave us the 'Stop' signal, and we floated, as the sea turtles came closer.

When they turned, Sam dived to below their depth, then swam parallel to their course, keeping his arms along his sides, and only barely moving his fins every few seconds. I'd never seen Sam look so sleek and graceful before. There were still things I was learning about this incredible man.

The turtles were diving deeper, and Sam followed, until he could no longer hold his breath. Then, he swam underwater towards us, and let himself rise in our midst. He went vertical, and asked how many turtles we had seen.

Julie and Linda were howling with delight. I thought we'd all seen the three turtles, but Sam started laughing, and asked, "But how about *those*?" He ducked his head under the surface and pointed. It was difficult to make out things, with everything a shade of blue. But not fifty feet away were another dozen or more turtles. Linda squealed again.

Sam led us toward the point, at the end of the cove, but suddenly dove down, turned right, and slowly advanced, hugging the lava rock. Then, he let himself float upward, and we saw that he was in the middle of a few hundred fish. Half were black, and the others were a light yellow, with several vertical dark stripes. They circled Sam, and then scattered, when he started kicking toward us.

His head out of the water again, he said, "The black ones are triggerfish, and the striped ones are convict tang."

Then he ducked his head under the water and pointed to the rocks near the surface. There were two fish chasing each other, both with bright yellow backs, and white bellies, with a wide diagonal black stripe. Again, he stuck his head out of the water, and spit out his snorkel.

He laughed, "Those are the famous state fish of Hawaii: Humuhumunukunuku'apua'a."

Linda yelled, "You're kidding."

Sam continued to laugh, "No, it's a type of trigger fish. Just pronounce it slowly: Humu-humu-nuku-nuku-apu-a-a." He gave the 'come along' sign, and we followed. We snorkeled above one of the lava ridges, the top of which was only about three feet under the surface of the water.

Sam stopped suddenly, and pointed. His hand followed a tiny fish, only a few inches long, but incredibly colorful. It was mostly dark green, but had a yellow and purple fin, an orange ring around it's 'neck', and a bright blue head. Sam informed us, "A saddle-back wrasse."

Then, Linda – her head underwater and eyes wide – was pointing, and trying to attract our attention with an insistent 'Hmmm hmm hmm'. Sam turned and followed her gaze. It was a huge fish – at least compared to what we had seen so-far; and it was also very colorful – mostly turquoise green around the edges, and brown, orange and pink in the center of its body.

Once again, Sam stuck his head out, and said, "Good catch! That's a parrotfish. They have teeth that can chew on the reef. And, at night, they sleep in a mucous cocoon." Then, Sam laughed, "I wasn't kidding about night snorkeling: There's really a lot to see. All kinds of things you don't see in the daytime."

We followed Sam to the point, where small waves were lapping up against the cliff. He dived down, and came up with a handful of brittle starfish, giving each of us one. They crawled around, and then Sam collected them, and dove again, putting them under a rock.

Continuing around the point, we entered a sandy area, probably 15 feet deep, and crystal clear. Sam held his finger up for us to wait, and he dived down, and disappeared into a narrow tube. Again, we followed his bubbles, and eventually swam in that direction. It was incredibly long, and Sam finally came out the other end.

When Sam surfaced he was panting, "Lava tube." Then, he turned, and we continued following him. I looked above the surface, and saw that we were aiming for a bunch of black rocks at the shoreline, above which was a small waterfall. When we got close, Sam put his finger to his mouth again, and we crept up slowly to the rocks.

Suddenly, five or six sea turtles jetted from the small pool under the waterfall past us into deeper water. Kathy let out a scream. Sam held the rocks, and pointed. There were still several sea turtles in the pond, munching on some underwater plants.

We continued on, stopping in a deeper area for Sam to let us know what we were doing. "We're going to snorkel across a huge expanse of blue-green coral ... and then snorkel into a sea cave. It will end on a small beach, and then I will lead you through a lava tube."

I looked at my friends, and there were only blank faces. We had no idea what would be coming.

We snorkeled across a spectacular area, acres of brightly colored coral. Then, as we followed Sam, it became dark. I looked up, just in time to see the cliff above us, vines hanging down, and pitch black ahead.

We *trusted* Sam. And we all followed him, ending up on a beach about ten feet across – just enough space to fit all of us, as we took off our fins.

Sam led us through more than 100 feet of a lava tube under the cliff. We could see 'light at the end of the tunnel', but it was pitch black where we were walking.

We finally came out the other side, standing on a tiny beach under the cave – more vines hanging above, and dripping on us. Looking out to sea, it seemed that the reef blocked any way of us leaving, except the way we came.

Sam took off his mask and fins, and walked out into the small pool, surrounded by boulders. It was probably the size of a hotel jacuzzi. We followed Sam into the water, and lay back, a gentle current moving us back and forth, as the waves hit the outer reef.

"It's like a hot tub!" Sam remarked. "We could snorkel another hour or two along the coast – and there are quite a few neat things to see – to the Princeville Hotel. Then, use their beach shower, take a dip in their pool, then walk the outside stairs up to the street, and walk back to the condo."

I sputtered a little of the saltwater out of my mouth. "Sam, I don't think any of us are up for another 'hour or two' of snorkeling." We had to have been snorkeling for more than an hour, already. Sam smiled, and nodded.

I lay back in the pool, the warm water comforting me. We had snorkeled as far as we would be going today. And, there were still one or two more 'events' planned for the day. The girls had been doing fine; they were strong swimmers, and comfortable in the water.

Opening my eyes, I gazed up: Blue sky filling most of my field of view, then the cliff, and vines hanging down, and dripping at the entrance of the cave.

Here I was, on the north shore of Kauai, in a private, idyllic setting – the 'hot tub', the beach, the tropical flora, and the blackness of the lava tube. I had once seen a Monk Seal here. And I was with four, beautiful, nude, young women – who trusted me, and who would accept my attention, and occasional attempts to satisfy them.

Kelly called, "Sam! What are we going to do, next?"

I stood on the sandy bottom, swaying back and forth with the current, and looked at Kelly and her friends. They all seemed happy. "You guys have done a great job, snorkeling this far. But we have to get back ... and it will be against the current."

I looked at each one of them, so that they would realize that I was serious. "So I suggest we leave soon. We're not going back through the lava tube ... we're going to snorkel directly back, this way." I pointed to the reef.

Then, I decided to begin planning ... "Could I ask a favor of you guys?" There were blank stares, and slow nods. "Unless you need to pee urgently, I'd like you to hold it, until we get back to the beach, and I can tell you about our next 'event'."

Once again, Kelly said – softly, this time – "Sam! What are you talking about?" I just smiled. I hadn't told Kelly or her friends about the next 'event'. If they could kick those fins – we would be back in fifteen minutes.

I looked around at the girls, "Follow me!" It was a bit premature, as I had to put on my fins, and mask/snorkel. And, the girls had to get ready, also. I snorkeled slowly to the right, along one of the deeper channels. Then, I stopped, staring down at the reef and rocks below me.

It had to be more than five minutes before I felt someone grab my fin, and pull herself alongside me. Kelly gave me the 'OK' sign. I looked back, and all of Kelly's friends were behind her. I slowly and rhythmically moved my fins, producing an efficient locomotion across the reef. I kept an eye out for anything interesting and, within moments, was halted by a sight I hadn't seen.

Pointing into the narrow channel, Kelly looked, and then her friends moved alongside, trying to see what was happening. There was an octopus, devouring the animal in a chambered nautilus shell. The shell was probably 18" long, and the octopus had enveloped it.

I moved forward, to let all the girls get a chance to see this act of nature. We snorkeled back to the point as quickly as we could. I looked back every couple of minutes; the group had spread out, but we were all making it. When we got to the shallow reef, I led the group down one of the channels, back to the beach where our sheet was spread.

The girls were tittering over the incredible snorkel tour. I checked my watch: It had been nearly two hours. I opened the cooler, and passed sodas around. "So how was it? Did you enjoy our 'snorkel tour'?"

Julie's friends couldn't stop raving, telling each other about what they'd seen. They were tired, but they'd had an epic experience. They all talked at once, then they hugged me – all of them; I was nearly smothered. We took off our booties, and drank our sodas, sitting on the sheet. It was a beautiful day, and nobody else had come to this beach.

The subject was opened, when Julie said, "Sam, I need to pee pretty soon."

Linda concurred, "Yeah, I don't know why you couldn't let us pee on the way back."

As Kelly asked me, "So what are we going to do, Sam?" I couldn't help but laugh.

"Well, after your submission challenge, there really isn't much that I can shock you with, anything that would embarrass you." I felt like I was getting slap-happy. "But, today, we're going to have a 'pissing contest'."

Kelly's mouth dropped open. "A *WHAT*?" Then, her eyes sparkled, and she shook her head. "You've got to be kidding ... but I know you too well." Kelly turned to her friends, "He's not kidding."

There were blank expressions, so I took the initiative. "Who has to go, the worst?"

Julie sheepishly raised her hand. She said, "I really can't hold it much longer, Sam."

Smiling, I brought everyone down to the water, and hopped up onto one of the smooth, black rocks that was wet, but warmed by the sun. I lay back, and said, "I guess the position will be something like this. We'll see how far each of us can pee ... and I expect all of you to make it at least to that next boulder" I pointed to the next small boulder, or large rock, at water's edge.

Julie shrugged, walked over to the rock, and I slipped down the side into the water. Julie hopped up, and sat back, reaching down and separating her labia. We all stood on the beach, as Julie's stream of pee arced through the air, and came down on top of the other rock.

Linda wheezed, and said, "I expected *something* like this." When Julie was finished, Linda walked up to the boulder, helped Julie down, and hopped up, herself. She looked at Kelly, and said, "Sam is *really* a pervert, you know."

Kelly nodded, "Yes Linda, I know."

Linda rolled her eyes, shrugged, then sat back, gauging the distance to the other rock. She reached down, and began peeing, rocking back and forth to aim the farthest, which was against the side of the rock. Her stream continued, her bladder obviously having been full.

Linda hopped off the rock, and walked past us, sitting down on the sheet, and shaking her head.

I looked at Kathy, who looked down, and told us, "I can't pee, yet, Sam." She held up a can of soda, and took a big swig.

Kelly's shoulders dropped, "Well, *I* can." She glared at me, "I can't believe you asked my friends to do this." She positioned herself on the rock, and her pee arced over the water, hitting the other rock, then petered off, splashing in the water, and eventually dribbling down the boulder on which she was laying.

I suddenly realized that I hadn't taken my phone out of the pack to capture these images. As I headed back to the sheet to console Linda, Kelly called out, "Where are *you* going, Mister?" I turned around, and Kelly looked stern, with her hands on her hips.

Except that she was nude, like the rest of us. Kelly crooked her finger, and signaled me to come over. "What?"

Kelly laughed, "It's *your* turn now, Mister."

Well, I *did* have to pee, now that I thought about it. I got up onto the rock, and stood on the slightly slick top. I reached down, and began to aim ... and Kelly yelled, "Oh no! That's not fair. You're going to do it like we did!"

Oh well. I had to expect that. I sat on the rock, and aimed myself. I started to pee, but it didn't reach the other rock. Then, I rocked back, and my pee hit the side of the rock. I leaned back more, and my pee – for a moment – flew over the rock, and splashed in the water beyond.

I seemed to be the winner of our pissing contest! The girls laughed, and I slipped off the rock, and walked back to the sheet.

Linda laughed, "That *has* to be all."

"All what?" I asked.

Linda said, "All that you can put us through. You really can't think of anything else. It's impossible." I grinned, and sipped my Diet Coke. Linda was right that we'd done a lot together. But I still had a few ideas left.

We were all tired from the long snorkel experience. As I lay back on the sheet and caught a few more rays, Kelly worked on her dissertation, and Kathy was on the other side of the beach, still hunting for puka shells. Julie and Linda were walking along the lava ledge next to the cliff, talking, but I couldn't hear what they were saying.

I flipped onto my stomach, and turned my head toward the other end of the beach. Kathy was bending over, her hand moving through the sand, when she looked up. There was a couple – about the age of Kelly and her friends – walking over the lava rocks to the beach.

Kathy turned back toward us, still searching through the sand; she was halfway back to us by the time the other couple began laying out their towels at the far end of the beach.

The girl was cute, similar in body type to Kelly, but shorter. She pulled off her tank, and took off her bikini top, then walked casually to the water and sat in the sand, the water lapping around her legs. Her breasts were smaller than Kelly's but just as firm and pointy – the mammaries of youth.

I offered to take Kelly on another snorkel and, surprisingly, she put down her notes and accepted. This time, we both went out nude, except for the neoprene booties.

We snorkeled around the rocks just off the end of the shallow reef, Kelly doing a nice surface dive and following me down a few times to examine the reef more closely. I had taken quite a few pictures on the long snorkel tour, making sure I had captured everyone, as well as the turtles, the waterfall, and the sea cave.

Now, I snapped a few more of Kelly, and had her free dive and swim underwater, her long legs kicking slowly to propel herself. As I watched her breasts and butt wobble, I decided to take a few videos, also. Kelly tried to swim down and come up in a large school of fish, as I had, but the fish had scattered by the time she reached them.

We made our way back to the beach, again following one of the deeper channels, and sat in the sand near the rocks near the middle of the beach to remove our fins and booties. As we were doing this, the girl walked in the shallow water toward us.

"Hi!" she said cheerily. We greeted her, and introduced ourselves. She asked about the snorkeling, and I gave her a quick orientation – the shallow reef, with holes in which you could see some fish, the deeper water with sand channels and lava ridges, and finally the area around the point with the waterfall and sea cave.

She shook her head, "I think we'll stay in the shallow part." Most tourists did confine themselves to the area in front of the beach, few venturing around the point or down the coast.

We found that they were from Colorado, and had visited Kauai a couple of times. They had found this beach through the recommendation of the condo at which they were staying, which was up another trail from the beach, across from the one we had taken.

Kelly and I went back to our sheet, joining Julie and Linda, while Kathy continued to search for shells. The next time I glanced across the beach, the girl had taken off her bikini bottom, and was lying on her towel nude, while her husband was still in traditional swim trunks.

I pulled out some of the snacks we had brought, and we all found something to munch on. A while later, Julie and Linda decided to snorkel again, as did the other couple, the girl now wearing her bikini bottom again. Kathy was sitting in the sand near the cliff, sorting shells.

Smiling at Kelly, I raised my eyebrows a couple of times. "What?" she asked.

I looked toward the back of the beach, where there were a few large boulders in the shade. Kelly shook her head, "I'm not really in the mood now, Sam." I lay down on the sheet and closed my eyes.

The next thing I knew, Julie and Linda were sitting down on the sheet, laying out their snorkeling gear, and talking about what they'd seen. I glanced to the other side of the beach, and saw the other couple packing up, then hiking over the lava rocks and disappearing around the other side of the cove.

A few minutes later, Kathy showed us a handful of puka shells, and I gave her the baggie that had held the grapes. She dropped in the shells, and sealed the baggie, then looked at me, and announced, "I guess I'm ready, now, Sam."

At first, I didn't know what she was saying, but she walked over to the large rock by the water, and hopped up onto it. I walked down to the edge of the water, and sat down, as Kathy lay on her back, and brought her knees up to her chest. A stream of pee sailed over the other rock, easily beating the distance record I'd set.

As we walked back to the sheet, I exclaimed, "Well, I guess Kathy's the champion of the pissing contest!" Julie and Linda laughed, but Kelly didn't seem to find it funny.

It was now mid-afternoon, and we'd all had enough sun for one day. We packed up, and hiked back up the hill to the car. Back at the condo, we all got showered and dressed, and I suggested that we go down into Hanalei. It was time for me to buy the girls their next 'souvenir' of the trip.

We drove down the hill, and walked around the small shops, stopping for a shave ice before I took them to a boutique that had my favorite island-style dresses. Sarah had loved this shop, and I again felt a pang of sadness.

Before we walked into the shop, I turned to the girls, "I'm only planning to buy you guys a couple more things during this trip, but one of them will be a unique tropical-style dress ... if you guys can find one you like." The girls squealed, and Linda hugged me.

There were a few dresses on display just outside the door, and the girls were already excited about them. We went inside, and the girls shopped. I pointed out a couple of dresses that I thought would look good on Kelly, and she decided to try one of them, and another one she'd picked.

I sat on a chair next to the dressing rooms, as Kelly and her friends tried on their selections. Each of the girls came out from the small curtained dressing areas, and modeled one or two of the dresses for me. I thought they were all beautiful – the dresses *and* the girls.

Back at the condo, I did some Internet research on Kelly's laptop, and found the website for a luau on the east shore. I had originally planned on going to a Japanese restaurant tonight, but decided that the girls should have a luau experience, early in the trip.

I made the reservations, and then went out onto the lanai, and sat on one of the chaises, as I explained the plans to everyone. "What would you guys think about going to a luau, tonight?" The girls nodded.

"A lot of hotels have luaus, but they're usually not that authentic; sometimes, they're pretty touristy. But there's one on the east shore where we can walk around some beautiful tropical gardens, then eat *Kalua* pig, and other typical luau fare, along with bottomless Mimosa's and Mai Tai's. And then, there's a pretty good show."

Linda was nodding vigorously, and Julie said, "That sounds great, Sam." I suggested that they wear their new dresses, and I swapped my cutoffs and tank for a better pair of shorts and a nice Aloha shirt.

We made a quick stop in Kapaa, where my friend said he would meet me, and I did a quick transaction, buying enough local pot to last the rest of the trip. Then, we continued south.

As we drove past the Wailua River, I said, "I'm not sure if we'll have time, but maybe later in the trip we can kayak on this river, up to the 'fern grotto'. It's really not much, compared to what we'll see on the Kalalau Trail, but it's an easy river to kayak."

I would really have liked to take the girls on a kayak tour down the Na Pali coast, but that would have been a full day and we would have had to go with a group. We would be seeing the coast by Zodiac on Friday, anyway.

We walked through the lush gardens next to the Wailua River, and then watched, as the pig was raised from the pit – first the hot rocks lifted with shovels, then the banana leaves pulled aside. The whole pig, now nearly unrecognizable, was lifted on a wire screen, and taken to the kitchen for preparation.

We sat at one of the long tables in the pavilion, drinking our Mai Tai's, and I thought how lucky we'd been that it hadn't rained too much, so far. The trip was working out great, but we had a lot more planned. It was hard to believe that this was only our third day on the island!

The show was OK – hula girls wearing coconut bra tops, fire jugglers, and a few other acts. The girls seemed to enjoy the experience; and I had enjoyed the Mai Tai's. I took a few group photos of the girls wearing their new dresses. They really were a cute bunch.

On the drive back to Princeville, I asked, teasingly, "I guess you guys aren't up for a night snorkel, tonight?" There was no answer. But they had done very well with the long snorkel tour today, and I decided that we would shoot for a night snorkel tomorrow evening.

It was Linda's turn to stay with me tonight ... or my turn to stay with Linda. Kelly and I got undressed, and we both put on a tank over our black bikini underwear. Then, I followed her into the other bedroom, where Julie and Linda were hanging up their dresses. Linda took off her bra, and put on her red dirt t-shirt.

Julie stepped up to me, and gave me a nice kiss. "Thank you, again, Sam." When I looked at her, she smiled, "For buying us the dresses, and taking us to the nice Luau." I hugged her, and she headed into the bathroom.

Kelly, Linda and I went out onto the deck, where Kathy was talking quietly into her cellphone. When we sat down, she ended her call, and looked up at us. "Christian," she said. "He's in Honolulu the rest of the week, but will be back on Kauai next week." It sounded serious.

The sky was clear, and a warm breeze caressed our bodies. Julie came out to the patio, and asked, "So are you going to share the smokes, Sam?" I hadn't planned to indulge tonight, but went inside, and pulled out my small plastic water pipe, a lighter, and the bag of grass.

We sat around the small table on the deck, passing the pipe around. I wondered whether the smoke we exhaled was being blown into any other of the condos. But it seemed that the place wasn't very full, this week.

Eventually, Kathy retired to the loft, and Kelly kissed me goodnight, and went into the bedroom with Julie. I wondered whether they would 'get it on' tonight. Linda and I sat on the lanai a while longer, then went into the master bedroom.

I went into the bathroom to pee, and when I came out, Linda was lying on the spread, parallel to the foot of the bed, watching television; it was a reality show called 'Naked Dating', couples meeting each other nude, and going on silly outings on some island.

Lying next to Linda, I lightly stroked her back, and asked, "How are you doing, Linda?"

She turned her head to me, and chuckled, "I guess I'm pretty tired. And drunk. And stoned." She smiled weakly at me, and I wondered whether she would be up for anything but sleeping tonight.

I smiled back, "Don't worry. I don't take advantage of women when they're drunk. And stoned." I put my arm around her waist.

"That's OK, Sam. You can do whatever you want with me," her smile broadened, "while I watch TV." Then, she chuckled again, "But maybe you shouldn't spank me ... it might be too loud, and I'd like to hear the program."

That was funny. But there were plenty of other ways I could 'play' with her, while she watched TV. I reached under her tee, and slowly pulled the pink panties down her legs and off, then reached for one of the decorative pillows. Linda lifted her hips, as I slipped the pillow under her.

I got a few 'supplies' from my suitcase, and sat on the bed next to her, deciding that I would show her each of my toys, and she could let me know if I could play with them. I showed her the rectal thermometer, and she nodded.

As she continued to watch her program, I separated her buttocks, and inserted the thin glass tube, moving it around, and then in and out of her slowly. Then, I lubed one of the small butt plugs, and again she gave her consent. I took out the thermometer, and slid the butt plug into her.

I massaged her bottom, then ran my hands up under the tee, and gave her a short back rub. Next, I lubed the short, fat butt plug with the thin neck and jeweled end. I showed it to her, and she shook her head. "Maybe I should put that one in you?" I shrugged.

Linda waited until the commercial came on, then she sat up – the small plug still in her – and I got into a knee-chest position. By the end of the commercial, the large butt plug was inside me, and Linda was again lying on the bed, watching TV.

I showed her a package of five needles, and asked, "How about one on each side, until the next commercial?" She shrugged. I swabbed each of her hips, and quickly inserted a needle on her left side, and then on her right. She didn't make a sound.

A few minutes later, I showed her two more needles, and said, "You can insert these in me." She said, "I'm watching the program. But I'll watch, while you insert them in yourself."

It wasn't what I was expecting, but Linda turned her head toward me, and I lay down, and did as she had suggested. Then, she turned her head back to the TV. I put my arm around her waist again, and we lay there, two needles and a butt plug in each of us.

The commercial didn't come on for a while, and the needles started hurting, but Linda said nothing. Finally, the commercial started, and I pulled each of the needles out of Linda's butt, dropping them into an empty soda can. Linda pushed herself up, and took the needles out of me.

Then, she asked, "Could you please take that plug out of me, now? It's getting annoying." I removed the butt plug, and – with mine still in me – walked into the bathroom, where I disposed of the can, and washed the thermometer and small plug.

I lay next to Linda again, this time on my side, rubbing myself slowly against her hip. By the time the program had ended, I was hard. Linda reached down and held me, her fingers curled around my shaft.

Then, she got off the bed, pulled the tee up over her head and off, and bent over to kiss me. She smiled, "Would you please make love to me now, Sam?" She lay on the spread, her head on a pillow, and I crawled up between her legs.

As I fingered her clit, what Linda had said hit me: She hadn't asked for sex, she'd asked for lovemaking. Perhaps it was semantics, but a pang rippled through me, as I thought about it. I'd had *sex* with Kelly's friends, but it was *Kelly* who I loved.

Kelly and I had talked about 'polyamory', and I thought about the feelings I had for her friends; especially Linda. I had deep feelings for her, and we'd already had sex a couple of times, but it still didn't seem appropriate for me to 'make love' to her.

I shook my head, and Linda lifted hers, looking down her body at me. "Are you OK, Sam?" I didn't know; it felt strange. It wasn't about sharing a bed with Linda, or 'playing' with her; or even having sex with her. But I wondered whether we'd taken it too far, now referring to sex as 'lovemaking'.

Nodding to Linda, I took my position, then lowered my head to hers, and kissed her. She returned the kiss, more passionately than I'd expected. She reached down, and put me inside her, and I lowered myself onto her, as I began plunging deep into her wetness.

Linda's vaginal muscles pulled me even farther into her, as we kissed again. Although my brain was confused, my heart wasn't: I did have strong feelings for Linda; perhaps it *was* love. But it in no way diminished my love for Kelly.

I could feel Linda's orgasm approaching, and that triggered my own response. As I kissed her neck, we came together, Linda's muscles clenching and unclenching, with each of my thrusts. I collapsed onto her, my head buried between her shoulder and her neck.

We finally got up, and went into the bathroom together. She sat on the toilet, while I bent over in front of her, and she pulled out the butt plug. I washed it, and then we washed our hands together.

Linda and I stood in the bathroom hugging, and then climbed into bed and turned off the lights. Our naked bodies next to each other, I stroked her hair. "Good night, Linda." I gave her a peck on the lips.

She turned onto her back. "Good night, Sam."

CHAPTER 9: FLYING HIGH

It was Wednesday, already. We'd done quite a lot, but it was still early in the trip. Despite not running every morning, we were getting plenty of exercise.

Sam had told us that today would be a bit different, hopefully easier than yesterday, but still with some excitement. I always had to wonder, with Sam, what kind of excitement he had in mind. He seemed to perpetually have *some* kind of excitement in his thoughts.

We sat around the coffee table, while Sam explained the plan for the day. "I thought we could tour a couple more places, this time to the east of Princeville, including some beach time." We were all smiling and nodding. "Then, we'll have lunch at the Princeville Hotel, and try out their pool."

My friends were even more excited. I knew that Sam had more plans for later in the day, but he didn't tell me, and I didn't ask.

He continued, "So first, we'll go to Kilauea, and I'll show you Secret Beach, the most official unofficial nude beach on the north shore. It will be a little hike, but if we're not going to run today, it will be good exercise. Next, we'll visit the Kilauea Lighthouse and nature preserve.

"Then, I'd like you to see Kalihiwai. There's a stream and a beach and, if we were interested in hiking, a trail that leads up to three pools, with waterfalls from one to the next."

He shook his head, "But we have quite a few more things for today; so we'll only see one more place – Anini Beach, where there's a nice park, with windsurfing and snorkeling. Then, we'll go have lunch." Sam always went overboard, planning more things each day than imaginable.

I waited for my friends to ask what else Sam had planned, but they didn't.

We packed up – a little lighter, this time – and headed to Kilauea. Sam said the lighthouse wouldn't be open quite yet, so he wanted to start the day with a visit to Secret Beach.

We drove by some very large properties, then parked and put on our packs. Sam wore flip-flops, but the rest of us wore trail running shoes.

Hiking the steep trail down the cliff, we could see that there were perhaps a dozen people on the beach, already. Most were nude. The lighthouse stood proudly on the top of the cliff at the point to our right, and there was a small island just offshore.

We walked down the beach and found a relatively uninhabited area, with some beautiful palms. Sam laid out the sheet, and we held it down at the corners with our packs, and promptly stripped down.

As we walked slowly toward the cliff leading to the lighthouse point, Julie asked, "Is nudity on this beach legal?"

Sam laughed, "It's a long story. The basic answer is that nudity isn't 'legal' unless a judge has ruled that it is. The beach we went to yesterday was in such a ruling, and may be the only truly 'legal' nude beach on the island. But nudity here is probably not *illegal*, either."

Julie retorted, "That's not logical. Let me ask another way: Are there laws against going nude?"

Sam laughed again, "Well, there are two laws that might apply: Indecent exposure, and open lewdness. They both require that the genitals are exposed ... so you guys could walk in downtown Honolulu topless, and in just a tiny thong, and it would be legal." Julie was shaking her head.

Sam continued, "And, it depends on whether the genitals are exposed in a public place, like on the side of the road, or in a more private place, like a beach with difficult trail access." It was getting more and more complicated.

"But 'open lewdness' requires that it's proven that someone intentionally tried to affront another person. So, if you're just lying on the beach, minding your own business, you shouldn't be breaking that law."

Still laughing, Sam concluded, "But the police would only respond if someone complains. Then, they probably wouldn't arrest anyone, if they covered their genitals. And, even if they went to court, there's a good chance they wouldn't be guilty of anything."

We had reached the cliff, and turned around. Sam pointed to the nearby island. "That's Moku'ae'ae Island, maybe a hundred yards across. There's some interesting diving around it – from shallow areas with lobster, to deep drop-offs with sharks, Lion fish and huge sea turtles."

Linda spoke up, "Lobster? Maybe we can catch some for dinner?"

Sam smiled, "That would be great, but lobster season ended last month, and we'd need a state fishing license. We could snorkel out there, but it might be challenging; there are currents and it sometimes gets rough between the point and the island."

Linda's lobster dinner disappeared. A moment later, Julie cried, "Look!" She pointed, and we saw something in the water; actually, *out* of the water.

Sam explained, "Those are spinner dolphin. Let's watch them for a few minutes. There are often pods of a dozen or more off this beach." He chuckled, "We could try to snorkel out to them, but they could disappear, and it would be a long swim back to the beach."

We had a long walk back to our sheet, and Sam decided to swim the distance. Julie joined him, and they first swam out about a hundred feet from the beach, and then paralleled us. Kathy, Linda and I got back to the sheet a good five minutes before they did.

Sam checked his watch, and said, "We can stay here as long as you guys like, or hike back up and see the Lighthouse, then go to the next beach." We decided to hike up the trail, which took considerably longer than the hike down. Then we drove a short distance to the Kilauea Point National Wildlife Refuge.

We got out of the car, and Kathy pointed: There were sea birds flying all around. Sam said, "Those with the long double tails are 'frigate birds', called *Iwa* in Hawaiian."

As we walked toward the lighthouse, Sam pointed to birds doing a courtship dance beyond the fence. "Those are Laysan albatross. I didn't think they showed up until October or November. They're courting, and will nest on this hill." They looked like large gulls.

We toured the lighthouse, and looked over the cliff to the island just offshore. Then, we went back to the car, and Sam drove us to another beach, called Kalihiwai. We parked in the midst of pine trees, and walked out on a spit of sand dividing a lagoon from a small bay.

Then, we walked back into the pines, and Sam pulled out his little water pipe. "Are you guys ready to get high?"

Nobody argued, and Sam lit up, passing the pipe around. We saw a rope tied to a tree, and Sam climbed up and released it.

Then, one by one, we swung out over the lagoon, and dropped into the water. We played around in the fresh water, and Julie and Sam took a swim on the ocean side. Then, we got back into the car, and drove to still another beach: Anini.

We stopped at a park, and walked across the grass to the water. There wasn't much beach, but the water was crystal clear. A few people were windsurfing out and back over the reef. Sam offered to let us snorkel here, but we opted out. So Sam drove us back to our condo, where we cleaned up, and put on nicer cover-ups.

It was less than a five minute drive to the Princeville Hotel, and Sam valeted the car in the *Porte Cochere*. We walked into the hotel, and immediately felt under-dressed. There were Italian columns and tiled floors, and glass windows circling the area, looking out on the Bali Hai view.

Sam brought us out to a small deck, and we had a spectacular view of Hanalei Bay. Then, we took the elevator down to the beach level, and walked out to the pool area. It was an infinity pool, framed by the Bali Hai ridge and Ha'ena point. Gorgeous!

We sat down in a small pavilion, and were immediately brought menus. The choice was limited, and the prices were high, but it was an incredible atmosphere. Sam and I shared a club sandwich, Linda got a spinach salad, Kathy the Cobb salad, and Julie had a burger.

The food was great. Although Sam had offered wine, we were still feeling the effect of the smokes, so we stuck with iced tea.

After a leisurely lunch, we took our tea, and picked up towels from the little beach hut, then found a line of chaises that we could commandeer. We tried the pool, which had a luscious feel, and the jacuzzi. Then, we walked on the beach, all the way to the outlet of the Hanalei River, across from Black Pot park and the pier.

We returned to the pool, and our iced teas were refilled. Kathy exclaimed, "Now *this* is what I pictured, coming to a tropical resort!"

It was true: Sam could have much more easily planned a relaxing week here at the hotel, with all of us lying around by the pool. But he never would have done that; if nothing else, Sam was an adventurous guy, and he wanted to share the adventures with all of us.

It was glorious weather, although big, puffy clouds floated by, and we felt a few drops of rain when we were in the spa. We were all relaxing, but Sam was suddenly checking his watch, and seemed in a rush to go.

Finally, he asked, "Are we ready for our next big adventure?"

My friends glanced over at Sam, wondering – along with me – what that would entail. Finally, Julie said, "Sure, Sam." Under her breath, I heard, 'Whatever you have in mind'. We retrieved the car, and Sam drove us back to the condo.

Linda asked, "We're having an 'adventure' in our condo?" I couldn't help but think, 'Oh no!', as we awaited Sam's response.

He laughed, "No. I just thought you guys would like to do a couple of things before the 'big adventure'.

Kathy asked, sourly, "What is that?"

Sam said, "Well, I thought we could get really stoned, and you guys can use the bathroom, and change out of your bathing suits, if you like." Then, he added, "But you can also go just the way you are."

Julie asked, "Go where, Sam?" He pulled out the pipe, and went out onto the lanai and lit up. Of course, we all partook, and Julie's question was not answered. We cleaned up quickly, and piled back into the car. Sam drove fifteen minutes to the Princeville Airport, and we parked next to a metal hangar.

When my friends saw the sign over the door, they went wild: We were going on a helicopter tour! Sam checked in, and we went to a waiting area. He said, proudly, "We have our own chopper!"

I wondered if my friends were as stoned as I was ... but I was pretty sure they were. Sam made sure we all had our cameras, and we boarded the helicopter, its blades already rotating. The pilot greeted us, showed us how to fasten the harnesses, and told us to put on the headphones.

A few moments later, we lifted off, made a quick turn, and headed toward the center of the island. Flying over Hanalei Valley, the pilot pointed out several waterfalls, and we flew very close to one. We continued into the island, now flying a couple of thousand feet above the ground.

We were really flying high ... in more than one way!

The pilot said that we were nearing the wettest spot on earth – that gets more than fifty *feet* of rain per year. We turned right, and were inside the crater of the extinct volcano, flying very close to the sheer vertical cliffs, waterfalls coming down all around us.

Then we flew up and over the edge, and Sam turned back to us and yelled, "That's the Alakai Swamp, where we're going to hike on Saturday." He smiled, "And I'm going to mud-wrestle Kathy." Julie, Linda and I looked at Kathy; she looked surprised, and shrugged.

The pilot was now pointing out Waimea Canyon, which Mark Twain called 'the grand canyon of the Pacific'. It looked like a miniature Grand Canyon.

We flew over a forested area, and learned that this was Koke'e State Park. Then, the canyon disappeared, and the ocean was ahead of us. The helicopter dipped, and dropped suddenly down through a narrow valley, winding left and right, then left again, down and down, until we crossed a beach, and flew out over the water.

We then flew parallel to the shore, along the Na Pali coastline, and Sam pointed excitedly. The pilot nodded, "To our right is Honopu Valley." There were two beaches and a huge rock arch. Then, the pilot pointed, "And that's Kalalau Beach, at the end of a world-class hiking trail."

Sam was pointing to the waterfall, and then up into the valley. He looked back at me and smiled, then wiped tears from his eyes. Sam had told me that coming to Kauai would be an emotional experience. He loved the island, but it was mainly the memories of coming here with Sarah that got to him.

Kathy and Julie leaned over to look out the window next to Linda and I; the view was spectacular, as we flew along the coast. There were narrow ridges, and deep valleys, with dozens of waterfalls and streams. Then, we flew just over the water, past a narrow rock arch that went into the water, and we could see bright yellow, orange, and blue kayaks gliding under the arch.

Ahead was Kee Beach, at the end of the road, and the pilot pointed out Tunnels Reef and Ha'ena. Too soon, we were flying by Hanalei Bay and Princeville. Sam pointed animatedly, and I recognized our condo and the small beach below.

We flew over the golf course, and soon were flying down the runway at the Princeville Airport. We hovered lower and lower, until the skids touched the tarmac in front of the hangar.

When I climbed out of the 'copter and stepped onto the ground, I realized that my knees were weak. I looked back at my friends, and they had ear-to-ear grins. Sam led us alongside the building back to our car, where it was quieter, then turned to us. "So that was our first 'big' adventure for the day."

What was he *talking* about? We'd hiked a steep trail to a nude beach, swung on a rope into a lagoon, visited a luxury hotel, and taken a helicopter tour of the island. There *couldn't* be any more 'big' adventures, today.

All three of my friends hugged Sam, and thanked him profusely. It had been an incredible experience: None of us had even been in a helicopter before, and in the past hour, we'd hovered next to waterfalls, flown down into narrow valleys, and skimmed over the ocean.

We hopped into the car, and Sam started the engine. Then, he turned back, and asked, "Would you guys mind, if we just brought in a couple of pizzas, tonight? We'll be going out a lot more, and it might just be easier, logistically."

We all nodded, not having any idea what Sam was talking about. Pizza sounded great. We drove back to Kilauea, where we went into a boutique pizza place, and ordered two large pizzas – one vegetarian, and one with meats, both incorporating some exotic ingredients.

When they were brought out, they smelled fantastic. My mouth was watering, although it seemed that we'd eaten just a few hours earlier.

As we drove back to our condo, Sam began apologizing. "I hope you're not starving, yet, because we're not going to eat for a while. And I know we've already had a big day, but I'm trying to fit everything in, and don't want you to miss this experience."

Once again, we had no idea what Sam was talking about. Linda spoke up, "What experience, Sam?" We turned into the driveway of the condo, and Sam parked in front of our unit. He turned off the engine, and turned around, looking at each of my friends, and then me.

Then, he answered the question: "Why a *night snorkel*, of course!" None of us said a word; I think we were all in shock. We'd already done so much today ... and the pizza was smelling so good ...

We went into the condo, and Sam stored the pizzas in the oven, then told us to put on our bathing suits. When we convened in the living room, Sam was spreading out equipment on the coffee table. He handed each of us an underwater flashlight, and we put our snorkeling gear into our packs.

Sam said we could relax for a while, so we went out onto the deck, while he prepared a salad which he stored, without dressing, in the fridge.

One moment we were looking out at blue sky, and the next, it was pouring rain. A huge black cloud passed over us, and headed toward the Bali Hai ridge, to the west. The rain only lasted a minute or two and, by the time Sam had finished the salad, there was blue sky, again.

We walked down to the beach, a slight fog rising from the now-wet path, and the plants and trees seeming even more lush, after the tropical downpour.

Julie and Linda were comparing their experiences, and the sights they had seen on the helicopter ride. Kathy was trailing, keeping up, but somewhat dazed, in her own world. Sam was leading the way, as usual, looking very fit, but I wasn't sure about the Speedos he was wearing under his tank top.

We walked over the grass barbeque area, and down the short trail to the beach, and followed Sam to the center of the small beach. The sun was low, and it was dark under the hala trees bordering the cliff. The water looked more agitated than it had been when we snorkeled yesterday.

Had it only been yesterday? Since that time, we'd gone to a luau, I'd made it with Julie, we toured three beaches and the lighthouse, spent time by the pool at the hotel, *taken a helicopter tour*, and now we were about to go on a 'night' snorkel!

Sam laid out the sheet, and we and our packs barely fit, as we took out our snorkeling equipment. Then he gave us an orientation. He loved to lecture, and would make a great professor at the college, if our company didn't work out. I listened well, as I was nervous about going into the dark water.

"A lot of people don't realize that on the reef – just like everywhere else – a lot of animals come out only at night. Creatures that are sedentary during the day, like the sea cucumbers and urchins, will move quickly across the reef at night. And some corals are luminescent; so when you look down on it, it seems like seeing a city from a plane, or from space."

I glanced at my friends, and they were listening intently.

Sam continued, "So, for your first 'night snorkel', I thought we would stay on the shallower part of the reef." We all nodded and there were a few smiles. Sam added, "We should try to stay together, but you'll never get lost: I'm going to hang a light from this branch."

He stood, and hung a flashlight with diffuser at the end, and turned it on. Clouds were now covering the sun, low in the sky, and it had gotten noticeably darker.

Sam looked at his watch. "We're going to go in as soon as you guys are ready. And, we'll make our way to the outer edge of the reef. We may go into a little deeper water, especially if it's still light, and we see some sea turtles. And, in deeper water, we can go vertical, and look to the west at the Bali Hai, as the sun sets.

"And we'll all look at the beach, and make sure we can see this light. Then, as it gets darker, we can work our way toward the beach ... but very slowly! Just let yourself drift, and look down at the reef, into the holes, and stay still. Hopefully, you'll see a few things."

Sam looked up at the dark cloud that was passing over us. "You'll see those red fish with big eyes ... I think they're called 'squirrelfish'. And you can carefully touch the spines of the urchins, like you saw me do, yesterday."

He glanced at his watch again. "I expect us to be out about an hour. By that time, it'll be pretty dark, and a lot of animals will come out.

"Now, go ahead and test your flashlight." We all switched them on, and back off. Sam smiled. He had brought them without batteries, and bought batteries at the market, after we got here.

"Good. You can use them as we go out; although you won't really need them, try shining them around, and you'll see the bright colors you may not have noticed before. And if you turn the light off for a minute or two, you might see those luminescent 'cities' I told you about."

He put on his booties, and rubbed spit on the inside of his mask. Then, he walked down to the water. There were no rocks to sit on, so he sat in the water, as he pulled on his fins.

I walked down to him and, as I was sitting down, Sam warned, "The water feels colder, now; although I doubt if it's gone down by even a degree." It *was* cold, and the air felt cooler, too.

Julie, Linda and Kathy were nearly ready, getting faster with every snorkel we did. There were a few squeals from Linda, as she got into the water. But soon, we were snorkeling away from the beach.

Sam and I were leading; he held my hand, so that we would stay together, and so that he could signal me, if he saw something interesting. I realized that I didn't need to kick at all, as Sam was pulling me through the water at an almost imperceptible speed.

It was amazing what bright colors we saw in the beam of Sam's huge underwater light: There were bright reds, yellows and greens. We didn't see anything that was much different than during the day, so we continued moving slowly toward the edge of the reef.

When we were all in an area of deeper water – perhaps ten feet – Sam went vertical, and looked around, then pointed. We could see the Bali Hai ridge on the horizon, huge dark clouds hanging over it, and backlit by the sun, with rays fanning across the sky.

Sam made sure we were all OK, and we snorkeled out a little further. He squeezed my hand and, in the beam of his light, we saw a sea turtle swimming by, slowly but gracefully, its small legs propelling it, and it's short conical tail sticking out from the mottled green carapace. The turtle glanced at us, and continued swimming.

I was getting chilled, now; perhaps a thin wetsuit would have helped? Sam had mentioned a Lycra body suit when we were in the dive store, but he did not buy one for us. Sam glanced at my friends, who's eyes were wide, watching the turtle, and gave them the 'OK' sign, which they returned.

Sam was vertical again, and pointing, so we all gathered near him, and pushed our masks to our foreheads. The scene was magnificent: The sun had set, and the clouds were now each a slightly different color, from pinks to purples. The sky itself had bands of orange and red, morphing from west to east into a dark blue.

Sam gave us the 'come along' sign, and we slowly drifted back over the shallow reef. We could now see the beams of all of our flashlights aiming around onto the reef. Looking into one of the holes in the reef, we saw squirrelfish, with their huge eyes watching us.

Sam squeezed my hand, and pointed excitedly. My friends gathered around and peered into the hole, and Sam pointed his light. The head of an eel was sticking out from under a ledge, its mouth opening and closing. Linda – or it might have been Julie – yelped, as the eel came out, and swam freely across the hole, and between two rocks.

The five of us drifted slowly over the reef, pushed slightly toward the beach by each small wave, and Kathy was now making sounds and pointing. Sam let go of my hand, and moved around to the beach side of the hole where Kathy was floating. He followed the beam of her flashlight, and gave her an 'OK' sign.

Lifting his head out of the water, he sputtered, "Candy cane shrimp!" We all looked, but I couldn't see anything until it moved: It was a red and white striped shrimp with two large antennae, peeking out from a small hole in the side of a rock.

We moved still closer to the beach, and Sam pointed again. We saw a large sea urchin that had long, thin needles with black and white stripes. Then, Sam pointed again to a smaller sea urchin with short, thick rust-red spines. Again, he lifted his head, and called out "Banded urchin, and slate pencil urchin."

Sam stuck his head down into a depression in the reef, and pulled up a small, black urchin that looked 'hairy', with no long spines. It had several small rocks and pieces of shell stuck to it. Sam raised his head, and said, "Collector urchin. It's sticky, so things collect on its surface."

He handed it to Linda, who's eyes were wide, and she quickly handed it to Julie, who handed it to me. It was like a 'hot potato' game. Sam took it from my hand, and showed Kathy, who nodded; then he reached down into the hole, and placed it carefully on the bottom.

It was quite dark now, and Sam suggested we turn off all our lights. It was a little scary being in nearly black water. But, as our eyes adjusted, we could see pinpoints of light from a few places in the reef below us, just as Sam had described.

Kathy pointed to the beach, and Sam nodded. We were all getting chilled. As we made a few small kicks of our fins, and slowly moved toward the beach, it started raining. We took off our fins, and walked in our booties up the beach to our now-soaked sheet.

Sam suggested that we leave the booties on, and we quickly packed our stuff, and walked to the path that led up to our condo. The booties worked well as a pair of comfortable 'shoes', but the water in them squished and sloshed with every step we took.

Back in the condo, we put all of our gear in the bathtub of the second bedroom, and Sam ran warm water, as he rinsed each item. Julie already had her suit off, and was ready to get into a warm shower, so Sam gathered the equipment, and laid it out on the deck near the sliding glass door.

Sam and I took a shower together and, as I was getting out, Kathy walked in to the bathroom, nude. She smiled at us, and Sam waved her over. As I dried off, Sam took a second shower with Kathy.

A while later, we were all in shorts and tees in the living room, and Sam turned the oven to 300 degrees to heat the pizzas, as he mixed the salad.

Julie and I set the small table in the dining area, and Linda brought in one of the patio chairs, so that we could all sit inside. It was no longer raining, but the patio table was wet, and we had to dry the chair that Linda had brought inside.

Sam was taking swigs of beer from a bottle, and opened a bottle of red wine, putting it on the table. I set out wine glasses, and Kathy brought the salad plates to the table. We were hungry by now, and dug into the salad, as Sam poured the wine.

He lifted his wine glass, and said, "I would like to make a toast to you guys. You really did great on our snorkel tonight. We didn't see that much, but we were only out there about an hour."

He smiled. "Now, if you guys really want to see more, we could hike down there around midnight, and snorkel into deeper water. We might find a parrotfish in its cocoon, or even some sharks." He was getting excited, "Or maybe even a lionfish!"

Julie's mouth hung open, and Kathy was shaking her head. Linda ventured, "I think we've probably done enough snorkeling for one evening." Then, she asked, "Is the pizza ready, yet?" We all laughed. Linda had done incredibly well limiting her food intake, and had only eaten a salad at lunch.

Sam took the pizzas out of the oven, and put them on the granite counter, along with a stack of plates. We all helped ourselves, and made a considerable dent in both pizzas. Sam poured the rest of the wine.

"I'd offer to open another bottle, or make some mixed drinks ... but I don't want you guys to have a hangover in the morning. We're going to hike to Hanakapiai Falls. That's two miles on the Kalalau Trail to the beach, and another two miles through the jungle to the falls." He smiled at us, "And then, we have to hike the four miles back to our car at Kee."

We all nodded, and Sam added, "And, if we're going to get a parking place, we'll need to start pretty early." We looked at him, and he frowned, and said, "OK, we can leave later. How about if we plan on getting out of here around 8AM?"

It was already after 8PM, and we were just eating dinner. Kathy finished her wine, and said, jokingly, "Well, so much for our relaxing beach vacation!" At least I *thought* she had said it jokingly. Sam *was* pushing us pretty hard. But I couldn't think of what we would have wanted to miss.

We cleaned up the dinner things, putting almost half of each pizza into the fridge. Well, it would be good for breakfast!

Then, we sat in the living room, as Sam connected his camera to the TV, and showed us some of the pictures he'd taken so-far, including a lot of underwater shots. None of us had brought our camera for the night snorkel; those images would have to remain in our memories.

Julie said something that I think we all had imagined: "I don't know, Sam. Snorkeling during the day was fun, but the whole time we were in the water tonight, I envisioned a huge shark coming up from behind, and eating me." We laughed, nervously.

Sam chuckled, "Well, there aren't that many sharks to worry about. And they usually don't swim over the shallow part of the reef." Then, he shrugged, "And I was trying to keep an eye on all of you."

Then, he laughed, "But on night dives, I sometimes have the same feeling. You just have to look behind you every once in a while, and shine the light all around." That wasn't very re-assuring, but Julie didn't comment further.

I got ready for bed in the master bath, then brought a few of my things up to the loft, where I would be sleeping, it being Kathy's turn to spend a night with Sam.

He hadn't told me much about his nights with Julie or Linda, but Julie and I had played around a little, in one of the small beds. I wondered whether Julie would visit me in the loft, where there was a queen-size bed to play on. Perhaps, after Linda fell asleep?

Kathy and I retired to the master bedroom, where we both undressed, and slipped under the covers. "Should I put on the TV?" I asked Kathy.

She replied, "Not for me, Sam. I'm pretty tired." She gave me a sheepish smile, "I wouldn't mind getting to sleep soon."

I nodded, leaned over, and kissed Kathy on the cheek. "No problem, Kathy. I'm tired, too." The girls didn't realize it, but I was getting tired every day of this trip, not just from the physical exertion, but from the stress of being responsible for everyone.

Kathy smiled at me, "You're a sweet guy, Sam."

Well, that wasn't exactly the response I had expected. And, I hoped that I didn't 'undo' the sweet guy persona, but I took the chance, and offered, "Would you like me to help you get off, before we go to sleep?"

Kathy wasn't fazed. She smiled again, and said, "Thanks for the offer. I wouldn't mind having an orgasm … but I'd prefer to take care of myself."

"Christian?" I asked, unnecessarily.

Kathy nodded. Then, she brightened, "How about if we lie next to each other and take care of ourselves?"

That was a good compromise. I pulled over the box of Kleenex on the nightstand, then leaned over, and kissed Kathy again on the cheek. "That would be fine, Kathy."

She turned onto her stomach, looked the other way, and reached both her hands under herself. The cover began moving slowly up and down, as she began a rhythmic motion. I turned off the light, and lay on my back, the covers pushed down to my legs.

I closed my eyes, and saw Kelly and her friends in the beam of my flashlight, their eyes wide as they watched the eel free swimming below them. Then, scenes from our helicopter tour passed across my mind's eye. I was stroking myself autonomically, only slightly turned on.

I briefly visualized Kathy and the others bent over the couch, waiting for me to give them shots, and my erection grew. But I couldn't focus.

As the image of the Honopu arch filled my brain, and the helicopter flying past the waterfall on Kalalau Beach, my thoughts went back to Sarah. A melancholy overtook me, and I realized that I was flaccid, again.

Kathy was moving in jerks next to me, and emitting quiet grunts, as she neared her orgasm. Perhaps it was the wine; or perhaps it was thinking of Sarah. But I was no longer turned on, and realized that I would not be in orgasmic bliss lying alongside Kathy tonight.

I turned away from Kathy, lying on my side, as I heard her moan, and the bed rippled with her ever-increasing motions. She inhaled deeply, and the bed quaked, as Kathy's body spasmed.

There was some panting, and I heard Kathy whisper, "Goodnight, Sam."

I smiled, then closed my eyes, "Goodnight, Kathy."

CHAPTER 10: WATERFALL WONDER

I woke early, alone in the large bed in the loft. Julie had snuck into bed with me last night, and we'd had a very intimate experience together. Sam was a good kisser, but Julie's kisses were somehow softer, more tender. I would even have to say more 'sensuous'.

I put on a bathing suit, then shorts and a tank. When I walked out onto the deck, the sunlight was still dim, and there were puffy gray clouds everywhere. Everything was wet, except our snorkeling gear lined up along the glass door. I had no idea whether we would be bringing it on our hike today.

I took a beach towel and dried off the chairs, then sat, staring out at the ocean. A sleek canoe with an outrigger passed in front of our condo, paddled by six strong guys. Then, another one came around the point and swept quickly by.

Sam came out, gave me a 'good morning' kiss, and sat down in one of the chairs. He wore water shorts and a tank, and his arms and legs looked distinctly more tanned than when we had left home. His nose, cheeks and ears were red, but they didn't look burned.

I smiled at him, and asked, "So how was your night with Kathy?"

Sam shrugged, "We just slept together." I knew *that*. I thought Sam might be a bit more forthcoming with the details; not that it mattered. I gave him an inquisitive look.

Sam smiled, "We just *slept*." I nodded, waiting for more. Sam added, "Kathy suggested we masturbate separately. I think she's really fallen for Christian." I knew that, also. Then, Sam chuckled, "I guess I was too tired, or had too much alcohol, to get turned on."

That was funny: Sam had gotten his chance with my friends, but Julie had had her period, and Kathy didn't want Sam's attention. I assumed that he'd had sex with Linda, but he hadn't given me any specifics. I guess Julie and I had been the most sexually active of any of us, last night.

Just as those thoughts went through my head, Julie came out to the lanai, still wearing her nightgown. She bent down and kissed Sam lightly on the lips. Then, she turned to me, took my head in her hands, and gave me a slobbery, wet kiss, her tongue probing my mouth insistently.

As Julie sat down next to us, I glanced at Sam, and he had a curious expression. Then, he blinked and smiled blankly.

Julie asked, "So how should we dress, today?"

Sam turned to her, and replied, "Just shorts and a tank would be fine. You can wear a bathing suit underneath, if you like, or just bring one in your pack ... or not worry about it. We will skinny-dip under the waterfall. Most people will probably be wearing suits on the beach, but I don't know if we'll be swimming there."

Julie nodded, and headed back to her bedroom. Sam made coffee, and I put out juices, fruit, and cereal, then helped myself and brought my own plate out to the patio. Kathy came out of the bedroom, wearing her red dirt t-shirt, and sat down next to me. I smiled at her, "Good morning, Kathy."

She smiled back, "Good morning, Kelly." She was quiet, as I ate my cereal. Then, she leaned toward me, and whispered, "Sam is really a sweet guy."

I nodded, "I know that." Then, I teased her, "It sounds like you guys had a wild time, last night."

She gave me a confused look, then laughed. "Yeah. I masturbated, while he went to sleep."

Then, Kathy became more serious, and said, "I hope he wasn't offended. He's been so nice to us, and kept us entertained; I guess I should have at least offered to give him a hand job."

I smiled, and shook my head. "I'm sure Sam's fine; he didn't really have any expectations." I laughed, "And I think he might have been too soused to get it up, anyway."

Kathy nodded, and smiled briefly. Then, she gazed out to sea. Finally, she looked at me, and said, "Kelly, I just can't get Christian out of my head." She looked down, and fiddled with the hem of her shirt. "I'm hoping that I get to see him again, while we're here."

Sam came out with a small plate of fruit and toast, and a glass of juice, and Linda followed him, with a bowl of cereal and a cup of coffee. Kathy got up and went back into the condo.

Linda smiled at me, then took a sip of the coffee. "Did you guys have fun last night?" I cocked my head, and Linda clarified, "You and Julie." Now, I wondered whether Linda had been offended that we'd had a romp, while leaving her to sleep.

"Julie thought you were already asleep."

Linda lifted a spoon of cereal and shrugged. I must have given her an apologetic look, and she said, "I'm OK with you guys playing around." She smiled, and turned to Sam, lifting her foot, and putting in his crotch. "I'm much more interested in the attention of a man."

Sam gave me a thin smile, and shrugged. Now I knew that they had made it, a couple of nights ago. That was fine: We all had our preferences, and Sam and I were happy to be able to share each other with my friends; at least the ones who were interested.

We drove to Princeville Center, and stopped at the market, where we each ordered a sandwich. Sam bought Tupperware containers that just fit one sandwich, and we each packed our lunch in the Tupperware that then went into our backpack.

We'd filled our water bottles, and Sam had brought his water filter/pump, but we still bought a few more drinks – Kathy selecting a Ginseng iced tea, and Julie and Linda picking Snapples. Sam found an IPA in a can, but I couldn't imagine that it would be cold enough to drink during our hike.

Then, we headed down the hill to Hanalei, and over another half-dozen one-lane bridges, until we arrived at Kee Beach, at the end of the road. This time, we found a parking spot close to the trailhead.

We hiked up the rocky steps, past the lookout spot we'd been to the other day, and continued higher and higher on the trail, as it wound around windy points, and curved across small waterfalls deep in the valleys. Some of the trail was muddy, some dry, and there were places with wooden steps, and others that were entirely rock.

Julie began to lag, and we waited for her to catch up. "We're not hiking this *again*, are we?"

Sam laughed, "Yes, Julie. This will be the beginning of our hike to Kalalau." She shook her head, and bent over, holding her knees. I was beginning to understand why Sam had wanted us to get into shape, before coming to Kauai. My legs were feeling it, but I wasn't winded, at all.

From one of the windy points, Sam pointed, and we saw the folds of hills along the Na Pali coast. Sam said, "On Monday, we're going to hike as far as you can see." Linda was breathing heavily, and Julie could only shake her head again.

We finally began descending, and had a brief view of Hanakapiai Beach far below. We walked through ruts and mud, finally coming down to a sign that warned of the tsunami danger.

Sam waited for everyone to catch up, and said, "If there's going to be a tidal wave, you would need to be above this point." The sign had to be at least 30-40 feet above the beach.

Around another curve or two, we finally reached the stream. It was a challenge crossing it, as we had to hop from rock to rock, then hold onto a rope that had been strung across. There was a lot of water rushing down, and it was crystal clear.

We turned onto the path going downstream, and climbed over rocks, finally arriving at the beach. There were less than a dozen people already here, some in shorts, some in bathing suits, a couple of girls topless, and one older man nude. We left our packs on a boulder, and walked down toward the ocean.

We crossed a small pond of water, and walked down the beach to the left, then explored a small cave in the side of the cliff. As we walked back, Sam told Julie, "Let's go for a quick swim. That'll get us cooled off. Once we're refreshed, we can continued into the valley."

Julie and Sam took off their shorts and tanks, and walked down the steep beach through small – but crashing – waves, into the water.

Julie and I swam away from the beach, then along the shore back towards Kee. When we were even with the stream, we stopped and treaded water. Pointing into the valley, I informed Julie, "That's Hanakapiai Falls, our destination for today."

Julie nodded, and said, "I'll try to keep up, Sam. You guys are in great shape!"

I frowned at her, "I know you're strong enough to do this. And our hike to Kalalau will be *much* more difficult." I pointed to the switchback trail rising above the beach on the other side of the valley. "Take a look. After this beach, the trail gets much rougher. That switchback climbs 800 feet, before it levels out."

Julie nodded, and we swam back to the beach, then got dressed, and joined the other girls. "Shall we have a snack, or do you guys want to get going on our jungle hike to the falls?" They had waited for Julie and I, and were now ready to start the next leg of our hike.

We walked through a thick bamboo forest, then came out under a huge mango tree. All of the branches were above our heads, but I managed to find a couple of mangos that had recently fallen. I took a bite, and passed them around.

Kathy exclaimed, "Yum! This is great – I *love* mangos!" Julie, Linda and Kelly also tried the fruit, which was nearly as big as an orange, but its smooth skin was green, yellow and red.

Continuing up the trail, we wound between trees, and climbed up sections holding onto roots. We all slipped a few times, and had to walk through areas that were wet and muddy. The girls were all wearing shoes, but I hiked in my flip-flops.

We saw no one else on the trail, and it was challenging to find the trail as it crossed the stream, and led up the other side of the valley. The sun was up, and the humidity high, as the wetness of the jungle began to evaporate.

We passed sections of the stream that had widened out into beautiful swimming holes, bordered by smooth boulders. I was tempted to stop, and let everyone rest and cool off in the pools, but wanted to reach the waterfall before other tourists arrived, and in time for lunch.

It was nearly 11AM, the hike to the beach having taken an hour and a half, after our late start at 8:30AM. And, we'd spent a half hour at the beach. At this rate, we would be doing well to get back to the car by 5PM. I wondered again whether our motley group could make it all the way to Kalalau in one day.

Climbing up muddy steps, while holding onto roots, we reached a narrow, rocky ledge, water streaming down over the rock. The girls were nervous, but we all made it across without slipping. Ten minutes later, we had our first view of the falls, through the trees.

"Wow! That's a high waterfall," Linda exclaimed. The girls were all looking up, Julie's mouth hanging open. Kelly smiled at me, and I gave her a peck on the lips.

"Yes, I think it's at least 300 feet tall, maybe more. But parts of it are against the mountain, so it won't be that painful, when we swim under it." All three of Kelly's friends looked at me with open mouths.

We hiked up to an open area with boulders, interspersed with lush vegetation. As we neared the pond under the falls, we felt the wind and spray blowing down. Kelly said, "It's *cold*, here." I laughed. Just a few minutes ago we'd all been sweating on the trail.

We put our packs on a huge boulder, and I took off my running shorts and tank, then fished out the can of beer, and walked to the edge of the pond. I put the beer under the water, between two rocks, and put another rock on top to keep it from floating away. I'd carried the weight up here, and didn't want to lose it, now!

Julie and Linda were sitting on a small boulder, and Kelly walked over to me. "What are we going to do, now?" I smiled at her, then turned, and stepped carefully onto rocks in the water, took a couple of more precarious steps, and dived in. It was just as cold as I'd remembered.

I treaded water, and turned back to Kelly and her friends. "The water's great! Come on in!"

The girls undressed, made their way to the water's edge, and dipped their toes in. Linda screamed, "It's cold!" The wind and spray coming down the falls had already chilled us, and the pond really wasn't *that* much colder. I swam slowly across the pond toward the right edge of the waterfall.

Behind me, I heard shrieks, as Kelly and her friends got into the water. Kelly followed me across the pond, her friends lagging behind. When they finally caught up, I was standing on a rock ledge at the base of the falls.

"Just a quick liability disclaimer, first: Please be careful, and don't stay under the falls too long, as there may be rocks coming down ... and you wouldn't want to get hit on the head with one."

I laughed, "It would be a very long way to carry you back on the trail. And the only access is a helicopter landing pad near the beach." Kelly stared at me, and her friends were shaking their heads.

"We can swim behind the falls, but don't kick too hard, or you may kick a rock, which would hurt. You can also try actually going under the falls, but it might sting." I swam slowly, my head out of the water, until we were all behind the falls. Everyone managed to find a rock or ledge to stand on.

Kathy's eyes were sparkling, "This is incredible! And we have it all to ourselves."

Not for long. I could see, through the sheet of water, that other hikers were arriving at the pond. We continued swimming behind the falls, until we came out the other side. Then we treaded water in the pond, and I pointed up.

The girls looked up, able now to see water falling in waves, sheets, and huge drops. I floated on my back, looking up the falls; it was quite a sight. The falls were at the end of the valley, coming through a notch in the mountain, with huge cliffs curving around to either side.

As we side-stroked to the edge of the pond, Kelly pointed, and I nodded. Another group of four younger people were sitting on a boulder looking at the falls. And we now saw a middle-aged couple hiking around the boulders, making their way to the pond.

We got out, and dried off. I left the towel around my waist, as did Kelly. Julie and Kathy pulled their pareos from their backpacks, and wrapped them around their waists. And Linda wrapped her towel around her body, now covered from the chest down.

"Anybody ready for lunch?" The girls all yelled, 'Me!', and we took out the Tupperware containers, and retrieved our sandwiches. Then, I remembered. I walked down to the pond, and found the beer can I'd left in the water. It was now suitably cold to drink.

The foursome went into the pond, the two girls topless, and the guys in surf trunks. As they disappeared behind the falls, the older couple undressed, and went nude into the water, the guy letting out a bellow when the cold water shocked him, and the woman following with a high-pitched yelp.

"So this is the beginning of the Na Pali coast. I can only tell you that the trail to Kalalau is much more difficult, and Kalalau beach and valley are much more beautiful than this." That might have been a slight exaggeration, but I wanted the girls pumped for the big hike on Monday.

After lunch, Kelly, Julie and I went back into the pond, and swam around for a while. As we were all getting dressed for the hike back, several other couples or groups of people arrived. By the time we left, there had to be more than a dozen people at the pond.

The hike back was somewhat easier, as the girls knew what to expect, and were much more confident. We stopped at one of the larger swimming holes, and took another dip, then laid out on the rocks for a while.

Some people passed by on the trail, but none seemed upset that we were all nude. Julie and Kathy lobbied to stay longer, but it was already 1:30PM, and we had nearly three hours of hiking to get back to the car.

It was a hot afternoon, the skies clear, and I decided to refill our water bottles using my purifying filter, before we left the swimming hole.

We hiked slowly but steadily, finally getting to the bottom, where we passed the helicopter landing pad, the mango tree, and the bamboo forest. We decided to not go back to the beach, and started the return hike on the trail.

It wasn't ten minutes before we were all hot and exhausted. Through gritted teeth, I explained that Sarah and I had called this uphill mile the 'never-ending climb'. And it seemed that way to all of us.

It took nearly an hour to reach the top, and another forty minutes to make it down the rock steps back to the trailhead. We decided to take a quick dip in the small lagoon at Kee Beach, then used the public showers to wash the salt off our bodies.

We'd cleaned up pretty well – not that much mud left on our shoes or clothes. As we drove back toward Hanalei, I asked, "So how did you guys like the hike?"

Kathy spoke up, "It was amazing."

Julie chimed in, "Awesome! I've never seen a waterfall that tall; or swam behind a waterfall."

I nodded, "And that was just a preview of what we'll see next week, hiking to Kalalau."

Linda said, "It's only Thursday. It seems like in another couple of days we would have seen most of the island. So I can see why most people only come here for a week."

I frowned, "Are you ready to go back, already, Linda?" I felt energized, and just getting started, and I wondered whether Linda – or any of Kelly's other friends – were already getting bored with the island.

After a moment, Linda said, "I'm having a great time, Sam. But we've done so much already, I can't imagine how much more we'll see or do in the next week."

Under her breath – but obviously loud enough for all of us in the car to hear – Kathy said, "I'm not ready to leave, yet. I haven't even visited Christian." Nobody laughed; Kathy was quite serious.

As we passed Lumahai Beach, and wound around the hill, I asked, "Would you guys be OK with going to a funky bar-restaurant tonight? We wouldn't have to go back to the condo and get dressed. And I think it's 'fish taco' night."

The girls all nodded their assent, and I parked in Hanalei. We got to the restaurant early, better to find a table. While we waited for the restaurant to get going, we ordered drinks. Their Steinlager on tap hit the spot for me, while Kelly and Julie ordered Mai Tai's, Linda ordered white wine, and Kathy had an Island Punch.

I think Kathy was shocked that her drink was so alcoholic; perhaps she thought it really would be 'punch'? We had pulled a couple of tables together, which would not have been possible twenty minutes later, as the restaurant opened, and was filled quickly.

Julie, Kathy and I ordered the fish tacos, while Linda had a big salad, and Kelly had a nice-looking burger. As we were finishing, I asked, "Anybody up for a night snorkel?" I only got glares and stares, and was lucky there was no more food on anyone's plate that they could throw at me.

We drove back up the hill, and arrived at our condo in time to see the sunset. Once again, it was truly atmospheric, including a rainbow that crossed our entire view. As the sun set, I described the 'green flash' effect, and held my breath. It wouldn't take many clouds on the horizon to prevent seeing the green flash.

But the horizon was clear, and as the last bit of sun hit the horizon, we all saw the light turn a pure green color, and everyone cheered. We heard cheers from other condos, as well; although our deck was quite private, we now realized that there were a lot of other people staying in these condos, and watching the sunset.

"So, if we're not going to do any night snorkeling, there are still the tequila shots ..." No glares, but a look of resignation – that was the way I was always going to act. "OK. I can make Margaritas, or Mai Tai's, or even an 'Island Punch'."

Kathy's eyes brightened, "That so-called 'Punch' at the restaurant was great."

I turned to Kelly, and said, quietly, "We'll need to go to the market tomorrow – to replenish our supplies, and get food that we can bring to Kalalau."

Kelly looked confused, "I thought it was a backpacking and camping experience."

I had to laugh: It probably *should* have been a traditional backpacking trip. But I'd wanted to provide the girls more comfort, more luxury. So, in addition to bringing packaged food for the first night or two, I was making and freezing things that would be transported to us by Zodiac. Especially the most important things – beers and wines.

I planned to make spaghetti sauce, and a specially prepared ahi for the first night after the delivery. If my friend's boat broke down, or something else happened, we would be stuck, and probably have to make the 12-mile hike back out.

Taking everything out of the fridge, I poured the rest of the orange juice, pineapple juice, guava nectar, dark rum, the añejo, and Cointreau in the largest container I could find, and dumped in about half the ice in the icemaker of the fridge. Then, I cut up and threw in oranges and limes.

I brought glasses out to the patio table, and presented my special concoction, in a large pitcher, as I stirred it with a wooden spoon. The girls' eyes lit up.

Then my eyes focused on the spoon – probably about fifteen inches long ... I sucked all the drink from the spoon, turned around, and smacked my own bottom a few times. Then, I held up the spoon, pondering it, and glancing at the girls.

Linda held out her glass and said, firmly, "I'll take the drink, not the spoon." Then, she batted her eyes at Sam, and said, "But if you want me to beat you with that spoon later, just ask, Samo." I poured Linda's drink, and filled all the other glasses, as everyone laughed.

Kelly put her hands on her hips, and said, steadfastly, "Sam's mine tonight. I gave him to you, to play with ... and now, I'm taking him back."

I bent over, laughing. "Is *that* what you were doing?" I looked around at Kelly's friends. "Did you get to 'play with me' enough?" The girls laughed.

Then, Kathy said, "Well, I thought he was a gentleman." She smiled, "Or he was just too drunk." Kelly thought that was funny, but I wasn't laughing.

Julie said, "I'll second that. I had to almost *force* him to let me help him." She looked me and winked, "But he was too weak to say no to coconut syrup." Kelly, Linda and Kathy gave us a look, but Julie didn't comment further, and nobody asked us for an explanation.

Linda put her arm around mine, and said sweetly, "I love being with Sam. He really is a gentleman. And his performance is *much* better than most of my other boyfriends." Kelly was hysterical.

I didn't recall hearing how many 'boyfriends' Linda had. But, somehow, I detected that this was meant as a barb for me; anyway, I thought Kelly and her friends usually talked about 'hook-ups', not 'boyfriends'.

The hiking – and perhaps also the Island Punch – was hitting me, and I turned to Kelly. "Do you think we could hit the sack early, tonight?" I looked at my watch: It was after 9PM.

Kelly took my arm, kissed my cheek, and said, "Yes, dear. I'll walk you home, safely. Shall I make your evening laxative tea? Or, perhaps, an enema?"

I shook my head, then pulled Kelly toward the bedroom, looking back and waving to Kelly's friends. I yelled, "Finish that pitcher. I don't want any leftovers!"

As Kelly and I closed the door to the bedroom, I realized that I hadn't told everyone about tomorrow's plans. But it was a day we could sleep late, and nobody was pressing for the schedule.

We undressed and, realizing that we'd only had a cursory shower since our waterfall hike, we hopped into a hot shower together. We bathed each other, but I was a little out of it. As Kelly washed my 'private' parts, and I didn't respond, she stopped, and said, "You're going to have to do a lot better than that, Mister!"

Our heads finally hit the pillows, and it felt so good! Kelly twirled the hairs on my chest. "Are you OK, Sam?"

I nodded, my eyes closed, "I'm just tired. And, maybe this high altitude is making the alcohol affect me more."

Kelly was too smart for that. She flipped the covers down, and sat on top of me. Then, she fell forward, and pinned me to the bed. I put up token resistance, but was too tired to fight. Kelly sat back up, still straddling me.

I said, "You know, one of our upcoming events is what Kathy requested. We'll be driving to the other side of the island that we flew over in the helicopter." Kelly looked at me. "A mud wrestling match." Kelly was shaking her head, *her* eyes now closed.

Kelly stroked me, and I closed my eyes again. I knew it would take focus. I visualized the four young women bent over the couch, as they had been on the first night. But, in my fantasy, I *would* have spanked them, inserted butt plugs, and inserted needles ...

My concentration was broken, as Kelly was putting me in her. I had gotten hard without even realizing it. It was a luxurious feeling, and my thoughts drifted. Yes. After the needles, I would take each of them from behind.

Kelly was panting, and I was suddenly brought into an acute focus, as I orgasmed, filling Kelly, but not yet satisfying her.

I continued to move, and she brought one hand under herself. It couldn't have been even a minute more before she climaxed, drawing in huge gasps of air, and trying not to let out a scream that might wake her friends, or people in the neighboring condos.

Kelly collapsed onto me, and I held her and pulled the covers over us. "Sorry I wasn't more energetic, tonight."

Kelly laughed, "You were pretty energetic on the trail. I could barely keep up, and my friends were really being pushed."

I gave Kelly a 'Duh!' look. "I needed to push them today, to see what they could do, and to let them get used to the terrain, before I would be comfortable taking them to Kalalau."

Kelly gave me a dubious look, "It's not really *that* difficult of a trail, is it?"

I smiled, and pulled her head down onto my shoulder. Maybe it wasn't as world-class for a bunch of twenty-somethings; but I remembered it as being quite challenging.

Reaching over and turning off the light, I whispered to Kelly, "We're going on a boat ride, tomorrow. And you'll get to see the Na Pali coast from the water."

Kelly yawned. She must be tired, also. Everyone did great on the hike, although I knew that Julie would have to push herself to keep up, and finish the trek to Kalalau.

"We can sleep late, if you like. Our boat trip is at 10AM, and I have nothing planned before that. Unless you want to go for a run ... or do a morning snorkel at the beach below us."

Kelly yawned again, and put her arm around my waist. "We can see in the morning. Sleeping late might not be a bad idea." Then, even in the dark, I could see her open one eye, and say, "And, knowing you, I bet our little 'boat ride' will be challenging, too."

I could only smile. The conditions were calm, but no doubt it would still be an adventurous day.

CHAPTER 11: ZANY ZODIAC

We all had a good sleep, and got up on our own schedules. By the time I went out to the lanai to say good morning to my friends, Sam was coming in the door from a morning snorkel at the beach below us. He smiled, and looked very invigorated.

I poured some coffee, and sat at the small table on the lanai with Julie and Linda. They were pointing to the grass below, near the edge of the cliff: There were two huge birds, looking like twins, and both had metal bands around their skinny legs.

Sam looked over the railing, and said, "Those are *nene*," he pronounced it 'Nay-nay', "they're Hawaiian geese. The nene is the rarest type of goose, and the state bird of Hawaii." He chuckled, "I figured we'd see them down at Kalalau, but I didn't expect to see a pair in Princeville!"

Sam sat in a chaise, and I realized that Kathy was on the phone again, in the living room. She bounced out to the lanai, and sat at the table with us. Then, she turned to Sam, and asked, "Would it be OK, if Christian came to Julie's birthday party on Sunday?"

Sam laughed, "Of course, Kathy! He would be welcome with us any time." He looked at Julie apologetically, "but Julie's party is actually part of a larger gathering. I think it's also the birthday of one of the local building contractor's daughters."

He squinted, looking at Kathy, "I'll have to give you the directions, so you can explain where it is to Christian."

She smiled, "Christian's pretty familiar with the whole island ..."

Sam shook his head, "Maybe, but this is a pretty special place; I'm not sure how many people know about it." Then Sam thought, and added, "But if he's a local, I guess he should be able to find it."

Linda pointed out the nenes to Kathy, and then turned to Sam. "So what's the plan, *today*, Sam?"

Sam leaned forward, and the chaise tilted into its most upright position. His legs straddled the lower part of the chaise, and he looked handsome ... and much younger than his chronological age. Then, I chuckled; he would look even more handsome in surf trunks, rather than his small Speedo.

Sam smiled at us, and said, "I forgot to tell you the plans, last night, and thought you would never ask." Linda pursed her lips, and waited for an answer to her question. Sam asked, "How would you guys like to go on little boat ride, today? With lunch, and some snorkeling?"

Julie grinned broadly, and Linda was nearly popping out of her seat. Sam explained, "If we were here another week ... or two," he looked at us, and I noticed that we all had very different reactions, as Sam continued, "I'd love to take you kayaking down the Na Pali coast, and around to the west side."

He looked up at the ceiling of the lanai, where a gecko scampered to the corner behind Sam, and then halfway down the wall. "And, it would be great to do some sailing in Hanalei Bay." Now, Julie was nodding enthusiastically.

"I have a friend who has a Hobie Cat on the beach – you may have seen it, near the Pavilion; but he's out of town, and would need to be here, so I can get the sail and other parts for it."

Sam looked at me, "And we could take one of the commercial sailing outings, maybe a sunset cruise, on a boat just big enough for our group. That would probably be from the south shore." Sam grinned, "Or maybe even a fishing excursion on the north shore."

Directing all of his attention to me, Sam said, "And I would *really* like to see Kelly certified in SCUBA, so that we can take dive trips." I nodded; we had discussed it, and diving was something I wanted to do.

"For example, we could take a boat across the channel to Niihau, the private island where native Hawaiians continue their culture. The diving off Lehua Rock can be incredible, with a visibility of 200 feet or more!" Sam was getting excited, now. I knew that he loved boats and the water.

Sam took a deep breath, "But today we're going down the Na Pali coast in a Zodiac." Linda and Julie both clapped their hands. "We'll see the rugged coast 'up close and personal' and probably even go into some sea caves. And, the ride back might get a tad rough ..."

My friends gave Sam an acid expression, and he shrugged. "OK, not 'rough', but maybe 'exciting'." Sam choked, as he tried to get a laugh out, then whispered to me, "Especially if you're straddling the tube, as we go 'uphill'." I wasn't sure what he was talking about; but I was pretty sure I would find out.

Sam asked, "What time is it?" I told him that it was just after 9AM. He stood, and said, "We need to leave in a half hour ... forty five minutes at the most." Linda asked how we should dress, and Sam said, "In a bathing suit and tank, or cover-up. I wouldn't wear the pareo, as it might get blown off."

Then Sam stepped inside, and picked up one of his waterproof bags. "And, you can put shorts and a top in here, if you want them to stay dry." It almost sounded like our jet boat experience in the Niagra River.

As Sam and I got our things together in the bedroom, I asked, "Do we need to bring lunch?"

Sam shook his head, "No, lunch is included. And my friend is the captain – it's his private boat. So I don't know exactly what he'll be bringing. Let's just put some drinks in the cooler."

We drove down to Hanalei, and parked at the end of the beach road, next to Black Pot park, and the Hanalei River. As we pulled our things from the trunk, Sam walked over to a guy who had backed a trailer into the river, and was now unloading a black inflatable boat.

Sam had bought each of us a small waterproof bag that had a waist strap – basically a waterproof fanny pack – and we put our sunglasses, cameras, phones, and a few other items into them, and put them around our waists. I lifted out the large bag that Sam had brought.

We walked past the end of the road to the mud ramp, where Sam was standing knee-deep in the river, holding the boat. His friend was driving the trailer into one of the long parking spots.

I passed the large waterproof bag to Sam, and he tossed it into the boat; then, I handed up the small cooler, which Sam stowed in the stern of the boat. His friend was walking down into the river, and Sam introduced him: "This is RJ. One of the characters who has lived on the north shore for the last forty years."

RJ smiled, and shook our hands. He was very 'rough', and appeared to be much older than Sam. A stubble of gray hairs grew from weathered skin, with more creases than I'd seen on anyone's face. He was slightly shorter than Sam, and looked scrawny, until he jumped into the boat, and started lifting things, including what looked like a pretty heavy anchor.

Then, he signaled us, and we climbed over the black rubber tube, and made an ungraceful entrance onto the aluminum deck. The boat looked pretty big, perhaps twenty feet in length. It had two large outboard motors that RJ was lowering into the water, as Sam walked the boat farther into the river.

Standing at a center console, RJ flipped some switches, and the motors roared to life. He nodded at Sam, who took another step or two, then pushed the boat into the river, while hopping onto the tube.

RJ didn't wait for Sam to be fully onboard, but gunned the engines, and we headed out the mouth of the river, and into Hanalei Bay. It was a spectacular morning, blue sky with a few puffy white clouds, and people fishing off the end of the Hanalei pier.

We sat on the tubes, and held a rope that was looped around the boat. There was also a string of rope loops on the floor, for our feet. Sam was still straddling the tube, riding the boat like a bucking bronco; but it was only bucking slightly, as the waves were small.

RJ hollered, "Everyone hold on, now!" He gunned the motors, and the boat flew across the water, leaving a straight foamy wake behind us. Julie and Linda cheered, and even Kathy looked happy – more upbeat than we'd seen her in the past few days.

Sam pointed out Lumahai Beach and Wainiha Bay, and RJ headed out farther, taking a wide track around Tunnels Reef. He pulled in toward the Ha'ena Beach park, and put the motors in neutral, letting us drift a couple of hundred yards offshore.

The lush tropical vegetation and Bali Hai ridge were just as beautiful from the water as they had been from the beach. RJ pulled off his tank top, his chest a forest of gray hairs. He opened a fishing box, and pulled out a joint, then lit it, and handed it to Sam.

Smiling at me, Sam took a big hit, then passed it to Julie. The joint made its rounds, and I indulged, also. But I wondered about RJ captaining the boat down the Na Pali coast stoned. I gave Sam a look, and he shrugged.

"RJ is one of the 'old timers' on this coast; he knows it like the back of his hand." RJ lifted his hand, and it seemed to be slightly shaking. Sam continued, "But he's not the usual boat captain ... sometimes he gets a little crazy."

RJ looked at Sam, "Who, me?" He laughed, "Sam, I used to *swim* this coast. On acid." That didn't make me feel any better. He squinted, "Sometimes, Bobo and I used to do a night swim down to Kalalau." He sighed, "Those were the days!"

The joint finished, RJ fired up the motors, and we continued down the coast, passing Kee Beach, then Hanakapiai Beach.

The ocean was still calm, and Sam pointed to the side of the mountains, where we could barely see parts of the Kalalau Trail, winding around the cliffs, and back into the valleys.

Suddenly, RJ turned the boat toward the cliff, and we entered a huge sea cave. He pulled the throttles back, and the engine puttered, as we glided through the water slowly, the darkness enveloping us. We couldn't see the back of the cave.

RJ said, "This is the Pirate Cave." He maneuvered the boat in a wide arc, the ceiling of the cave nearly coming down to our heads. Then, we slowly motored through the cave entrance, and passed under a waterfall, soaking those of us on the port side.

Kathy was still wearing her tank, which clung to her chest, nipples showing prominently; fortunately, the rest of us only wore our bikinis, and the water felt good, after the past hour of the sun baking on us.

RJ continued down the coast, and we again motored slowly near the cliff, and then passed under a rock arch that extended from the cliff into the water. Once again, we passed under a small waterfall. Linda was howling with laughter; and it wasn't just because she had gotten high.

The boat motored along, close to the cliffs, and then turned into a very small cave – not much wider than the Zodiac. As we entered the cave, there was a narrow waterfall coming through a circular hole in the top of the cave. Julie and Linda shrieked, their voices echoing off the rock walls of the cave.

The cave got much darker, but RJ seemed to know where to go; he curved to the right, around the edge of the cave, and we saw a much larger opening back out to the sea. Again, we passed directly under a waterfall at the cave entrance, this one soaking all of us.

RJ pushed the throttles forward, and we sped out toward the horizon. Then, he made a very sharp turn, circling around 180 degrees, and heading back to the large opening of the cave.

At an unbelievably fast speed, we passed under the waterfall, and nearly ran up on a rock beach deep inside the cave, before turning sharply left, and zipping through the small side of the cave, back out to the ocean.

Sam yelled, "This is 'two-door cave'." He glanced at RJ, and added, "Usually people go through it the *other* way!" He stared at RJ and shook his head. RJ just chuckled, as he stood at the console, and turned the boat down the coast.

The motors roared, as we raced along the cliffs, the boat bouncing gently. I noticed that my friends were now holding on to the rope with both hands, and I put a foot under the rope loop on the floor. Sam was standing at the console, next to RJ, shouting something into his ear. RJ nodded and smiled.

Ten minutes later, we were slowing, the boat paralleling a long sandy beach. Sam pointed, "This is Kalalau Beach, the destination of our hike on Monday. Up ahead," Sam pointed to a gradual rise, and a waterfall cascading down from the mountain above, "is the area where we'll be camping."

We saw a couple of kayaks pulled up onto the beach, and a few people walking – all of them nude. Sam pointed again, "We could also sleep in that cave." The cave was wide, but only about twenty feet high. Then, I looked up, and realized that the mountain rose a couple of thousand feet above the cave.

Continuing along the shore, we saw several more happily clothes-free people walking along the beach, and a few more caves. Then, RJ pulled back the throttles, and we drifted around the corner … and saw an incredible curved vertical cliff – at least a thousand feet high – backing another beach. There was a huge sand dune in the middle of the beach.

Kathy gasped, and yelled, "Look!" Our eyes looked ahead, and we could see a rock arch extending from the mountain over the beach and into the water. It was huge. There was a small stream meandering under the arch.

Sam nodded, "This is Honopu Beach. It's where the '70s remake of the '*King Kong*' movie was filmed. As well as parts of '*Six Days and Seven Nights*' and '*Raiders of the Lost Ark*'.

"Honopu is considered a sacred beach – there are a lot of Hawaiian temples and burial grounds in Honopu Valley. It's also called the Valley of the Lost Tribe, as there were Hawaiians living here until a couple hundred years ago, then they disappeared."

The boat was still drifting, and Sam turned to the stern and pointed at the end of Kalalau Beach. "*That's* where we're going to have to swim ... from the end of Kalalau, around the point to Honopu." He smiled with satisfaction, "And it looks like it will be nice and calm for us."

Linda asked, "Can we land here?" Sam shook his head, "No. Boats (and helicopters) aren't allowed to land. We could swim to shore, but we'll be there next week, so won't take the time to do that today. We'll be spending an entire day here."

RJ pushed the throttles up a little, and maneuvered the boat around the end of the rock arch, and then idled the motors, drifting along another beach. Sam pointed, "There's a waterfall here, where we can play; but it's not nearly as tall as Hanakapiai Falls."

RJ looked at Sam, who nodded. The motors growled, and the boat headed straight out to sea. It was getting choppier here, and we all hung on. Then, the boat turned around, facing the island, and RJ idled the motors, again.

As we looked at the Honopu beaches and arch, we could see the valley behind. Rising up hundreds of feet were numerous spires of rock. Sam said, "Honopu is also sometimes called 'Cathedrals Beach', since those eroded mountains look like the spires of a cathedral."

He explained, "Kauai is the oldest of the main Hawaiian islands; we saw the extinct volcano, Mount Wai'ale'ale, during our helicopter ride. Over the past six million years, rain and wind have eroded these mountains, producing the sharp spires and steep cliffs that we see now."

RJ pushed the throttles forward, and the boat continued cruising down the coast. Another ten minutes, and we were motoring slowly along the cliff; then, we turned toward it, and a sea cave came into view. This time, it looked light inside.

Sam pointed, "That's 'open ceiling' cave." RJ steered the boat slowly through the entrance, and into a circular area, with steep cliffs all around, and a tiny island of rocks in the center. He cut the engine, and we rocked, as the boat drifted into the cave.

We all looked up at the sky, through the 'ceiling' of the cave. It was incredible. Sam asked, "Anybody up for some snorkeling?" Nobody responded, so Sam put on his booties, and grabbed his fins and mask.

"I don't think there's much to see, but maybe I could take a quick look." He glanced at RJ, who shrugged, sat down on the tube across from us, and pulled out another joint.

Sam did a backflip off the tube into the water, and snorkeled around the rocks, then did a surface dive. We could see him swimming below us in the crystal clear water. The only sound was lapping of the tiny waves against the rock walls of the cave.

RJ held the joint out, and Julie took it. She and Kathy took a couple of tokes, while Linda and I passed, this time. I was still feeling stoned from our earlier smoke. And this entire coastline felt like a dream; it was too picturesque to be real.

Sam surfaced next to the boat, and handed RJ something; it was a mask and snorkel that someone had lost. RJ threw it in the stern of the boat, and Sam climbed back on board. We motored slowly out of the 'open ceiling' cave, and headed further down the coast.

Another ten minutes at full throttle, and we slowed again, RJ maneuvering the boat through the opening in a reef. Sam announced, "We're now at *Nu'alolo*; the beach is called *Nu'alolo Kai*." There were several other boats already there, with at least a dozen people on each one. Sam winced at RJ, and said, "Oh, no!"

RJ shook his head, "Most of the tour boats will leave in the next half hour. We got here a little early." RJ laughed, "The sea is calmer than usual – still summer conditions. Why don't you take the ladies for a snorkel, and I'll get lunch ready?"

Sam asked, "Will we be having lunch on shore?"

RJ shook his head, "I don't have a permit to land. You guys could swim everything to shore, if you want ... but it might just be easier eating on the boat. Then, you can swim ashore to explore, if you like."

We got our snorkeling stuff together – all of us finally able to get snorkel-ready without much delay. Sam was already in the water, his mask looking ahead through incredibly clear water to the reef a hundred feet in front of us. Julie, Linda, Kathy and I went over the tube into the water clumsily.

Sam led us around on a snorkel tour, but I don't think he was very familiar with this reef. We circled around, as he dove, and explored small lava tubes and sea caves 20-30 feet down. I surface dived down, but couldn't clear my ears well enough, and they were hurting by the time I was halfway down to Sam.

We saw two sea turtles, that seemed to be lonely, as they stopped and looked toward us, before swimming on. Sam was pointing to a lava tube that was only about three feet in diameter, and indicating that he would be swimming through it.

My friends snorkeled alongside, and we watched, as Sam dived down at least twenty feet and stuck his head into the tube. He gave a strong kick, half his body entering the tube ... before he suddenly pushed back, and quickly spiraled to the surface, gasping for breath.

I was about to ask him what had happened, but he was frantically pointed down. I looked back down, and saw a large shark slowly emerging from the lava tube, then swimming off to deeper water.

I glanced at my friends, and they had all backed-up, Linda splashing about, as she kicked the surface with her fins, retreating from where the shark had been.

Sam gave the hand signal to ask if we were all OK, and everyone replied with the same thumb-to-forefinger sign. We snorkeled back to the boat, all of us happy to get out of the water for a while.

As we were drying off, Sam was excitedly telling RJ about his shark experience. "I was just going to dive through a small lava tube ... or maybe it's just a hole through the reef. But I knew it came out, and decided to show off for the girls."

He glanced at us; we were finishing drying and folding our towels, and Kathy already had her top off. RJ was looking at us, also, with a bit more than a casual glance. He smiled, and pulled a beer from the cooler – and handed one to Sam.

"Anyway, I took a big breath and dove down, and quickly entered the tube, without looking first. It was at least 90 feet to go down, swim through the tube, and surface, and I didn't want to get stuck in the tube with no air."

Sam took a swig of beer, and continued, "So I just ducked into the tube and kicked my fins ... and came face-to-face with a little white tip reef shark. The tube was too small for both of us, and it was getting upset that I was cornering it." Sam laughed, "I was upset, too. Fortunately, I could push myself back quickly, and give it some room."

I shook my head, "That was a 'little' shark? It looked pretty big, to me."

Sam said, "No, it probably wasn't more than four or five feet long."

RJ stopped chugging the beer for a moment, and explained, "Reef sharks can breathe without moving forward; so it probably could have backed out, if it wanted."

RJ glanced at Kathy again, and gave her a lecherous smile. Then he announced, "Who's ready for lunch?" We all raised our hands, like we were in school, and RJ chuckled. "I have a 'plate lunch' for each of you."

Sam helped RJ take out the lunches from the huge cooler that also served as a seat in front of the console. Taking the foil off the top, and handing the plates to us, RJ said, in a faux-pigeon local accent, "Plate lunch: two scoop rice, one scoop macaroni salad."

Then he smiled, "I picked up some *huli huli* chicken in Anahola this morning." He pointed to the plate I was holding, "And teriyaki sauce, in those little containers."

We started eating, a lot of 'Yum!'s coming from my friends. Sam picked up a drumstick, bit into it, and smiled. "Yes! This is classic huli huli chicken, smoked on an outside grill, probably over a combination of woods – apple, hickory, and a few others."

The rice was plain, but the macaroni salad was pretty good. Then, I saw Sam pouring the teriyaki sauce over one of the mounds of rice on his place. It was quite salty, but I ended-up doing the same. It was a pretty good lunch, for an impromptu tour on one of Sam's friends' boats.

It was a gorgeous day. The wind blew my hair, the sky was blue, and the ocean had a dark blue hue, small dots of white accenting the waves. It looked pretty choppy farther out, now, although it had been a very calm morning. RJ followed my gaze, "Yeah, the wind's coming up. There are already some whitecaps out there. Perfect windsurfing conditions!"

Sam looked at us, as he finished off his last piece of chicken, "We can swim ashore, if you guys want, but it might be better to head back," Sam smiled at RJ, "uphill."

RJ nodded, then laughed, "Well, it won't be anything like it can get in the winter, with two feet of chop on top of huge swells. But it might get a little exciting today ... if you know what I mean."

Sam laughed also, then tilted his head back, finishing his beer. "I know what you mean, RJ. But the girls are going to have to find out for themselves." RJ chuckled, then collected the plates, giving Kathy an extra-long look. She gave him a friendly smile.

I glanced at RJ, his back to me, as he put things back into the cooler. Then, I turned to my friends, "Maybe we should get a little sun on our tops – to even out our tan; and to give RJ a little treat?"

Julie and Linda grinned; Julie was nodding, looking forward to being a 'trouble causer', and Linda shrugged. I took my top off, and they followed suit – bathing suit. We were putting them into our waterproof fanny packs, when RJ turned around, and stared. Then, he laughed – loudly, and naturally.

"Well, it's great to have you guys on board today." He turned to Sam, "You can give me a call, anytime, Sammy! I'd be happy to take you and your friends out."

Sam smiled, "That's great, RJ. I *am* counting on you to deliver our stuff on Tuesday morning. And then pick us up on Thursday morning."

RJ was nodding, as he turned a key, then pressed two buttons on the console. The engines came to life, then idled, as RJ went to the bow and pulled in the anchor line. The boat drifted closer and closer to the edge of the reef, until RJ finally pulled the anchor onboard, along with several feet of chain.

Then, he came back to the console, backed the boat as he turned it to face out to sea, and pushed the throttles forward. We were underway again, and the wind picked up as we headed away from the shore.

As we turned to go up the Na Pali coast, and back to Hanalei, the wind was stiff, and spray came over the boat, hitting us in the face and chest. I looked at my friends, and they were smiling, their bare tops dripping, and ...

The bow of the boat rose up, then came down heavily, pounding the water, and already diving into the next wave. A huge splash of water came over the bow, hitting us like someone had thrown a bucket of water in our faces.

I looked up at Sam; RJ had ducked under the front screen of the console, but Sam had nowhere to go. He had tried to duck, but was now soaked. He was just wearing his Speedo, and I'm sure he was starting to feel as chilled as we were.

My friends were bouncing on the tube, hanging on with hands and feet. Julie and Linda – along with me, of course – were too big on top to bounce gracefully. We should have kept our tops on, but now couldn't let go long enough to retrieve them.

RJ looked back at the bouncing breasts of the bouncing girls, and laughed. Then, he faced forward again, just as the boat was jumping from one wave to the next, crashing down with a jarring 'thud', before accelerating again, and leaping off the crest of the next wave.

After twenty minutes, we were approaching Kee Beach, and Sam waved his arms. RJ throttled back the motors, and the boat rocked in the now-choppy water. Sam reached into his river bag and pulled out a windbreaker shell.

The four of us got our tops and put them on. Kathy and Julie also put their tanks on. But we were so wet, it didn't seem that it would make any difference.

The boat headed out to sea, and then cruised around Tunnels Reef. Another twenty minutes, and we were back in Hanalei Bay, motoring slowly toward the Hanalei River. The tide was low, and RJ asked us to hop off the boat. Sam also got off, and helped push the boat over the sandbar.

We met Sam and RJ at the muddy ramp, and Sam handed me the bag, and Julie the cooler, as well as the car keys. We got everything packed, while Sam tilted the motors up, hopped off the boat, and held the Zodiac by its 'painter' line, and RJ backed the trailer into the river.

Sam climbed up on the boat again, and handed RJ's huge cooler down to Julie and I. As we had a minivan, we were able to fit it behind the last row of seats. Sam finished making the plans with RJ, and we headed back up the hill to our condo.

It was late afternoon, but earlier than I'd expected when we got back up to Princeville. I pulled into the shopping center, and told Kelly and her friends that I needed to do a little shopping. I would be preparing two nights of our 'camping' dinners, that RJ would transport down the coast.

The girls came in with me, and shopped for their own supplies – more fruit, breakfast items, and snacks. I picked up everything needed for the two dinners and re-stocked our alcohol, and we met back at the check-out stands, where I paid for everything. We had bought four bags of ice, that we stored in the cooler, piling the paper bags of food on top and around the cooler in the back of the minivan.

After we'd returned to the condo and put all the food away, I took drink orders, and we all decided to open a bottle of crisp, cold white wine. The girls were still in their bathing suits, but all had tanks or another cover-up they'd donned before going into the market.

We sat around the table on the lanai, and sipped wine, as the girls yammered about the boat tour. Kelly teased me about my shark experience, but most of the memories were of the sea caves and the rough trip back, as we pounded our way uphill into the wind and current.

I had pointed out the Kalalau trail, high up on the cliffs, winding its way around each windy point, then into each wet valley. But the girls wouldn't appreciate how 'world-class' the trail was, until Monday, when we hiked it.

Julie commented, "That RJ was quite a character." And that was quite an understatement; RJ had been around, doing crazy things on the north shore of Kauai for nearly four decades. I let out a quiet 'If only you knew ...' under my breath.

Linda reminded us that we'd been on the island nearly a week. With one more day for touring, even the single-week trip would have been memorable. But I was hoping that we would all have a few more great memories, before we headed home.

Checking the time, I realized we would need to get ready for dinner, soon. "We have reservations at the

Princeville Hotel, for their Friday night seafood buffet, out on the deck overlooking Hanalei Bay."

I explained, "That is something they used to have, then they stopped it, and now they have it again. Sarah and I used to enjoy it on each of our trips here." I tried not to get emotional again. "I suggest you guys wear the island dresses I bought you, or another dress that you brought."

I chuckled, "People *do* come very casual, but this will be the nicest dinner we're going to have here."

Then, for full disclosure, I added, "I reserved a table for six as far out as possible on the hotel deck; we'll have a spectacular view ... but might get a little damp, if it starts raining."

Linda retorted, "Couldn't get any more 'damp' than we got on the boat, today!" We all laughed, but it was true: The girls were now nearly acclimatized to the island, not worrying about a little water – whether rain or salty ocean spray.

And on the Hanakapiai trail, they had gotten used to some mud. But nothing like what we would experience tomorrow. I was planning to satisfy one of Kathy's requests ... although I didn't know if she remembered she'd made it. It would be fun.

But how could it *not* be fun, when I was traveling with four beautiful, young women?

We drove the short distance to the hotel, and were seated at our table without a wait. It was still a half hour before sunset, and the view of Hanalei Bay and the Bali Hai ridge was beautiful.

It was very 'atmospheric', as usual, with the sun's orange rays poking between puffy clouds that grew pink against a dark blue sky.

We had just finished a bottle of wine at the condo, so we ordered iced teas, sodas, and juices. But I spoke with the waiter, and told him to wait a while, and then bring us a bottle of Champagne to celebrate nearly finishing our first week on Kauai.

The girls headed through the glass doors to the main dining room, where three large round tables were set-up, a huge ice sculpture of a dolphin in the middle. Then, there was a buffet line-up of hot foods, not to mention the two grill stations outside – one cooking steaks and the other fresh seafood.

Each of the girls came back with her own interpretation of the buffet. Kathy returned first, with a large plate of green salad, fruit, and a few sushi rolls.

Linda's plate had a selection of salads, meats, and smoked fish. Julie's plate had a great selection of sushi rolls, along with pickled ginger, and a small dish of soy, next to which was a mound of green wasabi.

Finally, Kelly returned, carrying a plate with a few small portions of salads, a few sushi rolls, a small mound of boiled shrimp, and a pile of crab legs.

Everything looked great. Linda looked at Kelly's plate, and nodded, her mouth already full. She swallowed, and said, "I haven't gotten to the shellfish table, yet. It looks great!"

As the girls began tasting the variety of dishes, I headed to the buffet. Although I wanted to taste a lot of dishes, we still had the Kalalau trail to hike – in only about 60 hours – so I limited the taste of each dish to one spoon. But there were a lot of dishes ...

When I returned to the table, the sun was setting, the sky deep orange to the west, and dark blue to the east. There were still puffy clouds dotting the sky, now in a multitude of hues. A sailboat was beating into the wind, as it departed Hanalei Bay, and headed to the east.

"How's everybody doing? I want to make sure you don't go home hungry, tonight. You need to build your strength for our hike on Monday."

Linda looked up from her plate, "We're not going hungry, Sam. My stomach's already getting full. But I am looking forward to having some grilled fish, and shrimp and crab." Linda blushed, and started to chortle, as she said, "And did you see that dessert table?"

We all laughed. But I knew that they had some great desserts. And, the girls hadn't even seen the hot buffet, yet. I had peeked: There was paella, crab cakes, Mongolian beef, spare ribs, roasted vegetables, and many more delicious-looking choices.

The waiter came with the Champagne, in a silver ice bucket. Kelly's eyes widened, and she gave me a questioning look, and Linda clapped, a huge grin on her face. The waiter poured, and I held up my glass.

"I just wanted to thank you – for coming on this trip, being so open, and trying new adventures. And, I want to congratulate you – all of you – for doing so well hiking, snorkeling, and surviving the rough and wet boat ride.

"You guys, as usual, have been really good sports, and taken everything in a positive way. It's incredible that there could be five of us who are able to get along so well, no drama ..." Kathy coughed, and Linda gave me a 'look'. "OK, maybe a little 'drama' from me, but you know what I mean!"

I tasted the Champagne – it was from France, but I hadn't heard of the winery. Linda approved, "This is the best Champagne I've ever had." I'd served sparkling wines, and I thought I'd served a French Champagne, to Kelly's friends.

Kelly raised her glass, "Thank you for taking *us*, Sam. I love the trips you design ... and I think you're a generous man to bring my friends on this trip." Kelly looked at Julie, Kathy, and Linda, "I think it's been fun! I'm really glad we've gotten close in the past year, and happy that you guys would come here with us."

Kelly's friends were slowly shaking their heads, and seemed emotional. Julie said, "It's been a great experience – both being with you guys, and doing the adventurous things we've done." She raised her glass, "Thank you, Sam." Then, she turned to Kelly, "And thank you, Kelly, for allowing us to come with you ... and sharing Sam with us."

We sipped more Champagne, then Linda raised her glass. "You guys are great, and I agree that Sam's been very generous to bring us here. And, to buy us cameras, and packs, and lingerie, and dresses." Julie and Kathy were nodding. Then, Linda laughed, "Even if he didn't take us to Paris ..."

Julie exclaimed, "Linda!" But we all knew that Linda was joking.

Kathy said, "Well, Sam, I might have to wait a few months before I'll know exactly how much to thank you for this trip." I started to ask, but Kathy added, "Depending on what happens between me and Christian."

We all went back several times to try more of the dishes, and we finished the Champagne with our plates of desserts. I offered the possibilities of going down to the pool area, or sitting in the lounge to listen to the music, but everyone was tired, so we headed back to the condo.

The girls got undressed, and put on t-shirts (their salty tank tops went into the washer), then we sat out on the lanai. Linda asked, "So what's on the schedule for tomorrow?"

I looked at Kathy and smiled, "Mud wrestling."

Getting a bunch of stares, I reminded the girls, "Kathy thought she could out-wrestle me, and I told her we would get the chance to find out. So, tomorrow, we'll be driving around to the other side of the island, first to Koke'e State Park, where we can look out over the Kalalau Valley."

I smiled, "Then, we'll hike around in the Alakai Swamp."

Julie laughed, "A *swamp*?"

I nodded, and explained, "As you know, the central part of this island gets the most rain of anywhere in the world. And the water collects on the plateau that we saw from the helicopter, then cascades over the north side, creating all the waterfalls, streams, and rivers we see here on the north shore."

Julie nodded, blankly. I elucidated, "Alakai is more of a 'bog' than a swamp. Most of the walking is on a 'boardwalk', but we'll be doing a few side hikes, also, including to a beautiful stream ... where we'll have the wrestling contest." The girls just shook their heads.

"So, if you guys aren't interested in a night snorkel, we should get to bed soon. You can pack the backpacks for hiking, but we'll also bring our snorkeling gear in the car, in case we have time to get in the water on the south side."

Linda laughed, "Are *you* up for a night snorkel, Sam?"

I shook my head. "No, Linda, I'm pretty stuffed ... and I seem to be feeling the alcohol." Then, I brightened, "But we *could* go skinny-dipping in the condo pool. There aren't many people here, and I doubt that anybody will be in the pool this late."

The girls turned down that option, also. It was probably a good thing, as just after I said this, it started raining again.

Kelly and I retired to our bedroom, and got undressed. "So what did you think of the 'seafood buffet' tonight?"

Kelly didn't hesitate, "That was the best buffet I've ever had. Everything was incredibly good. That fresh fish from the outside barbeque was fantastic."

I had forgone that, as well as the steaks being cooked on the other barbeque. The hot dishes included duck, beef Wellington, and several other things that I couldn't resist. And, of course, I'd had to leave room for the desserts.

I kissed Kelly, and we made love, passionately, slowly. We hadn't discussed the issue brought up when Linda spent the night with me: Was I having sex with her, or making love to her? Perhaps it was all semantics. I knew who I loved, and with whom I wanted to share my life. And Kelly knew that it was her.

CHAPTER 12: SWAMP THING

We got started early on Saturday morning, Sam acting as the tour guide again, as he drove us around the island – first along the north shore and down the east shore to Lihue, then on the Kaumuali'i highway through Kalaheo to Ele'ele, then highway 50 to Waimea, and finally up the hill on highway 550 stopping at several lookouts over the canyon.

Near the end of the road, we parked at the Kalalau Valley lookout. None of us had believed we really needed warm clothes, but were glad Sam had insisted that we bring them, as it was quite chilly up here at a 4,000 foot elevation.

Sam had warned us that the lookout might be in a cloud, and there *were* low clouds hanging right over us, but the view of Kalalau Valley far below was incredible.

Then, we drove to the Pu'u O Kila lookout, at the end of the road. Our backpacks on, we began our hike on the Pihea trail, skirting the top of the cliff at the back of Kalalau Valley.

Sam told us that several trails headed in the opposite direction to lookouts over the valleys we'd seen from the Zodiac. Then, he admitted that he wasn't sure how long this hike would be, as there were several possibilities, and he wanted us to see parts of the Alakai Wilderness Preserve and then make it to the Kawaikoi Stream.

Whatever. The views of Kalalau were spectacular, and the trail was easy, so-far. In less than an hour, we were at the junction of the Alakai Swamp trail.

The trail consisted of boards that passed through a picturesque area of trees, then out into an open area with bogs of mud that would have been impassible without the boardwalk. Sam had suggested that we all wear our trail running shoes, although we also carried our flip-flops in our backpacks.

Sam frowned, "Well, maybe I should have bought all of us some 'tabbies' – sock-like shoes with a rubber sole. They look pretty dorky, green with yellow stripes, but they do work well in the mud." But it was too late, now!

There were few people here, and we decided to jog along the boardwalk, Sam leading with his arms out like the wings of a plane. We banked one way and then the other, stopping every few minutes for a photo opportunity.

The clouds descended, and we were now in an eerie fog. We finally reached the Kilohana Lookout, and were amazingly lucky that the clouds hovered just above us, affording an incredible view of the north shore, from Wainiha Valley to Hanalei Bay.

After a few snapshots, Sam looked at his watch, and shook his head. Then, he began jogging back on the boardwalk; this time we had to dodge several groups, but finally made it back to the junction of the Pihea trail.

We headed downhill, slowly jogging down a switchback. It was obvious that we would need to hike back *up* this switchback to get back to our car.

We crossed the Kawaikoi stream, and continued on the trail; Sam was unsure of where we needed to cross it again to reach the Kawaikoi Stream loop trail. At some point, we saw people across the stream, and managed to cross it, walking on a log, then hopping from boulder to boulder.

It was a beautiful area, and we hiked part way along the trail, and then 'cross country' through ferns and other tropical plants, until we found a nice swimming hole where the stream widened. There was a considerable amount of mud here, despite the fact that Sam said there had been less rain than usual over the past week.

Sam found a large boulder, and put his pack down, then took off his water shorts and tank top. We all followed his lead, and walked through mud to the edge of the stream. There were already spatters of mud up and down our legs.

Sam said, "So who wants to mud wrestle?" None of us answered, but Kathy bent down, took a handful of mud, and slung it at Sam. It hit his stomach, and slid down, through his pubic hair, before most of it fell back to the ground. "Oh! I see we have a 'taker' ... Kathy, who said she wanted to wrestle me!"

Without further warning, Sam reached down, picked up some mud, and – as he approached Kathy – he threw it at her. Rather than backing off, Kathy stepped to Sam, and they began wrestling.

Somehow, Kathy managed to trip Sam, and he fell into the mud. He let out a bellowing 'Arrrggh!' before grabbing Kathy's leg, and pulling her down into the mud with him.

Kathy straddled Sam, and leaned forward, pinning his arms to the ground. Sam had been holding his head up, but now, it fell back into the mud. Sam bucked his middle up and down, giving Kathy quite a ride, but she didn't let go or fall off him.

Sam rocked from side to side. Finally getting one of his hands free, he grabbed some mud and pushed it into Kathy's wavy light brown hair; there were now no more blond streaks, and Sam reached for another glob of mud.

Kathy lowered herself onto Sam and reached for his arm before he could put more mud into her hair. Sam continued to rock, then turned suddenly, flipping Kathy onto her back. Sam growled, and Kathy growled back. This was a really fun mud fight to watch!

Sam now straddled Kathy, but couldn't pin both of her hands. Kathy reached up and slapped mud onto Sam's face, then rubbed it around, the mud covering Sam's lips. He kept his mouth closed, and lowered himself onto Kathy, and gave her a muddy kiss – wiping the mud from his lips to hers.

Kathy's hair was now on top of the mud, and Sam pushed it deep under the thick, reddish-brown muck, perhaps thinking that would keep Kathy down. But Kathy reared up, globs of mud now stuck in her hair. Her head fell back into the mud, but she raised a leg, her thigh just missing a good impact into Sam's balls.

Kathy's arms flailed, her hands trying to reach Sam's face, but he pinned her down by her wrists. Both contestants were panting, now; this was turning into an animalistic display of raw energy.

Sam let go of one wrist and grabbed another fistful of mud, slapping it onto Kathy's forehead, smoothing it back into her hair. Kathy took advantage of one of her arms being free, and pushed up on Sam's chest; but she didn't have the leverage to push Sam away.

Suddenly, Sam let go of Kathy's other wrist, and pushed himself up; then, as Kathy lifted her upper body off the mud, Sam flipped her over, facedown, and straddled her, sitting on her butt.

As Kathy pushed herself up, Sam pushed her shoulders down with both of his hands, and quickly flipped himself around, now sitting on Kathy's upper back, his legs still straddling her.

Sam leaned forward, and gave Kathy a few spanks on the bottom, causing wet mud to fly off her – spattering Sam, as well as Julie and I. We backed off, stepping into the stream. Julie kicked water over Sam and Kathy, which didn't add much to the mud bath they were taking.

Now, Sam filled both hands with mud, and slapped them onto Kathy's butt, massaging it in. Then, he ran one of his fingers down her butt crack, and wiggled it, the slippery wet mud lubricating it enough to enter Kathy's rear. She roared, and tried to push herself up, but Sam was putting considerable weight on her upper back.

Then, Sam leaned forward, his legs now on each side of Kathy's head, and his head just above Kathy's bum. With one finger still in her, the fingers of his free hand dug into the mud, and he pressed a glob into Kathy's butt crack, pushing it down over her anal area, as he withdrew his finger.

Kathy was panting and groaning, now, still not able to push herself up. It took all of her energy to keep her face out of the mud. Sam pulled himself down Kathy's body, and pulled mud from between her legs toward her crotch. We couldn't see whether he was stuffing her cunt with mud, but Kathy was struggling, and managed to flip herself over again, under Sam.

Now, she was raising her legs, her knees bent, and I thought Sam would get a knee in the nose. But he continued to move down Kathy's body, his legs now holding her waist, and his arms reaching for her ankles.

Kathy was able to raise her upper body now, and I thought she would take Sam by the balls ... but she needed her arms to support her, and Sam sat up, then let himself fall backward onto Kathy's front.

Falling back into the mud, Kathy circled Sam's chest with her arms. Then, she pinched both of his nipples, and

Sam let out a cry. Sam rolled over, freeing Kathy, but as she sat up, Sam threw himself across her, his middle now over Kathy's, both of them reaching for more mud.

Kathy threw mud onto Sam's back and, finally able to sit up, she slapped Sam's bottom hard. Mud went flying again. Sam was momentarily surprised, and twisted to look at her, but Kathy used the opportunity to extricate her legs, and roll over onto him.

Sam was facing down into the mud, and couldn't lift himself with Kathy sitting on his rear. Suddenly, Sam bucked his middle, and we heard a surprised, 'What?!?', as Kathy leaned forward, pressing both her hands down on Sam's shoulders, forcing his face into the mud.

Then, we saw what had surprised Sam: Kathy was peeing on Sam's backside, rivulets of pee and mud streaming down Sam's butt, and pee flowing down his butt crack to his balls. Kathy leaned forward, and lowered herself, putting her full weight onto Sam.

Her hands reached forward, smearing mud into Sam's ears, and onto his cheek, as he tried in vain to lift his head. In the meantime, Kathy's legs pushed Sam's apart, and she slid her body down Sam, until she could reach between his legs. As she grabbed Sam's balls, he bellowed, and pushed himself up, tossing Kathy off to the side.

Both Sam and Kathy scrambled to take advantage of the situation, both of them on hands and knees. They raised their bodies, facing each other on their knees, and Sam grabbed for Kathy's small breasts.

Kathy reached down to grab Sam's cock, and it appeared to be a standoff, until a fountain of pee shot up from Sam, hitting Kathy in the chest. Instead of letting go or backing off, Kathy grabbed Sam's dick, and aimed it until he was peeing on his own chest, the stream now decreasing as Sam's bladder emptied.

I turned to Julie, "Shall we stop the match, now?" Julie shrugged, and I half expected her to join the fight. Despite the peeing, both wrestlers had played fair – no hair being pulled, no mud slung in the eyes, or forced into the mouth. But Sam and Kathy were now completely covered by the thick reddish-brown mud.

Sam reached out, and pulled Kathy to him, his big arms clamping her upper arms as they circled around her back, his fingers clasped. Their bodies were in full contact from their hips to their chests. Both of them were gasping for breath, and Sam put his mouth to Kathy's ear. "Would you like to call this a draw?"

Kathy struggled for a moment more, and said, "OK, Sam." Then, she chuckled, "I won't try to bite your ear off. Or kick my knee into your balls. Or slap mud into your eyes." Sam pushed back, and they disengaged from each other.

Sam sputtered mud from his mouth, and laughed, "Yes, I'm sure you could do a lot of damage, if we didn't play fair." He took a step back, and both Sam and Kathy looked down at their bodies. They were truly covered with mud, from head to toes.

Julie, Linda and I applauded, and Kathy and Sam looked at each other. Then, they smiled, a non-verbal communication passing between them. They both bent down, taking huge globs of mud in their hands ... and threw them at Julie, Linda and I.

It was unexpected, and we let out a shriek. Then, Sam and Kathy took a few steps, Kathy tripping Julie, who fell onto her butt into the mud; and Sam making like he was going to hug me, then twisting me onto the mud.

Not to be left out, Linda grabbed handfuls of mud, and slung them at us. She was standing at the edge of the stream, and barely had any mud on her. Sam smiled, and jumped across the mud to Linda, then pulled her toward him, until they both fell backward into the mud.

Julie threw a fistful of mud at me. "Julie! I thought it was going to be us against them!" She shrugged, and gathered up more mud, throwing one handful at Linda, and another at me.

Linda had fallen on top of Sam, but he rolled her over, and pinned her to the mud. But instead of wrestling, he leaned forward, and kissed her. Sam's face was full of mud, and he turned one cheek and then the other, wiping some of the mud onto Linda's cheeks. She laughed.

Then, we ganged up on Sam, Julie pressing a gob of mud onto his rear, while I pinned his legs. Kathy took two hands of mud, and reached around Sam's head, rubbing the viscous mess around his neck, and up to his ears.

The three of us flipped Sam onto his back and, as we piled mud on Sam's chest and stomach, Linda freed herself and knelt by Sam's middle. Sam was spent now, no longer flailing his arms and legs, and Linda took another handful of mud, and pressed it around Sam's cock.

Julie and I laughed as we realized what Linda wanted to do, so I pinned Sam's wrists while Julie pinned Sam's ankles. I wasn't sure that Sam was turned-on, but Linda stroked Sam, and we could see that he was responding nicely.

Kathy crawled across Sam's chest and put her mouth to his. They had a muddy kiss, and Kathy said, "Thank you, Sam, for the nice wrestling contest."

Sam was no longer fighting us, and Julie moved between his legs, then reached under him. When Sam's middle bounded up, I knew that Julie's finger must be inside him. I moved to Sam's head, and massaged mud into his hair, giving him a muddy shampoo.

Leaning over him, I said, "That's a good boy. Now just relax, while we take care of you." Linda was working on him in earnest, now, and it wouldn't be much longer for Sam to be 'taken care of'.

He scooped some mud in his hand, and reached up, smoothing it over Linda's hip. Then, he closed his eyes, and relaxed his head back into the mud, as he thrust his middle up several times, culminating with a jet of cum that left a white trail from his chest down to his stomach.

Sam lay there, as we all dismounted and stood, looking down at our muddy bodies. Cakes of mud had dried on Sam, and were now cracking, as he tried to move his arms and legs. I reached down to pull him up, but he pulled me down onto him, the mud and cum and bits of plants in a layer between us.

I kissed Sam, and ran my hands over his muddy cheeks, and through his muddy hair. "Would you like me to bathe you in the stream, or are you planning to wrestle with Julie and Linda?" Sam nodded, then shook his head.

I got up, and held out my hand; this time, Sam let me help him up. He was still breathing heavily.

He walked over to Kathy, who was standing in the stream, and kissed her. "Thank you, Kathy. That was a good wrestling match." He smiled, "You're pretty strong ... for a girl." Kathy shook her head, "Are you trying to ask for more, Sam? Because if you can't be nice, you're going to get it!"

Sam shook his head, then stepped to Julie and gave her a peck on the lips. "Will you give me a rain check? I *know* you're strong; it would be an even match."

Julie laughed, "Sure Sam. But it looked like a pretty even match between you and Kathy." Sam shrugged, not wanting to admit that little Kathy could keep him pinned.

Sam walked over to Linda, and ran his hand through her shoulder length hair, before giving her a quick kiss. "And thank *you*, Linda, for the 'happy ending'. That was a nice way to end a wrestling match."

Linda chuckled, "I thought you were going to take Kathy, after you had gotten on top." I had thought the same thing.

Sam shrugged, "I really wasn't looking at it that way; I thought we were really wrestling, not just engaging in foreplay." We all laughed, then sat in the shallow stream, as we all helped bathe Sam, and then each other.

Sam whined, as we peeled some of the dried cakes of mud from his back. We would be getting most of the mud off ... but I knew that there would be plenty left – in our hair, and in a few other nooks and crannies.

The fog had dissipated, the day now warm, and Sam lay back on the pebbles in the stream, as we continued to bathe him. "It was lucky that nobody else came down the trail," Sam said.

Julie and I laughed. "Actually, there was a group of four older people hiking by; but one look at us, and they quickly disappeared around the bend." Sam shook his head, probably wondering when the park ranger would show up.

When we were all mostly mud-free, we walked down the stream, climbed over a couple of boulders, and jumped into a wide swimming hole. I wrapped my legs around Sam's waist, and my arms around his back, and he held me, kissing me lightly all over my face. At least these weren't muddy kisses.

As we dressed, Sam offered some snacks – we had beef jerky, pretzels, and trail mix. Then, Sam pumped water into each of our water bottles, and we put our backpacks on, and continued around the short looping trail.

Sam didn't know if there was another way back to the car, so we hiked back up the Pihea trail, now climbing the steep switch-backs, and passing the junction to the Alakai Swamp trail. We were all very tired by the time we reached the car, and surprised that it was already mid-afternoon.

We headed back the way we had come, and Sam pulled into the main parking lot for Koke'e State Park. A couple of us had to use the restrooms, as Sam and Kathy – already relieved – walked around the small museum.

Behind the building there were some open showers, and we rinsed off again, our clothes now completely soaked. As Sam drove down the hill, we all changed into clean clothes.

Driving through Waimea, Sam pointed, "This is the west side. There's a large military base that way, and Polihale State Park, where there's some great body surfing waves. But we just don't have the time."

A little farther down the road, Sam said, "And we don't have time to visit the south shore. There is a blow hole, and some good snorkeling, and a couple of nice hotels we could visit – including one with a meandering pool and waterslide."

Linda broke in, yelling "Waterslide! Waterslide!" Sam glanced in the rearview mirror, and shook his head.

"And there's the salt pond, and a Buddhist temple we could visit. And you guys haven't seen Na'wili'wili harbor." But as we came to Lihue, Sam turned north, along the east shore, heading back to Princeville.

Then, he asked, "Is anybody hungry, yet?" We were all starving, having had a small breakfast and only a few snacks.

Sam decided to drive to a small beach park, where we could sit on benches looking through the pine trees and palm trees to the ocean, while he showered and changed into a clean pair of shorts and an Aloha shirt.

When we were all presentable, Sam asked, "How would you guys like some Japanese food, tonight? There's a nice restaurant, and they have *teppanyaki* tables." Linda clapped her hands excitedly, and the rest of us nodded our assent. Japanese sounded perfect for tonight, although none of us was dressed for anything fancy.

We got to the restaurant as they opened at 5PM, which was a good thing, because we didn't have a reservation, and it was Saturday night. Fortunately, they did have a *teppanyaki* table, which Sam managed to get for just our group. We sat down, and looked at the drink menu.

They had all kinds of fancy island-style drinks, with little umbrellas stuck through pieces of pineapple and cherries. We all ordered strong rum drinks, along with glasses of water, as we felt dehydrated.

Sam ordered a few sushi rolls for the table, to start, and then we decided on our dinners, most of us settling on steak and shrimp, except for Kathy, who ordered chicken and shrimp.

When the drinks arrived, Sam held up his glass, and asked, "Are we having fun, yet?"

Kathy sipped her Lava Flow – a concoction that Sam said was like a Piña Colada with banana, and strawberry puree swirled through it. "I thought it was pretty fun." Then, she batted her eyes at Sam, "But next time, I won't be so nice: If I were really in a fight, I would have shoved mud up your nose, into your eyes ..."

Sam smiled, "Wow, Kathy, I've never seen you get this aggressive, before."

Kathy took another sip, "Maybe it was the sun ... or the elevation?" Pointing at her drink, "Or maybe the alcohol?" Kathy lifted the umbrella, and ate the skewered piece of pineapple. "But I'm feeling pretty good, now ..." She smiled, "I just talked with Christian."

When we all gave Kathy questioning looks, she explained, "I called him when we were at the beach park."

Kathy turned to me, "He's still in Honolulu, but will be returning tonight. He needs to be in Honolulu again on Monday through Wednesday, but said he could come to Julie's birthday party tomorrow ... if you don't mind."

Sam shrugged, "Of course not, Kathy! It would be great to have him join us."

Then, Kathy put down her drink, and looked at Sam, "And he invited me to visit him at the end of next week. He said he could pick me up on Thursday, and drive me back to the north shore on Friday evening."

Sam nodded, "That's great, Kathy. Maybe we can come down to the Wailua River and do some kayaking, and Christian can meet you there."

Kathy nodded, and said, "And he said he would love to take us to dinner on Friday night, if we're available."

"Sure! It would be great to have dinner together on Friday night. But let him know that I would be happy to pay. We'd love to meet him!"

Kathy picked up her drink, and sipped through the straw, the drink now down to the foam. "Thank you, Sam. I know you've taken me on this trip, and I feel bad, leaving you for a couple of days." Then, she looked at Julie, Linda and I and chuckled, "Stuck with those chicks."

Sam laughed, "You shouldn't feel bad, Kathy. This is a great opportunity for you to get to know Christian. We're happy for you." Then Sam looked at us, and waved his hand, "And, I don't mind being stuck with those 'chicks' ... too much." I reached down and pinched Sam's butt.

Sam looked at me, "Thanks for testing me, but I really don't think I'm dreaming." I didn't immediately understand, until I thought about the pinch. No, he wasn't dreaming; this experience was very real.

———————————

I was happy for Kathy, but even happier that she would still be coming to Kalalau with us.

The sushi came, and looked great. "So I think we should designate the next 24 hours – or maybe 30 hours – as Julie's belated birthday ... if that's OK with you, Julie." Julie smiled, nodded, and finished her Mai Tai. We ordered a second round of drinks.

"The party tomorrow is in a beautiful little valley, next to a stream; it's not far off the highway, but tucked behind a mountain, so only locals know about it. As I told you, we're 'piggy-backing' onto another party ... but I told them I'd bring beer, sangria, and potato salad."

Then, I remembered, "And I plan to pick up a birthday cake tomorrow morning at the market. Julie – you're welcome to come with me and pick it out, if you like."

I looked at Julie, then Kelly, "I'll need to cook a little tomorrow morning. I'm planning on making spaghetti sauce to take to Kalalau. So maybe you guys will want to go to the beach down below our condo."

Then, I remembered something else important, "And, we need to move to the house tomorrow. We should do that around noon. Then, we can go to the party."

I laughed, "But we'll need to get some sleep tomorrow night, because we get up very early on Monday to begin our hike. You guys won't have a problem with it ... and after we're in Kalalau, the boat will deliver supplies, and bring us back – so it should be a pretty easy excursion."

The chef took his position behind the table, and began his performance – juggling knives, chopping the vegetables, tossing the rice, and expertly cooking our steaks ... and chicken. As he served us, I lifted my refreshed drink, and toasted, "Happy birthday, Julie!"

Everyone sipped their drink, and Kelly put her arm around Julie, and rubbed her back. "Happy belated birthday, Julie."

Then, Kelly leaned over and kissed Julie. Linda and Kathy smiled, but the chef dropped his knife; fortunately, it bounced off the grill, and the chef caught it, and continued flipping it, as if that were part of the show. Maybe it was?

Kelly sat back, and picked up her drink, as if nothing had happened. It was nothing out of the ordinary ... for us. I looked at her, and then at Julie, "Maybe we should have a special group sex experience for Julie?"

Kelly laughed, "You mean it's not also for you? Or me?" She looked at Julie, "But it would be fun, if we can find something to do that you might like." She batted her eyelashes at Julie.

Julie picked up some rice with the chop sticks, struggling a bit to avoid losing most of it on the way to her mouth. "That sounds nice. But I think Linda and Kathy should participate, also." It hit me again: We really were a sort of 'family'.

Back at the condo, I offered Julie, "OK, as the beginning of your birthday celebration ... would you like to go skinny-dipping in the condo pool, or walk down to the beach, maybe starting a campfire, and do a night snorkel?"

I saw the frown on Julie's face, "Or, just stay here ... and maybe have some fun together?" I raised my eyebrows, and she smiled.

"Thank you, Sam. All those things sound pretty good, but we've done a lot of hiking today. And I'm not in the shape you guys are. But I wouldn't mind a little 'playing around' with you guys ... all of us."

She raised her eyebrows, and laughed, "You're the creative one, Sam. What would you suggest, that's not too strenuous?"

"Do you trust me, Julie?" That was really teasing her, as she obviously trusted me. And, she gave me a 'dumb question' look.

So I looked around at all the girls, and clapped my hands loudly, "Go to your rooms, use the bathroom, if you need to, and come back in just thong underwear. How about in ten minutes?"

The girls looked at me blankly, and nodded. As they'd demonstrated on multiple occasions, they trusted me, and would play along with most of my games. And, most of the time, I think they enjoyed them.

Kelly gave me a 'look', but then smiled, and kissed me, as she went into our room to get undressed. I had to make sangria, and pulled out the large Tupperware pail that I'd bought at the market. Then, I took the fruit out of the refrigerator, and found the cutting board.

I poured two magnum-size bottles of hearty burgundy, a can of peach nectar, a can of guava nectar, and a bottle of apple cider into the pail. I dissolved sugar into lemon juice and water, then added my 'secret' ingredient, brandy – from a couple of miniatures I had been given on the plane.

I washed the fruit, and cut oranges, lemons, limes, and apples into large pieces, then dropped them into the pail, now nearly full – more than a gallon of Sangria, ready to steep overnight. I was about to put the pail into the refrigerator just as the girls were returning.

Setting the pail back on the counter, and opening the top, I showed Julie and Kathy the Sangria. "It will take overnight for the good fruit flavors to infuse, but I added guava, peach and apple juices already."

Julie shrugged, "That looks good ... but we've already had a lot of alcohol tonight," she smiled at me, "so I'd prefer to turn on." She smiled, as she put her arms over my shoulders and pressed her bare breasts into my chest, "In more ways than one."

I smiled, too. "I think that can be arranged." I put the Sangria in the fridge, and got the smokes. We sat on the lanai, looking out over the incredible ocean view, a crescent moon now rising behind us, it's light illuminating the clouds.

By now, we were all totally comfortable with each other, no matter what we were – or weren't – wearing. But it still amazed me that I could be so lucky as to have met Kelly, *and* be able to develop this close relationship with her friends. They were all very special people, and we had grown together in many ways.

When we were suitably high, we sat on the living room floor, in a circle on a towel. I retrieved one of the empty magnum bottles of wine, its cork now back in place, and put it in the center of the circle, then spun it.

Linda laughed, "'Spin the bottle'?"

I nodded, "It's just an idea. Maybe Julie should spin the bottle, and one of us would have to offer her something – something you would do to her, or she would do to you." My brain was now flooded with ideas, and possibilities.

I asked, "We could have different categories – I'll suggest a couple, then you guys can suggest some? And we can each spin the bottle. Whoever the bottle points to must offer something in that category."

Julie frowned, "Like what kind of 'categories'?"

I replied, "Well, the first might be hugging and kissing, the next a spanking, the next stimulation, and so forth."

The girls shrugged. Kelly said, "We can try it."

Julie spun, and the bottle pointed to Linda. She crawled over to Julie, knelt before her, and held her head; then, she gave Julie a very passionate-looking kiss. As she crawled back to her place, I saw Julie's mouth drop open. I'd never seen Linda showing any interest in playing with Julie.

Linda spun the bottle, and it pointed to Kathy. Kathy smiled, and walked over to Julie, then faced her, squatting until she was sitting in Julie's lap. She smiled at Julie, then lowered her head, and licked Julie's nipples, playfully biting them, and then twirling them between her fingers.

Then, Kathy ran her finger across Julie's lips, and hugged her tightly, putting her head on Julie's shoulder. After some time, Kathy looked at Julie, and kissed her delicately on the lips. Then, she returned to her place.

Julie looked at me, "Well, Sam, I'm enjoying your 'Spin the bottle' birthday game, so far!" We all laughed. Then, Kathy spun the bottle. It pointed to Kelly; I would be the one not participating in this round.

Kelly turned to Julie and whispered something, and Julie put her legs out and lay on her side. Kelly scissored her legs between Julie's, their crotches pressing tightly together. Then, they leaned toward each other and kissed, as they gyrated their hips, and ground their clits together.

It was enthralling to see. As close as we'd become, I saw that Linda had a hand over her mouth, and Kathy had a huge smile on her face.

I wondered whether Kelly and Julie were going to consummate their act, but they stopped, and separated themselves, sitting back up in their places. I knew they both had to be dripping, by now.

"OK, time for the second round, some kind of spanking." Linda smiled, Julie seemed neutral, and Kathy gave a slight frown. Kelly spun the bottle, and it pointed to Linda.

Linda laughed; it was almost a cackle. "I'll let you give me an OTK spanking – twenty six hard swats." Linda again crawled over to Julie, and positioned herself across Julie's lap. Then, she said, "I'm ready, Miss."

Julie smiled at us, then looked down at Linda's thonged bottom. Linda still had a full figure, even though her butt was noticeably smaller, now that she'd lost the weight. It seemed pretty flabby, however, when Julie's first spank rippled Linda's tissues from side to side.

Linda gasped a little, but remained quiet and in her place. Julie gave Linda what she'd asked for: A hard hand spanking. It was given slowly, maybe a spank every three or four seconds; but it was given hard, Julie using her strength, and perhaps surprising Linda a little.

Linda's bottom was quickly turning red, as Julie alternated sides, the slaps sounding like high frequency gunshots, and I wondered what the 'neighbors' would think. Linda was now grunting with every swat, Julie pouring it on, making the last few even harder.

When it was over, Julie rubbed Linda's bottom, then said, "You may rise."

Linda knelt in front of Julie, and gave her another serious kiss. "Thank you, Miss." Then, she took her place again.

The bottle spun again, and it pointed to me. Shrugging, I said, "You may have the option of me spanking you, or you spanking me. Twenty six swats, similar to what Linda just did."

Julie smiled at me. I wasn't sure which option she would take. Finally, she said, "It's supposed to be my birthday celebration, Sam. So I'll spank you." My bottom was hurting, already.

Then, Julie added, "I saw Kelly giving her approving look, when I spanked Linda; and, you asked for it. I think I have enough strength left in this arm." She flexed the muscles of her right arm.

I crawled over to Julie, and positioned myself across her lap. She rubbed my bottom, and I tried to relax, my head turned so that I could only see Linda, on the other side of the circle. Julie gave me a hard spank on my right buttock, the pain not sinking in for a second or two, but then feeling like searing heat.

Then, a spank on my left side. Then on the right. Julie was spanking hard, but faster, now. I held my hands together in front of me, and put my forehead on the carpet. Julie had become a very good top, and she continued to make my bottom very sore.

When it was over, and Julie told me that I could get up, I knelt in front of her, as Linda had, leaned forward, and kissed Julie on the lips. Julie looked down and laughed. She said, firmly, "Put your hands on your head, young man! And turn around, now!"

I did as she had instructed, and shrugged. My penis had grown too large for my small European thong, and was popping out of the top. Kelly chuckled, "Did that spanking get you a little excited, Sam?"

I went back to my place, and spun the bottle. It pointed to Kelly. I stuck my tongue out at her; she was now going to get *her* payback. Kelly smiled demurely, and said to Julie, "I'll spank *you*."

Julie wasn't surprised, but I was. I had thought that Kelly would take the spanking. Julie went over Kelly's lap, and Kelly immediately began spanking her hard and very fast. The twenty six spanks were over in as many seconds, and Julie had been too surprised to hold herself still. She hadn't stuck her hand behind her, but was bucking and kicking her feet.

Julie got up and gave Kelly a peck on the lips, and Kelly went back to her place.

I announced, "Well, that's the end of the second round."

Linda laughed, "What's next, Sam? Needles?"

I had thought about that ... but wasn't sure what Julie would accept as something 'nice' for her birthday. "What would *you* like to do, Julie?"

Julie thought, and responded, "I don't mind needles. But I'm feeling pretty horny, Sam."

It didn't take me long to suggest, "Then why don't we go into the bedroom. I have a few ideas." I stopped at the entrance to the kitchen, and asked, "Would any of you like to taste the Sangria, before we get started?"

Everyone – even Julie – nodded, and I ladled the purple-red liquid into small glasses. We toasted again.

Linda immediately said, "Yum!"

Kathy got excited, "That's fantastic, Sam. I like wine, and I really like juices ... and this is a great mix."

I pointed at the huge pail, "I hope I made enough for tomorrow." I got some 'dumb comment' looks, but none of the girls knew how many people would be at 'Julie's' party, tomorrow. I was picturing nearly a hundred people.

We went into the master bedroom of the condo, and pulled off our thongs. I whispered something to Linda, and handed her a few things. She briefly went back out to the kitchen, as the rest of us got onto the bed.

I sat on a decorative pillow, my back against another pillow between it and the headboard. Then, I spread my legs, and had Kelly sit between them, then lay back. Finally, I had Julie straddle me. Linda returned, and got onto the bed, crawling over to my side, and putting a small bowl on the bed.

As I reached down to 'do' myself a little, Linda got on the bed, "I'll take care of that!" She took my erection in her hand, and stroked expertly. Kathy was on the other side, crawling over to me, and gave me some nice kisses.

Linda told Julie, "He's ready," and Julie lowered herself onto me, as I guided myself into her. She was kneeling, almost in a sitting position, moving herself up and down on my shaft.

Then, she leaned forward, and Kelly adjusted her position, to allow Julie access. Kelly's feet were on the bed, her knees up, and fallen apart, as Julie lowered her head to Kelly's privates. Julie moved herself back and forth on me, as she took care of Kelly's needs.

I had a great view of Julie, and signaled to Linda and Kathy to kneel next to Julie's hips, which were right in front of me. Linda handed Kathy an alcohol swab, and Kathy looked at me.

I explained, "Julie is going to get 13 needles on each side. I'd like you to insert at least three or four. Then, if you prefer, I can do the rest."

Julie's head rose suddenly, "What?"

Laughing, I told her, "One for each year. They're small; you probably won't feel them much." Julie harrumphed, and I added, "If they hurt too much, just tell us, and we'll take them out. OK?"

Julie reluctantly said, "I guess so." Then, she lowered her head and went back to her ministration of Kelly.

Linda and Kathy tore the wrappers of the alcohol swabs, and I pointed to Julie's butt, "All around." In a few seconds, Julie's butt was shiny with a thin layer of alcohol. I nodded, and Linda handed a needle to Kathy – unwrapped, but still capped.

They nodded to each other, picked sites on Julie's bottom, and inserted their needles. Julie didn't make a sound or react.

Julie had stopped moving, and – in my position – I couldn't effect much movement, so my 'other' head was getting frustrated. On the other hand, I didn't want to come too quickly, so maybe it was better, this way.

Linda continued to hand Kathy needles, and they inserted them nearly simultaneously, in symmetrical positions in Julie's rear. After Kathy had inserted five needles, she turned to me, "You can do the rest, Sam. I think it's time for me to give myself some attention."

Linda handed me the next needle, and I took off the cap, and inserted it while Linda inserted hers. We continued in this way, inserting three or four needles per minute into Julie's butt.

A few minutes later, Julie had 26 needles in her bottom, the blue hubs pressed against her skin, and an inch and a half of stainless steel deep in her tissues.

Kelly was writhing now, squeezing her feet against my thighs, as Julie concentrated on her task. Now, both Linda and Kathy were lying on the bed alongside us, their heads near the foot of the bed, masturbating, the bed now a jumble of vibrations and sounds.

It was too bad that I hadn't thought of preparing a butt plug for Julie. But my finger would have to do. I put the middle finger of my left hand into my mouth, and lubricated it with saliva. Then, I massaged Julie's anus with the tip of my finger, and gradually went deeper, finally inserting it fully, and moving it back and forth.

Julie got the hint, and began moving back and forth on me again, and I thrust as much as I could (which wasn't much) into her. My right hand glided over the blue hubs, slightly moving them in different patterns.

Kelly let out a brief scream as she came. Julie lifted her head, but continued to do something with her fingers. She was now moving forcefully against me, each time also moving back against my advancing middle finger in her rear. Kathy came with several violent jerks, and continued to lie on the bed, her hips moving slowly.

A minute later, Linda came, with a few grunts and spasms. She turned onto her side, facing Kelly and Julie, then got up, and knelt alongside Julie's hip again. She looked at me, and I nodded.

I gave her a 'wait' signal, and pulled all of Julie's needles halfway out, a forest of stainless now gleaming across her bottom. I gave Linda the 'OK' sign, and she began pulling each of the needles fully out, and dropping them into a Coke can.

Kelly had sat up and leaned forward, and it now appeared that she and Julie were kissing. I pulled one of the needles out of Julie and held it, while Linda finished pulling the rest out, and dropping them into the can. Then, Linda took an alcohol swab, and rubbed Julie's rear again, to clean up a few dots of blood.

I smiled at Linda, and told Julie, "And now for the final three."

Kelly, Kathy and Linda called out in unison, "One for good health." I jabbed the needle into Julie's right buttock and wiggled it for a few seconds, then pulled it out. "One for good wealth." I jabbed Julie on her left side, and did the same. "One for long life." I put the needle against Julie's rear, and pushed slowly, until the needle popped in.

I pulled it out again, and dropped it into the can that Linda was holding. Then, I lay back against the headboard and closed my eyes. I thrust as hard as I could and, fortunately, Julie did the same. When I was ready, I leaned forward, and held Julie's hips, then shot my hot fluid into her.

Continuing to thrust, I reached under her, and rubbed in a fast circular motion over her clit. Julie continued to thrust back on me, as I shrank, eventually sitting up, and pressing down on my hips. Finally, she came; I was still in her deeply enough to feel *her* warm secretions envelop me.

Julie lifted herself off me, and sat on the bed. We were all panting, looking around at each other, and smiling. I signaled with my hand for everyone to sit around me. Then, one by one, I kissed each of the girls – a brief, but sincere, open-mouth kiss.

Then, one by one, they kissed each other. We did a group hug, and got off the bed. Kelly went into the bathroom, and Linda went into her bathroom, while Kathy told us goodnight, and headed up to the loft.

Julie and I went out to the lanai, both of us still nude, and lit up another bowl, sharing tokes, as we looked out at the water. Kelly came out just in time to take one hit from the water pipe.

Julie and I rose, and she hugged me, then gave me a serious kiss. "Thank you, Sam. That was a pretty 'exciting' experience." As she let go, and headed through the sliding door, she added, "I can't imagine what you have planned for tomorrow." She said goodnight, and left Kelly and I on the lanai.

Well, I *could* imagine a few things we might do tomorrow. It was going to be a busy day. Again.

CHAPTER 13: JULIE'S BIRTHDAY BASH

Kelly and I woke early. We had talked last night about giving Julie a few more 'special' experiences today, so I got out of bed and tiptoed, nude, to the other bedroom. I pushed open the door a crack, and Linda waved to me. Julie was still sleeping.

Sitting down on the edge of Linda's bed, I asked, "Everything OK?" She nodded, and I bent over and kissed her. Then, I explained, "I came in to give Julie a little 'birthday nooky' ... if she's in the mood."

Linda chuckled quietly, "I think she's *always* in the mood. She masturbated last night after she thought I was asleep. And she had just had that multi-way experience with you and Kelly! She acts like a nympho."

That was interesting. I had viewed Julie as a forward kind of person, easy talking with the opposite sex, and very teasing; perhaps a vixen. But she didn't push to have sex when we were together. At least, not every time.

I whispered to Linda, "I hope you don't mind."

Linda shook her head, "Not at all, Sam. I understand." She smiled, "I could probably masturbate while you're making it in the next bed ... if you don't mind. Otherwise, I can go to the kitchen and make some breakfast."

I shrugged, "I'll let Julie decide. But after an experience like last night, I can't imagine she would care."

Then, I tiptoed to the other side of Julie's bed, and quietly climbed in, under the covers. I did not touch Julie or lie next to her ... just lay on my side, watching her. Notwithstanding a woman never wanting a man to see her in the morning before she cleans up, Julie looked very cute; I would say she was pretty, but not quite 'beautiful'.

But, with her vivacious personality, openness, and assertiveness, she really was a turned-on person. I didn't know if she craved sex, but it was obvious that she enjoyed it. She seemed to like me, and she obviously liked – or loved – Kelly.

Julie was flirtatious with me, and accepting of all the challenges I threw at her; but she was seriously infatuated with Kelly – I could see it in her eyes last night, during our 'Spin the Bottle' game. Perhaps *Kelly* should have been the one to come in and give Julie some nooky?

Julie's eyes popped open, focusing on me, and she smiled. I brought my head to hers, and kissed her lightly on the lips, "Happy birthday, Julie." Then, I chuckled, "Or at least happy *belated* birthday. Sorry we're ten days late."

Now Julie slid over to me, sideways, facing me, and put her hand behind my head, grabbing my hair, and pulling me toward her. We kissed – passionately, this time – and I let my arm drop casually over her waist. Julie had slept in the nude and, of course, I was still nude.

I smiled at Julie, "You're beautiful. I was watching you sleep. I came over to give you a little 'birthday nooky'." Julie smiled, her face seeming slightly flushed ... but it was still too dark in the room to really tell. Then, I had to offer, "But I just realized that you might have preferred Kelly to come into your bed. I can go get her, if you want ..."

I had said it in a joking way, and certainly hoped that I wasn't kicked out and Kelly invited in. But I would have been happy for Kelly, and I knew that Julie and I would have more experiences together.

Julie shook her head, "No, silly! I'm glad you're here. And I'm looking forward to that nooky." We kissed again, less passionately, somewhere in between the kiss of a lover, and the kiss of a close friend. With Julie, I think for both of us, it was 'having sex', not 'making love'.

I wondered how many male friends Julie had ... and how serious they were. She had assured me that she had not slept with anyone over the past six months since we'd first had sex ... at least, intercourse. But I guessed that men were always after her, and she would certainly be the first one of Kelly's friends to find a mate, and get married. At least, that's what I assumed.

Smiling at Julie's smiling face, I whispered, "I spoke with Linda. She will leave, if you want; but she also said that she could masturbate, while we were making it. I'm OK with whatever you decide."

Julie shrugged, then turned her head to face Linda, "Good morning, Linda. I'm going to take Sam up on his offer of a little morning sex. But it's OK with us, if you want to stay in bed."

I heard Linda say, quietly, "Thanks, Julie." I heard some sheets rustling, and Julie turned back to me. Then, taking me in her hand, she held me, and moved her thumb in a circular motion over my frenum.

"So what is your preferred position, this morning, m'lady?" I gave Julie a peck on the lips.

She shrugged, "Anything with you in control, but I want to be facing you."

That was a good offer; although 'over the corner of the bed' was one of my favorite positions. I got under the covers, and between Julie's legs, as I went down on her. I swirled my tongue under her hood, and around her clit, and then used my fingers to rub over her clit in a circular motion.

Julie's hands came under the sheet, and pulled me up to her. Her knees came up, as I moved up her body, first kissing her breasts, and then her mouth. I tried to rub myself on her, and was happily surprised that – despite her lack of pubic hair – her 'stubble' was stimulating. And Julie's stroking had achieved its goal.

I entered Julie, the feeling glorious – not better or worse than with Kelly, but different. Julie squeezed her pelvic muscles as I thrust into her, and we kissed deeply. Then, I lifted my head, and smiled at Julie. She knew that I was asking something, and gave me a curious look, then a very subtle nod of her head.

Sliding out of Julie, I flipped back the covers and sheets, and crawled backwards to the foot of the bed, pulling her by the ankles, as I slid off the bed. Then, I pulled until her butt was just beyond the spread, and I lifted her legs, resting them on my shoulders.

Julie smiled, as I reentered her, grasping her hips, and pulling her even further toward me, until my front was slapping against her bottom and thighs on every thrust. I leaned forward, and Julie crossed her ankles behind my neck. I took one big thrust into her, and leaned forward until the crook of Julie's knees were over my shoulder.

Julie reached up and held my shoulders, as she pulled herself up, and I put my hands around her shoulders, bringing our heads together, as I began to thrust again. Julie pushed my shoulders, as she lay back down, turned her head toward the wall, and closed her eyes.

I realized that she could thrust much better this way, and she was now gyrating wildly, a desperate, pained look on her face. Or, maybe that was ecstasy? My mind was receding as I approached my own orgasm and, somehow, Julie and I came together, both of us grunting and moaning, panting, and gasping, as our bodies spasmed together.

It was on my third or fourth final orgasmic thrust into Julie that my eyes fluttered open, and I saw Linda smiling at me. She was still in the next bed, the covers over her, but her hand (or hands?) reaching under them. She closed her eyes, and reached her own climax a minute later, as I bent down to kiss Julie.

I whispered, "Happy belated birthday, Julie. I hope you have fun, today. I have a few things planned; but if you don't like them, just tell me. I want you to be happy."

Julie lifted her head and kissed me briefly. "You're sweet, Sam. I *am* happy." She chuckled, and I could see thoughts running through her head, "And I *will* tell you, if there's something I don't like, or don't want to do." We rubbed noses, and I stood, and went into the bathroom to clean myself.

A minute later, Julie came in and sat on the toilet. She smiled, "Come over here, and I'll suck that off, if you like." Then, her vixen-like cackle. I had already used a warm washcloth, and declined her offer.

I stepped over to her, bent over and gave her a quick kiss, and said, "I'm going to get dressed and started in the kitchen. When you're ready, meet me there, and I'll give you a few choices for breakfast." Then, I smiled, "Unless you'd like to have 'breakfast in bed'?"

Julie shook her head, "That won't be necessary. I'll come to the kitchen in a few minutes."

I cut fresh papayas into quarters, and put them on small plates. The girls had their cereals. And I had bought eggs, and could even make 'country potatoes'. But Julie selected pancakes. We had fresh berries, and she decided on blueberry pancakes. Linda walked into the room, and said, "*That* sounds great!"

A few moments later, we heard Kelly yell from the lanai, "For Kathy and I, also!"

So I made a big batch of pancake mix, then fried up some bacon, and got out the pure maple syrup that I'd bought at the market.

Linda set the table out on the deck. Julie poured fresh orange juice for everyone, then brought out the plates of papaya. It took several rounds of pancake-making to have stacks for the girls, and I made my own while they were eating out on the lanai.

I asked Julie if she wanted to come to the market with me to select a birthday cake (and maybe pick out a few pastries to bring back ... not that any of us needed them). But she suggested doing it on the way to the party. That was a good idea – assuming I didn't need anything else from the market for what I was cooking.

I'd told our hosts that I would bring a big bowl of potato salad, and sangria, and beer. I think the beer made their decision, and we were all invited to the 'local' party; but it wasn't that local, because a lot of *haoles* were part of it – providing beer, playing music, and setting up the food tents.

And, I wanted to pre-cook at least one meal for Kalalau. Spaghetti sauce seemed the easiest, and – in the spirit of our camping, I made it vegetarian, to be more minimal. But this wouldn't be a real backpacking trip: We were getting a delivery from RJ by boat.

We would have coolers of ice (a real delicacy in Kalalau) and beer (of course, another special commodity), and frozen or cooled food, as well as a real barbeque grate that I'd bought at the market.

It was a cross between backpacking and car camping. But when the boat departs, it is one of the most remote places in the world. At least, it seems that way.

"Don't forget that we'll have to be packed up by noon, to move to the house." There were a few groans.

Kelly said, vibrantly, "We're going to do a little snorkeling, at the beach below."

Nodding, I said, "I know you don't need me to tell you to be careful ... but the ocean's very powerful, and there can be rogue waves. So, at least try to either be in shallow water, or deep water, but don't hang around the edge of the reef." I smiled at them, sorry to have sounded like I was lecturing, like a worried father – although that's really how I felt. "Have fun!"

Julie, Linda, and Kelly picked up their snorkeling equipment, and their cameras, as they passed through the living room, then exited the condo. Kathy had decided to stay and get packed-up, and ready for the party ... and Christian. I would be interested in really meeting him, as I'd only seen him glancingly in the plane.

Two hours passed quickly, Kelly and friends down at the beach, and Kathy in her loft, or on the lanai talking with Christian; at least I assumed that's who it was, as she was talking very softly.

Everything was done, and I'd packed myself and all the stuff from the kitchen, ready for the short drive down the hill to Hanalei. I'd also packed three waterproof bags and two coolers for the boat drop-off.

Kathy put her rolling case and backpack next to the front door, with mine. She wore a pareo wrapped around her waist, going down to her ankles; and tiny bikini top that seemed to match. "That looks cute! I'm sure that Christian will love it. That top matches perfectly."

Kathy said, "Yeah, that was lucky. They made me buy the matching bottoms." She smiled at me, and added, "But I'm not wearing them, today."

I shrugged, having easily already seen that she was wearing a thong under her pareo. I glanced down, "The thong from last night?" Kathy laughed and nodded.

The girls came up, excited about the things they'd seen on their snorkel adventure, and had some great pictures – something that would have required equipment costing thousands of dollars just a decade or two ago. Kelly and I got into the shower together, and I wondered whether Julie and Linda were taking a shower together ...

Julie, Linda and I had experienced an amazing snorkel adventure. We'd seen an octopus, a baby eel, and some huge schools of fish in the deeper water. Neither Julie nor Linda had been comfortable about venturing out that far, but the conditions had been calm, and they'd had confidence in me.

We all had tried some surface dives, and I learned how to dive slowly, so that the fish wouldn't be disturbed. Finally, on the last few dives, I managed to clear my ears.

I snapped out of my reverie, as Sam drove through the town of Hanalei. I asked, "Do you know where you're going, exactly?"

Sam nodded as he concentrated on the road ahead of him, "I think so. It came up on the map app, and I saw a satellite view." He glanced at me, apologetically, "It's *not* on Hanalei Bay ... one of those would have cost a fortune. But it's supposed to be on a stream, and have a lot of land."

I couldn't understand why we would need a so much land; the condo had been great, with the beach an easy walk below. But Sam's friend was willing to charge him for only half the nights, as we would be in Kalalau half the time. Sam was a good negotiator.

Sam turned left into a long driveway, hidden by thick growth of tropical vines and an occasional palm on each side of the narrow track that was dirt, with grass in-between. We drove across a huge grass expanse to the house, which was a small Hawaiian-style place, dark green with white trim around the windows. Sam pulled into a car port, and we got out.

The house was at least six feet above the ground level, and we had to lug all our stuff up the stairs. Inside, it was spacious and airy, with skylights, and light wood construction. The floor had huge tiles, 'soft' and not cold to the feet.

As with the condo, there were two bedrooms and a loft – which would remain empty, if Kathy stayed with Christian. I wondered whether her infatuation with him was a backlash to her experience a year ago in Mexico.

The back of the house was a huge screen-covered lanai that looked out into the backyard – really a bamboo jungle with large trees beyond. We could see a trail leading into it from the back of the grass yard, bordered by papaya trees along the side, and huge plumeria trees in the corners.

They were blooming, and Sam said he would make me a lei, when we had a chance to relax. He had worked hard, preparing the trip, and now shepherding us. We left the coolers with the food, sangria and beer, and the spaghetti sauce in the back of the minivan. Taking up the rest of the room were Sam's waterproof bags.

Finally, everything was inside the house, and we were unpacked again. It was easy, as the layout was very similar, and we all took our same spots. There was another half-bath in the house, along with a laundry room, pantry, dining room, and the screen room.

Linda, Julie, and I changed into our party clothes. Linda wore the dress Sam had bought her in Hanalei, as did Julie. I wore shorts and a safari blouse, tied at the waist, the sleeves turned up.

Sam was in his casual shorts and Aloha shirt, with new flip-flops he had bought in Hanalei. They had a tire tread on the bottom – the better for hiking Kalalau, Sam said. But he'd also told me that he would be wearing trail running shoes on most of the hike.

Sam looked at his watch, and suggested we leave for the party. We stopped at the market, and Sam and Julie went in, while I sat in the back with Linda telling Kathy about the snorkel she'd missed. But, by her reaction, it seemed that she hadn't missed anything.

When Sam and Julie got back, Julie sat in front; but before Sam started the car, he turned around, and I could see him laughing already, although he hadn't made a sound. "I was going to do this with Julie privately,"

Julie interjected a quick "What?"

Sam nodded at her, and continued, "but I thought – since we've all been so open with each other – that I should share this with you guys."

Oh no; not again! "Sam, what are you talking about?"

Sam reached into the center console, and pulled out a small box, then opened it, and pulled out the device. "You've got to be kidding! That's not nice." I knew what was about to happen.

Turning to Julie, Sam handed her the contraption, and explained, "This is the radio-controlled vibrator that I built – the one that was inside Kelly when I first met you guys at the French restaurant." Suddenly, Linda had her hands over her mouth, and Kathy was nodding, a big smile on her face. We had to expect that Sam would do something like this.

Sam turned to Julie, "Please take off your underwear." He gave her an unusually evil smile, "You won't be needing them, today."

Julie looked up at the ceiling, and then complied, taking off her panties as people wheeled their groceries by.

Sam asked Julie to insert the thingy, and she did, the antenna wire hanging out like the string of a tampon. It really wasn't uncomfortable ... until Sam pushed one of the buttons.

When Julie had inserted the vibrator, and put down her dress, Sam said, "We'll have to test it, of course." He was laughing now. As he pushed the first button, and Julie jumped, I had to laugh, too.

Then Sam said, "Level two." Julie jumped even higher, and let out a yelp. Finally, Sam said, "Level three."

Julie squealed, then yelled, "Sam!!!" She looked back at us, and said, "That thing gets annoying!"

I laughed, "Tell me about it. That's what I was dealing with, when you stopped by our table on Linda's birthday. That was the end of the first weekend that I spent with Sam." Well, it hadn't *caused* the end ...

Linda asked, "You mean the one that was all BDSM and spanking?" She was laughing (as she knew the answer).

I replied, "What do you mean, Linda? That's how *all* my weekends are with Sam." We were laughing so hard that people going in and out of the market looked over at us. Sam started the minivan, and put up the windows. Then, we headed to Julie's birthday party.

"Sam, remind me how you picked the site for Julie's birthday party?"

Sam glanced back, "Sarah and I had gone to a couple of parties there, and I knew some of the people who organize them. I originally had thought of Anini Beach –

where we saw the windsurfers, that nice park; but then I found out about a party being held here. Where we're going is not someplace that most people can see. It's private land. And it's beautiful."

Then, Sam looked back at me – specifically me, looking into my eyes – and added, "And it fits my *purpose*, beautifully." Well, I knew that he would want to give Julie her birthday spanking, although I wasn't sure how that was going to happen at a big party. I couldn't *believe* that he would do it publicly; on stage, as he and I had done in Toronto. Well, I guess I *could* believe it ...

The memories of our Toronto and Niagra Falls trip returned, and I drifted for the next ten minutes. We were all in our own worlds – of dreams and expectations, past experiences and future adventures.

Sam turned up a mountain road, and into a parking lot. There were probably fifty cars there already! We heard the music as we got everything out of the back – Julie carrying the sangria, Kathy and Linda the beer, and Sam and I the large cooler with the potato salad and some *huli huli* chicken he bought at a roadside stand in Anahola, on the way here.

It was spectacular! We walked into a small valley – bordered by a mountain on one side, where the music was set-up on a stage, and a meandering stream – nearly a river – that curved around, bordering the other side, with a slope up to another hill on the far side of the river.

The entire valley was green grass – *very* green. There were palms and papaya trees, and banana trees, and a few pineapples near the base of the hill. We passed plumeria trees, with their sweet scent, and a large mango tree, fruit already falling – and being picked up and eaten by kids at the party.

We walked up to a central tent, under which were several picnic tables of food. At the end of the tables was an area with a keg and several coolers of beer. Sam showed us where to put the potato salad, chicken, and sangria, then we put the cooler with the beers alongside the others.

Linda and I perused the food at all the tables – it was an incredible spread – salads, desserts, Hawaiian dishes, casseroles, sushi, Mexican, and more desserts.

Against the mountain was a stage that looked as if it had been built with leftover wood from the hurricane. But the music was good – there were several bands, playing reggae, classic rock, metal, and blues. It looked like it was going to be a fun day – even without the extra 'fun' that Sam had planned.

Sam introduced us to the host, who was part Hawaiian, and to two or three people he knew, who had helped organize the party. When he told everyone that it was Julie's birthday, he reached into his pocket, and Julie jumped.

As we walked toward the stage, Sam shouted, "Fancy meeting you here, you old scallywag!" Sam shook RJ's hand, "You remember the girls ... it's Julie's birthday!" As RJ hugged Julie, Sam must have hit the second or third button, because Julie yelped, and jumped into RJ's arms. That really wasn't nice; but I was starting to laugh, myself.

RJ gave her a curious look, and she improvised, "I think I've got ants in my pants." RJ bellowed with laughter, and held up his beer. Sam suggested that we all get drinks and, as he walked toward the sangria with Julie, she was whispering to him, and poking him in the ribs.

Kathy came over, and Sam served us all a big cup of sangria. We toasted to Julie's birthday and Sam sent another vibration through Julie. "Sam!" She turned to me,

"How can you put up with him?" I shrugged. Sam had to put up with me, too.

We listened to the music, and Sam and I danced; then, Sam danced with Julie and with Linda. I turned around to find Kathy, and saw her walking towards us with a huge grin, her hand in Christian's.

The music ended, and as the next band got set up on the stage, Kathy introduced us all to Christian. He was tall, dark, and charming. He had long black hair, pulled into a pony tail, and strong jaw; a rugged but cultured look.

He wore khakis and a safari shirt, not that different from mine. And he wore sunglasses, pushed up onto his head. I now saw that he also wore an earing on the left side, and a leather band around his wrist.

Christian shook our hands, my immature Sam feeling the need to goose Julie with the remote controlled vibrator again; she nearly jumped into Christian's arms, and Christian gave a surprised look – first to Julie, and then to Kathy.

Kathy coughed, and said, "I'll explain later."

Christian spoke softly with a French accent. He seemed very mature, but must have been only in his mid-thirties.

He and Sam immediately hit it off, discussing diving, and talking about the Kalalau hike tomorrow. It turned out that Christian did 'bow hunting', and has spent a lot of time on the trail and in the valleys of the north shore.

He was evidently also experienced at spear fishing, and fishing from an ocean kayak, as he told stories, including one about the huge ahi that got away. We walked to the food tent, and tried some of the dips and the sushi.

Kathy was beaming, but eventually pulled Christian away, and they walked off toward the base of the mountain.

Sam took another chip and guacamole, and asked, "Well, Julie, are you ready for your birthday spanking?"

Julie looked surprised, and I hoped that Sam wasn't going to make a spectacle. Linda whispered to Sam, "Where are the bathrooms? I need to pee."

Sam said, "Well, you could walk back to the parking lot, and use the porta-potties ... or I can show you guys the stream, and you can find a place behind a rock or a tree." Linda smiled and shrugged.

After taking a few more chips, Sam led us along the stream, which bordered the grass area, then made a bend, behind the mountain. We walked on large rocks at the edge of the stream, which was quite wide, but very shallow. We passed the generator that was supplying electricity for the sound system, and walked up the river, into a hollow.

As we walked around the corner of the mountain, the sound of the music and people suddenly quieted, and we heard only the rushing of water over the rocks in the stream.

Linda sat on a rock, facing the stream, then lifted her dress, and pulled the crotch of her panties aside and peed. She smiled at Sam, but he continued walking along the stream, searching for something.

Finally, he pointed and ran over to a flat-topped boulder, not that different from the one in his back yard. Sam took off his flip-flops, slapped the soles together, and put them on the boulder, then sat down and patted his lap.

Julie walked slowly to Sam, standing before him, and Sam held her hips as he explained, "I'm going to take you across my lap, and spank your bare bottom. I think a hundred spanks will be a good warm-up. Then, I'll slipper you with the flip-flop ... unless you want Linda and Kelly to each help warm your butt."

I stepped up to Julie, turned her around and gave her a slobbery kiss. When we came up for air, Julie said, "OK, Kelly. I know you would like to spank me, too." Linda joined us, and Julie shrugged, "And you, too, Linda."

Sam clapped his hands loudly, "Then it's settled: Each of us will give you 100 spanks, and *then* I'll slipper you. Julie shrugged, and Sam took her hand, and gently guided her across his lap. He pulled up Julie's long dress until it was above her waist in back.

Glancing down the stream, I didn't see anyone else, but wondered whether the sound of the spanks would carry to the party. But the music was probably loud enough to mask any sounds we might make.

Sam rubbed Julie's bottom, and Julie said, "I'm ready for my birthday spanking, now, Sam." She glanced over her shoulder, smiling at me, almost a dare. But she knew that Sam wouldn't hesitate to redden her bum.

Then, Julie lifted her head again, and asked, nicely, "Could you please take that thing out of me, first?" Sam chuckled, and reached between Julie's legs and under her. It only took a moment for him to find the antenna wire and pull the device out of Julie.

He put the thingy on the boulder next to his flip-flops, and asked, "Are you ready, *now*, Julie?" She chuckled, and put her head in her arms that rested on the boulder. Then we heard an 'Ummm hmmm'.

Sam stopped rubbing Julie's rear, and said, softly, "OK, Julie, here we go." His first few spanks were very hard, and Julie yelped and squealed a few times, before settling down. Sam continued spanking her – not quite as hard, alternating sides, and finishing in two minutes.

Julie was bouncing on Sam's lap, and kicking a little, despite her efforts to remain still. By the time Sam finished, Julie's bum was already bright pink all over. But we all knew that she had a long way to go.

Sam helped Julie off his lap, and Linda sat on the boulder, and pulled the front of her dress up, while Julie positioned herself across Linda's lap. She looked up at us and smiled, then put her head down by Julie's, "Happy birthday, Julie."

Without further discussion, Linda began spanking Julie – with almost the same speed and intensity that Sam had demonstrated. Julie was whimpering and kicking her legs as Linda finished her part of the spanking.

It was finally my turn, and Julie knew that I would give her no quarter; she gave me a serious look, but I just smiled sweetly at her and shrugged. She got over my lap, and her dress came up for the third time. Julie's bum was red, now, and I knew that she would be feeling the spanking through the rest of the party.

I put my hand under her, and stroked a few times, as Julie wiggled on my lap, thrusting her pelvis onto my hand. Then, I withdrew my hand, and gave her a quick and hard swat. Julie screeched. "Kelly!"

I repeated what Sam had once told me, "When we give spankings, we don't play around, Julie." Of course, we *were* playing around. But my arm needed some exercise, and Julie's bum was a beautiful target.

Like Linda, I decided to give Julie a stinging spanking. My technique was improving, and by the fiftieth spank, I was wondering whether we were overdoing it. Julie was moaning and sniveling. But I didn't let up; Julie was going to get her money's worth from the three of us.

When I was done, Julie was like a ragdoll across my lap. She was quietly sobbing, but managed a 'Thank you, Kelly." I rubbed her bottom and slipped my hand under her again, and Julie quieted.

We traded positions again, Julie over Sam's lap for the second time. "You're twenty seven, now?"

Julie was shaking her head, "Twenty six, Sam."

Sam nodded, "Got it. You're twenty eight." He laughed, then stuck his hand under Julie and she jumped as Sam squeezed her clit. Sam removed his hand, and rested it on Julie's right butt cheek. "OK, Julie. Twenty six hard swats with the slipper. Please count them."

Sam picked up one of the flip-flops, and bent it, examining the tread on the bottom. Then, he laid it on Julie's rear; it covered a good portion of her bum, and it was clear that the swats would overlap. Julie really *would* be feeling this spanking the rest of the day ... and evening.

Raising the slipper, Sam said "Happy birthday, Julie." Then, he brought the slipper down with a loud 'THWACK!' on Julie's rear. Her legs flew out straight, and her free hand was waving in the air, but she brought it back onto the boulder, and counted, "One, Sir."

Sam gave Julie one swat every ten seconds or so, and the scene repeated: Julie bouncing and crying out, then giving Sam the count, as he rubbed her redness. After a half dozen swats, Sam slowed down, putting his hand under Julie and stroking several times between each swat.

"You're getting your dress wet." Julie lifted her middle, allowing Sam to pull the front of her dress up, so that her crotch was over Sam's right thigh. I looked down the stream again, but nobody from the party was venturing in this direction.

Sam continued Julie's birthday spanking, finishing with a last few zingers, the rubber sole of the flip-flop making a solid sound against Julie's bum. Julie was sobbing and panting, and Sam rubbed her bottom, then slipped his hand under her again.

Looking up at us, Sam said, "Maybe we can skip the extra three, since we did an extra three last night?" Linda and I nodded, and Julie let her head drop.

"Thank you, Sam." I didn't know if Julie was thanking him for the spanking, or for agreeing to not give her an extra three swats.

As Sam's fingers did their magic under Julie, Linda stepped up to them and began massaging Julie's bottom. I positioned myself in front of Julie, bending over the boulder and taking her head in my hands. Julie and I kissed, as Julie's breath became more ragged, Sam really focusing now on his task, and making good progress.

We all worked on Julie quietly, the only sounds being her panting breath and the gurgling of the water in the stream. Julie began gyrating her hips, then bucking her middle, as Sam brought her to the edge. My tongue entered Julie's hot mouth, as Julie's motions became arrhythmic, her body jerking and trembling as she came.

When she had calmed, Sam helped her up, and let her dress drop. Then, Sam stood and took Julie in his arms. "I'm sorry we had to celebrate your birthday late ... but so glad that I could bring you here – to the island, and to this place for your party."

Julie draped her arms over Sam's shoulders, "Thank you, again, Sam. This has been an incredible trip." Then, as an after-thought, Julie chuckled, "I just hope I can keep up with you guys on the hike tomorrow."

Sam cocked his head, "You mean the spanking hurt so much, you might not be able to walk?"

Julie pushed Sam away, "No, silly. I'm not sure my legs are going to have the stamina. Just the first part of the trail that we hiked was pretty rugged ... and you said that was nothing, compared to the full hike."

Sam nodded, "That's true. It'll be challenging, but I know you'll make it." He gave her a peck on the lips, and we headed back along the edge of the stream to the party.

The first people we saw were Kathy and Christian, who were walking slowly near the stream, talking. As we approached, they looked up, and Kathy asked, "Did I miss anything?"

Julie reached back and rubbed her bum through her dress, and smiled thinly at Kathy.

Christian was confused, and looked at Kathy, who explained, "Sam just gave Julie her 'birthday spanking'."

Linda chimed in, "We all did."

Christian must have thought we were all joking, but Kathy goaded Julie, "Maybe you should show him?"

Julie shrugged, turned her back to Kathy and Christian, and lifted the back of her dress. By the time it was up to her waist, Christian was staring, silently; then a big grin formed on his face, and he looked at Kathy.

"My birthday isn't for another month." She glanced at me, and stared at Sam; then, still looking at Sam but talking to Christian, she offered, "I guess I could let you give me an early birthday spanking, if you want."

Sam smiled, obviously delighted that he was going to see Christian spank Kathy. But Christian was confused and tongue-tied. Finally, he whispered to Kathy, "Maybe we can do that when you visit me."

Julie let her dress drop, and said, brightly, "I'm starving. Shall we see what's for dinner?" We all laughed, and made our way across the expanse of grass to the food tent. Sam pumped beer from the keg, and we each took a paper plate and sampled the variety of dishes everyone had brought.

Christian tasted the potato salad, and exclaimed, "Now *this* is really good!" Kathy chuckled, "Sam made that. He's a very good chef." Christian began telling Kathy about his cooking experience, and they drifted off toward the stage.

Julie, Linda, Sam and I sat on the grass with our plates of food, and our sangrias and beer, listening to the music. Linda pointed, and we watched as Kathy and Christian had their first dance together. They had started dancing separately, but Christian took Kathy's hand, and spun her around, now dancing a swing together.

They made a nice couple, and Kathy looked perfectly dressed in her Tahitian pareo and bikini top. Christian was quite a bit taller than Kathy, perhaps a little taller than Sam. The more I looked at him, the more I realized how fit he looked; how virile. I had to agree with Kathy: Christian was a real hunk.

Sam and I danced a little, then Julie and Linda joined us, and we all danced together. The bands were pretty good, the rock and reggae now softening into blues and Hawaiian, as the sun set. There were pink clouds above us, and the mountain quickly made the valley dark, tiki torches now illuminating most of the party.

Sam kissed me, and pulled me away from the dancing, leading me around the stage toward the mountain. We could barely see, but Sam led me up a trail, around some vegetation, between a couple of boulders, then followed a switch-back, until we were high above the party, behind the stage, looking down on everyone.

We positioned ourselves behind a waist-high boulder, and Sam gave me a loving kiss. Then, he whispered, "Are you as turned on as I am?"

I chuckled, "Probably not ..." We laughed.

Then, I got a little more serious, "But Julie took her spanking quite well, and you seemed to get her off pretty quickly."

Sam nodded – I could barely see him now – "She's a sexy woman." He laughed so loud that I thought people from the party would hear us, then he said, "Linda thinks that Julie might be a nympho."

That was ridiculous, although I could easily see how Linda might say that; but she knew better, also. Julie had a healthy sex drive, and an aggressive personality; she usually got what she wanted from men. I realized that Julie used men to pleasure her; but she wasn't sex-obsessed.

Sam reached around and undid my belt, and unbuttoned my shorts. "Really, Sam? We're right above the stage; anybody who looks up here can see us."

Sam unzipped my shorts and lowered them, and I took my legs out of them. Then, Sam lowered my underwear, and removed them from my legs. "Anyway," he said, "we're behind a boulder. We can watch the party as I hammer you from behind."

"Hammer me? That's not what I had in mind."

Sam chuckled, turned me around, and gently pushed me until I was bending over the boulder. He rubbed himself on me, and I reached under and put him inside me.

It was a surreal experience watching the party, while Sam took me from behind. I was feeling the sangria, and my eyes glazed over, seeing the flickering lights of the torches, as a Hawaiian group – three huge guys – played ukulele and guitar, and sang 'Hanalei Moon'.

Sam bent over me, contouring his body to mine, and kissing my back, as he thrust into me. I hadn't thought that I would be in the mood, but the combination of the soft island atmosphere, the island music, and the sangria combined to make me horny, and I started pushing back against Sam's thrusts.

I looked up, and a thin, crescent moon was rising above the mountain on the other side of the stream. My mind melted, and my body fused with Sam's. It was truly romantic ... although it might have been more romantic with us facing each other.

Sam must have heard my thoughts, because he slipped out of me, spun me around, and hoisted me onto a flat ledge on the side of the boulder. Then, he entered me again, as I held on, my arms around his neck, and my legs around his hips. He lifted me off the boulder and toward him, his shaft now pumping deeply within me.

My muscles spasmed, and I came, remembering at the last moment not to scream. Sam exploded into me, and he pushed me back against the boulder, as we continued thrusting until we were both wasted. He extricated himself, and set me down, then handed me my panties and shorts.

We walked down the trail, feeling our way in the darkness; although Sam had a small flashlight in his pocket, he was afraid to use it, lest people would see us. Not that it would have bothered anyone to see two partygoers walking down the trail.

Christian said his goodbyes, and Kathy walked him back to his car. Sam bumped into RJ, who said he would be leaving soon, and the two of them went to the parking lot to transfer the coolers and waterproof bags to RJ's pickup.

When Sam returned, Linda and I were trying out a few of the cakes and cookies people had brought. It was a good thing that we would be using a lot of calories on the hike tomorrow!

Sam pumped another cup of beer from the keg, and set out to find Julie. Linda and I sat on the grass, listening to the music – now modern jazz being played by a talented quartet, consisting of a guy on the sax, one on guitar, one on standup base, and a woman on the drums.

It was getting late, and I decided to find Sam and Julie. Walking toward the stream, I passed the generator, and saw Julie ahead. Then, I saw Sam standing behind her; very *close* behind her.

As I approached, Julie waved, "Hi, Kelly." She glanced over her shoulder at Sam, and laughed, "Thanks for sharing Sam with me ... again."

It wasn't until I had walked around Julie that I saw her dress lifted in the back, and Sam pressed against her, moving a slow grinding motion. "You've got to be kidding! I'm surprised you could even get it up, again."

Julie laughed, "Well, he got it up, and in me, but I don't think he's getting very far."

Sam slipped out of Julie, and looked dejected. "I *thought* I could give Julie one last treat for her birthday ... but maybe I had a bit too much sangria ... and beer."

Julie smoothed her dress, and turned to me; I informed her that Sam and I had just made love on a boulder above the stage.

Julie laughed, "So *that's* what everybody was watching, up on the mountain!" I hoped that was just a joke.

"Very funny." Then, I felt bad. "If you guys really think you can get it on right here, in front of everybody, don't let me disturb you. Linda and I can have another piece of cake, while we wait."

Sam turned to Julie, "Let them eat cake!" but Julie was shaking her head.

Julie kissed Sam. "He's given me everything I wanted for my birthday." She looked at me in the dim light, "And I think we're all getting tired."

As we started walking back to the food tent, Sam added, "Yeah, we need to leave the house by 6AM tomorrow morning."

Julie and I turned to Sam, and said "What??!?" Julie finished the thought, "Why so early?"

Sam was shaking his head. "You guys just don't realize. The trail will take us a long time, and we need to get to Kalalau before the sun sets ... or it could get dangerous."

Julie chuckled, "What? There will be snapping turtles coming to get us on the trail?" She began pinching Sam's butt, both her hands squeezing like the claws of a crab. That looked like fun, so I joined Julie, and we pinched Sam all the way back to where Linda was sitting.

She looked up, "It looks like you guys are having a fun time."

We laughed, and Julie informed Linda that we'd have to be getting up very early. Linda stood, and brushed the grass off the back of her dress. "I'm ready to leave. I don't think I can eat another piece of cake!" That was the old Linda, but we knew she was joking. She had controlled herself pretty well, considering all the food that people had brought to the party.

Sam had already brought the cooler back to the car, filling it with the 'extra' beers that we'd left in the car, and leaving the beers we'd brought to the party – if there were any left. As we made our way to the parking lot, Kathy was walking toward us.

"We're leaving," Sam said. "There wasn't enough food, and we couldn't dance to the music." Kathy laughed.

I said, "It looked like you and Christian were dancing pretty well together."

Kathy nodded, "He's quite a guy. And a terrific dancer!" She turned to Sam in the dark, and added, "He really liked you, Sam."

Sam mumbled, "I liked him, too. Maybe someday he'll take me bow-hunting." I didn't know that Sam hunted; I thought the only thing he shot with was his camera.

We drove the two-lane Kuhio Highway along the north shore, passing Princeville, and going down the hill and across the one-lane bridge into Hanalei. The town was mostly shut-down, only a couple of restaurants still open. When we got to the house, we all went to our rooms, or bathrooms.

A while later, we reconvened in the screen room at the back of the house, and Sam lit the pipe and passed it to Julie. She took a toke, and passed the pipe to Linda, Kathy and me, and then Sam re-loaded it, and the pipe made the rounds again.

We were all exhausted, and still had to pack our backpacks for hiking and three nights of camping. Sam pulled out a checklist, and went over it with us, and we retired again to our rooms to pack and then hit the sack.

As Sam and I climbed into bed, he said, "I thought that worked out pretty well."

I kissed him, and agreed, "Yeah, it was a great party. And I think Julie enjoyed it."

Sam pulled up the covers and laughed, "And we *know* that Kathy enjoyed it." We snuggled together, and Sam said, "Christian seems like quite a guy."

Yes, that was an understatement; he really was a sexy hunk of a guy.

CHAPTER 14: TRAIL MIX

The alarm on Sam's watch went off at 6AM, and we groggily got out of bed. Sam went to the other bedroom and loft to wake my friends, and I went into the bathroom. Somehow, we were all ready in less than 45 minutes, and piled into the car with our backpacks, and water bottles.

Sam drove to the end of the road, where we easily found a parking spot next to the trailhead. He was grumbling that we should have been on the trail by 7AM, but it was 7:30AM by the time we began climbing up the rock steps.

It was more difficult climbing the steps with our backpacks on; ours were about 25 pounds, while Sam's was closer to 45 pounds. Fortunately, a lot of the heavy stuff would be delivered by boat.

The trail was cool, and there were occasional minutes of rain, but we were all warm due to the exercise, despite wearing only our running shorts and tanks. Sam pushed us hard, and we were at Hanakapiai Beach in well under an hour, a huge improvement from our first time on this trail.

There was no time to stop, so we began hiking up the switchback trail, climbing some 800 feet over the next hour. The trail was very narrow in places, and there were steep drop-offs down to the ocean below. Sam yelled, "The gate!" and we walked through a short length of fence with a gate in it.

Sam waited for all of us, and then pointed at a huge boulder that seemed to be balanced halfway over the ledge. "This is 'space rock'. We're at one of the highest points on the trail, about 800 feet over the water." We looked down and saw a small cove with spectacular blue water.

Sam passed around some trail mix, and we took a short break. Julie pointed out, "This trail seems pretty dangerous ... there are steep drop offs, and you sometimes can't even see the trail."

Sam nodded, "Yes. I don't have the statistics, but a few people have died on this trail – fallen off the cliff, or been hit by falling rocks."

Then Sam looked at each of us and chuckled, "I wasn't going to tell you this until we got to Kalalau tonight ... but this trail is rated by Backpacker Magazine as one of the ten most dangerous hikes in the U.S. And it was rated by Outside Magazine as one of the 20 most dangerous hikes in the world."

We were all very quiet. It was mid-morning, and we hadn't seen anyone else on the trail. The intermittent rain had stopped, and the sky was blue, with just a few puffy clouds.

Sam put the trail mix in the side of his pack, and stepped to the edge of the trail. Then, he stepped back. He pulled the crotch of his running shorts aside, and peed over the edge. He mumbled, "I sure hope there aren't any kayakers below us!" When he finished, he announced, "Ha! I am the grand pissing contest winner – 800 feet!"

Then, Julie smiled, and climbed up onto space rock, and walked to the edge. Sam cautioned, "Please be careful, Julie. You wouldn't survive an 800-foot fall into the water."

Julie chuckled, and pulled the crotch of *her* running shorts aside. Then, standing straight, she reached down, and we saw a stream of pee arcing over the edge of the rock. When she was finished, she jumped down from space rock, and stuck her tongue out at Sam.

"Ha, yourself! I am the *grander* pissing contest winner – 806 feet!" Sam shook his head, and we all laughed.

As we continued hiking the trail, Sam whispered to me, "That was really scary! I wasn't sure I could pee far enough to get over the edge. I was almost getting vertigo, as it was!"

We continued on the trail, getting into the rhythm: Walking deep into the valleys, feeling the heat and humidity, and sometimes crossing small streams; and then walking around the viewpoints, with steep drop-offs to the water, and the wind blowing.

Passing the four-mile marker in Hoolulu Valley, Sam checked his watch, "Well, we're doing OK: We've been on the trail for about two and a half hours, and made it a third of the way." He gave us a serious look, "With an hour lunch break, we'll have to keep up this pace, if we want to get to Kalalau before dark."

We hiked out around the point, and along the trail hanging high above the water, and then turned into the next valley. As we passed a small waterfall, and crossed the stream, Sam smiled, "This is Waiahuakua Valley. This stream is the one that we went under in the Zodiac, when we came out of the two-door cave."

The trail into the valley was downhill, but going back out of the valley it was a steep uphill climb. We were all getting tired.

A young couple passed us, going in the opposite direction, and we spent a few minutes talking with them. When Julie commented on the difficult trail, and steep drop-offs, they laughed, "Just wait 'till you get to 'crawler's ledge'!"

As they hiked back along the trail, Sam laughed again. "Yeah. That's something *else* I wasn't going to mention. You'll find out soon enough!"

We passed the five-mile marker, and turned into another valley. It was huge, and Sam informed us, "This is Hanakoa Valley. We should be at the halfway point soon – keep an eye out for the six-mile marker."

Linda groaned, "Only *half*way? My legs are going to be sore tonight!"

Julie was nodding, but had to catch her breath before she could comment. "I sure hope we can take a break, soon. My feet are already sore."

Sam laughed, "Yes – we'll have lunch when we get down to the stream. This valley is the only official camping place, other than Kalalau. There's no beach, and quite a lot of insects. But there *is* a beautiful waterfall in the back of the valley – which requires another hike, once we get to the stream."

We passed the six-mile marker, and finally got down to the stream. It was beautiful! Sam took off his shoes and socks, and waded in the shallow water, then sat on a rock and took a few snapshots. Then, he put his pack on a boulder on the other side of the stream, and took off his running outfit.

By the time my friends got to the stream, Sam was already lying back in a shallow pool, his head under a three-foot waterfall. Julie and Kathy stripped down and joined Sam in the refreshing water. Then, Linda and I decided we might as well get in, also.

Sam opened his pack, and pulled out a bunch of snacks for lunch. We hadn't brought sandwiches this time, and I had no doubt we would be hungry by the time we got to Kalalau. We drank from our water bottles, nearly emptying them, and Sam pumped water through his backpacking filter to refill them.

We put on our running clothes again, and Sam suggested that we wear clean socks. He also cut a few pieces of moleskin to cover the start of a few blisters on several of our feet. Finally, we got going again, having only taken 45 minutes for our lunch break.

The trail was winding and up-and-down again; Sam pointed behind us, and we had a glimpse of Hanakoa Falls at the back of the valley.

Now, the trail switchbacked down, and Sam pointed ahead, to a section of cliff where we saw an incredibly narrow trail, then no trail. "That's called the 'balcony'. It's another scary place, like 'crawler's ledge'."

Julie and Linda were shaking their heads. Sam said, "It's not that bad, just keep your balance, and don't look down, until you have a good place to stop."

Then, Sam glanced at me, and whispered, "This is my worst nightmare; I wanted you guys to experience it, but this trail is something that challenges me, too." He closed his eyes, then opened them, "Just don't look down!"

It *was* scary! It looked like the trail had ended, but there was a small ledge to walk around the corner, where the trail picked up again. There was beautiful crystal clear blue water far below us, but I was trying to keep my eyes on the trail.

We continued on, and as the trail led to a point, it narrowed again. Sam looked back at us – each of us about a hundred feet behind the next person – and yelled, "And this is 'crawler's ledge'!" He waited until everyone had caught up, and walked carefully along the foot-wide path, holding onto rocks and roots, then disappeared around the corner.

This part was even scarier: As I inched my way to the point, holding on to anything I could grab, the wind gusted, and it felt like my pack was pulling me over the edge. In all fairness, it *wasn't* a vertical drop-off; there were a few steep slopes, and ledges. We probably wouldn't have fallen more than two or three hundred feet ...

Just past crawler's ledge, the trail was eroded, a steep slope of scree. There was only minimal indication of where the trail should be but, fortunately, there was a rope about ten feet below us – obviously for a faller to grab onto, before she continued down the slope and over the edge.

The trail went on and on. My mind was a blank, now, and none of us had talked for a while. We walked through another small valley, and passed the eight-mile marker. Sam didn't point it out, but we were only two thirds of the way to Kalalau.

It was already past 2PM, and getting very warm. We took a short break, and Kathy took off her running outfit and put on a pair of bikini bottoms. The sky was blue, and I hoped that she didn't get sunburned.

The trail climbed, and switchbacked, then climbed some more, and switchbacked again. Kathy and Julie were falling behind; they were still around the last corner, as I looked back. Sam kept up a mean pace, and I finally had to shout to him to wait for all of us. Our water bottles were nearly empty again, and we were all slick with sweat.

Sam pointed ahead, "We just have to get to the top of Red Hill, and then it's all downhill from there." We walked and walked – the hill Sam had pointed to unfortunately *not* being Red Hill. We hadn't seen the nine-mile marker, yet; this had to be the longest mile I'd ever hiked.

Finally, the trail narrowed between two rocks, and another portion of fence. Sam stood, waiting for all of us, and announced, "This is the top of 'Red Hill'." He smiled,

"I think we're going to make it!" His joke wasn't humorous to any of us; we just wanted to get there.

Red Hill was mostly dirt – red dirt – eroded into ruts, with thick roots crossing our path. It wasn't that difficult, but Sam pointed out, "You know, we've had great weather, hardly any rain for the past week. But you can imagine after a few weeks of rainy weather, how dangerous this trail would be."

We focused on each step, as we descended, stepping over roots and ruts, and finally coming down to the Kalalau Stream. As we crossed the stream, hopping from rock to rock, Sam said, "And the most dangerous part of this hike can be flash floods in the streams." Then, he softened, "But the conditions sure are good, now."

A short distance from the stream, we finally saw the beach. The trail straightened, and paralleled the beach, and we began to see cleared areas for campsites. Then, we walked through a grassy helicopter landing area, and a bit further on, we passed a tent, then another.

Sam pointed out the composting toilets, and we continued walking up a slight grade, where the ground overlooking the beach was terraced, each terrace being a campsite. But there were only a few tents. Sam had said there were forty permits per night, but it didn't look like that many people were actually here.

Sam surveyed the campsites, and selected two neighboring terraces. He took out a king size sheet, and laid it out on the lower terrace, holding it down with small rocks. There was a narrow path down the bluff to the beach, and enough vegetation that the campsites were fairly private. Then, He took the tent out of his pack, and pitched it on the upper terrace.

Taking off his clothes, Sam smiled, and said, "Welcome to Kalalau!" We followed him a short distance to the end of the main trail, where a beautiful waterfall was tucked into the corner of the cliff.

Two girls were bathing under the waterfall, nude. Sam stepped down to the edge of the small pond. and waved at them, and they waved back. The water from the falls meandered down to the beach, lush vegetation growing along the narrow streambed.

The girls finished bathing, and walked past us, down another trail that led along the stream to the beach. Sam stood under the waterfall, rinsing himself, his head against the rock, the water flowing over him. He stepped over to us, "I'll get a real shower in a while – I've still got a lot of work to do.

"But you guys can get cleaned up; there's soap in a little recess in the rock." He pointed to the top of the waterfall, "I have to warn you that rocks can come over the edge, and have been known to conk people on the head. You really can't predict it, so don't stay under the waterfall for too long."

We all stepped into the small pond, and up to the waterfall. I leaned back against the rock, as Sam had, and let the water flow over me. It was cold, at first, but then it felt terrific; I felt better already, just getting some of the dirt and sweat off my body.

Julie, Linda and Kathy took turns under the waterfall, as Sam and I stood on one of the rocks leading back up to the trail. Sam pointed, "Look at their smiles!" My friends were having a great time; I turned to Sam and hugged him.

"It was a challenging trail, as you said it would be … but now that we're here, I think it was worth it."

Sam chuckled, "Wait until we hike up into the valley tomorrow!"

I put on a mock pout, "*More* hiking?"

Sam said, "Only a couple of miles, and it's easy. And we'll be hiking down to the end of the beach, and swimming to Honopu on Wednesday." I shook my head. Sam's trips were always packed with adventures; he wasn't the 'relaxing' type.

There was no need for a towel, as our bodies dried within minutes. Sam said, "I still have to set up a few things, but how about a short walk down the beach?" We were all happy now, and followed Sam down the short trail to the beach, then turned left. It was an incredibly wide beach, probably a couple of hundred feet from the water to the cliff. It looked like there were some small waves, and the wind was picking up.

After a five minute walk, we saw a cave, and Sam headed over to it. He stopped, and pointed along the ground at the hundreds of small rocks in the sand, in a line under the cliff. "You can see that rocks really do fall."

He walked quickly beyond them, and we walked just inside the cave. It was huge – perhaps fifty feet deep and more than a hundred feet long, open to the beach. There were several tents set up inside the cave, and we waved at a couple of groups of people.

We continued walking, and came to an area where the cliff formed a semicircle; there was a tornado-like column of sand, as the wind whipped around the circle.

"Wow," Linda said, looking up. "That's neat. And how high is that mountain?"

Sam chuckled, "On the way back, we'll walk along the water, so you can look up and see. There's about 4,000 feet of rock above these caves."

There was a small pond that went into another cave. This one wasn't as wide in front, but evidently went pretty far into the mountain. We walked into the cave, along the side of the pond, until it got too dark to see anything.

Sam said, "I suggest that you have a small flashlight handy from about sunset on. It gets pretty dark out here. And I *hope* that it will be clear at least part of the time, so we can see the stars. We will be able to see the Milky Way arcing across the sky."

We walked back out of the cave and across the beach to the water. The wind was really blowing now, and there were whitecaps out to sea, but the waves didn't look that big. Sam stopped and pointed, and we all looked up.

Julie's mouth dropped open, "Oh my God! That's a huge mountain!" It was. The cliff went up a few hundred feet, and then there was a slope, and another cliff, towering a couple of thousand feet above the beach.

When we were across the beach from our campsite, Sam excused himself – he needed to get the dinner organized – and we decided to continue walking down the beach. Linda bent over to look at her blisters, and shrugged. "They're not so bad ... they haven't popped."

It was amazing: Just an hour ago, our feet were dying after the 12-mile hike. Now, our bare feet were stepping through the cool water that lapped up onto the beach, and we all felt great.

I headed across the beach to our tent, as I watched the girls walk down the beach, the four of them nude and very relaxed. We had made it here by 4PM, around eight and a half hours – an hour longer than I'd targeted; but we'd done very well, nobody complaining, and no injuries.

I was ready to relax, also, but had to get a few things done before dark. It all depended on the weather ... which was not dependable on Kauai. It could be mostly clear all night, but a cloud or two could come over and rain hard for five or ten minutes.

We would need to have enough shelter for all of us. I'd brought my backpacking tent, which was nominally 4-person, but which I'd always used just for Sarah and I. I also brought a large fly – a long triangular tarp that had it's own tent poles. The tent was on the upper campsite, and I would put up the tarp on the lower terrace.

And I hoped that we could sleep on the beach at least one night – under the stars.

I assembled the fly, and put two ground cloths down, then put the rain fly over the tent, and pounded in a few more stakes and a couple more guywires. These were against the gully between us and the next campsite, so out of the way of anybody tripping.

Then, I started the dinner. I went to the waterfall, and half-filled a pot with water, then poured it into a 2-cup plastic measuring cup, dumping out the rest of the water, and putting the 2 cups back into the pot. I put on the top, and set a baggy of rice next to it – which I'd already measured out to one cup.

I dug into my pack, and found some of the heaviest items I had carried: five different foil packages of Indian dishes, actually made in India. I had been buying these for years from one of the specialty markets.

I filled the camping stove with fuel, and lit it. Fortunately, it worked (I was pretty sure it would, as I had tried it at home before the trip). I put on the pot of water, then went to the waterfall again, to pump clean water into all my water bottles.

Digging into my pack again, I pulled out the last few ingredients we would need, along with my knife. I put lemonade mix into one of the water bottles, along with two miniatures of vodka. It was more efficient than beer – which would be delivered tomorrow (I hoped). I would have preferred tonic ... but didn't want to pack it in.

Finally, I took out a baggie of cashews. If we had made a fire, I would have roasted them, but I would have to use the camp stove, tonight. I cleared off the big sheet, and put the utensils, cups, cashews, and a lime – along with my knife, into the center. Fortunately, the wind wasn't blowing too hard, and the sky was still clear.

I turned off the stove, the water near boiling, and surveyed the dinner preparations. I would need the set of plastic bowls that I'd brought, so I pulled those out of my pack and put them on the sheet.

With most of the work done, I walked the trail a hundred feet to the waterfall. There was nobody here, and it seemed that people weren't taking advantage of their permits ... unless they were camping up in the valley.

I rinsed off, then took the thin bar of soap that always seemed to be in a recess of the rock next to the waterfall. There had been debate about using only 'camping soap', but the bar looked like normal soap to me, and there had been no ecological disasters here, so far.

I took my time bathing, the water quite cool – very refreshing, even invigorating. I was facing the cliff, letting the water splash over my head and down my back, then turned around to see Kelly and her friends standing by the small pond, watching me.

Running my hands through my hair, I stepped out onto the rocks. I should have asked 'How was your walk?', but it came out, "Do you like what you see?"

The girls went under the waterfall, taking turns; Julie and Kelly were bathing each other. I didn't offer to help; just watching them seemed to validate our lifestyle. As I was pondering this, someone stepped next to me, and I eventually turned to see who it was.

"Sam?" she said. I was struggling to remember her name, but she was a friend of Sarah's and mine, who lived here part of the year. Finally, it popped into my head.

I smiled, "Ashley! It's great to see you! I had no idea that you were on the island, let alone in Kalalau." We hugged, and when I stepped back, I took a long look at her.

She was a well-proportioned woman, a few years younger than me, probably Sarah's age. She had shoulder-length sandy hair, with a few strands of grey, that showed that she hadn't dyed it. I remembered that she was a very 'natural' woman.

Ashley wore a pareo around her waist, her breasts as nice-looking as I had remembered, and perfectly tanned with no lines. She was a beautiful woman, and had a younger perspective on life.

I compared her to Alex: Both of them had great bodies, and took care of themselves ... but Alex comported herself very elegantly. Alex was a mature woman. In contrast, Ashley, with a more vivacious personality and direct way of speaking, seemed more like a girl.

"You look great! Not a day older than the last time I saw you. And I love your tan!"

Ashley looked past me to the girls, "So how is Sarah?"

It hit me: She didn't know. I looked down, and quietly told her about Sarah's accident. My voice was cracking, not just talking about Sarah, but talking about her here in Kauai, where we'd shared some life experiences.

Ashley hugged me, our bodies pressed together, her arms clutching me around the back. "I'm so sorry, Sam." She stepped back, looking past me again, "Are those your daughters?" A flicker of confusion crossed over her face, and she said, "You have two *sons*, don't you?"

I nodded, "Yes. A little over a year ago, I met Kelly," I turned and pointed, "who's the daughter of one of our close friends. She's going into biotech, and we started a company together." Ashley was nodding uncertainly. "And, we've developed a very close relationship."

I couldn't help but add, "And those are three of her friends. I decided to bring them all to Kauai ... to experience some of my own feelings for the island."

Kelly walked up to me, and cocked her head. "This is Ashley; Ashley, this is Kelly." I explained to Kelly, "Sarah and I met Ashley years ago. She lives in Colorado in a log cabin ... and in Hanalei." They shook hands, and there was a moment when I knew they were giving each other the once-over.

Julie, Linda, and Kathy stepped up to us, and everything would have been fine ... until Julie took my cheeks in her hands and kissed me; *way* more passionately than appropriate – at least in front of Ashley. Kelly turned my head toward her, and gave me an even more passionate kiss.

I turned to Ashley and shrugged. Ashley smiled, then looked at each of the girls, "Glad to meet you." Then, she smiled at me, "Call me, if you'd like to get together before you leave."

Ashley took off her pareo, put it on a rock, and walked under the waterfall.

Kelly said, "She seems nice." She looked at me, "You'll have to tell me the story, sometime." There wasn't really much of a story; but I nodded, and the five of us walked back to our campsite. The girls decided to 'dress' for dinner.

I turned on the backpacking stove, and heated the cashews. Then, I put the pot of water on the stove and dumped in the baggie of instant rice. Within a couple of minutes, it was boiling, and I turned off the stove, and took off the pot. After five minutes, I transferred the cooked rice to one of the bowls. Then, I went to the waterfall, and filled the pot again, and put it back on the camp stove.

About this time, the girls were sitting in a circle on the sheet, and I served the vodka lemonades – only enough for one cup for each of us, and the warm cashews. "Here's to everyone making it safely to Kalalau! Nobody fell off the trail, was washed down the stream, or got attacked by a wild boar."

Linda screamed, "Wild boar? You didn't tell us about *those*."

I nodded, "There are a lot of bow hunters along the Na Pali, like Christian, who hunt goats or wild boar. After they clean what they've caught, they have to carry the carcass back to the road. It takes a lot of effort."

I sipped and savored the warm, and warming, drink. "Anyway, you guys did great. And we're going to have two days that I hope you'll find amazing." The girls raised their glasses, and tasted their drinks.

The water was boiling, so I took off the top and carefully inserted the five foil packets of Indian food. There was *Punjab Eggplant*, *Aloo Gobi*, *Saag Paneer*, *Murgh Tikka Masala*, and *Madras Dal*. The food would be cooking for another five minutes, so I finished my drink, and had a few cashews.

The girls got their water bottles, and Julie and Kelly took up my offer of mixing lemonade powder into them. I did have a few more bottles of vodka ... and we would be receiving the wine and beer tomorrow, so I pulled them out of my pack, and put them on the sheet.

I turned off the stove and dumped the water out of the pot. Then, I pulled out each foil pack, ripped the top off, and dumped each Indian dish into one of the plastic bowls. With the rice, we now had a six-course Indian meal that I set on the sheet.

"Bon appétit!" Everyone sampled the dishes, putting them on their paper plate. I had made a crude fire pit, but we hadn't collected enough wood for cooking; at least, I would be able to burn the plates ...

As we ate, Kelly pointed, and we watched the sunset. Even though we were only twenty feet above the water, we saw a clear green flash. We all cheered, and there were also cheers from elsewhere on the beach and the campground. The sky was clear, the color morphing from red-orange through blue and purple.

I cut the limes, some of us using them as a garnish for the Indian food, and a couple of the girls dropping a wedge of lime into their lemonade and vodka.

The girls sat cross-legged on the sheet, Kathy in her pareo (this time, tied above her breasts, and coming down to her knees), Linda in her red dirt t-shirt, and Julie in a tank and her bikini underwear. Kelly wore a bikini top and a clean pair of running shorts.

When we were done, I pulled a garbage bag out of my pack, and dropped in the foil packages, the aluminum foil, and a few other bits of trash, twisted the top, and put a tie around it. Fortunately, there were no bears on Kauai that could get into the trash.

I pulled a small flashlight from my shorts pocket, and headed toward the small trail down to the beach. "I'm going down to the beach to pee."

As I started down the trail, Kathy stood, and said, "I think I'll join you."

Then, Linda stood, "Me, too."

We walked down the trail, and across the beach, almost to the water. The girls squatted, and we all peed in the sand. It was already dark, and we could barely see each other. I knew a crescent moon would be rising, but it was behind the mountain at the back of the campground.

As we walked back, we could see a couple of fires inside the huge cave, where at least a dozen people were camping, including Ashley. We climbed up the trail to the campsite, and Kelly's friends set-up their sleeping bags on the ground cloth under the fly.

"If it suddenly starts raining hard, and you guys are getting wet, you can come into our tent." It briefly occurred to me that we could have a different threesome every night in the tent; but we were all tired, and I wasn't going to suggest anything 'exciting' tonight.

The market had already stocked candies for Halloween, and I'd bought a couple of small bags of bite-size candies that I opened, and passed around. We weren't going to worry about calories today, as we had expended tremendous energy on the hike.

Kelly and I walked to the waterfall, and then a bit down the stream, and I washed out the bowls and utensils, as Kelly held the flashlight. There was amazingly little to clean up, after having a six-course meal.

I pumped water into everyone's water bottles, and took a handful of the candies, giving one to each of Kelly's friends. "Chocolates for your pillow."

Linda laughed, "Yeah. It would be nice, if we *had* pillows."

Julie chided her, "Just wrap your t-shirt over some soft clothes, and put it on your pack." Linda gave her a dirty look; it wasn't the same as having a real pillow. But we were camping, and had to 'rough it' a little.

I made sure that the girls took a look at the incredible canopy of stars that now filled the sky. The Milky Way was clearly visible cutting diagonally across the heavens.

I kissed each of the girls goodnight, and said, "You guys can sleep as late as you want, tomorrow morning."

Chuckling, I amended the comment, "Or ... sleep as late as you can. Tomorrow should be a relaxing day."

Kathy coughed, and I heard Linda mutter, under her breath, "Likely story!". I went out to the trail, and up to the next terrace, where our tent was set-up. Kelly had already undressed, and had put on *her* red dirt t-shirt.

We decided not to zip the sleeping bags together; it was too warm to sleep next to each other. Kelly lay on her back on her open sleeping bag, and I crawled over, and between her legs. We made love silently and, within minutes, we were asleep on our own sides of the tent.

CHAPTER 15: FAR OUT CAMPING

When I woke, the light was dim, and I lay in my sleeping bag, listening to the sound of the waterfall. Birds squawked somewhere outside the tent. I looked over at Sam; he was on his stomach, sleeping soundly, the top of his sleeping bag folded back so that only his legs were covered.

The Indian dinner last night had been great, but I was now urgently needing to go. I took the toilet paper from my pack, put on my flip-flops, and walked to the composting toilets in my tee and panties.

The first step was to throw dried leaves, from a trash bin, into the toilet. I stepped in and closed the door. It was a little stinky, but functional.

Sam was up when I returned to the tent, sorting through items as he packed the top portion of his pack, which he had removed to use as a fanny pack for today's hike into the valley.

He smiled at me, "Good morning!" He pulled things out of his pack, and asked me to put them on the sheet: A large baggie of cereal, a few oranges, the trail mix, and some small boxes of raisins. "I don't think we have much else for breakfast, until RJ arrives."

Then, Sam gave me a serious look, "I *hope* he arrives. He's not the most reliable person, but at least the surf's not up." Sam chuckled, then turned serious again, "We would be in trouble, if he didn't show up."

My friends came into the campsite, and sat on the sheet. Sam offered, "I can make coffee, if anyone wants." Julie and Linda nodded, and I decided I could use some caffeine, myself.

As we munched on the breakfast fare, Sam went to the waterfall, and filled the pot. He lit the camp stove, and took out a small jar of instant coffee; it was nothing that he would normally drink, but fine for camping. Ten minutes later, he poured the coffee into cups; but they were too hot to pick up for a few more minutes.

Linda asked, "So what's the plan for today, Sam?"

Sam swallowed his raisins and nodded, "I have to stick around until about 10AM for RJ. He's supposed to bring two coolers and three waterproof bags – we'll have wine and beer, plenty of food, some extra clothes, another tarp ... and a few more items." Sam smiled, and I had an idea of *what* items he might have brought.

"In the meantime, we can do whatever you want. I wouldn't mind walking down to the end of the beach with you – we can explore some more caves, and I can show you where we'll be swimming tomorrow. Or we can go for a swim, or just take it easy."

Sam popped a few more raisins into his mouth. "After we get our supplies, I'd like to take you to 'Ginger Pools'. It's only a short – and very easy – hike; but it's a truly idyllic spot." Sam looked at me, "Much better than our pond at home."

He took a swig of lemonade from his water bottle. "If you guys want more of a challenge, we could hike up into the valley; some parts might have to be 'cross country' – without a trail. There are gardens up there, waterfalls ... it's beautiful."

Julie said, somewhat sourly, "Relaxing sounds better than challenging, Sam. We had our challenge yesterday."

Sam smiled, "What? You don't think we should have a daily challenge?" Julie shook her head; so did Kathy. "OK. You guys will have a challenge tomorrow, actually a couple of challenges; so I guess we can relax, today."

We finished eating, and Julie asked, "How should we dress for our beach excursion?"

Sam replied, "Any way you want. I'm usually nude while I'm here, unless it rains hard or gets cool at night. You could wear a bathing suit, or shorts and a top. But my suggestion is to wear something comfortable. Or nothing."

Julie nodded. "Can we have 20 minutes, before we leave?"

"Of course, Julie. We can leave whenever you guys are ready." Then, Sam stood, "I'm going to take a quick shower." He walked toward the waterfall, as my friends went back to their campsite. Twenty minutes later, we re-convened, and walked down the narrow, steep trail to the beach.

We were lucky again: The weather was beautiful. I watched, as the girls negotiated the short trail down to the beach. Kelly, in the lead, was nude, as was Kathy. Kathy had a good all-over tan, I guess due to her trip to Mexico. Linda wore her red dirt t-shirt, and what looked like a bikini bottom.

Julie wore only a white thong; she looked the sexiest, topless and in a skimpy bottom. On this remote beach, at least half the people were nude, and it seemed like the 'natural' thing to do.

We walked along the water, past the large cave, and the small cave with the pond. Near the end of the beach, there was a jumble of rocks, and the entrance to another cave.

We peeked in: It was huge inside, with a ceiling at least fifty feet above us, but was mostly filled by another jumble of rocks. At the far end, the top of the cave was open, admitting light that formed rays cutting diagonally down to a large boulder.

I looked at Kelly, "It looks fairly dangerous. The lava rock isn't stable; people get hurt all the time, trying to climb it as they would granite." She nodded; I didn't think that any of her friends was interested in spelunking, today.

The beach narrowed, as we approached the end of the sand – the 'jumping off point' (literally) for our visit to Honopu, tomorrow. The small inlet, surrounded by rocks, was as calm as I'd ever seen it; hopefully, the conditions would hold until tomorrow.

Pointing to the water, I explained, "Here is where we'll start our swim tomorrow. It really isn't very far, but this little inlet can sometimes be very rough. But it's only a little choppy now, and I know you're all good swimmers."

Then, I walked to the edge of the water, and pointed, "Honopu Beach is just around the corner. It's actually two beaches, divided by a huge rock arch, as you saw from the helicopter, and from RJ's boat. And there's a waterfall, and a little stream. It's my favorite place on the island."

I walked out on some rocks, but still couldn't see the beach. "It's a sacred place, and boats can't land there. So, we should be the only ones on the beach." I really hoped that would be true.

As we walked back, Kelly pointed, "Is that him?"

Squinting, I saw a Zodiac heading along the beach, just offshore. "I think it is." I wasn't wearing my watch, but didn't think it was ten o'clock, already; RJ was early.

I ran down the beach, trailed by Kelly, and we were panting by the time we were even with our campsite. RJ's Zodiac bobbed in the water a hundred yards offshore. I waved to him, and he waved back. "Does anybody want to help me ferry some things into the beach? It'll be a pretty long swim."

Both Kelly and Julie decided to come with me. Again, it was very lucky that there weren't big waves crashing on the beach, and we made it out easily, taking only five minutes to swim out to the boat.

RJ lifted the large cooler over the tube, and handed it to me. It floated, and he had sealed it with duct tape. Then, he began handing the waterproof bags to us, as we treaded water. Kelly took two, and I took one. Then, RJ handed the second cooler to Julie, grunting. I knew that must be the important one – with the beers.

I waved to RJ, "So tomorrow afternoon? Maybe around 4PM?" RJ gave me the 'OK' sign, and started the motor. Then, he waved again, and headed offshore. I turned back once more, and saw him putting out fishing lines, as he motored away from the beach.

Julie, Kelly and I swam the coolers and bags to the beach; it took a while, but everything floated, so we just had to drag it along, as we side-stroked in. Kathy and Linda helped Julie and I carry the coolers, and we finally got everything up the trail and to our campsite.

"Isn't it about lunchtime, now?" I was joking, but as I looked through the bags, I pulled out a few boxes of ramen, and held them up. Surprisingly, all of the girls nodded, and I got the camp stove started again, and went to the waterfall to fill the pot.

There were several people there – two guys in surf trunks, the female partners in bikini bottoms, and an older couple (probably my age) who were nude. Everyone took turns in the shower, and I managed to stick my pot in, and fill it quickly.

People seemed nicer here, more cooperative than most people you would meet in a city. Accepting of other people, no matter their skin color, or whether they were dressed or nude. I walked back to the campsite, and boiled the water, then made the ramen.

When everyone was eating, Kelly looked up at me, "Aren't you going to eat?"

I laughed, as I bent over, opened one of the coolers, and pulled out a beer. "I'm going to drink my lunch." Linda chuckled, and Kelly shook her head.

After our early lunch, we walked along the trail, heading back to the Kalalau Stream. Kelly and Julie had put on cover-ups, but I decided to hike *au naturel*, wearing only my flip-flops, and a fanny pack. I carried two towels. Kelly and Linda had their cameras, and all the girls wore their running shoes.

We turned up another trail near the stream, and headed into the valley. Suddenly, the wind stopped and it felt hot. We walked uphill on a dirt path, past a boulder field, and Century plants. The flora was huge, dwarfing us, and we were still just at the entrance to the valley.

The ground leveled, and we walked under a canopy of trees, past a huge mango tree, and along a winding path covered with leaves. I pointed, "These are ancient ruins, walls from the time Kalalau Valley was heavily populated, with a few thousand native Hawaiians here." We passed a couple of *heiau*, or Hawaiian sacred sites, just up from the stream.

As we continued walking, I told the story of *Koolau*, a *paniolo*, or Hawaiian cowboy, who had gotten leprosy, and was banned to the leper colony on Molokai. "But he escaped, and brought his family to Kauai, hiding out in a cave high in this valley. That was in the 1890's. People tried to find him, but never did.

"This valley was also famous for the *menehune*, the so-called 'little people', who may have lived here 1000 years ago, before Polynesians came here in sailing canoes." We walked up, from one terrace to another, passing a series of ancient rock walls.

We got to a stream, and I pointed to the other side, where a trail wound up the hill, "That's the main trail into the valley. A lot of the trail is along the stream, and there are some great pools and waterfalls."

Then, I turned left, "But we're just going to stay in the lower valley; I think you'll like Ginger Pools."

A few minutes later, Linda exclaimed, "A teepee!"

We looked at the crude structure, and I explained, "It's a 'sweat lodge' built by locals. They heat up stones, and then bring them inside, and it gets really hot." We looked at the oblong hut. "It can be dangerous, but I've always wanted to try it; like going into the sauna."

Finally, we turned onto a tiny trail, through lush tropical vegetation, and came out on a large flat surface of rock next to one of the offshoots of Kalalau Stream. Kathy exclaimed, "This is beautiful!" And it was.

There were huge boulders, making up several pools, one below the other, with bright red torch ginger, ferns, and many other tropical plants surrounding the pools, almost as if a landscape designer had created it.

The gurgling of the water was very relaxing, and we were the only ones here. But I knew that wouldn't last for long. I opened my fanny pack, and held up my pipe, "I was so tired, I forgot last night that I had brought this; but, maybe we could partake now, if you like?"

Julie's eyes lit up, and both Kathy and Linda were nodding. So I filled the bowl of the pipe with grass, and we passed it around, as we admired the scenery around us.

In between puffs, I pointed upstream, "There's a 'slippery slide' up there that leads down to this pool. And, if you want, we could explore the stream – swimming across each pool, and then climbing up or down the boulders to the next level."

The girls had their shoes off, and took off what little clothes they wore. Kathy laid out on another boulder, while Julie and Linda walked across rocks to the stream, and then climbed up to the next level. I heard Linda shout a 'Wow!', and Kelly and I joined them.

There was a cascading waterfall, only about five feet high, but the fast-flowing water made numerous small falls into a shallow pool below. Julie was lying back in the water, her hair under one of the small waterfalls.

Kelly nodded, "It's *really* beautiful, here."

I agreed, "Not that many visitors to Kauai actually see Kalalau Valley. There weren't many people camping on the beach, and you may have noticed that quite a few were European. They seem to be more adventurous than most Americans." I always strived to not be cast in with 'most'.

Near the downstream end of the pool was a narrow channel. I had never tried this without a bathing suit, but it felt pretty smooth. I sat down, and turned my head back to Julie and Linda, "And here's the slippery slide!"

I pushed off, and slid down the rock, shooting over the edge and down a few feet into the lower pool. The water splashed up on the rock were Kathy was. "Sorry!" Kathy raised her head and smiled.

A moment later, Kelly came sliding down, and splashing in the water. Then came Julie and finally Linda. Kathy got up, and slipped into the cool water of the pool with us. It wasn't much bigger than a big jacuzzi, and was tight for the five of us; but I always enjoyed being 'tight' with the girls.

When we got out, I pulled out the rest of the trail mix from my fanny pack, along with some dried mango that I'd packed in one of the waterproof bags. Passing around the snacks, I noticed the lack of insects here; for the past week we'd not had a problem with mosquitos. It was probably the unusually dry weather.

We were all relaxing on the rocks, the only sound the babbling of the water in the stream, until we heard voices. Two young couples – the ones I'd seen this morning in the waterfall – came through the foliage, and onto the boulders of Ginger Pools.

The two guys eyed Kelly, Julie, Linda and Kathy – all now lying or sitting nude on the boulders. The girls giggled, and pulled off their tops, then jumped into the small pool. The guys followed, and there was a lot of splashing and joking around.

They finally got out of the water, and the two guys decided to explore downstream, while the girls sat on one of the boulders. They were whispering, and finally both took off their bikini bottoms, and lay on the warmth of the boulder – one on her back, and one on her front.

The sun was getting hotter, and it was humid. Ginger Pools was again silent, save for the sounds of the water. A while later, we heard some shouting and laughing, and the two guys climbed back up to the rocky ledge over the pool.

The two girls sat up, and the guys walked over to them, leaning against the boulder, and whispering to them. I got the feeling that the guys hadn't expected the girls to go nude. There was some shaking of heads, then the girls slipped off the boulder onto the rock ledge.

The guys were still shaking their heads, but pushed down their trunks, and they all jumped into the pool. I walked over to Kelly, and sat with her in the shade of a huge palm. "So what do you think?"

Kelly laughed, "I think I could live here. If I didn't have school, or work, or a career." I nodded; that was how I felt, too. Not that we would be living in Kalalau, but I loved the island, and this place was accessible – either by hiking the trail or, even quicker, kayaking down the coast.

The four kids climbed out of the pool, and there was a sudden downpour. They ran over to their small packs, got dressed, and ran across the rock, quickly disappearing down the trail.

It was still drizzling, and we all got back into the pool. The water was crystal clear. Kathy asked, "Is this water safe to drink? It *looks* clean."

I shook my head, "No. All of the streams here – including the waterfall by our campsite – are polluted by the animals living higher in the valley. They're known to have *leptospirosis*."

Linda scrunched her face, "Lepton spirals?"

I laughed, "Leptospirosis is a bacterium that can infect you. Then, you would need antibiotics, or it could get serious: It could lead to kidney or liver damage, meningitis, or even death." Linda's eyes went large, and now both Julie and Kathy were listening.

"You can be infected by getting water onto open sores, drinking it, or even through mucous membranes – such as your nose, mouth, or eyes. But as long as you don't have open cuts or drink the water, you should be safe."

Then, I had to add, "I *told* you this was an adventurous place ... and that means there is some danger." I laughed, "But I'll try to make sure nobody dies here."

Julie said sarcastically, "Gee, thanks, Sam."

Linda chimed in, "Yeah. I didn't come here to die of a tropical disease." I thought she was saying it as a joke, but her concern sounded serious.

"I don't think many people die from leptospirosis; only if you're infected and don't take the antibiotics."

Then I remembered, "Sometimes, people visit a tropical place like this, then go home and feel like they have a flu. If they don't tell their doctor where they've been, he might not think of leptospirosis. That's when it can get dangerous."

I pushed off from the rock on one side of the pool, and glided to the other side, then made my way to the little waterfall coming down the slippery slide, and stuck my head under. The water was cool, but felt perfect on a hot, humid day like this.

The rain stopped, and we got out, and I passed a towel around, then we sat on the rocks a while longer. Finally, we decided to head back to the beach. "Let's try to find some dead wood that we can carry, so that we can have a campfire tonight."

We walked the winding trail back, collecting whatever branches we could find on the ground. Stopping under the mango tree, I was able to find three ripe mangos that had just fallen to the ground. Kelly and I shared one, and Kathy ate a whole one, savoring the delicious fruit.

The mango tree looked quite old, and had to be at least forty feet across. Unfortunately, the branches were too high off the ground to collect any more mangos, so we continued down the trail.

By the time we reached the beach, we all had an armful of dried branches. We brought them back to the campsite, and put them under the tarp, lest it rain again and soak them.

It was late afternoon, and I pulled a rosé wine from the cooler. Using the corkscrew on my knife, I opened the bottle and poured cups for everyone. We sat under the shade of a tree that separated our campsites, looking out at the whitecaps now dotting the water, and watching two kayaks land on the beach.

I told the girls, "I originally wanted us to kayak down, and then hike the trail back, but the logistics were too difficult."

I sipped some wine, and explained, "RJ couldn't fit five kayaks on his boat, not even three. And towing them back uphill to Hanalei would be a pain – not to mention preventing RJ from fishing along the way. So we'll have to kayak down here another time ... then all the way around to the west side."

The wine didn't last long, being split five ways, and I grabbed a can of IPA from the cooler, and began working on the fire pit. I built up the sides with rocks, then pulled the grate I'd bought at the market from one of the bags, and placed it across the rocks.

When I had everything adjusted, I put the grate on the sheet, and arranged some scrap paper, small twigs, then larger pieces of branches in the center of the pit. Kelly walked over, "What's for dinner?"

Julie, Kathy, and Linda came over, and we all sat on the sheet. "First, we have more wine – red and white – and also a couple of kinds of beer. Also in the cooler are a dozen bottles of water and a few six packs of soft drinks. I don't have much for appetizers, except the beef jerky and dried mango.

"I made a nice salad in the condo, and put it in a large baggie, and I brought a bottle of dressing." Then, I smiled at the girls, "Tonight, we're going to have fresh fish, grilled over a wood fire." There were smiles all around, and Linda was licking her chops.

"I'm not sure what RJ provided for us; I had suggested ahi, but it depended on what he caught yesterday."

I took another swig of beer, and added, "And we will bake potatoes. I was going to bring the potato salad, but decided to leave it at the party – it was mostly finished. So I bought some nice big potatoes yesterday morning, and partially cooked them in the microwave. Hopefully, they'll get finished on the fire."

I hoped that we would have enough wood. Some of the branches were quite thick, so they would burn for a long time. I decided not to tell the girls about the dessert; they would have to find out later, but I had a feeling they would enjoy it.

It was getting hot again, "Anybody for a quick swim? Then we can shower off, and I can serve the salad." The girls looked at each other and shrugged. Somewhat reluctantly, they stood, and we all walked across the beach.

The girls ditched their clothes near the waterline, and we swam out past the small waves. I floated on my back, looking up at the sky; it was still mostly clear, but a few clouds were gliding past us.

I hoped it wouldn't rain until *after* dinner. A heavy rain right now might foil my dinner plans. And I knew the fresh air had made us all hungry.

We stayed in the water quite a while, drifting slowly along the beach, and finally getting out about halfway to the end of the beach. Then, we walked across the hot sand, and took a waterfall shower together.

The sun was low by the time the girls were dressed for dinner and sitting around the sheet. We didn't have a mixing bowl, so I poured dressing into the baggie with the salad, sealed it, and shook it to 'toss' the salad.

I served the salad, and asked the girls what they wanted to drink. Kelly said, "I wouldn't mind some white wine."

Kathy decided on a can of guava nectar, Julie and Linda decided to go with wine, and I took another beer. We ate our salads, a treat to have fresh, cold vegetables. And even more of a treat – for me, at least – to have a nice cold beer; or three.

I started the fire and, when the large branches were burning well, put the grate over the pit. I wrapped each potato in foil with a pat of butter, and put them on the grate. Then, I sat with the girls, drinking our drinks, and watching the sun creep lower to the horizon.

There were a lot more clouds, now, and I hoped it would clear enough to see the stars; and possibly sleep out on the beach. The sun disappeared behind clouds on the horizon, and I realized there would be no green flash this evening.

But just after the sun set, the clouds became a kaleidoscope of colors; it was spectacular. Kelly and Julie took a few snapshots of us sitting on the sheet, our tent in the background, with the colorful sky above.

Then, they ran down to the water, to take pictures of the cliffs, '*Na Pali*', bathed in the orange glow of the sunset, the eroded spires towering thousands of feet above our campsite.

I moved the potatoes onto the burning branches, now red hot, and turning into charcoal. Then, I opened the package of fish. It was *mahi mahi*, sometimes called dorado or dolphinfish, although it was a true fish, and not a dolphin. RJ had prepared five beautiful steaks, probably a half a pound or more each.

Shaking some salt and pepper on the fish, I put the filets on the grate. The fire was now mostly embers, but smoke was also rising through the grate. Fortunately, the slight breeze blew it over the bluff toward the beach, and not toward our sheet.

The fish didn't take long to cook, and I placed a filet on each plate. Then, I gingerly pulled the potatoes out of the fire, squeezing them to test their doneness, and unwrapped them, placing one on each of the plates. I pulled a small cutting board and knife from one of the bags, and cut some lemon wedges, which I used to garnish each plate.

I put the butter into one of the small bowls, and handed it to Kelly to put in the middle of the sheet, along with the salt and pepper. Then, I made a sour cream sauce for the baked potatoes, cutting up some chives, and mixing those into the sour cream with seasoned salt and pepper.

We passed around the plates, and I poured more white wine, taking a cup myself. I turned to Kelly, "Did I forget anything?" I looked around, but it appeared that our dinners were complete.

Kelly shrugged, "Sit down, Sam. I think we're all doing OK." I tasted the fish, and it was incredible; RJ had outdone himself, providing us with something that couldn't be bought at the market.

"Yum!" Linda cried, as she tasted the fish.

Kathy nodded, "This is really fantastic. Maybe the best fish I've ever had." I nodded. It was very good, but I couldn't decide whether it was better than the ahi steaks we'd had a week ago in Hanalei.

This was our tenth day on the island, and I felt satisfied that Kelly and her friends had gotten a good feel for Kauai – including the scenery around the island, and some of the adventurous activities available here. I hoped to snorkel again, if the ocean stayed calm, but we had already done most of the things that I loved here.

Kelly looked up at her friends, "Sam really will make a great wife, someday. In all the time I've been with him, his cooking has never disappointed me." Linda was nodding her head, as she dug into her fish.

I laughed, "I call this 'luxury camping'. We're about as remote as you can get, but the boat delivery enabled us to have fresh fish and cold drinks."

Then, I filled them in on the plans. "Our permits allow us to stay here tomorrow night ... and I brought spaghetti and made spaghetti sauce for dinner ... but I decided to tell RJ to pick us up tomorrow afternoon. I hope you guys aren't disappointed." The girls shook their heads.

I felt I had to explain, "First, we've really been lucky with the weather, and I didn't want to push our luck another day. Second, we need to get Kathy down to Wailua on Thursday, and leaving here Thursday morning would put us on a tight schedule. And, third, we've got the house, which I think will be much more comfortable than camping out a third night."

Julie said, "That sounds fine, Sam. We're getting a pretty good feeling for the camping experience, and what's here in Kalalau."

Kathy said, sincerely, "Thank you, Sam. That's very thoughtful of you. I'll need to pack a few things before we meet Christian." She smiled, "And, I wouldn't mind taking a *real* shower, before I see him." We all laughed.

We had all finished our plates. "Did everybody get enough to eat? If you guys are still hungry, we could have a second course of spaghetti ..." There were groans all around, and Linda said, "We've had plenty, Sam."

"Then I guess you wouldn't be interested in dessert?" Now Linda was all ears. "I didn't bring any cakes or pies ... but what's camping without marshmallows?"

Linda and Julie were both clapping their hands, when I added, "And, if you want something really traditional, I brought everything to make s'mores."

Now, Linda and Julie went wild, and Linda crawled across the sheet to kiss me, nearly tipping over Kathy's guava nectar, and a couple of cups that still had wine. I looked at her, "I thought you were on a diet?"

Before she could find a suitable retort, I said, "Linda, I'm just kidding. It's because we all dieted and got into shape that we could even be here. And, we've gotten plenty of exercise. So this is just a little reward."

Julie and Kelly cleaned up the dinner things, and went to the stream to wash off the utensils and the plastic plates we'd used. I used a couple of small branches to remove the grate from the fire, setting it aside next to the back guy wires of the tent. I would either be bringing it back, or giving it to one of the other campers.

I put a few more large branches on the fire, and they flared up, lighting our campsite in flickering orange light, in the now-dark evening. The stars were coming out, and the crescent moon was already in the sky over the mountain behind the campsite.

When the large branches were all embers, I took my knife and stripped a few of the smaller, greener branches, and handed them to the girls. We pulled the sheet around the campfire, and sat down in a semi-circle. I took out the graham crackers, a few chocolate bars, and the bag of marshmallows.

As Linda skewered a marshmallow on her branch, and twisted it over the embers, I held up the chocolate bars, "I have a couple of regular milk chocolate bars, and one with dark chocolate and 70% cacao."

The girls were now fighting over positions for their marshmallows over the coals, the white cylinders now puffing up, and darkening around the edges. Julie's caught on fire, and she blew it out, then put an edge of the marshmallow in her mouth, and pulled it off the branch. "I love this! When was the last time we roasted marshmallows over a campfire?"

There was silence, and then Linda volunteered, "We had to be in middle school. It must have been in girl scouts."

Even Kathy seemed to be enjoying the sugary dessert. Everyone was now roasting their second marshmallow, and preparing the s'mores with two graham crackers, and four squares of chocolate broken off the bar. As they moaned with delight, I roasted a marshmallow, and popped it into my mouth.

I smiled at the smiling faces, and said, "I think I brought a few miniatures of brandy or liqueurs, if you guys would like that with your s'mores."

There were shaking heads all around. I finished the little bit of wine left, drinking it from the upturned bottle. Then, I opened the drink cooler, and passed around cold water bottles.

All our fingers were sticky, and we walked to the waterfall, using our flashlights to light the way. The water felt much cooler now, and none of us actually took a shower, but we all washed our hands. We sat around the fire a while longer, until the embers were white, and had burned mostly down to charcoal and ash.

Looking up at the sky, we saw millions of stars, and only one or two small clouds illuminated from behind by the waxing moon. I pulled the tarp out of one of the river bags, and walked the trail down to the beach to lay it out, holding it down with rocks.

I went up to the campsite, and told the girls, "It would a great experience to sleep out under the stars tonight. And it looks clear. But it could always rain. So I'll leave it up to you guys. I suggest you bring your sleeping bag, maybe unzip it, and we can all sleep on the tarp next to each other." I smiled thinly at them, "And, if it rains, we can run back under the fly or into the tent."

We all put on our red dirt t-shirts, carried our sleeping bags and water bottles down the trail, and laid them out next to each other on the large tarp. Kathy walked across the beach toward the water to pee, while the other girls unzipped the sleeping bags, making one large bed for the five of us.

Kathy came back, and got into our 'bed' on the opposite side from me. Linda was next to her, and Kelly next to me, with Julie in the middle.

I sat up, "May I visit with each of you for a few minutes?" The girls shrugged and nodded. It was quite dark, and we could barely see each other in the light of the crescent moon. I walked around the tarp, and climbed under the sleeping bag with Kathy.

There was no room to lie next to her, so I straddled her hips, and lowered my head to hers. I gave her a light kiss on the lips. "How are you doing, Kathy?"

Kathy put her arms around me and hugged me. "I'm fine, Sam. This really has been an incredible trip."

"But you're a little preoccupied ... with Christian?"

Kathy closed her eyes, then opened them and looked into mine, "Sorry, Sam."

I gave Kathy another peck, "Not at all, Kathy. I understand. You'll be with him in 40 hours. Just try to have fun in the meantime."

Kathy smiled, "I am, Sam. Ginger Pools was fun, and the dinner you made was great."

We rubbed noses, "Good night, Kathy." She lifted her head, and kissed me on the lips.

"Good night, Sam."

I crawled sideways off Kathy and straddled Linda, lowering myself onto her. "How about you, Linda. Are you OK?" I ran my hand through her hair. Linda put her hand behind my head, pulled me down to her, and we kissed.

I put my hand under Linda's tee, and took her breast in my hand. I let my hand run down her side, and held her hip. Linda smiled, and I raised my eyebrows.

"Not tonight, Sam. Let's just sleep under the stars, like you suggested." I gave her a pouting look, and she put her finger on my lips, "I'll make it up to you." And I was sure that she would.

As I began to crawl over to Julie, I realized that she was turned to Kelly. I tapped her on the shoulder, and she turned onto her back. "Do you want to join us, Sam?"

I straddled Julie, "I guess I don't have to ask how *you* are." I lowered my head and gave Julie a deep kiss. Then, I chuckled, "Well, I'm pretty tired. So let me tell Kelly good night, and then you can have her."

I was joking, but knew that Kelly and Julie might really get it on, squeezed between Linda and I. And that would be OK with me. Not that I wouldn't have liked to make it with both Julie and Kelly. I began to fantasize about making it with all the girls together.

Crawling sideways one last time, I straddled Kelly, and kissed her. "Did you have a fun day?"

Kelly chuckled, "It was great, Sam." She smiled at me, "Let's make love and go to sleep." Now, I was confused.

"I thought you and Julie were going to get it on."

Kelly gave me a 'silly boy' look. Julie had turned the other way, and I got between Kelly's legs, and entered her. We made love slowly and quietly. Then, we lay on our backs and drifted off, looking up at the multitude of stars.

Yes, it had been quite a day. I had no doubt that tomorrow would be, also.

CHAPTER 16: HEAVENLY ARCH

It was really annoying: Here I was still asleep, and Sam was nibbling on my toes. Not that I wouldn't like it another time; when I was awake. Ow! He was getting a little rough. I opened an eye, and looked to my side.

Sam was lying there, snoring softly, obviously still asleep. My body propelled itself into a sitting position, and I looked down at my feet. My toes were sticking out of the bottom of the unzipped sleeping bag ... and a huge bird was pecking at them!

I couldn't help but yelp. There was another bird pecking at Linda's toes ... or maybe they were Kathy's. I pulled my feet under the sleeping bag, and tried to shoo the bird with my hands.

A moment later, Linda groaned, then lifted her head, and looked toward her feet. Instantaneously, she was on her feet, stamping on the sleeping bag, then taking a few steps toward the bird, until it finally waddled over to my side of the bed.

Linda looked at me with an incredulous look, her mouth open, and I nodded and smiled. Sam opened his eyes, "What?" I hadn't said anything.

I leaned over and kissed him, then said, "We have visitors." Now, Sam's head popped up, and he saw the birds; he began laughing, and within a minute both Julie and Kathy were awake.

Sam said, "*Nenes*, Hawaiian geese. They're usually pretty friendly."

I shook my head, "Yeah, really friendly – they were chewing on my toes."

Sam was still laughing. "I'm sure they didn't eat much. Should I kiss your toes to make them better?"

Julie and Kathy sat up in time to see the two birds take a few steps down the beach, and take off. In the air, they were beautiful. But it was still a rude way to be awakened.

We brought everything back up to our campsites, and Sam boiled water and made a pot of coffee, then a pot of oatmeal. He put out a small Tupperware of fruit, and the leftover maple syrup from our pancake breakfast.

Sam suggested that we take a couple of hours to get cleaned up and pack everything for the boat extraction this afternoon. Then, we would begin our next adventure.

It was already 10AM when we had the tent and tarp taken down, all the packs packed and put on the sheet with the tarp over them, and our fanny packs put into a garbage bag and then into one of the coolers.

Sam had decided that we should spend the day at Honopu, so we brought all the cold drinks we wanted, a bunch of snacks, a few clothing items, and our shoes, packing everything in the cooler.

RJ had put the duct tape in one of the bags, so that Sam could seal the coolers to bring them to the boat, so he sealed one now, putting the duct tape inside before running the tape all around.

Sam looked at the sealed cooler, and shook his head, "It may not be worth the effort to carry this down the beach and swim it around the corner ..."

But I grabbed the handle on one side, and Julie on the other, and soon we were all heading down the beach. When we got to the end of the sand, Sam pointed, and we put down the cooler. Sam sat on it, his back to the water, and facing a bunch of large rocks. The rocks and beach were still in shade, as the sun hadn't yet risen from behind the mountains. We all sat down, and awaited Sam's instructions.

Sam looked at the small inlet, circled by rocks, just a ten-foot beach from which we could safely swim. Although it seemed calm looking out to sea, the inlet was choppy, from one side to the other.

"I hope today will be special, for all of us. First, the beach is very special – the only way to get there is to swim, either from here, or from a boat." He pointed to the inlet.

"The valley is a spiritual place; it's called the 'Valley of the Lost Tribe,' because until about 150 years ago, there were people living here."

Sam continued his lecture, "Because it's spiritual, the local chiefs were buried in caves in the mountains, and there are temples and burial grounds in the valley." He smiled, "Also, Honopu Beach has been used in a lot of movies – the 1970's *King Kong*', and *Raiders of the Lost Ark*', among them." Sam had told us this, already.

Rubbing his eyes, Sam looked down, "Sarah and I came here as part of a helicopter tour organized by Club Med, which was located above the Hanalei River, in the old plantation house from the movie *South Pacific*'. I'll tell you that story another time ... but Honopu will always be special to me."

Now he looked at each of us, "I'm hoping that nobody else will be on the beach; you can see why most people don't swim there ... it can be dangerous. We're very lucky it's calm today, and I know you guys can make it."

He pointed to the cooler on which he was sitting, "I want you guys to swim – probably the crawl to get out of this inlet, and then you can side-stroke, if you want. I'll float the cooler, and if any of you are having problems in the water, you can use it as a floatation device to rest for a few minutes."

Sam coughed, "And, I would like you guys to consider today a 'submission' experience. It shouldn't be too challenging, but I'd like to suggest our activities there ... and you can probably expect that I'll pick one or two of my 'favorite things'."

Linda glanced at me, and I heard a quiet, "Oh, no." I had no idea what Sam was planning.

Sam smiled, "On the other hand, I have the responsibility to take care of you, make sure you're OK, and ensure that you're having fun ... at least, most of the time. And I take that responsibility seriously."

We all nodded, and Sam knew that we would all cooperate with anything he wanted to do. It was a matter of trust – that Sam wouldn't ask anything too much of us; and he'd already tested all of us to find out how much we could take.

And we *trusted* Sam. Of course, we knew that he was turned on by certain things – spanking, medical stuff; but we'd already experienced everything Sam could throw at us, and we all knew we would submit to Sam. And some of us were even turned on by the same things.

Sam stood, "So are we all ready?" We stood, and nodded. We were a motley group: Kathy, Sam and I were nude, Julie wore a thong, and Linda was in a bikini – her body looking incredibly good after her weight loss ... and despite everything we'd eaten here on Kauai.

Sam dragged the cooler to the edge of the water, the choppy waves splashing up against it. "I could swim each of you out of this inlet, but you're all strong women, and should have no problem swimming yourself. I'll swim out with the cooler, and wait for you in the open water, far enough out that we won't get bashed into the rocks."

He waded in, up to his knees, the rocking of the cooler nearly making me seasick, just watching it. "Then, you guys should swim out one-by-one, with the strongest and most confident of you going last. When you get to me, you can tread water or float, or head in to the beach."

Sam pointed, then turned, and side-stroked out, one hand pulling the cooler. It didn't look that bad, and Sam did fine.

We all followed – first Linda, then Kathy. Julie and I looked at each other, and she smiled, "You can go next." I shrugged, and swam out, easily making it to Sam, although the waves had pushed me back and forth, with the rocks only a few feet away.

Julie was right behind me, and we all treaded water next to Sam and the cooler. "Great job! Now, we just have to swim in to the beach. There are usually breaking waves, but it looks calm, today."

We all swam toward the beach, but it was a lot farther than we'd thought. Linda had to rest a couple of times, and we all stopped with her. There *were* some waves breaking on the beach, but they were small, and we all made it safely with no problem.

Sam dragged the cooler up onto the beach, and we all stood around it. "Welcome to Honopu, otherwise known as Cathedrals Beach!" He looked up and pointed, "This curved rock cliff must be five hundred feet high, and that 'little' sand dune isn't so little when you try to climb it."

He smirked at us, "And we *will* be climbing it ... and doing a few other things."

I glanced at my friends, and none of them were complaining; their mouths were hanging open, and they were staring at the beach, the sand dune, and the incredible vertical cliff backing the beach.

Sam pointed down the beach, "And there's the famous Honopu rock arch. It's about a hundred feet above the beach. And you can see the stream coming through it, creating that little lagoon on the beach."

Sam and I carried the cooler along the harder sand near the water, then walked up alongside the lagoon and stream, until we were under the arch. Sam pointed to a boulder, and we carried the cooler and placed it on top of the large, flat-topped rock.

We all looked up: The 'ceiling' of the arch *had* to be a hundred feet up, as Sam had said. There were ferns growing out from the rock, and water dripping in many different places. I wondered how safe we were, under here.

Sam pulled off the duct tape, and opened the cooler, taking out the trash bag containing all of our stuff. He handed us the fanny packs, and put on his own.

Julie took off her thong, and Linda removed her bikini, stashing them in the trash bag, and Sam twisted the bag, and held it down with a couple of rocks. I now realized that the thousands of rocks sitting on the sand under the arch had probably fallen from the ceiling.

Sam reached into the cooler, and pulled out a water bottle for each of us. He chuckled, "Unless you're ready for beer or wine?"

We shook our heads, and he looked at Kathy, "Or sodas, or your juice ..." There were no takers, so Sam led the way through the arch, following the stream to the left of a sand dune. Walking over some rocks, we reached a small pool, and waterfall.

The waterfall wasn't very tall, but there was a lot of water coming down, as well as a cool breeze that chilled us, as we were still in the shadow of the mountain.

Sam pointed, and we climbed up on some rocks a little above the pool, where there was almost no wind. He pulled his fanny pack around, and unzipped it. "You don't have to submit to this ... it's only a suggestion, if you want to do it."

We all looked at him, his serious face cracking a smile as he pulled out the pipe, a lighter, and a small pill bottle of finely ground marijuana.

Once again, nobody complained, and we passed around the pipe, smoking local weed which, Julie noted, was better than anything we could get at home. Sam filled it again, and then a third time; we were all quite stoned by the time he put everything away.

And it was a good thing he'd given us the bottles of water. Of course, it wasn't an accident: Sam planned out everything ... at least, he tried to, when he could.

Sam pointed up the steep sand dune, and smiled. It was difficult, but we followed him up, taking advantage of the few rocks as foot-holds.

When we reached the top, there was a breeze again, and we had a magnificent view of the ocean ahead, the beach below and, to our right, the rock arch with the stream below, and the bright sand of the beach on the other side shining through the opening.

Sam suggested that we spend some time exploring, so we all made our way down the sand dune to the beach, then walked from one end to the other, before going back through the arch to the other beach, stopping to retrieve our flip-flops, as the sun was now above the mountain, and the sand was starting to get hot.

We walked to the far end of the beach, the cliff going around the corner to Kalalau, from where we'd swum. Then, we walked to the back of the beach, next to the towering curved cliff, and behind the sand dune.

It was amazing: As soon as we walked through the narrow space between the cliff and the sand dune, it was silent; the sound of the ocean – which we'd barely noticed – was now muted.

Sam gave me an evil smile, "I've always wondered ..." He looked at Julie, "Would you mind continuing, until you're out from behind the sand dune? On the beach?" Julie shook her head, questioningly. "I'd like to know if you can hear the spanking."

Kathy groaned and Linda smiled. Sam looked at me, "Would you like to volunteer?"

I shrugged, then stepped up to the cliff, bent at the waist, and put both my hands against the cool rock. "I'm ready, Sir."

Sam swung his hand; there was a loud 'CRACK!' as it impacted my bum. Sam gave me a hard swat every few seconds, six in all. Even here, the sound was hushed, with no echoes. Sam walked out to Julie, and they both walked back behind the sand dune. "Julie couldn't hear it."

Julie laughed, "And I was standing just at the corner of the sand dune."

Sam said, "OK. Just one more test." We all walked around the sand dune, and Sam asked Julie, Linda, and Kathy to walk down to the water. I followed Sam up the side of the sand dune – we were both carrying the flip-flops, our feet sinking into the soft sand.

It took several minutes to reach the top; Sam hadn't been kidding about how huge this dune was. He waved to my friends, then had me bend over and hold my knees, facing the ocean. He gave me another six hard swats, and I heard a distinct echo from the rock cliff behind us.

We walked down the steep front of the dune, and joined my friends on the wet sand. Sam asked, "So could you hear the spanks that time?" My friends all nodded.

Kathy said, "It's like an amphitheater: The sound was focused by the cliff. We could hear you pretty well."

We walked back to the arch, Linda, then Julie, stopping for a moment to pee, along the way. Sam opened the cooler, and pulled out a bunch of food that he stuffed into his fanny pack.

We each selected a drink – Sam, of course picking a beer, and the rest of us sodas. There was a bottle of white wine in the cooler, and Sam decided to bring that, along with several plastic cups. Then, Sam pulled the large sheet out of the garbage bag, and put the rocks on it again.

Sam stood and smiled at us, "So where would you like to have a picnic? There's the top of the sand dune, the beach below, next to the lagoon, here under the arch, on the other beach, on the sand dune above it, or by the waterfall?"

I chided, "You're giving us too many choices!"

Linda spoke up, "How about by the pool under the waterfall?" Kathy and Julie seemed to like that idea, so we set out again.

There was only a small 'beach' area with sand, and then an area with tiny rocks, like gravel. We set out the sheet, and sat in a circle. The breeze was still cool, but the sun was baking down on us now, so it felt good.

Sam set out several paper plates. On one, he placed a large bunch of grapes, a couple of apples and oranges; on another, he put a slab of cheese and a small salami, along with his knife. And on a third, he put a baggie that he had packed with pieces of seeded baguette. He also produced a plastic knife, a small baggie with the remainder of the butter, and a tiny jar of Dijon mustard.

Sam opened the bottle of wine, and pushed the cork back in. Then, he put the wine in the shallow water of the pond, surrounded by rocks, so it wouldn't float down the stream. The wine was already cold, but the pond would keep it that way, until we were ready for it.

As we ate, Sam reminded us that the leftover snacks were still in the cooler: The trail mix, dried mango, and beef jerky. He had also brought a bag of chocolate chip cookies.

We all knew, by now, that Sam went overboard on nearly everything he did. And he never wanted us to go hungry. I wondered whether we would have to go on a diet again, after this trip. At the least, we would probably keep running every morning.

We took our time enjoying the picnic. It was a beautiful location, the food was good, and we were all close friends, now, and very comfortable with each other. When all of our sodas were drained, Sam poured the wine.

By the time we finished the picnic, we were all very relaxed. Kathy walked back under the arch, retrieved a towel, and continued down to the beach, lying in the sand to further her all-over tan, which was already nearly perfect.

Julie and Linda washed off under the waterfall, and decided to sit on the wet sand on the beach on this side of the arch. As they began hiking down the stream, Sam called to them, "Kelly and I are going to be behind the sand dune for a while."

"We are?" I said. I wondered if Sam had not been satisfied, only giving me a dozen spanks. It didn't matter; I was quite willing to do whatever Sam asked of me.

Sam smiled, "We haven't had much time alone together, so I thought we could play around a little ... and you could let me satisfy your needs."

We headed over the rocks and along the stream under the arch, and Sam grabbed a towel.

As we walked past Kathy, and headed to the huge dune, I thought about Sam's statement. It was true that we'd spent most of the time with my friends, but that hadn't stopped us from making love, even last night, when we were all lying next to each other.

And, I wasn't sure what Sam meant by 'playing around', as just about everything we did fell into that category.

And, it was obvious whose needs would be satisfied! Sam was a very sexual being. I briefly wondered if *he* was a nymphomaniac; maybe he would be called a '*Satyr*', but I wasn't sure of my Greek mythology.

There were several people kayaking a few hundred yards from shore, but they continued on, and fortunately did not land on the beach. Sam had told us that landing any boat, even a kayak, was forbidden on this beach.

We walked into the narrow passage behind the sand dune, along the cliff, and the ocean sound disappeared again. Sam laid out the towel, and we sat down, cross-legged and facing each other.

I laughed, "So how would you like to 'play around'?"

Sam shrugged, "I don't know." Then, he looked into my eyes, "But I'm very much in love with you ... and would like to make you happy."

I leaned forward, and gave Sam a peck on the lips. "I *am* happy, silly! This has been an incredible trip. I think we're *all* having fun."

Sam nodded, "Yes. It's been nice traveling with your friends. They're adventurous enough to appreciate this island. And we all seem to get along very well."

That was true; it was amazing that five of us could be together so much without getting on each other's nerves. And I really didn't feel 'slighted' by bringing my friends along on our island adventure.

Sam leaned forward, holding my head, and kissing me ardently. I reached down, and held his cock, which was already beginning to stiffen. His hands went down to my breasts, kneading them and tweaking my nipples. I thought again about the possibility of getting nip rings.

When Sam was fully erect, I straddled him, and sat in his lap, my feet around his waist, and his length inserted into my already-wet depth.

We rocked back and forth, as we kissed, Sam running his fingers through my hair ... until they hit a knot. I couldn't help but yelp, and Sam pulled his hand out of my hair, and put his arms around me.

I closed my eyes, as we continued to rock, Sam occasionally thrusting further into me. He dropped his arms, putting his hands between us, his thumbs applying slight pressure, as they glided over my hood.

Suddenly, I was incredibly more turned-on, and I let my mind drift, as I visualized scenes with Sam in the past ... and in the future. I held his head, and our mouths fused, tongues swirling, as Sam continued his 'two-thumb' technique.

Sam really knew how to 'press my button' (or 'ring my chime'?), and our mouths separated as I threw my head back, eyes still closed.

We were hypersensitive to each other, and Sam could read me well. He thrust his pelvis toward me, and my vaginal muscles squeezed repeatedly on his cock. Now, we were both thrusting, the crescendo of our feelings peaking.

Sam made one final thrust, holding himself deep inside me, and I orgasmed, letting out a shrill cry. Then, Sam put his hands under my bum, and lifted me toward him, as he thrust several times more, then came, emptying himself into me.

My arms were still around Sam's shoulders, my head tilted back, and I opened my eyes. The view shocked me for a moment, as I had forgotten where we were. My entire field of view was filled, on one side, with the cliff, and on the other with the sand dune. In between, there was a ragged line of bright blue sky.

It was like the central sky in a Baroque ceiling fresco, the eye focused to infinity, reaching to heaven. This place *was* heavenly.

I looked at Sam, who had a bemused expression, having been watching as I stared at the sky. "Thank you, Sam. That was really nice." We leaned toward each other and kissed again, then Sam came out of me, and used a corner of the towel to clean himself.

We walked back under the arch, and continued to the waterfall for a quick bathing, finding Julie and Linda playing under the cascade of water. Sam and I stuck our heads under, and washed ourselves, the water temperature now feeling perfect in the hot afternoon.

As she looked at my rear, Linda chuckled, "Well, it doesn't look like he spanked you *that* hard."

I laughed, "He didn't spank me, Linda; he made love to me." A silent 'Oh!' formed on Linda's mouth, and she smiled and nodded.

We all walked down to where Kathy was still sun-bathing. Sam warned, "I hope you don't get burned." Then, he laughed, "It might limit your activities with Christian." Kathy gave him a mocking scowl.

Sam brought the cookies down, and we nearly finished the bag. It must be the fresh air; at least that was my story, and I was sticking to it.

He said, "I checked my watch, and we only have another two hours until the boat comes. And, I have one more 'experience' for us."

There were blank nods all around, but we followed Sam up to the cooler and packed everything, our fanny packs in the cooler inside the garbage bag; except for Sam's, which he wore – the *only* thing he wore.

We carried the cooler down the beach until it was even with the center of the sand dune. Then, we followed Sam, climbing to the top of the dune. We looked out at the ocean, which was a deep, dark blue, whitecaps speckling the farthest waves.

Sam said, "We haven't really played around much, since we've been here," there were already groans from my friends, "and this is a very spiritual place ... so I thought we would have our own ceremony." We waited to hear what Sam had in mind.

He explained, "This will represent our friendship, our intimacy, our trust of each other, and our willingness to accept some pain or discomfort for each other." Now, we could guess the direction Sam was heading.

"Please line up next to each other, facing the ocean, and get into the 'standing' position." We spread our feet apart in a wide stance, stood straight, and put our hands on our heads.

I looked back, and Sam was taking the camera from his fanny pack. He took a few snapshots from behind, and then a few from in front, all of us smiling at the camera.

I realized that my friends were exhibiting ultra-trust, allowing Sam to photograph them nude ... again. He had done it many times before, sometimes covertly, and we all trusted that he wouldn't put them on the internet, or use them to embarrass us.

He instructed, "Now, bend over and hold your knees. You may bend your knees a little, if you like." Nobody complained. Sam took another set of pictures from behind, facing the ocean, and from in front, facing the cliff, all of our heads raised to look into the camera. Then, he took a few from the side, with the rock arch in the background.

Sam took off the fanny pack, putting his camera back into it, and setting it on the ground behind us. Then, he stepped in front of us, one of his flip-flips in his hand, which he was casually bending and straightening.

"I'm going to give each of you a nice hard swat on each side of your bottom with the slipper." Linda was shaking her head, but still smiling; Kathy was also shaking her head, but not smiling so much.

Sam continued, "Then, I'll get at the end of the line, and the next person – Julie – will spank us all. Then, she'll get at the end of the line, and it will be Linda's turn, then Kelly's, and finally Kathy's.

"If you're up for it, I suggest we do three rounds, so we would each get 24 swats, a nice bottom-warming."

He looked at Kathy, and said, "And it will be OK to give each person harder or lighter swats. You can do whatever you like, but I'm going to go easier on Kathy, and harder on Kelly ... and Linda."

I could see that Linda was about to make a sarcastic comment, but closed her mouth and nodded, silently.

Sam said, "If you're ready, we'll get started. Let's do this without talking, facing out to the ocean as you feel the sublime pain of the slipper."

Julie couldn't help but comment, "Sublime?"

Sam stepped behind Julie, ignoring her comment. "Prepare yourselves. And please think about the trust we have in each other to do this. It will be our own Honopu ceremony."

We all lifted our heads, and looked out to the ocean. I heard a 'WHAP! WHAP!', then another pair, then another, as Sam worked his way down the line. He gave Linda somewhat harder swats, and Kathy much lighter swats.

I took a breath as Sam stepped behind me. Then, I felt the stings – first on the left, quickly followed by one on the right. It may have been the wine, or the atmosphere, or my experience with spankings, but it tingled more than hurt.

Sam walked down to Julie, and handed her the slipper, then took his place at the end of the line, to my right, and bent over, holding his knees, and looking at the ocean.

Julie walked down the line, giving each of us two swats, making Kathy's lighter than Linda's and mine about the same.

Then, she stepped behind Sam, and I heard two very loud 'WHAP!s' coming from Sam's bum. Julie walked back to Linda and handed her the slipper, then took her place next to Sam.

The process continued, with Linda and I taking our turns. Kathy was less inclined to spank hard, and her swats were very mild, until she got to Sam. Somehow, the strength in her arm suddenly increased, and she gave Sam two zingers.

Sam took the slipper, and stood behind Julie. "I have a new idea." Groaning all around, again.

Sam said, defensively, "Well, we don't have to follow my idea, but I was going to suggest that we only have one more round of spanks, and then a round of kissing."

That sounded better to everyone. Sam announced, "Round two!" Then, we heard the double-swats coming down the line. Once again, we each took our turn, and Julie and Kathy seemed to be a bit easier on Sam, this time.

When the second round was done, Sam announced, "Round three!" He stepped in front of Julie; she stood, and they kissed. Then, she bent over and held her knees again. Sam worked his way down the line, kissing each of us, his intent clearly sincere. And my friends were clearly returning the feeling.

It was hard to believe that only fifteen months ago, Sam was concerned about kissing even me. Although, I did remember that he had smoked with all of us at my birthday party, so had shared saliva ... and then, the following morning, my friends had gone down on him. In any case, he seemed to be getting a lot more relaxed.

The kissing round continued, Julie kissing each of us, then Kathy, then me. While Kathy had seemed distant since we'd arrived – probably because of Christian – she didn't skimp on her kisses. It was the first time that Kathy and I had kissed with real feeling. And it looked like she gave the same attention to Sam.

We were all bent over, holding our knees again, and Sam rummaged through his fanny pack. He shouted, "Eyes forward!" but I heard the clicking, and immediately recognized the sound, and knew what he was going to do.

Sam walked in front of us, his hands behind his back, pacing back and forth like the captain of a ship. "As you guys know, I think every spanking should have a 'corner time'." He looked at me, "And our corner times are usually rectal insertions." Now, both Linda and Kathy groaned.

He continued, "Today's corner time is going to last until we return to Kalalau Beach. And, I don't think any of you have experienced *this* kind of insertion ... except for Kelly." Sam took his hands from behind his back, and held up the string of three metallic anal beads.

Kathy rolled her eyes, and Linda – still bent over – put her hands over her mouth. Julie was chuckling, but quickly quieted, as she would be the first recipient of Sam's 'gift'.

I could see that Sam had already lubricated the beads. He would have never backpacked the heavy anal beads here, so obviously took advantage of RJ and his boat. I wondered if RJ had any idea of some of the things Sam had brought. I hoped not.

Julie was making some quiet sounds, but finally let out a big breath, as Sam stepped behind Linda. I glanced to my left, and saw Linda's face scrunched, her eyes closed. She was silent, until the moment that the last bead popped into her, when she squealed.

After inserting Kathy's beads, I was next. Sam took his time, moving each bead in slowly, then – sensing my reaction – pulled it back out, repeating the process, until he could pop the bead through my anus without hurting me. The last bead hurt a little, but only for a moment.

Once the beads were in, my anus was relaxed, but the weight of the beads made me feel like I had to poop. I tried to relax my muscles, and the beads didn't feel that bad.

Sam walked in front of us, and said, "OK, ladies, you may stand, now. Just relax."

Linda laughed, "Yeah – relax with two pounds of metal balls inside us!"

Sam nodded. "So the final event on this beach will be running down this sandy slope," he chuckled, and nearly coughed, "with those beads inside you."

He turned to me, and winked (something he rarely did), "I really like the clicking sound, when you're running or doing jumping jacks!"

Then, he turned back to my friends, and said, "OK, so what we're ..."

I broke in, "Sam! Haven't you forgotten something?" At first, he was confused, but within moments, he couldn't help but smile, then he stereotypically scratched his head, looked up at the sky, and said, "No ... I don't think so."

This was *my* chance! I commanded in a loud voice that echoed from the rock wall behind us, "OK, Mister! Standing position. Now!"

Sam was initially surprised, but jumped when I said 'Now!', immediately taking the standing position, facing my friends. There was a lopsided grin on his face.

I walked over to Sam's fanny pack, and unzipped it, "You *better* have brought another set ... or you're going to get mine."

I felt inside the pack – Sam had it stuffed with various 'emergency' items – and found the last set of anal beads. They were in a large baggie that had KY in it. I held up the beads, then zipped his pack again.

"Turn around. Now! And put your hands on your ankles!" Sam started to groan, but complied. He had to bend his knees, which caused his butt cheeks to separate, and kept his anus open.

Stepping to the side, I stuck out my straight hand, palm up, directed to Sam's butt, and waved it with a flourish, as an announcer might when introducing a new act. Linda chuckled, and Julie tittered; Kathy just stood there with a frown on her face. I doubted that Christian would put her through the things that Sam had.

Kneeling behind Sam, I began inserting the beads. The first two were easy, but the third one was a lot more challenging. "Relax, Sam!" I instructed, loudly. We finally managed to get the third bead in, Sam screeching as I pushed the thickest part through his sphincter.

I stepped back, and looked at my friends; I was having one of Sam's 'brain farts' – thinking of strange new things to challenge people with. "OK, Sam. You can stand up and turn to us."

He did so, getting back into the standing position. His dick was a little hard, pointing downward; this would be perfect! "Now, you're sharing the anal bead challenge with us." I smiled sweetly at him, "But, for your bad intent and dishonesty, you'll have to be punished."

Sam's mouth fell open, but he said nothing. I decided to draw this out, and tease him. He deserved it, after all. I picked up one of Sam's slippers and bent it, the way he had. Slapping it in my hand, I asked Sam, "How many, do you think?"

Sam shrugged. Finally he said, "Ten?" The pitch at the end of his question kept going up, until he was squeaking.

I slapped the slipper in my hand hard (it hurt!), and commanded, loudly, "Twenty five!" Sam started to shake his head, and I tossed the flip-flop down with Sam's other one and the fanny pack.

A confused look flashed across Sam's face, and before he figured it out, I barked, "Twenty five jumping jacks." I laughed, "So my friends can hear the clicking sound." Sam had asked for it.

Sam hadn't started, so I crossed my arms and stamped my right foot on the sand. He closed his eyes, then opened them, staring straight ahead in a daze, and began doing jumping jacks. Sam was very good at it, coordinated, but trying to land softly. Finally, he gave up the effort, and we heard clicks each time he came down. His dick bounced up and down, finally finding its own rhythm.

My friends laughed, and I took my place next to Kathy. "OK, Sam, you may continue."

Sam nodded once, then stepped toward us gingerly. "When I count down and say 'Go!', we're going to run down to the water." Sam glanced at me, "I was going to say that the last one would be spanked ... or something ... but we can just have a 'fun run' down the dune to the water."

I had a feeling that I knew why Sam was saying that. And, my feeling was confirmed, when Sam did the countdown, and we all ran down the hill, with Sam walking slowly down, himself. I chuckled, the last person still may have to be punished. Then I groaned, feeling the beads jostling inside my butt.

Julie was in the lead, but tripped, and fell, head-over-heels, down the sand, immediately getting back up and continuing alongside Linda. Kathy and I were taking it a bit easier, and safer, by doing a fast walk down the dune, our feet sinking into the sand with every step.

As expected, Sam straggled in, last. He bent over, panting, then stood, and looked back at the dune. Suddenly, he yelled, "Oh! I forgot! I wanted to take pictures of you guys lined up at the top of the dune – from here; with the cliff in the background ..."

I shook my head, "Forget it, Sam. We're not climbing back up there!" He looked dejected, as he slowly walked to the cooler, and dragged it along the wet sand. I reminded him, "Seal it?"

Sam smiled at me, and shook his head. He took the duct tape out, ripped off a six foot piece, then put the duct tape, and his fanny pack and shoes, into the cooler and sealed it with the tape.

I helped him lift the cooler into the water, and we all stood knee deep, the small waves coming in, and foam sliding out between our legs. Sam said, "OK, guys. You *know* you can do it. I'll try to swim just behind you, and you can still use the cooler to rest, if you need to."

He looked out across the water to the end of the cliff, and we could see huge boulders piled up, but not the inlet. "Let's assemble just outside the inlet, and we can swim in one-by-one – in the same order as last time."

We walked further into the water, then began swimming. Now *THAT* was different! I hadn't thought about how the beads would feel, as I swam. It didn't hurt, and was actually an interesting feeling. My friends were swimming fine, and not complaining.

This time, it must have taken at least twenty minutes to swim around the corner to Kalalau. Each of us swam in to the tiny beach. It wasn't that difficult, if you were OK being thrashed around in the water. I was surprised that none of us got seasick, swimming the last fifty feet.

Sam grinned, "Great job, ladies!"

We put the cooler down where it had been before, and Sam sat on it. "OK, each of you come here, and I'll take the beads out and give them to you, for washing in the ocean. Then – if nobody else is there – we can wash them with soap in the waterfall."

Now, I pictured Sam's friend, Ashley, appearing just as each of us was washing a set of anal beads. I broke out in hysterical laughter, Sam turning, and my friends smiling, but wondering what the joke was. I stopped long enough to say to Sam, "Continue on!"

Sam nodded, and called, "Kathy!" Kathy stepped in front of Sam and bent over. She helpfully held her own buttocks apart, and Sam pulled the beads out, Kathy making three little yelps. Sam whispered something to her, and she turned around and kissed Sam on the cheek.

Then, Kathy took the metallic balls, holding them by a loop of string, at arms length, as she marched to the water. Sam shouted, "Linda!" and Linda stepped up to Sam, gave him a kiss on the other cheek, then bent over.

Linda followed Kathy's example, also holding her butt cheeks apart for Sam. There was a loud 'Eeeeeh' when the first bead came out, but Linda was quiet after that.

Sam took Julie's beads out the same way, all three of my friends now down by the water, washing their beads. I bent over, and Sam patted my bum. "Are you sure you don't want to keep them in for the boat ride back?"

I laughed so hard, I nearly fell over. I *remembered* how rough the water had been, and how the boat had bounced, sometimes pounding into the next wave with a shudder that passed through all of us.

I turned to Sam, and put my hands on my hips. "Do *you* want to keep those beads in, for the whole boat ride back?"

Sam shook his head slowly, and looked down sheepishly, "I guess not." Then he brightened, "But, you have to admit, it *would* be another unique experience."

It sure would: One that I wasn't interested in having today. "No thanks, Sam. Just pull the damn thing out!"

Sam obliged, and held the beads, while bending over so that I could take *his* beads out. He whimpered when the first bead came out, but after a few moments, we were walking to the water together.

We un-taped the cooler, and put on our fanny packs. Then, we each took a drink – they were still quite cold, not all the ice having melted in the cooler. Sam, of course, had another beer. He only had to swim two coolers and three river bags through the surf, and out to the boat.

Julie and I carried the cooler back, and we left it just above the waterline. Then, we all went back to the campsite, took a quick shower under the waterfall, and brought our packs down to the beach, along with the river bags. Sam rummaged through one, then the next, cursing quietly. He finally pulled out three more river bags – new ones, still rolled up.

Holding them up, he went 'Phewww!' and said, "If these had not gotten in, we would have a tough time getting the hiking packs back to the boat." He laughed, "Although I've done it once with garbage bags. And that was in high surf conditions."

Soon, everything was packed into the coolers or the large waterproof bags, and the coolers were sealed. We put our bathing suits into the small bag, along with a few other items for use on the boat.

Less than a half hour later, we saw RJ's Zodiac cruising along Kalalau Beach. He stopped about a hundred yards offshore, and we divvied-up the coolers and bags.

Sam offered to take both coolers, but Julie insisted on taking one; and Sam took one of the large waterproof bags. Kathy, Linda, and I took the other three bags, and I also took the small bag with stuff for the boat.

It was difficult to swim with the bags, and the saltwater kept splashing into my face, but we all eventually made it out to the Zodiac. RJ took our coolers and bags, and stowed them on the boat. Then, he offered to help each of us get on the boat, by now realizing that all of us were nude.

Julie hopped up onto the tube by herself, as did I. But Linda took RJ's hand, and he pulled her onto the boat. Then, Sam pulled Kathy onboard.

RJ tossed his cigarette overboard, and smiled, "Well, I guess you guys got all relaxed in Kalalau!" We hadn't talked about it, but were happy to give RJ some 'kicks' at seeing all of us nude.

But Sam grabbed the small bag, and pulled out his water shorts and put them on. He was still uncomfortable nude around other men, despite his progress with his son and partner, and with Justin.

The ride back 'uphill' was as exciting as the first time, water splashing over the bow onto us, as the boat ploughed through some waves, and smashed onto others. The tubes kept us bouncing, and I couldn't imagine doing this with those anal beads in me.

Sam stood next to RJ at the helm, again, which seemed like a smoother ride, as he could flex his knees as we went up and down on the waves.

Soon, we motored back into Hanalei Bay. RJ turned around, "You gals ought-a get your suits on, now." Sam had told us that some of the locals weren't happy about *haoles* going nude. And we would be passing the pier and Black Pot park, where there were a lot of families.

I decided that if I ever had a family, we would be open, and not worry about Victorian sensitivities; but I knew that we would always be in the minority.

We all put our bikinis on – Julie wearing a thong bottom ... except Kathy, who shrugged, "Sorry. I can pull out a tank when we get the bags on dry land, but I didn't bring the top to this suit."

She got a couple of looks from guys on the beach near the pier, but we made it back into the river, and unloaded everything, Kathy finally being able to get her pack and put on her tank. Julie wrapped a pareo around her waist, and Linda put on her red dirt t-shirt, while I slipped on a pair of shorts.

Sam threw the car keys to me, and we put everything in the back, as he helped RJ get the boat connected to the trailer, and pulled out of the water.

RJ told us goodbye, and offered to take us on the boat anytime, if we returned to Kauai. I certainly hoped that Sam and I would have the opportunity to spend more time here. We waved, as he drove the Zodiac down the beach road, and Sam sniffled and wiped his eyes.

I still didn't know what experiences had made Sam so emotional about Kauai, but now we'd had our own experiences, and I could see why he loved the island.

Sam started the car, then turned to us, "I'll give you a choice: We can have the spaghetti tonight – in which case, I'll stop at the market to pick up a few things ... or, we can forget about the spaghetti, and I can take you for a hamburger tonight ... or whatever else you have in mind."

Linda said, "I love your cooking, Sam. And spaghetti sounds OK to me." Julie and Kathy nodded.

Sam drove to the small shopping center in Hanalei, and went into the market, while my friends and I walked around the center. We got back to the car, and Sam still hadn't returned. When he did, he pushed a basket with at least three large bags of groceries.

"We needed *that* much stuff? We'll only be here another three days."

Sam nodded, "I bought ingredients for a salad tonight, and dessert, some Italian sausages to go with the spaghetti, more breakfast stuff, snacks for the next two days, a couple of bottles of wine, and a bottle of rum, coconut syrup, and pineapples for making Piña Coladas." As usual, Sam had gone overboard with the food and drink.

We hauled everything into our rental house, and Sam said, "Get yourselves cleaned up, and I'll start the dinner and make a pitcher of drinks."

Then, he smiled, "And I'd like to see you all lined up in just your Victoria's Secret panties in the living room, in one hour." Here we go again! I hoped that Sam hadn't planned anything too challenging, as we'd already had a pretty challenging day.

CHAPTER 17: VIDEO SHOW(S IT ALL)

I took a quick shower, and went into the kitchen, where I heated the spaghetti sauce, and made a 'Caprese Caesar' – my usual Caesar salad topped with slices of heirloom tomatoes and mozzarella. Then, I cooked the sausages until they were browned, and dropped them into the sauce.

I opened a bottle of chianti, leaving it on the dining table to breathe. I set the table, then cut up one of the pineapples, and got set-up to make the drinks in the blender.

Then, I retrieved the bag of stuff I had bought a week ago at the small shop in Wainiha, on the way back from our Hanakapiai Falls hike.

Julie and Linda were already sitting on the couch, topless and in cute bikini underwear, as I had instructed. They were sharing pictures of our hiking and camping experience with each other.

Kathy and Kelly finally wandered into the living room, everyone looking fresh and clean after a nice hot shower. The waterfall at the campsite hadn't been that cold, but we all appreciated getting back to the conveniences of modern life, including a flush toilet. I was especially looking forward to sleeping in a real bed, with a soft pillow.

I walked into the living room, which was open to the dining area and kitchen, and had a vaulted ceiling with huge wooden beams. Fortunately for our activity tonight, there was a large screen television mounted to the wall facing the couch. I quickly checked the connectors to make sure I had a suitable cable to hook up Kelly's laptop.

The girls were cute in their panties, but we'd all been nude together so much that it didn't faze any of us. I was wearing my usual shorts and aloha shirt. I decided to be quick, this time, and not tease them too much.

I began, "You're probably wondering why I called you all in here for a meeting ... in your underwear ..." I got blank stares and a couple of smiles. "Please stand in a line behind the couch." They did so without comment.

Starting on the left end, with Linda, I asked, "May I please kiss you?" Linda nodded, and I gave her a nice kiss. Moving to Kathy, I whispered, "If you'd rather, I can kiss you on the cheek?"

Kathy shook her head, "It's OK; you may kiss me, Sam." I gave her a quick peck on the lips.

When I moved over to Julie, she didn't wait for the question, but took my head in her hands, and gave me a slobbery kiss. Then, I moved to Kelly and gave her a loving kiss.

Stepping back, and facing all of them, I said, "That is a small 'thank you' for coming on this trip, trying some new things, being open, and submitting to a few challenges."

There weren't actually that many – mainly the pissing contest, the mud wrestling, and the 'ceremony' we'd had in Honopu today ... especially swimming back to Kalalau with the anal beads.

As I opened the bag, I told them, "And here's one more small 'thank you'."

I pulled out the t-shirts, handing one to each of the girls. They smiled, and put them on. They didn't come down as far as the other tee's I'd bought for them, so weren't quite as good a cover-up, their underwear still showing beneath the hem of each shirt.

They modeled the shirts for each other, and read the message on the back: 'I Survived the Kalalau Trail'. Julie hugged me, "Thank you, Sam." Then, I got hugs and thanks from Linda and Kathy, and a big smile and passionate kiss from Kelly.

I went into the kitchen and, within a couple of minutes, blended the Piña Coladas and poured them for each of us. We toasted, and I gave them an evil smile, "There's just one more thing …"

Linda groaned, not even knowing what I was going to say; but she knew me …

"You guys know that I've videoed some of our experiences, and taken some pictures of you." There were slow nods all around.

"In fact, I have hours of video from the first day that Kelly came over. And hours more from her birthday party. Not to mention you guys lined up and getting your shots at the doctor's office."

Now, Kelly's mouth slowly dropped open. I'd told her I was working on a big project, but hadn't given her any details. "So over the past month, I've spent quite a bit of time finally looking at the videos, and editing parts of them together."

I looked at Kelly, "Not including the ones from our trips." Then, I remembered, and had to laugh, "Except for the video Justin sent to us from our performance at the wedding." Kelly started to crack up, remembering the thrashing she'd given me, in front of a hundred or more wedding guests.

Taking a sip of my drink, I announced, "So tonight will be the premier of my mockumentary, *Challenges and Submissions*." Linda's hands covered her face, and Kelly gave me a wilting smile. Kathy sat there with a blank expression, while Julie started laughing, then cackling.

Kelly's expression was becoming angry, as she thought about everything that I'd filmed. I finished my drink, and said, "I've told all of you that the videos and pictures would be private, but I thought we were all close enough that they could be shared within our group."

Kelly slowly nodded, not looking quite as upset. We'd all been together for many of the experiences, except for Kelly's first experience with me. And I hadn't videoed our long weekend together, which had been quite intimate.

I made another pitcher of Coladas, and refilled all our glasses. Looking through the kitchen window, I saw the field next to us, with two horses prancing around. The sun was setting, and the clouds were pink. Then, I saw what appeared to be the end of a rainbow.

Carrying my drink, I shouted, "Come with me!" We all went through the screen room to the backyard, and the girls gasped: There was a full rainbow framing the mountains behind Hanalei. In fact, it was a double rainbow, the outer, dimmer one having colors inverted from the main bow.

I pointed, "That's Mount Namolokama, in the center, with the double waterfall, flanked by Hihimanu, on the left, and Mamalahoa on the right." There were numerous small waterfalls in the folds of the mountains.

Kathy exclaimed, "That's *beautiful*!" We were all nodding. There were more waterfalls than we'd seen up to this point in the trip, at least a dozen being visible from the backyard of our rental house.

As a warm breeze blew softly, rustling the fronds of the palms, my emotions suddenly hit me again; I really wasn't sure exactly why. I turned to Kelly and kissed her. "It's hard to explain, but I hope you all understand why I wanted to bring you here."

I sipped my drink as the clouds turned from pink to orange. I shook my head, "It's really a magical place." We all hugged each other, then went inside.

The girls sat at the dining table, and I served the salad, each plate decorated with layers of tomatoes and mozzarella over a traditional Caesar salad. Then, I poured the wine. I decided to make one more toast, "Here's to Kathy's new friend, Christian. I hope you have a great couple of days with him!" Kathy smiled and nodded.

Everyone enjoyed the salad. I had not made garlic bread, as I'd bought a couple of desserts. I cleared the table, and washed the salad plates and forks, then stirred the sauce one last time, and turned off the heat.

I invited the girls to serve themselves, as I knew I'd pile on too much spaghetti, if I served them. But they were all hungry, and took plenty – even Kathy, although she passed on the sausage.

Linda smacked her lips, "You really are a good cook, Sam." Turning to Kelly, she said – not so jokingly – "I really would take him, if you ever decide to get rid of him." Kelly just smiled and shook her head.

I looked at Linda – really looked at her. She had a beautiful face, a well-proportioned oval, black hair coming down past her shoulders, dark brown eyes, and a Mona Lisa smile, the corners of her mouth turned up in a bemused, but knowing way.

Linda had always had a great personality, a combination of humorous and witty, with quick sarcasm and she was – as we'd learned over the past year or so – extremely sensual and sexual.

But I could see that her additional weight hadn't been a help in finding a partner. I had probably had a different 'vision' of her because of her weight, but have learned to accept people, and relish their uniqueness. I guess not everyone was like that.

Now that Linda had lost weight – and evidently not gained it back in the past ten days we'd been here – she looked incredible. Her body would always be curvy, with C-cup breasts and wide hips; and she would always be a fun 'spanking partner', her bottom now smaller, but still substantial.

It was unfortunate that so many people judged others based on their weight or body shape; but I was willing to bet that Linda would have more 'luck' with men, looking like this.

Linda glanced at me, with a questioning look in her dark eyes. "Sorry. But I was mesmerized: You look great!" Then, I had to add a quiet, "Not that you didn't, before ..."

I was feeling the wine. Or maybe it was the Piña Coladas? I looked around, and it appeared that everyone's plates were nearly empty. "We have plenty of spaghetti and even more sauce left. And maybe one or two sausages. Help yourselves!"

Linda put her fork down, "Sam! How could you tell me I look good one moment, and then goad us to eat more?" She looked serious, but then cracked a smile, "But, I feel weak, and will probably take more ... and worry about calories later." Kelly and Kathy laughed.

There were a lot of possible replies. "I wasn't 'goading' you. And we all used plenty of calories in the past few days ... and didn't eat that much." Now, I was flustered, "And you *do* look great." I looked at Kelly for support, but she remained quietly amused at our exchange.

I asked, sheepishly, "Shall I pour the rest of the wine for anybody? I think I've had enough." More laughter.

Julie reached for the bottle, "I'll have some, Sam."

I passed her the bottle. Yawning, I said, "I hope we can all stay awake for the show." Then, I remembered, "Oh! And the dessert." Kathy groaned. I turned to her, "You don't have to have any. Or, you can save some for breakfast."

Linda asked, "What is it, Sam?"

I glanced at Kelly, "Actually, I got two desserts." Now, Kelly groaned; but Julie thought it was hilarious.

Looking at Julie, I asked, "How much of your birthday cake did you get, at the party?"

Julie smiled, "I had some of Linda's; I meant to go back for some, but it was gone, when I finally remembered."

I nodded, "I never got any, either, and it looked really good." I smiled, "So I bought another one ... at least, it's very similar. I think both markets use the same bakery."

Then, looking at Kathy and sticking out my tongue at her, I said, "And I thought Kathy might like to try the pineapple upside-down cake." I put my palms up, "It *is* a little sweet, but it has fresh pineapple that's caramelized."

I turned to Kelly, "At least, it looked good, to me."

Kelly patted my back, "That's my Sam. I hope *you* keep your athletic form." She laughed, but it wasn't funny.

Kelly got up, and said, "There's an espresso machine here, that uses cartridges – several different flavors. Maybe that might help keep us awake, for a while? If you want to watch Sam's little show."

Linda and Julie screamed a chorus, "Of course!" Linda said, "Although I'm not overjoyed at the prospect of seeing myself getting an enema on the big screen." We all laughed.

Kathy nodded, "That video *better* not be shown to anybody else!"

Shaking my head, I laughed, "No, Kathy." Then, I pretended that a great idea flashed into my mind, "It *would* have been interesting to have Christian here tonight, so that he could watch it. I wonder what he would think?"

Kathy gave me a mean look, "Don't even think about it, Sam ... or talk about it. That's not nice." Then, she made a crooked smile, "It wouldn't help my chances with him. I don't think *anybody* else would or could understand the relationship we've all had with each other."

Kathy ate the last of her spaghetti, "And it's all your fault, Sam. It started at Kelly's crazy birthday party."

I tipped the wine glass, so the last few drops rolled into my mouth; then I remembered that I'd already had enough, and put it down.

"Actually, Kathy, it started when Julie and Linda came over, the first weekend that Kelly stayed with me. Linda took her birthday spanking, and Julie masturbated over my lap." I had to reach into my shorts and adjust myself.

We all gave our espresso orders to Kelly; except Kathy, who poured herself a tall glass of orange juice, with some guava juice falling through it. Like a 'tequila sunset'. I hooked Kelly's laptop to the large LCD screen, and inserted the flash drive on which I'd stored the finished video.

My shorts were feeling a bit tight, so I went into the bedroom, and changed into my red dirt t-shirt and European underwear.

When I came out, Julie, Linda and Kathy were on the couch, facing the screen. I set-up my iPhone as a remote, and sat on one of the comfortable chairs around the coffee table. Kelly served the coffees, then sat down in the chair on the opposite side.

I got up and turned off the lights, only the dull glow of moonlight through the windows illuminating the room. Then, I tapped the iPhone screen, and the show began. It was a compilation of short clips from more than 40 hours of multi-channel video. Overall, there must have been well over 100 hours.

I'd had to watch most of it – although I'd 'scrubbed' through the boring parts, and then, from each scene that I wanted to show, selected a short clip – between ten seconds and a minute. The editing program was great, but it took an inordinate amount of time. One of my retirement projects ... in addition to starting the company with Kelly.

The video began with a short clip from the contract discussion with Kelly, with me saying 'You're supposed to have fun'. Next was the discussion when I was playing the role of a professional spanker, hired by Kelly's parents. The girls were hysterical after the first 30 seconds. Then, Kelly was bending over for needles, since she hadn't followed the rules.

Then, there were a half-dozen ten-second clips, with increasingly heavy implements. The views were obviously very intimate, the cameras having been set-up and located precisely to record the action.

Kelly sat there, smiling. We'd now done most of this with her friends; so what we thought was such a huge deal a year and a half ago, seemed relatively tame – at least within our special group.

Then, there was an image of me, standing in front of the coffee table with a partial erection. The girls were even more hysterical, Julie choking, and even Kathy clapping. The next scene was me – from behind – as Kelly punished me. I reminded them that it was because I had made a comment about Kelly's young age.

Kelly put her hand on her forehead, as the scene was now of us in the exam room. She glanced at me, and it occurred to me that she hadn't been aware that I'd had three cameras there, also. That was my best lighting!

Now, the video was a time-lapse, with me running around, putting Kelly in different positions, and doing different things. But, again, not that different from what I'd done with Julie, Linda and Kathy.

The next clip had me explaining our 'game of chance', then another time-lapse of rolling the dice and giving each other shots in the rear, all sped-up.

There was no video of us in the shower or the sauna, but a series of still pictures flashed on the screen: Showing Kelly at the restaurant, a couple of the needle play and candle wax snapshots, some pictures of Nurse Kelly, and some snapshots showing Kelly's rear after her first caning.

But we had no photos from the pool or jacuzzi, no massage, not even a snapshot of the playroom set-up for our first lovemaking, with a rose petal path, and all the candles lit. No pictures of our Kama Sutra experience, or our picnic at the pond, where we'd met Alex and Fiona.

Julie turned her head, suddenly, "You mean you didn't video the spankings you gave Linda and me ... or my masturbation scene?"

"You don't know how much Kelly and I would have loved to have those scenes ... but I didn't video you guys, because I didn't want to have to tell you about it, and wouldn't have done it without your knowledge." Julie shrugged.

Then, I volunteered, "I *also* didn't video our ménage." Julie was nodding, with a smile growing on her face, as she remembered.

Next on the screen was a slideshow of pictures I'd taken of Kelly and Fiona, in the backyard. Kelly knew what was coming, next.

"Sam! I'm not sure you should be showing Fiona, without her permission."

I nodded, "Yeah. I guess we should show Fiona a portfolio of the images I took during your ..." At that moment, the slideshow changed to Fiona and Kelly's girl-on-girl experience. They were hot!

Glancing at Kelly and her friends, I saw Kelly's hand over her mouth, and the mouths of all three of Kelly's friends hanging open. It was *really* hot!

Julie was staring at Kelly. Kelly glanced over to her and shrugged.

At that point, the screen said "Intermission", and I paused the video. Everybody had finished their coffees, and I suggested that Kelly might make a second portion for everyone, and I would put out the cakes on the coffee table, and pass around plates.

Real plates! Sitting in a comfortable chair! I enjoyed camping, and Kalalau was very special, but it was nice to get back to civilization.

When everyone's plates were full, I decided that I had to have a taste of both of the cakes. I started the show again, and the video showed the pirate flag waving on the yardarm, high above the pool.

Kathy clapped, and Julie cheered, but Linda started choking. Julie patted her on the back, and she was OK. Linda whispered to Julie, "You *know* he's going to have a video of us on that stupid turntable."

There were clips of us on the sheet on the grass, our group massage in the jacuzzi, and then the pirate scene. I had left in most of the video, from when Kelly came out in her Victorian dress, and I surprised her in the pirate costume, to me taking her over the boulder by the pool – which only showed our heads.

I had forgotten, but Julie's punishment for blabbing about Kelly's adoption was also included – the six swats with the school paddle, and her corner time.

We were all laughing, as the turntable ('Lazy Sam') scene came on. I had included a video capturing each of the girls from behind, as I turned the turntable ... a tampon string hanging down from each of them. Then, I'd made another time-lapse, with all the rest of the 'Spank Poker' game taking only a minute. I thought it was pretty funny.

Kelly's birthday spanking was next; then her demonstration of the 'Triple Treat' rabbit dildo. I had forgotten that I'd played a starring role, especially, when I was in the chair position, Julie and the others inserting the butt plugs into me, and then giving me a hand-job.

Unfortunately, I didn't have any video of the slumber party; of course, the room had been pitch black most of the time. Then my technical brain realized that I could have videoed the room in infrared. But we had enough video; there was no need for any more.

Also, I had not been recording video during the ménage with Julie. I couldn't remember exactly why I hadn't done that. But it would remain a private experience in the memories of the three of us; a very special experience.

Then Linda's hands covered her face again. Her 'schoolgirl' scene was now on the big screen. I'd only used a few clips, which did include her hard paddling and exam room experience, but didn't show Linda and I in front of the desk, as Kelly punished us, then rewarded us.

I put my hand under my tee, and adjusted myself, as I saw the girls bent over the exam table at the doctor's office, getting their third set of shots. I had edited the scenes of each girl – a rear view, showing her getting the shots, and a front view, showing her smiling and putting her thumb up.

Now, we saw scenes from my own birthday party: Me prancing around as Samo, the puppy – including when I lapped Kathy to a climax; then me as baby Sammy, in a diaper, sucking on Linda's breast; and me again, on the turntable, as the girls each took their turns.

Then the best part – as far as I was concerned: The challenge experience, with the girls lined up in the pool room, their legs tied to the wall, and an enema tube coming out of each one of them. Then, there was the spanking competition, for which I had used a combination of time-lapse and 10-scond clips.

And finally, the girls' enema squirting contest. I realized that Kathy had won that one too; as well as the pissing contest. Until Julie and I had peed more than eight hundred feet!

I paused the video, and we all took another slice of one (or both) of the cakes. The coffees had kept us awake, and I decided to sip some of the añejo rum, as we'd be leaving soon, and not be able to take it.

Kelly announced, "And now, the *piece de resistance*, when Sam volunteered to get spanked in front of a hundred people at the wedding." The girls had already seen it, but were still tittering. I shrugged, and sat down with my rum. Then, I hit 'Play' on the remote.

I didn't think I would want to watch it again – my bottom was already hurting just thinking about it – but I had to admit that it was a pretty good show. The professional videographers had captured the expressions of people at the tables, and also had a few close-ups of my pained expression, as Kelly strapped me with the belt.

It went on and on, and then the video ended, and the screen went dark, the girls' mouths hanging open, again. Linda swallowed the last of her cake, and said, "Wow, Sam. You put on a pretty good show for them."

I nodded, "Well, it *was* a sex club. Although most of the wedding party probably had never been there."

Kelly laughed, "It could have been *really* shocking, if Fiona and Justin had romped on the bed with us ... like we did in the playroom." Julie looked at Kelly, then me, with a −hopefully − mock angry expression. We both shrugged.

I turned on the lights and unhooked the computer. Linda yawned, "That was a good show, Sam." Both Julie and Kathy were nodding.

Kathy leaned forward. She was looking at me, but talking to everyone, "You know ... I never much liked the spanking, and certainly not the shots." I nodded, and she smiled, "But with all of us together, I didn't mind playing along ... too much."

Now, she was looking at me, "I'm pretty uninhibited, and being nude − or even you examining my privates − wasn't a big deal." She looked at me sweetly, "And we all trusted you, Sam."

Chuckling, she said, "Actually, we trusted Kelly. But she was right: You are a nice man ... a sweet man." I was about to protest with a comment about spanking her, but Kathy held up her hand.

"But, now that we've done so much together, it's not shocking any more − not even to see ourselves on the screen ... in a 'compromising' position."

She looked at Kelly, then Julie and Linda, "And we have become much closer. At least, much more open with each other, sexually." We were all nodding.

Kathy chuckled, "So, I'm not so sure about your methods, but the result seemed to be good: We're all very open and trusting with each other, have shared some intimate experiences, and have an even closer friendship."

Kelly leaned over and hugged Kathy. "I probably should have felt bad, introducing you to Sam, and then having him push you guys so much. But, I enjoyed it, too. I had no idea that any of you would accept so much of Sam's weirdness." What? I wasn't weird! Not *that* much.

I chimed in, "And, with everything we've done together, I feel really close to all of you," I glanced at Kelly, and she smiled, "and I think I love all of you."

Before they could respond, I said, "I don't know what kind of love it is; sometimes, it feels romantic, and all of you turn me on. But most of the time, it's like love for a sister. Or maybe, just love for a very close friend."

We were all solemn, now, and I hugged each of Kelly's friends. Then, I squeezed into the large chair with Kelly, and turned to her, "But my love for Kelly transcends everything else." I looked at the girls on the couch, "You guys know that." They were nodding.

I kissed Kelly long and hard, nothing else in the room encroaching on my thoughts or feelings. We got up, and I said, "It's been a pretty long day!" We had awakened in Kalalau this morning, and had enjoyed nearly a full day in Honopu. That now seemed very far away.

Each of Kelly's friends kissed me, as they filed off to bed. Julie held me, "Thank you, Sam, for bringing us on this trip – and taking us camping. That was really an incredible experience."

Kelly and I crawled into bed together, and I said, "That worked out pretty well." I had been talking about the camping trip, getting back safely, and the dinner I'd made with the leftovers from the trip.

But Kelly was thinking about the video. "I just hope you don't show that to anybody else." She chuckled, "Maybe not even to us, again."

She climbed on top of me, pinning me to the bed. Then, she lowered herself onto me, and moved her hips rhythmically, as the underside of my penis slid along the stubbles of her pubic hair.

Kelly lifted up, and put me inside her. There were no words, just feelings, as we coupled, the exquisite sense of our bodies conjoined, our warmth shared.

I saw the crescent moon through the window, then closed my eyes, as millions of stars shone brightly in my mind's eye. We climaxed together, and stayed coupled as long as we could.

Something clicked in my brain – again. I knew that I wanted to spend my life with Kelly, experience new things together, and share our joy with her friends – and maybe even children. I wanted to travel more with Kelly, taste the world, and take our time exploring remote places.

But it seemed to be a pipe dream: Kelly hadn't even finished school, yet, and had a whole career ahead of her. It might be a long time before we could spend the time together that I craved.

I resolved that we would be together, and that I would wait as long as necessary; but I knew that we would ultimately consummate our relationship more formally, committing ourselves to each other. For all the future.

CHAPTER 18: SPIRIT OF ALOHA

We slept late, and I made omelets for everyone, along with toast and jams. We put out all the fruit – fresh pineapple, papaya, mango and berries, as well as orange juice and guava nectar. It was raining outside, and I saw a horse in the field next door standing by the rickety wooden fence.

Kathy packed her rolling case and her pack, and I laughed when she put them next to the front door. "You *will* be coming back here, won't you? We don't leave until Saturday night."

Kathy shrugged, "Probably. Christian wanted to take us all out on Friday night, so I guess he'll be coming to the north shore." She smiled at me and shrugged, "But, I may as well be prepared ... for anything."

Kelly had done a load of laundry for all of us, and I put on my water shorts and tank. Kathy wore shorts and a halter top, while the rest of the girls wore bathing suits and a cover-up, or with shorts and a tank top over them.

We drove to Wailua, on the east side, and parked at a launching point, where we would rent kayaks. Christian was already there, talking animatedly with another local-looking guy. Then they gave each other a Hawaiian handshake, clasping their hands, and then their fingers.

Kathy drove off with Christian ... 'and then there were three'. We pushed our kayaks into the slow-flowing Wailua river, and began paddling upstream on one side of the wide expanse of water. It wasn't five minutes until there was a downpour ... but only for a few moments, until the cloud passed over us.

We had been lucky on the trip, so-far, but had to have a little wetness and mud to really experience Kauai!

I had hoped that we would beat the tour boats – actually barges – that plied the river up to the famous 'fern grotto', but there were already a few boats on the other side of the river making their way upstream, the amplified voice of the tour guides audible across the otherwise-quiet river.

We stopped at the fern grotto, and pulled our kayaks ashore some distance from the barges, then walked up the winding path through the lush jungle.

We couldn't quite hear the spiel, so I explained to the girls, "This has been a favorite place for weddings, usually with Hawaiian music. It was an easy natural place to get to, with lush tropical plants and flowers. But it got commercial."

As we watched one tour group file down to their barge and another walk up to the grotto, I continued, "It was destroyed in a fire around forty years ago ... and then mostly destroyed again, during Hurricane Iniki that flattened Kauai in 1992 – actually, on *September 11, 1992*."

We walked around a few minutes, then back to our kayaks, and continued up the river. We finally came to the start of a trail, unfortunately marked by a several kayaks tied to trees or pulled up on shore.

We walked in our flip-flops along the muddy trail, coming out into an open area with a spectacular waterfall, probably more than a hundred feet high, splashing into a beautiful pool. Despite having been to Hanakapiai Falls, this one was pretty impressive.

There were a half dozen people sitting around the pool, only one young couple standing waist deep next to the waterfall.

The girls didn't hesitate to strip down to their bikini bathing suit bottoms, but Kelly shrugged, and took them off. We all decided, 'what the hell', and went into the pool nude, not worrying about the few other tourists here ... who didn't seem to mind.

I had brought a small river bag with some snacks, but there were no takers. A larger group appeared at the end of the trail, and we got out, dressed, and headed back to our kayaks. We took our time paddling downstream, getting soaked by rain a couple more times before reaching the take-out.

It was still early afternoon, and we had time, so I drove up to the lookout over the Opaeka'a Falls. Then, we drove down the hill to the Kamokila Hawaiian Village, where re-created ancient structures and cultural traditions were displayed.

After all the exciting things we'd done on the island, this was a let-down. We drove down to the main highway, and a short distance to a beach park. Sitting on the benches, in the pine trees, we looked across the narrow beach out to the ocean.

"So what else would you guys like to do, on Kauai? There's a Buddhist monastery, a couple of botanical gardens ..."

Then I said brightly, "Or – if one person wants to drive back to the north shore, the others could run from near here, up a fire road, and ridge trail, across the center of the island to Princeville."

Nobody commented, so I said, "*My* suggestion for tomorrow would be to go back to the little beach, and do some snorkeling."

Linda nodded, "That sounds good." She smiled, "Just no more contests ... or ceremonies!" I laughed; there weren't any planned. But now that I thought about it ...

We were getting hungry, and I suggested that we have an early dinner, if any restaurant was open. Sam snapped his fingers, "I know a good hamburger joint in Kapaa." He smiled, "Then, maybe some dancing ..."

I laughed, assuming that Sam was joking; but perhaps he wasn't? I wondered how much nightlife existed on this island.

Sam's face was blank, and a quick flash of darkness passed across it. "Are you OK, Sam?" He nodded, and we headed for the car.

The hamburgers were great. Sam ordered a chili bowl, and slopped the thick stuff inside his burger. Then, Linda pointed, "Sam, is that you?" We all looked up at the small pictures surrounding the room, near the ceiling.

Sam put his hamburger down, and nodded. "I thought I could come here and not notice ... or maybe they had gotten rid of it."

I looked at an image of Sam and Sarah. They were standing together smiling, with the ruins of Machu Picchu in the background.

Now I noticed that all the pictures were of customers who had traveled internationally: One was of a couple on the Great Wall of China, another of a young boy in front of a wide waterfall - the lettering on a sign said 'Victoria Falls', and still another boy was standing next to a sign that denoted the equator, somewhere in Africa.

I rubbed Sam's back, and kissed him on the cheek. "I'm OK," he said. But he was quiet through the rest of our dinner.

Sam drove us back to Hanalei, and we returned to the house before sunset. We sat in the backyard, smoking grass, and looking at the beautiful mountains. The peak of Mount Namolokama and the twin waterfalls were now in the clouds, and it appeared that there were many more waterfalls than we'd seen yesterday.

We went inside and sat in the screen room, and Sam noticed the mattress on the floor under a window at the far end of the room. "I was planning to offer Kathy – and the rest of you – a massage ... but now I don't know when that will ever happen."

Linda smiled, her eyes sparkling, "I'd love a massage, Sam." Then, she glanced at Julie, "Unless Julie would like to take the first one?"

Julie shook her head, "I'm OK, Linda."

She looked at me, "Maybe Kelly and I will take a little walk on the beach." Sam was quick to inform us that there was a small trail to the beach directly across the main highway from our driveway. That sounded good. Then, Julie asked Sam, "May we take the pipe with us?"

Sam chuckled, and gave Julie the pipe, a lighter, and a small pill bottle of powdered weed. We each took our fanny pack with cameras and bottles of water, and headed out the door, down the steps, and across the highway.

The tiny trail passed between two houses, and came out at the cul-de-sac of a small street, where it intersected a small parking lot on the beach.

We walked to the left, away from the pavilion and the pier, and sat down under some pine trees next to a shallow stream that wound its way across the beach to the water. Julie filled the pipe, and lit-up again; it was really too much for the two of us, and we each took half a dozen tokes, feeling very stoned by the time we were finished.

Julie put the smoke stuff in her pack, then leaned over and kissed me lightly on the lips. "Thank you, Kelly, for letting us come on this trip with you and Sam." Then, she started to chuckle, but burped, "And thank you for sharing him."

I smiled, and nodded. It had been my pleasure to see Sam and my friends close, even satisfying each other's near-term needs. I thought again whether I might have voyeuristic tendencies, as I was much more turned on than turned off by seeing Sam with Julie or Linda.

Kathy had seemed aloof, and I didn't think that Sam had had sex with her on this trip. But their mud wrestling had been pretty hot, Kathy really getting into it.

Now, Kathy had another love interest; it would be interesting to see whether it would last, with Christian here on the island, and Kathy on the mainland.

Julie caressed me, and said, softly, "I don't know how to say this, Kelly ... I hope you don't get upset ... I certainly don't want to interfere with your relationship with Sam ..." I was starting to get nervous, not sure I wanted to hear what Julie had to say.

She leaned over and kissed me again, and said, "I love you, Kelly." My eyes must have gone wide, and I pulled back from Julie. She had a gentle smile, "Don't worry, Kelly, I won't attack you, or try to pull you away from Sam." I knew she wouldn't do the first, and couldn't do the second.

"But I love being with you ... holding you, and kissing." Julie sat up and smiled, "Of course, I still love men, too. They're fun to play with ... and tease." She looked into my eyes, "I love Sam, the way he described that he loved us. And he's really fun to play with ... I wouldn't mind having another ménage, if you guys are game."

I nodded. It was something Sam and I had discussed, and that we would both be interested in repeating.

Julie continued, "But my truest feelings seem to be for you. I don't consider myself a lesbian, but certainly bi." Maybe, it's just that I haven't met a man for whom I could have such deep feelings."

I didn't know what to say. "Julie, you know that I love you too; also, in the way that Sam talked about. It's a blast playing with you – and all three of us playing together."

Now, I looked into *her* eyes, "But you *know* that I am only satisfied by Sam. I love him deeply, and nothing you and I do will lessen that." I smiled, "Just like him playing around with you guys; I can understand that it is just playing, and nothing that will draw Sam away from me."

Julie nodded. "I know." She held my shoulder, "Maybe, you should propose to him?"

I laughed. It wasn't a crazy idea, but it wasn't time; I had to at least finish school. I knew that when it *was* time, Sam would propose to me. And I looked forward to what would probably be done in his overly-romantic style.

We got up and walked to the end of the beach, then back toward the parking lot, and the trail to our rental house. The sun had set, and the sky and clouds were again an incredible sight.

I thought about the future, but it was impossible to know how it would roll out: How long would it take me to graduate? Would we put KS Biotech on the map? How many years would I have to work in my career to have some level of success? Would there ever be children?

Overall, the main questions were: How would Sam and I ever have enough time to be together? And, how could we ever afford to travel and explore the world as we wanted to? I could imagine working hard in my career at least ten years, and then having a family for another decade.

But would Sam and I ever have a family? His vasectomy would limit the possibilities. We could adopt, but I just couldn't visualize myself as the 'soccer mom'. That thought led to thinking about my father, and my mother ... and then I had a vision of my birth parents – the same image I'd imagined for years.

My mind's eye saw the glass of the nicely framed image breaking, and my mother fading, while Jake became a monster.

"Are you OK, Kelly?" Julie was asking.

I focused on the beach ahead of us, and shook my head, trying to rid myself of some of these thoughts. Not realizing it, I had stopped on the beach, and Julie was now looking at me, worriedly. "I'm fine."

We kept walking, past the parking lot, and toward the pavilion and pier. The light dimmed, an orange glow now bathing the mountains behind us. The tail of the dragon; 'puff' the magic dragon. Man, was I stoned!

We didn't have massage oil, but I had plenty of vegetable oil, and filled a measuring cup. Then, I scrounged through the cabinets, until I found some sheets.

Not wanting to get oil onto the mattress, I retrieved my small tarp, and covered the double size mattress, tucking it in underneath. Then, I put a sheet over the tarp and tucked it in. Finally, I pulled the mattress away from the wall.

I heard the toilet flush, and Linda came out of her room, and walked nude across the living room, into the screen room. The temperature was perfect, and there was a slight breeze from the ceiling-mounted fan.

Linda asked, "How do you want me?"

I laughed, "Let me count the ways ..." I pointed, and Linda lay on her stomach on the mattress. I told Linda, "I'd like to try giving you a 'Thai' massage – using my entire body, like I've heard the women do in the Thai massage parlors."

Linda gave me a 'look', then shrugged, putting her head on the mattress. Her hips were still wide, and her butt was a little flabby, now, but her body really looked great. Perhaps she could lose another five pounds? It was amazing that she'd been sufficiently motivated to lose so much weight in only a couple of months.

I undressed, got onto my hands and knees above her head, and began, as usual, with my hands doing a deep massage from Linda's shoulders and neck, down her back, feeling each vertebra.

I inched my way down, my legs now on the mattress on either side of Linda's head, drizzled more oil on her back, and lowered myself onto her, so that my stomach was 'massaging' her back, and my hands were focusing their efforts on her gluteal muscles.

Continuing my way down her body, my legs squeezed against Linda's side, as my stomach passed over her butt, my hardness now between her legs. I massaged each leg and, pulling myself further down her body, gave her a foot massage, my weight now on her hips and legs.

I turned around, and straddled Linda's hips, my partial erection settling into her butt crack, and I leaned forward and massaged her back, which resulted in my stroking myself against Linda, at the same time.

Linda turned over, as I continued to straddle her hips, and I leaned forward, massaging between and around her breasts. Then, I lowered myself completely onto her, breasts squashed against my chest, my length against her stomach, pointing toward our heads.

I reached up and massaged Linda's forehead, ears, and neck. My hands ran across Linda's chest and over her shoulders. I licked and kissed her nipples, then my hands gave her a light breast massage.

Now fully erect, I lowered my head to Linda's and whispered, "Would you like a 'happy ending' ... or, maybe, a 'happy middle'?"

Linda chuckled, "It seems like *you're* the one who needs a 'happy middle'." Linda lifted her head, and smiled at me, "And you may take me, any way you like." Then, Linda gave me a severe look, "But, if you come before me, you will agree that I can give you a thousand spanks."

Linda was laughing, now, my retort being, "Your arm couldn't last for a thousand spanks. I'm not sure either one of us could count that high ..." I knew that she *could* actually give me that many spanks, but I was pretty confident that I could make her come first.

I had always given massages as professionally as possible in the past, no sex involved ... except perhaps a 'happy ending', if the massagee desired. This was more of a sensual body contact, rather than a massage. But Linda wasn't complaining.

Turning her over, I sat on my heels, and pulled her up to me. Fortunately, she helped slip me into her, as it took all my effort to pull her up to me by her hips. But once she was in me, she was able to thrust back into me, freeing my arms, which I put around her, my fingers over her clit.

I had gotten Linda off several times, and paid close attention to her response, in order to intensify her experience. My fingers worked, moving forward and down, into Linda, as she thrust her pelvis back to meet me.

Although I stayed hard, I focused on satisfying Linda, and not fantasizing. Soon, Linda was bucking against me, and I felt her vaginal muscles squeeze me, and her hot secretions creaming me. Linda was panting and moaning, as I thrust into her, my fingers continuing their pressure, without movement, over her clit.

I visualized the girls lined up on the first night, bent over the couch, waiting for needles to be stuck into their rears. As I savored the feeling of being inside Linda, I saw myself taking each of the girls from behind.

I took handfuls of Linda's hips, and pulled her against me, as I came repeatedly. Linda continued her thrusts, and I felt that I was near passing out.

When I slipped out of Linda, I turned her over, and lay flat against her, from head to toes, with only slight weight on my knees that straddled her. I kissed her deeply. Then, I laughed, "I guess that was only a partial massage. But I hope you were as satisfied as I was."

Linda kissed me back, "It was wonderful, Sam. Thank you." I rolled off her, and she lifted her head, "I think we need to take a shower." I couldn't have asked for a better invitation, so we went into Julie and Linda's bathroom and bathed each other.

When we came out, Kelly and Julie were back. "How was your walk?"

Kelly shrugged, "It was OK." Then, she smiled, "It's really a beautiful bay. Especially at sunset." Then, she looked at me, wearing only my running shorts, and Linda, in a t-shirt with nothing underneath, "How was the massage?"

I laughed, "Now I know why only *women* give Thai massages ... it's just too easy for me to get turned on, and too hard for me to last long enough to give a good massage." Kelly nodded and laughed.

Linda was shaking her head, and looked at Kelly, "Sam gave me a great massage." Looking at me, she chuckled, "You were turned on already when we started!" All I could do was shrug. I'd tried.

And I wondered how much of Linda's pleasure came from me being in her, or from just my manual stimulation. I had set out to please her, but it ended-up being much more a sexual experience than a conventional massage.

We all watched television for a while, and finished the cakes. It was raining again, the sound loud against the roof of the small house. I put my feet over the side of the couch, and lay back in Kelly's lap.

The next thing I knew, Kelly was telling me it was time for bed; I had dozed for two hours! Sinking in to the comfortable bed, I spooned Kelly, and must have dozed off instantly, as I remembered nothing after that.

Sam was out. I knew that, in spite of the playing around he did with my friends, the trip had been stressful for him. He took very seriously the responsibility of keeping us safe, and we'd done quite a few adventurous things. But there had been no casualties, so far, and there was only one more full day on the island.

I got out of bed, brought my laptop into the screen room, and worked on my dissertation for the next two hours. Then, as I listened to the patter of rain on the roof, I spent another hour thinking about my discussion with Julie, and my future with Sam.

In the morning, we packed our snorkeling gear and a few snacks, and put a bunch of sodas in the small cooler. We drove up to Princeville, heading toward the condo we'd stayed in, then turned into a residential area, and parked by a trail on the bluff.

We hiked down, and came out on a huge expanse of dark lava bordering the water. There were tide pools, and palms overhung the lava from the edge of the hill. Sam pointed, "That's called 'Queen's Bath'. It's calm enough that we can get in."

We walked to an area where the lava made a small inlet from the ocean, water swelling up and draining in an eternal rhythm.

It was already warm outside, and the water temperature was not much different than that of the air. Leaving our bathing suits on, we climbed down into the 'bath', sitting on a rock ledge, as the water swirled around us, similar to a jacuzzi.

Sam pointed out to the water, and we saw the backs of several green sea turtles, as they swam slowly along the edge of the lava. Sam said, "We *could* do an 'epic' snorkel ... from the little beach where we were before, all the way down to the Princeville Hotel."

A larger-than-normal wave rolled into the Queen's Bath, and splashed against the lava, as we floated up and down in the natural pool. Sam continued, "It's a neat trip, but would take more than two hours. And I would need to leave the car at the hotel, and run back to the beach trail."

"It sounds interesting, Sam ... for another time. Why don't we just relax, today?" Sam shrugged and nodded, then closed his eyes, and let his body move with the current.

After a little more exploring of the lava tide pools, we drove to the trailhead, where we could hike down to the little beach. We were all familiar with the trail, now, and it didn't take long to get to the beach. There appeared to be somebody lying in the sand on the near-side of the beach.

As we got closer, we realized that it was an animal. Sam whispered, "That's a Hawaiian Monk Seal. It's an endangered species – only about a thousand left. So, let's try not to bother it." We stepped onto the beach, and stayed near the waterline, moving quickly past the sleeping creature, to the far side of the beach.

We laid out the king size sheet, holding the corner and edges down with rocks from around the beach. Julie and Linda had their suits off before we had even sat down. Sam decided to go on an exploratory snorkel, and asked if I wanted to come.

I told him I would go out later. As he snorkeled quickly across the shallow reef, heading for deeper water, I opened my pack, and took out my laptop and notes. Julie and Linda were near the end of the crescent of sand, sitting on a couple of rocks, talking, their feet in the water.

Poring over pages of handwritten notes and a few printed images, I pulled out the drawing of intracellular biochemical pathways, another of the bacterium *Borrelia burgdorferi*, along with a table of DNA sequences with the proteins they coded for.

A thought had passed through my brain late last night, and I needed to determine whether it was a dream, or something that might be useful. I lay on the sheet, my backside getting it's all-over tan, while I stared at the three sheets side-by-side.

It could work … I put my head down on the sheet, as helices of DNA floated through my consciousness. It wouldn't take much modification of the experiment – just a little programming. I drifted off, the warm sun baking one side of me, and the cool sand cooling the other side.

I woke up with a start, realizing that Sam was sitting next to me. He smiled, "Good morning, sleepyhead!" Then, he looked at the papers, and my laptop balanced on top of my pack, and frowned, "You're *working*?" I nodded. I hadn't told Sam that I'd stayed up late last night.

Ignoring Sam, I made a few important notes, putting a box around them, and put everything back into my backpack. "How was the snorkeling?" I finally inquired.

Sam nodded, "It's good. But not quite as good as the last time – a little choppy out there, and less visibility."

He took off his tiny black thong, and pulled a Diet Coke from the small cooler, tilting his head back, as he took a large swallow. It could have been a scene from a Coke commercial.

Surveying the beach, I saw Julie and Linda still talking at one end of the beach, and the Monk Seal at the other end, evidently unperturbed by our presence.

It was a beautiful day again, bright blue sky, with just a few clouds, but more wind, the dark blue ocean already becoming speckled with whitecaps. A large sailboat near the horizon was beating its way upwind, perhaps sailing to Oahu, or even the mainland.

Sam followed my sight, and commented, "That was the other possibility for today: Going out on a sailboat, either here on the north shore, or on the west side." He snapped his fingers, realizing the he had forgotten something,

"We could have taken Christian and Kathy sailing; the small harbor is pretty close to where Christian lives." I shrugged; it was nice just relaxing on the beach, and not having to drive a couple of hours.

There was a buzzing in Sam's backpack, and he reached in and pulled out his phone. I was flabbergasted, "You brought your phone? And it actually works, here?"

Sam answered the call: It was Kathy. There were a lot of 'Umm hmm's, and 'OK's, and Sam hung up. Turning to me, he said, "Christian insists on taking us to dinner tonight, at a gourmet fish restaurant in Poipu, on the south shore. He suggested that we meet for drinks in the bar of the Grand Hyatt at 6PM."

"Did she say anything else? Give you any hints of how she's doing?"

Sam shook his head, "Not really. But she sounded happy, and said they were going horseback riding. Evidently, Christian has horses."

Linda said, "Horses?", as she and Julie sat down on the sheet with us.

Sam nodded, "We'll be having dinner with Kathy and Christian; they're going horseback riding this afternoon."

Linda grinned, "I *love* horses!" Her hands were in her lap, and she was casually touching herself. I hadn't had much experience with horses, myself, but had heard a few women say that they could be a turn-on, both mentally and physically.

Sam took out the snacks, and we had a small lunch. Then, Julie and Linda went snorkeling together on the shallow part of the reef. As they were coming back in, Sam and I put on our booties, and carried our mask, snorkel, and fins down to the water.

He looked funny wearing only the booties and his thong. But I could see how it would be scary snorkeling only a few inches from the holes in the reef – home to octopus, sea urchins and eels – with a 'dangling appendage', as he called it.

Sam held my hand, as we snorkeled quickly off the reef, and around the corner of the cliff to the left. We snorkeled near the waterfall again, sea turtles crowding the small pool and feeding on the seaweed.

Then, we snorkeled into the sea cave, the water suddenly feeling cooler, as we passed into the shadow of the overhanging rock. We walked through the cave, and sat in the warm pool, protected from the ocean by the reef and several large boulders – leaving our snorkel gear, and Sam's thong, by the entrance to the cave.

Sam sat on a submerged rock, and pulled me into his lap. We held each other and kissed, the warm water swirling around us. There appeared to be tears in Sam's eyes, but it may have just been splashes of the water.

Chuckling, he adjusted his hardening shaft, now vertical and pressed between us. Then, we continued kissing and caressing each other. When we came up for air, Sam looked down, and I nodded. I lifted myself a bit, and put Sam's cock inside me.

We rocked, and thrusted, and hugged and squeezed each other's bodies. Our eyes closed, and no words necessary, we felt the exquisite oneness of our souls joining. The only sounds – those of the waves and splashing of water, and wind in the trees – faded, as we climaxed together.

I hooked my feet around Sam's hips, and he touched my lips with his finger. "I love you, Kelly." He hugged me tightly, and now I was sure that there were tears in Sam's eyes. I looked at him, and waited.

Sam shrugged, "I would like to tell you something ... *ask* you something. It's a simple question, but there will need to be a lot of discussion." Sam shook his head, and looked down. He mumbled, "Maybe it *isn't* such a simple question ..." I had no idea what he was talking about.

Sam lifted me off him, and I stood in knee-deep water; then, he took my hand and led me to the entrance of the cave.

It was a spectacular setting: The dark cave; an arch of rock with ferns and vines hanging down, water dripping; a fine sand beach descending into the shallow pool, the light blue water corralled by the reef; and gradations of blue out to the midnight color of the deep ocean, still dotted with whitecaps, that now looked like frosting on a cake.

Then, Sam was kneeling before me, taking my hand. Before I could consider what Sam was doing, whether it was a joke, he looked up into my eyes. "Kelly, will you marry me?"

My knees felt weak. Tears were streaming down Sam's face, and he held my hand firmly, not wanting to let go. It didn't seem real: We were just going on a little snorkel. Now, Sam had asked a question that could change both of our lives.

I fell to my knees, and leaned forward, Sam hugging me. He kissed me, then looked into my eyes and waited.

I loved this man. I wanted to be with him, always. My eyes glazed over; I realized that although I'd thought about the possibility of Sam proposing at some point, I'd never imagined when or where it would be. This was certainly a romantic setting, and a place I would always remember.

Sam was right – we would have a lot to discuss. But his question *was* simple: Would I marry him? It felt like I'd known the answer forever.

I kissed Sam, and held is face, "Yes, Sam. I will marry you." We hugged, and now tears were streaming down my own face.

Sam led me back into the warm pool of water, and held me, his back to one of the boulders. "I love you, Kelly. I want to always be with you ... and never lose you." We hugged again.

Then, Sam smiled, and said, "But the devil is in the details. I've felt like this for a long time, and decided that I was ready to pop the question, ready to make the commitment. But I'm not suggesting we get married tonight, or elope to Las Vegas next week." Las Vegas?

Sam continued, "I'd like to see you get your degree, and we have a lot of work to develop the first KS Biotech product, and get the company going. And, I want to be sure that you can accept not having kids," Sam chuckled, "unless we adopt or we use a surrogate."

Then, Sam took his arms from around me, and floated a couple of feet away, "You might want to punish me for saying this – and you're welcome to, if you feel it's appropriate – but I also want you to think again about our age difference." It was going so well, until this upsetting statement ...

Sam said, softly, "In twenty or thirty years, you'll be in the prime of your life, and I'll be an old man." He laughed, "Even older than I am, now. A *really* old man." I was shaking my head, but he'd at least softened the message by being a little humorous.

Sam took my hands, "And we *could* have a long term relationship without getting married. I don't think a license and a ceremony are the key factors. It's a matter of commitment."

He looked into my eyes, "And, by proposing to you today, I wanted to communicate my willingness to commit ... if it's something you want, something that will make your life happy."

My mind was filled with thoughts, in fact a jumble of thoughts. But there was one clear over-arching fact: I loved Sam, and I didn't want to lose *him*, either.

Sam said, "And there's your parents. I should really ask permission for your hand from your father ... although I'm not sure he would give it."

Before I could reply, Sam said, in a sardonically sad tone, "And I should have had a ring to give you ... but I had no idea that I would be proposing on this trip."

I shook my head and held Sam. "My parents love me, and they will accept my decision." I smiled at Sam, "And I think they really like you – not as their friend, but as their daughter's partner." Sam didn't look so sure about that.

"And a ring is certainly not necessary ... although I might let you buy me one when we're ready to publicize our engagement."

Sam asked, "What about your friends? Can you – do you *want* to – keep this a secret from them?"

I really didn't know. But, as I thought about it, I wasn't sure if I could keep this a secret. And my friends and I – and Sam – had shared intimacies and trust. "I would like to tell them," actually, I felt like shouting it to the world, right now, "if it's alright with you."

Sam nodded, "I would like them to know, as long as they can keep it among us. I wouldn't want your parents to find out from one of them." That was a good point; but I trusted my friends. Sam had made sure that even Julie would respect our private information.

I stood, and waded to the small beach. "Shall we snorkel back, and tell them?"

Sam smiled, and we collected our gear, walked back through the lava tube, then snorkeled out of the sea cave, and back to the point of the hill. This time, we got out of the water and walked back to the beach along the rocky ledge, Sam carrying his thong, and now only wearing the dive booties.

Julie and Linda had repositioned the sheet in the shade of the hala trees, and were now talking to two older women (probably Sam's age), who were wearing bathing suits and carrying snorkel gear.

We dropped our equipment onto a corner of the sheet, and greeted the two women. They were staying in a condo above the beach, and asking about the snorkeling. Julie and Linda had evidently given them a lot of information, already.

As Sam and I sat on the sheet, the women thanked Julie and Linda, and headed down to the water, taking their time to put on their fins, and adjust their mask and snorkel. We all watched them, until they were snorkeling slowly on the shallow part of the reef.

Sam handed me a soda, and Linda asked, "So how was your snorkel tour?"

I smiled at Sam, and he gave me an tiny nod; or, maybe I imagined the nod. I smiled at Linda and Julie, and replied, "Well, we didn't see that much ... but Sam proposed to me." I started to take a swig from the can, but couldn't hold it in, anymore, and started laughing.

Linda's mouth fell farther open than we'd ever seen it – probably about the same as it would be at the dentist's office. Julie screamed, "Kelly! That's wonderful!" Julie hugged me, and gave me a big kiss on the mouth.

Recovering a bit, Linda smiled, "Congratulations! Both of you!" She leaned over and hugged me, then Sam.

I had to be careful to set expectations, "Sam and I are committing to each other, and we want to spend our lives together." My friends were nodding, and grinning broadly.

"But the actual wedding may have to wait until I have my degree, and we get the company off the ground." I looked at Sam, "It isn't really important *when* the wedding is, as long as we both know that we've made the commitment." Sam nodded.

I added, "There's no ring, yet, and we'll have to figure out the best way to break it to my parents." I looked at Linda and Julie seriously, "So we'd like to keep it private, for now. You guys and Kathy will be the only ones to know."

Sam rolled his eyes, shook his head, and looked at me, "And we'll have to figure out how to let my sons know." That would be a lot easier than telling my parents.

I asked nobody in particular, "I wonder whether we should not tell Kathy until she comes back with us tonight?

The dinner should be focused on her and Christian." My friends shrugged.

Sam said, "That's OK, but I might have to buy a bottle of Champagne for all of us." We laughed.

Julie offered, "I don't think it would be a problem telling Kathy ... as long as you don't mind Christian knowing, also." I didn't think that would be a problem.

Sam suggested, "Let's play it by ear."

We all toasted with our sodas, and Sam explained, "You guys know that the word '*Aloha*' means 'hello' or 'good bye' or 'love'." We all nodded, and Sam continued, "But the 'Spirit of Aloha' means something deeper. It was taught to Hawaiian children as a way of life, including a connection with nature."

Sam finished his drink. "Part of the teaching went something like this: 'Aloha is being a part of all, and all being a part of me. When there is pain - it is my pain. When there is joy - it is also mine.' Now, that's supposed to mean we share the pain and joy of nature ... but I'm interpreting it to mean that Kelly and I share each other's pains and joys."

We nodded, uncertainly. Sam added, "And the literal translation of Aloha in Hawaiian means 'joyful sharing of life energy'." He leaned over and kissed me softly on the lips, "And that is my intent with Kelly – to joyfully share our life energy."

The 'Spirit of Aloha'. It seemed to perfectly fit our relationship and philosophy of life. It felt like a dream.

CHAPTER 19: TOGETHERNESS

Sam pulled out his watch, and said, "Why don't we head back to the house? We can re-pack, and drive down to the Hyatt early, and use their pool – as long as we're having something from their bar or restaurant."

He added, "You guys would have to change, but we can bring our dinner clothes, and change in the hotel's restrooms ... or in the car." That sounded OK.

Actually, everything sounded OK to me, right now. My body was tingling, and I was pretty sure it wasn't due to the snorkel tour.

We hiked up the trail, and drove back to the house, where we all got showered. We wore shorts and tops over our bathing suits, and brought our underwear and dresses in a single rolling case.

Forty five minutes later, we were driving under the 'tree tunnel', and through the small town of Koloa, to Poipu, on the south shore.

Sam decided to make a slight detour to the famous 'Spouting Horn', a blowhole just off the highway, and then we headed to the Hyatt. We parked and walked through the lobby, and then down to the pool area, and sat in their outdoor bar/restaurant.

Smiling, Sam said, "We could order the Champagne now, but it might be nicer to share it with Kathy and Christian." We all agreed, and Sam suggested iced teas.

But Julie looked at the drink menu, and decided to try the Lava Flow, Linda ordering the same, while I went for the Lilikoi Margarita. Sam gave in, and ordered a local pale ale. He also decided to order spring rolls that we split as an appetizer.

Julie and Linda finished their drinks, took off their shorts and tops, and went into the huge meandering pool. A few minutes later, they came back, excited about the waterslide. But Sam and I decided to relax at the table ... and bask in the glow of our new commitment to each other.

Around 5:30, we went back to the car, and the three of us changed into our dresses, while Sam sat in the front watching us.

All three of us were wearing the tropical dresses Sam had bought for us down in Hanalei. Then, we went into the hotel, and disappeared for fifteen minutes in the restroom, where we did our hair and makeup.

We came out, and Sam beamed, "You look beautiful." Then, he whispered to me, "I swear that you have an aura surrounding you."

We picked a large round table on the terrace of the main bar, overlooking the pool, lagoon, and Keoneloa Bay. A few minutes later, Christian and Kathy walked in, Kathy also wearing the dress Sam had bought her.

Shaking hands with Christian and hugging Kathy, we greeted each other, and sat around the table, and the waitress came to take our drink order.

Christian perused the menu, but Sam pre-empted his selection. "Since Kathy insisted that we let you pay for dinner, please allow us to pick up the drinks. And, if you guys wouldn't mind, I thought we'd get a bottle of Champagne."

When the bottle arrived, and glasses were poured, Sam lifted his, and began his toast. "Tomorrow will be our last day here, and I wanted to first toast to the trip; I hope everyone will agree that it's been quite an experience."

Everyone raised their glasses, and Sam continued, "We should also celebrate Kathy and Christian's new friendship."

Then, he gave Kathy a curious look, and said, "At least, I hope it's something you guys are OK celebrating." Kathy and Christian answered by smiling and kissing each other. We raised our glasses again.

Finally, Sam gave me a smile, and looked at Kathy, "And, just one more thing ..." He loved to draw out the suspense. "We went down to the little beach today?" Kathy nodded. "And, I took Kelly snorkeling to the sea cave?" Kathy nodded again, now getting impatient.

Sam concluded, "Well, when she was standing under the entrance to the cave, I got down on one knee and proposed marriage to her."

Kathy screamed, pushed her chair back, and ran around the table, hugging me, and then Sam. "That's fantastic!" As she sat down, "So when's the big date?"

Sam looked at me, and I answered, "We've just made the commitment to marry each other ... but there are a lot of details to work out. And I don't think it's going to be anytime soon, as we've agreed that I should finish school first."

I glanced at Sam, "And we want to get the business going. And I have to let my parents know, in a way they won't kill me. So, it might not be for quite a while ... maybe a year or more." We hadn't discussed timing, but neither of us was in a rush.

Christian smiled broadly, displaying a gleaming set of teeth, "Well, congratulations! This is a nice place to get engaged ... or married."

That was something else: We would need to decide where to have the wedding ... and where to go on a honeymoon – assuming we had the time and money to take one. My mind was again filled with a jumble of thoughts, and I couldn't focus on any of them.

Kathy told us about Christian's estate, and their horseback riding experience today. "We rode bareback – something I'd never done before. Christian is a great equestrian; he's even competed, doing jumps and everything." Christian was modestly waving his hand as if he was shooing flies away, and shaking his head.

Christian's parents had come from Tahiti, and Christian learned both Tahitian and Hawaiian customs. He spoke fluent English, French, and Hawaiian; and he demonstrated that he could also 'talk pigeon' as he told some local jokes.

We drove a short distance to the restaurant, and had a fabulous dinner, an incredible array of fresh fish on the menu, as well as some amazing preparations and sauces.

Christian picked up the check – which was by no means small – and we all thanked him for the wonderful evening.

Sam asked Kathy, "Where are you guys parked? We should transfer your stuff."

Kathy shook her head, "No, Sam. I'm staying with Christian tonight. He'll drive me up to the house tomorrow morning. He's flying to Honolulu a little earlier than our flight to LAX."

A crooked smile formed on Sam's face, and he nodded, "OK, Kathy. How about getting to the house by noon? If we're not there, we might be on the beach at Hanalei Bay. But we'll leave the house open."

Sam hugged Kathy and shook Christian's hand, "Thank you, Christian. It's been a fun evening. And some great food." He glanced at Kathy, "We'll see you around noon, tomorrow."

Christian waved at Julie, Linda and I, and put his arm around Kathy's waist. As he turned into another lane of cars, he squeezed Kathy's butt.

The hour-long drive back to Hanalei started out quiet, all of us lost in our own thoughts – or feeling the bottle of Chardonnay Christian had ordered; oh – it was two bottles. Not to mention the Champagne Sam had ordered at the hotel ... and the drinks by the pool.

As we were passing Wailua, Julie asked, "So now that you guys are engaged, how will it change your lives ... like how you play with us, and other people?"

Sam frowned, and I exclaimed, "Why should anything change?" Out of the corner of my eye, I saw Sam looking at the road, nodding his head.

"I don't think Sam and I have talked about changing our lifestyle, or relationships; *especially* with you guys." Sam shook his head in agreement.

Then, I had to add, "And, Sam *knows* that I still intend to take the Domme course from Mistress Elena in London." Sam flicked his eyes sideways for an instant, and gave a resigned look to the road.

It was dark when we got back to the house. We'd had a relatively easy day, for our last full day on the island. Sam said, "We need to use up all the alcohol, so I can make pitchers of Piña Coladas, or Mai Tais; whatever you like."

I was going to argue that we *didn't* need to 'use up all the alcohol'; we could dump what we didn't finish ... or just leave it in the house. Then, Sam followed up with "But I'd like to take you all down to the beach, so we can experience Hanalei Bay at night, one more time."

Julie and Linda nodded, and we all used the bathroom and put on shorts and a tank. Sam went out the back door to survey the sky, then came back in and picked up a guitar that was in the corner of the living room.

"I didn't know you played the guitar!" Could there still be things we didn't know about each other?

Sam shrugged, "I took piano lessons when I was small, but rebelled, and taught myself guitar; I was in a rock group for a while." Both Julie and Linda were as surprised as I was to hear this, and I could see that they both were searching for a sarcastic comment, but neither provided any comic relief.

He had a shocked look on his face. "Oh, no!" He glanced at me, and smiled at Julie, "We have to finish-up something *else*, before we fly home tomorrow." He brought out his pipe, and the small container of grass, and put it in his fanny pack.

Sam carried the large sheet and the guitar, and we each took our small camping flashlight and a towel, and followed Sam along the trail to the beach. There were no other people, as we had expected, and Sam walked a bit farther, until we were under some palm trees at the edge of the sand.

"I thought we could take a night-time skinny-dip." He leaned over and kissed me, "But I want to sing a song for you, that I've always loved." Sam pointed up, above the mountains behind our house: There was a half-moon, glowing brilliantly.

Sam chuckled, "If we were here much later, the moon would be low over the water, and we would see the silvery reflection. But it's not such a bad view of the moon through the palm fronds."

Sam lit the pipe, and we passed it around. We talked about Christian, and speculated on whether Kathy would maintain a long-distance relationship with him. Sam filled another bowl, and the pipe made its rounds, again.

The soft wind caressed us, the atmosphere thick, and the bay dark, save for a few lights in windows of boats anchored on the other side of the dark water.

He tuned the guitar quickly, and apologized, "I love to play music, when I get the chance ... but I'm not a good singer." He looked at me, "But somehow I feel compelled to sing this to my new fiancé." It took a moment to flash on the fact that I was now a 'fiancé'. It was unreal.

Sam played a couple of chords, and began to sing, very softly, perfectly in tune, but with a more scratchy than resonant voice:

> When you see
> Hanalei by moonlight
> You will be
> In heaven by the sea
>
> Every breeze
> Every wave will whisper
> "You are mine,
> Don't ever go away"
>
> Hanalei
> Hanalei moon
> Is lighting beloved Kauai
>
> Hanalei
> Hanalei moon
> Aloha no wau ia 'oe

He leaned over and kissed me, then stood. "Shall we try the water?" He pulled his tank over his head, and pushed down his water shorts, and Julie, Linda and I followed suit – or, in this case, no suit.

We walked down to the water, and waded in, then Sam picked me up, and continued to walk in, until I was floating in his arms.

We side-stroked out beyond the small waves, and floated on our backs, looking up at the 'Hanalei Moon', and a sky-full of stars. Then, we swam in, and stood in knee-deep water, the four of us hugging each other.

We went back to the sheet and dried off. Sam looked at Julie and Linda, "I'd like very much to have one more experience with you guys, if you're up for it ... tomorrow morning. But, maybe Kelly and I should spend some private time together now."

I was surprised that Sam was kicking my friends off the beach, but they understood. They got dressed, and headed for the trail back to the house. Sam pulled me over, and we kissed, then fell back onto the sheet.

Sam put his knee between my legs, and rubbed himself on my thigh, while he kissed me. Then, he positioned himself, and entered me. I put my legs around him, and we rocked until I was sitting in Sam's lap. The moon was nearly overhead, now, softly lighting our romantic tryst.

Sam let himself fall backwards, pulling me on top of him, and I took control. I straddled his hips, and moved up and down on his length. Then, I fell forward, and kissed him, as we both moved assertively against each other.

My tension had built to its maximum intensity, and I opened my eyes. Sam looked at me, and I smiled and nodded. Twenty seconds later, our energies detonated, Sam thrusting up into my depths, and me taking all of him, as he exploded within me.

We were spent, and I laid on top of Sam, as we continued to caress each other, our bodies tingling – not to mention our minds.

Sam's voice broke, "I love you, Kelly. I love you so much. I'll always love you."

My sentiments mirrored Sam's. It wasn't just pheromones, or the time we'd spent together; we had a primal need for each other, truly the matching piece to fill our own needs, to complete ourselves. And to complete us, as a couple.

It had been building for a long time. Not my deep feelings for Kelly, which I'd had for more than a year. But the deep-seated need to be with Kelly, to not let her go.

For most of the time I'd known Kelly, my love for her was tempered by my desire to let her find her own way, to not limit her future; more specifically, I was concerned that my age would take something away from Kelly's potential.

Perhaps it had been Fiona and Justin's wedding; or, maybe bringing her to Kauai, where I already had strong emotional ties. But, over the past few months, I'd begun to understand that I couldn't 'protect' Kelly; I had to free her to make her own decisions, even if it was to be with an older man.

I'd known that we were heading toward a commitment, although I hadn't been planning to propose to Kelly anytime soon.

In fact, I half expected *her* to propose to *me*. And, my logical approach and romantic thoughts should have led to me proposing on New Year's day, or on Valentine's Day. Although that would have been trite. I certainly hadn't planned to suggest marriage until Kelly had graduated with her doctorate.

But I had done it, here on Kauai. The sea cave *did* seem to be a romantic place for a proposal. I had fully expected to feel more nervous, perhaps have second thoughts; but I felt terrific, as if a weight had been lifted from my shoulders.

Perhaps the relationship with Kelly's friends, their acceptance of me as a friend and companion, showed me that my age was not relevant. But I still felt – to some extent – like a father or at least guardian to these young women.

Now, I realized that it was all in my own head, my own perceptions of myself, and the relationships I had with people around me.

Kelly had pushed me to overcome some of my own hang-ups – and I had not completely succeeded, yet, but my perspective was quite different now, compared to two years ago, before I'd met Kelly.

I kissed Kelly, and she opened her eyes, and smiled. I gave her another peck on the lips, then stood, and offered my hand to pull her up. We dressed, and folded the sheet, then headed back to the house.

Julie and Linda were watching television, and waved when we came in the front door. I offered to make the drinks, now, and we decided on using up the vodka, coconut syrup, and fresh pineapple to make Piña Coladas.

We sat in the living room, and toasted to each other. There wasn't much conversation, but there didn't have to be; we were all on the same wavelength, and – it appeared – all in a very mellow mood.

Finally, Linda said, "Congratulations, you two!" Then, she looked at me, "Sam, Julie and I have been talking, and we would be happy to have an experience with you tomorrow morning – whatever you want. We trust you, and we love you," she glanced at Kelly, "love you both."

As I poured the second pitcher (most of the ingredients now used up, except for a small amount of vodka), Julie chimed in, more seriously than her normal self, "Sam, we understand how much you've put into this trip – not only the money, but all your effort."

She sipped her drink, "And, as Kelly has reminded us, we know that you take responsibility for keeping us safe, and making us happy."

Another sip, and a smile, "And you've done a terrific job: It's been an incredible trip, and none of us got a scratch. As Linda said, we would be happy to 'play' with you tomorrow morning … assuming it's OK with Kelly."

Then, Julie burped, "And, the morning is a good idea, before Kathy comes back. I don't think she's quite as excited about satisfying some of your needs."

I nodded, "Kathy is a good sport; she let me spank her and put those beads in her at Honopu. But her mind is totally wrapped around Christian, now, and I know she really isn't interested in sex play with me."

Kelly finished her drink, and laughed, "I can't blame her, Christian's a hunk!" I could have tossed a throw pillow at her, but she was right: Christian was the kind of guy that all these girls should meet. Unexpectedly, I had a few pangs of insecurity and inferiority.

We cleaned up the kitchen, and I told Julie and Linda that I'd come in and kiss them good night. Kelly and I got undressed, and took a quick shower, as we were still crusted with salt from the ocean. Then, I walked to Julie and Linda's room, and knocked on the door.

There was giggling, and Linda's voice, "Who's there?"

I cracked the door open, and said, in my lowest voice, "The big, bad wolf!"

Julie said, "No, Sam. You're a good wolf." I did a few wolf howls, baying at the moon.

I went over to Julie's bed, and lay next to her. "Thank you, Julie for coming on this trip with Kelly and I. I think it's been really fun to have you guys with us. And I really appreciate your adventurousness."

Julie sniffed, "I'm just glad I made it to the end of that trail; I wasn't so sure, about halfway to Kalalau." Then, she chuckled, "As we said, Sam, it's been an incredible trip. You've taken really good care of us."

Then she pursed her lips, "And went way overboard, buying us cameras, and packs, and bathing suits, and dresses." She laughed, talking loudly, so that Linda could hear, "And, I hope Kelly makes enough money in her new career to support you in the life to which you've become accustomed."

We laughed, although I was sure that Julie knew that Kelly didn't have to work at all. But I respected her independence and interest in her career; she really was a good scientist, and I had high hopes that she would develop something truly important.

I held Julie, and kissed her, and she returned the emotion. She whispered, "I'm really happy for you and Kelly. You guys are a good match for each other." I rubbed my nose on Julie's, then got out of her bed, and walked over to Linda's.

Lying beside her, I repeated the message, "Linda, we're really glad that you could come to Kauai with us, and that you had a good time. You're a beautiful woman – and intelligent, and fun-loving. I have strong feelings for you, and always enjoy being with you."

We kissed, and I realized that although it was a long and deep kiss, neither of us were looking at it in a sexual way. It was an expression of true feelings toward each other – not romantic love, but love, nonetheless.

Back in bed with Kelly, I thanked *her* for allowing her friends to come with us. And for her letting me play with them, sometimes intimately.

"Sam, you know that I enjoy the company of my friends, also. And I enjoy seeing you pleased by them."

She smiled, and added, "And you've been pretty good on this trip – you haven't put them through many challenges."

Then, I smiled, "Well, let's see what you say after our 'experience' tomorrow morning."

Kelly shook her head. "We're way beyond being shocked by anything you want to do. You know that."

I nodded, "But you know that I still get turned on by many of the same things."

Kelly nodded, sleepily, "Yeah. I know." She turned over, and I slid over and spooned her. "Good night, Sam."

"Good night, my love."

It was Saturday morning, our last day on Kauai, and we would need to be out of the house by about 2PM. We planned to have dinner in Lihue before catching our red-eye flight to LA.

It was raining when we woke up, but the sun was out, a slight fog rising from the field and all the plants, by the time we'd finished breakfast.

We all spent time packing for the flights home, then we finished the rest of the grass, sitting in the chaises in the back yard. There were a few drops of rain, but the clouds passed over us quickly and, by now, we were immune to a little water.

When we were totally stoned, Linda asked, "So what would you like to do with us, today, Sam?" That was a good question; I'd thought of many possibilities. But they all had common elements, and I hardened just thinking about it.

As I had explained to Kelly long ago, much of my turn-on was from seeing people be very open and accepting – even of pain or embarrassment. But I also wanted to communicate my love for each of the girls.

In a way, it was too bad that Kathy couldn't be here, also ... but Julie had been right: Kathy might submit, but wouldn't really enjoy the things I'd planned. Her sexual focus was solely on Christian, which I respected.

I replied to Linda, "I'd like to finish what we started the first night on Kauai, when I had you guys bend over the couch. All the same stuff as usual – a few spanks, butt plugs, some needles – but, if you guys are willing, maybe you could take me in your mouths, and then I could have sex with all three of you." Linda shrugged, noncommittally.

Julie chuckled, "Do you have the stamina to 'get it up' three times in a row?"

I shook my head, "I was thinking more of going from one of you to the next ... 'musical sex' ... and finishing off with Kelly." I thought about it – something that I'd been totally against just a year ago: Sharing body fluids with multiple partners.

"But you guys would have to be comfortable with all of us sharing body fluids. Per my original definition, we'd all be having 'sex' with each other."

"We've done that, already," Julie said.

Laughing, I said, "Well, not quite in the way I'm picturing it." Then, I explained, "I had envisioned you guys wearing blindfolds, and maybe moving randomly from one of you to another ... but maybe the blindfolds aren't necessary. Unless you'd prefer them."

Linda and Julie shrugged, and Linda glanced at Kelly, "Whatever."

I suggested they use the bathroom, and dress only in their red dirt t-shirts. Kelly and I went into our bedroom, and changed into the tees, and I collected the supplies, while Kelly went into the bathroom.

When the girls were in the living room again, I pushed the coffee table away from the couch, and the girls lined up just in front of the couch. I still wasn't sure exactly what we were going to do.

"I see the main purpose of today's 'play' as demonstrating our close feelings for each other. I don't think I'll spank you. But, since you guys wanted to 'thank' me, maybe you can take a butt plug and a couple of needles for me?" The girls nodded their assent.

"I'm going to hug and kiss each of you, then I want you to get into the 'chair' position on the couch – your legs apart, back arched, butt in the air, and head down on the back of the couch."

I turned on the stereo system, and flipped through the channels, until I found some 'spa' music – basically new age stuff that seemed to fit well with our stoned condition. I planned on not talking at all, although it remained to be seen whether I could stick to the plan.

Starting on the left, I kissed Julie, and hugged her. I really did have strong feelings for Kelly's friends. Then, I moved to Linda, and gave her a sincere kiss and hug. Finally, I hugged and kissed Kelly. Each of the girls got into position on the couch after my attention. We skipped the blindfolds.

Although Kelly would be the true 'recipient' of my lovemaking, I planned to give each of the girls nearly the same experiences. I massaged each of the beautiful bottoms in front of me, moving left to right from one girl to the next.

Then, I put on an exam glove, squeezed out a dollop of KY, and inserted my finger deep into Julie's rear, twisting and moving the finger to lubricate her completely. Then, I repeated the process, taking a new glove for Linda, and then Kelly.

I lubed the three butt plugs – the ones that were a thick but short bullet shape, with a thin shaft to be held by the anus, and a jeweled end.

I took my time inserting the butt plugs, first into Julie, then Linda, and finally Kelly. Now there were three beautiful female bottoms with inch-diameter jewels facing me. I made another pass down the line, moving my hand under them, and stroking lightly.

Ripping the packages of alcohol swabs, I swabbed each of the girls' left buttocks, then their right. Then, I walked around to the other side of the couch, bent down, and kissed each of them.

Going around the couch again, I unpackaged six of the 25-gauge 1 ½" long hypodermic needles, leaving two on the coffee table behind each of the girls. I picked up three needles, and silently inserted them into each girl's left butt cheek, not touching them, so the timing of the insertion would be a surprise.

Then, I went around the couch again, and kissed each of them – this time beginning with Kelly, and working my way to Julie – my tongue running along their upper and lower teeth, and then doing a swirling dance around their tongues.

Back around the couch, I picked up the other three needles, and inserted them quickly, moving from Kelly, to Linda, to Julie. The girls were taking it all very well, facing ahead and being perfectly silent. There were now two blue needle hubs high up on each girl's hips.

As I stroked myself, I thought about getting my phone and snapping a few pictures, but decided that this experience would be only for our memories.

Then, I stroked myself in each of their butt cracks, moving randomly from one girl to the next, until I was hard. As I did this, I wiggled the needles a few times, and reached under them to run my palm over their genitals. Both Linda and Kelly seemed to be getting wet, already.

Now, I walked around the couch, and stood in front of Julie, my hard-on nearly horizontal, as I moved slowly toward her, Julie opening her mouth and taking my length, then moving her head back and forth, sucking me.

I moved to Linda, and she took me deep into her mouth. I wondered whether Julie or Linda were capable of a 'deep throat' technique. Kelly was getting better at it, but still occasionally gagged – which spoiled the sexy (if not romantic) atmosphere.

Finally, I moved to Kelly, and she glanced up at me and smiled, before demonstrating her oral techniques. I was completely turned-on, now, and realized that I would need to exercise incredible control to make this experience last, and not come too soon.

I went around behind them, and stroked a bit more, now moving from one girl to another randomly. My fingers were wet. One more time around, and they took me into their mouths, and – again – I moved between the girls, randomly.

Finally, I stepped behind Julie, and entered her from behind. She was dripping. As I moved slowly inside her, I pulled out both needles; then, I inserted one on her left side, about four inches to the side of the top of her butt crack, and the other symmetrically on her right side.

A few more strokes, and I had to come out of her, lest I blow the rest of the experience – literally. I pulled out the needles, then took her right hand in mine, and guided it below her. She got the idea, and stroked herself, moving her hips slightly, as she finished the work I'd started.

Moving to Linda, she reached under, and put me in her. It felt incredible ... but I was now concerned that I might come before I had given Kelly her turn. Trying to hold mostly still inside Linda, I pulled out the two needles in her hip, and re-inserted them, as I'd done with Julie.

Another couple of strokes, and I pulled out of her, then pulled out the needles. Linda didn't need any guidance: Her hand – still under her – was already doing its job, and she was now breathing heavily.

I saw Julie buck a couple of times, and she drew in a deep breath as she came. I watched Linda stroke herself, allowing my erection to slightly subside before moving to Kelly. Linda came, letting out a short squeal, and I went around the couch and kissed Julie, then Linda, running my fingers through their hair and rubbing noses, before I went back around the couch for the final time, and positioning myself behind Kelly.

I slipped into Kelly, and held her hips, as I thrusted slowly in and out of her wetness. I pulled out both needles, then inserted both of them simultaneously, one on each side. These insertions had been slow, and I watched the skin of her butt dent-in on both sides, before the needles popped in.

As I moved in long strokes, Kelly thrust back against me. I pulled out the needle on her left side, then did several quick insertions in different places, leaving the needle inserted in the middle of her left buttock. Then, I did the same on her right side.

Kelly was thrusting, and the only sound was her panting, as she neared her orgasm. Now, I was holding Kelly's hips, pulling her toward me, as I thrust myself deep within her.

Kelly climaxed with a high-pitched scream, and I noticed that both Julie and Linda were looking over at her. Moments later, I climaxed, shooting into Kelly's depths. I pulled out the needles, and went around the couch, holding Kelly's head and kissing her passionately.

I cleaned up everything, dropping the used needles into a Coke can, and throwing away all the supplies. I put a folded paper towel on the coffee table, then stepped behind Julie, pulled on the butt plug. Julie gave a push, and it popped out of her.

I repeated the process with Linda and Kelly, three goopy butt plugs now lined up on the paper towel. I reached over and pulled gently on Julie's shoulders, and she stood and turned toward me. I hugged her tightly and kissed her again. Then, I did the same with Linda and Kelly.

My voice cracking, I looked at Julie then Linda, "Thank you so much for being our friend; and coming to Kauai with us; and submitting to all my eccentricities." They nodded and giggled; I guess 'eccentricities' was a real euphemism, considering everything I'd put them through over the past year.

We all kissed each other, then I brought the butt plugs into the bathroom and washed them, while Kelly put on a pair of panties.

It was only 11AM, and Kathy (and Christian) wouldn't be arriving for another hour. When I returned to the living room, the three girls were sitting on the couch talking quietly, the coffee table now back in its place.

Kelly looked up at me, "Now that my friends have 'thanked' you and you've gotten your kicks, maybe you should give *them* a chance?"

I blinked my eyes, not expecting this, and not sure exactly what Kelly was talking about. "What chance?"

Kelly laughed, "You don't want to have to go through airport security again with all those needles, do you?" I shrugged; it hadn't been a big deal flying here. Kelly continued to look at me, expecting an answer.

Julie said, "You *know* that Kelly is turned on by your submission ... and Linda and I always love to see you squirm a little ... like you do with us."

Shaking my head, I replied, "I 'squirmed' along with you guys at Honopu – letting you all spank me, and," now giving Kelly a stern look, "letting you insert those anal beads. I had to swim back to Kalalau with those in me, just like you guys did."

"You *will* submit to us, won't you, Sam?" I guess they had this all planned out; Kelly knew that I would submit to her, if she asked me. And now, I guess, she was asking.

"I always submit to you. And I have also submitted to your friends." I shrugged, and looked down at the carpet, "But if you guys really want me to submit again, I guess I could do that." Although I still wasn't sure exactly what they had in mind.

Kelly took control, "Please bring the box of needles and swabs, one of the butt plugs, a few gloves, the KY, and a towel, Sam." She looked up at the ceiling, "And, you can also bring one of the blindfolds."

When I returned with the items, Kelly spread the towel on the coffee table, and said, "Knee chest position, please."

Still wearing my red dirt t-shirt with nothing underneath, I got into position as Kelly had requested. She handed me the blindfold, and I put it on. Now, my bare butt was high in the air, facing the three girls, my 'package' hanging down and swinging slightly.

A few moments later, I felt the cold of the KY on my anus, and a finger wormed its way inside me, moving around, and pressing on my prostate. Maybe this wouldn't be so bad, after all?

The finger came out, and another was inserted, and moved in and out of me. This was repeated half a dozen times, so I knew that each of the girls had taken their turns. Now, I felt the bulbous tip of the butt plug pressed against me, and I consciously relaxed my anal muscles.

It took a minute or two, but the butt plug was finally inside me. This was one of the ones I'd used on the girls, and the thin shaft was not too uncomfortable.

The girls started talking – about what they would be doing when they got back home, about buying a winter wardrobe, and other miscellaneous (to me) topics. Then, I felt fingers against my butt, and the butt plug was pulled out again. The central portion was thick, and it hurt a little coming out, but at least it was quick.

The girls continued talking, as the butt plug was shoved against my butt and inserted again. This process was repeated, and I assume that each of the girls had gotten their own 'kicks' invading my private space with the shiny metal device.

When the butt plug was inside me the third time, Kelly said, softly, "Please lie down on the coffee table, Sam." I turned ninety degrees, and lay down on the towel-covered table, my feet hanging off the end.

No sooner had I gotten into position than I heard the ripping of alcohol swab packages, and felt both sides of my butt being swabbed. I had assumed that the girls would insert two needles, as I had done with them ... but my entire bottom was being scrubbed.

I knew what was about to happen, so I tried to relax; there was nothing I could do – I had agreed to submit, and would let the girls do whatever they had in mind. A couple of needles wouldn't be a big deal.

As I thought this, I felt the sting of a cold steel needle being inserted into my left hip. I heard the girls moving around, and then there was another needle in my right hip. Then I was surprised by another two needles being inserted simultaneously in the middle of both buttocks.

I closed my eyes, even though the blindfold prevented me from seeing anything. The girls continued to talk, now about Kathy and their impressions of Christian. And I felt another needle being inserted ... and then another. "What?" I tried to relax and control my breathing.

Kelly laughed, "Just relax, Sam, there are probably at least sixty needles here." Oh, no! Was she planning on inserting *ALL* of the needles I'd brought? It was involuntary: I whimpered ... just a little.

Kelly seemed upset, now. "Sam, do you remember why you brought my friends on this trip?"

I nodded, "To thank your friends – and you – for putting up with some of the challenges during that long weekend."

Kelly calmer, now, said, "So just suck it up. We're not taking any needles on the plane." Then, she gave a fiendish laugh, "And we're definitely not going to waste them." I felt another sting, then another.

My eyes still closed, I thought of nice things ... being on a tropical island ... But I *was* on a tropical island! The girls were talking again, and I felt another sting from time-to-time, without warning. My bottom felt like a pin cushion; a sore pin cushion.

I heard one or more of the girls standing up, walking. It was quiet for a long time; well, at least several minutes. Now, I wondered what time, it was; I certainly wouldn't want Christian to come in and see me in this 'condition'.

I knew that Kelly was testing me. And I wanted to pass her test. But it hurt.

Finally, the girls came back in, and Julie asked, "Would you like us to take out the needles, now, Sam?"

I nodded, "Yes, please."

The sliding out of each needle did not feel good – but it was the lesser of the evils. I assumed that all three girls were working, as I felt the needles being taken out – then dropped into a can – very quickly; it was probably less than a minute for the last uncomfortable extraction.

"Knee chest position, please." That was Linda's voice. I got back into position for one of them – I guessed that it would be Linda – to pull out the butt plug. The girls had challenged me, but I had 'risen' to the challenge; although nothing else had risen.

It was only 11:30, although it had felt like hours. Kelly suggested that we all take a quick shower together, and get dressed before Kathy and Christian arrived. She, Julie and Linda were standing around me, nude, each carrying a towel.

Kelly handed me a towel, and led us to the outdoor shower, which was a concrete pad with a showerhead that produced a wide spray of water. And there was plenty of it.

The four of us bathed each other, with no conversation, but a lot of feeling. Bathing each other's (usually) private parts was natural to us – had been, for a long time, now.

We had certainly demonstrated today that our sensual and sexual proclivities would not be curbed, just because we were engaged, or even if we were married – *when* we were married.

Rather than tiring of dominance and submission, we continued to be intrigued by the feelings, and the possibilities – of things we'd never tried. And our love and respect for Kelly's friends continued to grow.

I knew it was a special time in our lives; Kelly's friends would find their own partners soon enough. And the relationship I had with Kelly would undoubtedly morph, perhaps not better or worse, but different.

We finished our showers, dried ourselves, and shuffled inside to get dressed. I 'dressed up' in my longer shorts and Aloha shirt, and the girls wore shorts, but would change into their dresses before dinner.

CHAPTER 20: ALOHA 'OE

The doorbell rang; right on time! Kathy came in, followed by Christian. Kelly hugged them both, and I walked from the kitchen and shook Christian's hand, then hugged Kathy. "Welcome to Hanalei!"

Christian nodded, "This is a nice place! I don't get up to the north shore often enough." Kathy turned to him, and they kissed; it was much more than a 'friendly' kiss.

As Julie and Linda were coming into the room, Christian waved, "Sorry, but I have to go. My flight is in a couple of hours; and I don't remember there being this many stoplights on the highway."

Then, he turned to Kathy, gave her another peck on the lips, and whispered, "I'll call you tomorrow night."

Christian disappeared down the stairs. Kathy closed the door behind her, and Kelly gave her an inquisitive look. Looking at each of us, then Kelly, Kathy smiled, "I think I'm in love."

Kelly hugged her, and I stepped up to her, "That's great, Kathy!" I gave her a quick hug. Then, I glanced at Kelly and back to Kathy, "Love isn't that easy to find."

As we drove down to Lihue I gazed out the window: There were the mountains, the ocean, the sugar cane fields; then, along the east shore, hundreds of palm trees. In between, we stopped in Kapaa, so that Sam could visit a dive shop, and say hello to the guy who had certified him.

I did some window shopping with my friends. Kathy actually went inside one of the stores, tried on an island dress, and bought it. She resonated with positive energy.

We didn't pry – Kathy would fill us in on her experience with Christian. Or, if she didn't by the time we got to Lihue, we would pry a little during dinner.

We rendezvoused back at the car, and Sam said, "We have a few hours before dinner ... is there anything you guys want to do? Shopping? Kayaking? Going to a beach park?"

We were all shaking our heads. We were all cleaned up for the plane, so weren't interested in anything too strenuous or in the water.

Sam suggested that we drive to the south shore, and visit a botanical garden. So we drove south, along the east shore, passing Lihue, and turning through the tree tunnel to Koloa, then down to Poipu.

We got out, and walked a while around Poipu Beach. Then, we continued along the beach road west, past the spouting horn. We'd seen it, but had not visited the nearby National Tropical Botanical Garden.

As we walked down the paths, Sam snapped pictures of some of the flowers, and we read the signs explaining the unique flora of the islands. After finishing the tour, we decided to continue on the same road to the Allerton Gardens, and Lawai Bay.

We parked, and walked out to the sand, then down the beach, and found a tree-shaded area of boulders. We sat down, and watched the waves roll in to the small bay.

Julie couldn't stand it any longer, "So, Kathy, tell us about your little side-trip with Christian." Linda, Sam and I were also awaiting her response.

Kathy shrugged, "After we left you at the Wailua River, Christian drove us down to Lihue. First, he showed me the marina, and his boat."

Linda squealed, "He has a *boat*?"

Kathy nodded, "A sailboat; it's pretty small – I think around thirty feet – but we went down below, and it will sleep four people." We watched as several frigate birds flew across the water, and Kathy continued, "Then, he took me to a the best '*saimin*' shop on the island."

Linda asked, "Saimin?"

Kathy nodded, "Noodles in a broth with pork and fried shrimp, and an egg on top. Then, we had mochi balls."

Sam laughed, "Well, at least he didn't starve you."

Kathy continued, "Then, he drove us back to his place – which has a couple of houses and a barn on a large piece of land. It's on a plateau that has an ocean view."

Kathy glanced at Sam, "Christian's a good cook, too. He barbequed steaks and made a big salad. Then, we sat outside and watched the stars. He taught me a lot of Hawaiian and Tahitian lore." Kathy smiled at us, "Then, we went inside."

The waves continued to roll in, funneling onto the small beach; we were the only people on this side of the beach, and there appeared to be only a handful of people on the other side. Above us were beautiful palms, leaning over the boulders as if in a painting.

Kathy said, "The house is kind of a Hawaiian-style single-family ranch house. Bamboo furniture, wooden and tile floors." Kathy looked at Sam, and remarked, "And he has a lot of high tech stuff too, Sam."

She grinned, "But his theater room isn't quite as big as yours ... and he doesn't have a bed behind the screen, or cameras in the ceilings." We all laughed.

Julie kept prying, "So did you guys get it on?"

Kathy nodded slowly, "The first night we played with his dogs – two Golden Shepherds – and met his housekeeper. Then, when she left, we got into his redwood hot tub – one of those original, old-style hot-tubs."

Sam leaned over to me and whispered, "Yeah, old-style, around my time."

Kathy smiled, "Christian is a gentleman. We held each other and kissed in the hot tub, then he showed me to 'my' bedroom and bath. He suggested we get showered, but then left me to take my own.

"I put on a long shirt, and met Christian in the kitchen, where he poured some white wine. He was wearing a light robe that hung as if from a statue.

"He wasn't going to push me, but we started kissing, and I went down on him; I think it surprised him, but he certainly enjoyed it. Then, he carried me – actually lifted me into his arms, and carried me – to his bedroom, where he tossed me onto the bed, crawled over me, and took control.

"We were very compatible, and he has quite a lot of stamina. He even got it up for a second time, and took me from behind, over the corner of the bed. Then, we slept together ... actually *slept*.

"Yesterday, he made coffee, and then taught me a little about taking care of the horses. He took me for a late breakfast at a local restaurant in Waimea, and then we got the horses ready and took a long ride. It was beautiful!"

As we finished walking the loop around the botanical garden, Kathy continued, "We got cleaned up, so that we could meet you guys ... and this time I suggested that we take a shower together."

She turned and looked at us with a sour expression, "And then I got my period." As we laughed she said, "But we did bathe each other. He has a *great* body; his chest, abs, those beautiful buns." We laughed louder.

Then, Kathy chuckled, "So, despite my having my period, Christian wanted me to stay another night ... and I wanted to stay. It was Friday night, and we met some of his friends, then we all went to a party. It was a reggae concert in the cane fields."

We got back to the Caravan, and changed into our clothes for the flight. Julie and I wore the dresses Sam had bought us in Hanalei; Linda wore slacks and a silk blouse, her 'new' body shown off well. And Kathy wore a wraparound skirt, and a halter top tied above her navel.

Sam drove back toward Lihue. We parked and walked along Kalapaki Bay, near the entrance to the harbor, and took a look at the pool at the Marriott.

Then, we went to one of the more popular tourist restaurants, and Sam managed to get us a table at the edge of the deck, just a few feet from the beach below. We all ordered tropical drinks, and toasted again – to Kathy and Christian, to each other, and to the trip.

We didn't need to be at the airport for three hours, and it was only ten minutes away, so we decided to have a leisurely dinner. Sam ordered several appetizers, including sashimi, coconut shrimp, and chicken skewers with satay sauce. A warm breeze flitted through the palms, and caressed our bodies.

Sam pulled the tiny parasol from his drink and ate the pineapple, then held up his glass, "I just want you guys to know that I've really enjoyed this trip – coming to Kauai, sharing the experience with you ... and spending time with you." How many times had he told us this, already?

He smiled, "Hopefully, you guys have enjoyed it, too ... and now understand a bit better why this island is so special to me. And our experience here over the past couple of weeks has made it more special."

Sam sipped his Mai Tai, and looked down; he was becoming emotional again. Then, he smiled at me, and lifted his glass again, "And this trip is even *more* special, and I will always have deep emotions for Kauai, since this is where I proposed to Kelly."

I leaned over and hugged Sam. There were tears in his eyes. "I love you, Sam." I looked around the table at my friends, "I love all of you."

Then, I flashed on a thought, "And, if it weren't for you guys playing with us ... and Sam trying to find a way to reward you, we might not have come here, and it may have taken Sam a long time to propose to me ... maybe years." I had said it facetiously, and Sam was shaking his head, but he didn't debate the point.

Kathy raised her glass and smiled, "And, if Sam hadn't taken us here, I wouldn't have met Christian." It still wasn't clear where that would lead, but Kathy seemed truly in love – the first time I'd seen her so head-over-heels about any guy.

We were all quiet for a few moments, thinking of the various implications of this trip, and our multi-way friendship. The waiter came, and we ordered dinner – ribs for Sam, and fresh fish for the rest of us.

I stared across the dark water of Kalapaki Bay to the lighthouse, it's light rotating around endlessly, guiding boats into Na'wili'wili Harbor. Sam had convinced me: This really *was* a magical island; and the friendship between all of us was magical, also.

Julie looked at Sam, and then me, and reiterated, "We love you guys, too." Then, she chuckled, "I used to think of myself as the 'open' one," and, glancing at Sam, "the 'wild' one. But, after the experiences that Sam has shared, and the challenges he's given us, my former life seems pretty tame."

Linda nodded, "Yeah. I was pretty shocked that first night at the French restaurant, when Sam suggested that he give me a 'birthday spanking' ... but we've all opened up to each other – in many ways – and our mutual friendship is now much deeper than I ever could have imagined."

I thought about Linda, who had always seemed rather staid and conservative; I certainly never imagined her as the sensual, sexual woman that she had been with us. Nor that we would be sharing all of the experiences and relationship developments that had occurred over the past 18 months.

Our 'last supper' on the island was great, both the food and the conversation. We ordered espresso, and Sam insisted that we try the 'hula pie'; we split two of the huge desserts between us.

I had to chuckle again remembering that first time at the French restaurant, when Sam was nervous about sharing a dessert – and our 'germs'. He had come a long way since then; we all had.

Not that we intended to be promiscuous; but the lifestyle we'd led over the past year or so would certainly not be accepted within mainstream society. I remembered Sam's rant against Victorian values; and there seemed to be no reason for many of them, other than social mores.

And, within our small group, we'd demonstrated that alternative social values can work. At least, it seemed that we were all happy, and nobody had regrets about the things we'd done. Once we had decided to be honest and open with each other, the rest naturally followed.

But I still could not envision the life that I would want beyond my career; or how the focus on KS Biotech might detract from the things that Sam would want to do.

ISLAND EXPERIENCE

We boarded the plane, and Linda decided to sit in the second row, behind Kathy and Julie. As we put our things in the overhead, she chuckled, "Maybe I'll get lucky, and meet a hunk, like Kathy."

Not likely; but Linda certainly did have an attractive physique in those clothes, although they didn't look the most comfortable for an overnight flight.

I got settled, and plugged in my music. As we taxied out to the runway, Sam reached over and held my hand; with his other hand, he wiped tears from his eyes. I looked at him, and he turned his head to me and smiled, then mouthed, 'I love you' and squeezed my hand.

It felt unreal: My friends and I had flown to Hawaii as single women, and I was flying back as a fiancé. Looking across the aisle, I saw Kathy staring out the window into blackness; only time would tell whether her relationship with Christian would become more serious.

Julie glanced at me and smiled. As Sam had predicted, it had truly been an epic trip, which had cemented the relationship that Sam and I had with my friends even more.

After we leveled off, and the drinks were served, Sam leaned over to me and hummed a tune – probably the most recognizable of all Hawaiian songs. He explained that it had been written by Princess Liliuokalani – before she became queen.

Sam wasn't clear on the full story, but evidently she had hummed the tune as a farewell, when she visited the ranch of a military official on the north side of Oahu, and wrote the words later.

Sam said, "I don't remember all the verses, but '*Aloha 'Oe*' means 'Farewell to thee', and the chorus talks about love. I interpret it as my love for Sarah in the past, my love for Kauai as we depart, and my love for you in the future."

For the second time on this trip – and since I'd met him – Sam sang to me, as tears streamed down his cheeks:

Farewell to thee, farewell to thee
The charming one who dwells in the shaded bowers
One fond embrace,
'Ere I depart
Until we meet again
Sweet memories come back to me
Bringing fresh remembrances
Of the past
Dearest one, yes, you are mine own
From you, true love shall never depart

Using the drink napkin, he wiped the tears away, then leaned over and kissed me. Sam was an incredibly romantic person, one hundred percent male, but with a rare sensitivity that most males either didn't have, or were afraid to show.

I closed my eyes, and visualized Sam on his knee, my hand in his, as he proposed under the arch of the sea cave. Then, a series of images formed in my mind's eye, morphing from one to the next like a slideshow.

I saw us swimming in the dark water of the wet cave, ducking under the rock wall into the 'blue room'. And, our first snorkel tour, seeing sea turtles, then snorkeling by a waterfall and into the sea cave.

The sound of the plane became the hum of the helicopter, flying into Mount Wai'ale'ale and along the Na Pali coast. Then, the sound became the splashing of the waterfall in Hanakapiai Valley. We hit a little turbulence, and I was transported immediately into the Zodiac, bouncing along the coastline, and motoring through caves and under waterfalls.

I imagined the beautiful valley and meandering stream, where we'd celebrated Julie's birthday. Then the Kalalau trail, hiking high above the water, our day at 'ginger pools', and showering under the waterfall in the campground.

Then I chuckled, as I remembered waking up to the Hawaiian geese nibbling at my toes. An image of the huge rock arch, waterfall and stream of Honopu formed, then I saw us on the sand dune looking out at the ocean during Sam's little 'ceremony'.

Fingering the material of the island-style dress Sam had bought, I thought about Sam's generosity, outfitting all of us, and bringing us to Hawaii. And, although he'd spent a night with each of my friends, he really hadn't pushed too hard, only 'challenging' us a couple of times during the trip.

And we'd rewarded him this morning with a multi-way sexual experience ... then challenged him with a needle experience he wouldn't soon forget.

I reclined the seat, and pushed my head into the pillow; Sam stood and took a blanket from the overhead, then laid it over me, and tucked me in. My Sam: My thoughtful, sensitive, perverted, but loving Sam.

I closed my eyes, and heard the refrain from *Aloha 'O*e. Then I was on the beach, Sam making love to me, with the moon high above. As I drifted off to sleep, the tune of *Hanalei Moon* filled the remainder of my consciousness.

CHAPTER 21: GRADUATING WITH HONOR

Kelly was working feverishly on her dissertation project – both the experimental and writing parts. She had told me about the idea she'd come up with on Kauai, a way to check whether the predictions by her software made sense; and she had now modified the equipment and software to check whether the DNA sequence of a specific bacterium might code for proteins that were part of the known biochemical pathways of the target disease.

We still ran nearly every morning, but Kelly's schedule at the university didn't allow for much time together, so I visited my son and daughter-in-law ... and, of course, my new grandson, for a week in October. It was hard to believe that it had been a year since our trip to Europe.

Kelly had met her friends for lunch – at the Mexican restaurant again – and told me that they had gushed about the trip to Kauai. Kathy was in contact with Christian daily, and she was going to visit him on her birthday.

Last year, Kelly and I had been in Europe, so we couldn't throw Kathy a birthday party ... or, even join her on her birthday. And, this year, she would be going back to Kauai.

I thought about our engagement: Kelly was still excited about our future together, as was I. But a key question was when we should inform her parents. We agreed that we would not set a date or let her parents know until Kelly had graduated.

Kelly was working nearly twenty-four hours a day on her dissertation, but I still expected Raj to hold her back to at least the summer.

There was no question that she was putting in the time, and had the creative ideas and analytical thinking ability ... but it *did* take a little luck, for one's hypothesis to be proven, and a doctorate granted earlier-than-usual.

I offered to make Thanksgiving dinner for Kelly's parents and us ... unless one or both of the extended families wanted to visit, like they had during Christmas, last year. Kelly didn't want to face the whole family until we were comfortable announcing our engagement. But, she was softening on the possibility of a Thanksgiving with just her parents.

I suggested that Kelly and I travel to Oregon to visit Robert, Jessica, and John Samuel, over Christmas ... but Kelly couldn't think about anything now, except her project. She was truly possessed: I'd never seen Kelly's determination, strength and stamina in a researcher, before.

It was mid-November, already, and I'd made great progress on my research and dissertation. Raj had agreed with the plan for testing my algorithm that I'd developed on Kauai. And, so far, everything was checking out. The writing of my dissertation had caught up with the research and, once the experiments were complete, I would be able to finish quickly.

Raj had asked me whether I really wanted to graduate at the end of this quarter, which would require defending my dissertation in front of a panel of professors. And, it could jeopardize doing further research at the university ... unless Raj could arrange a post-doctoral position for me.

My decision was to finish as quickly as possible, and worry about continuing the research as a second step.

Sam was in discussions with the university, and in the process of negotiating the patent rights. His proposal was that we would pay for the continuing patent prosecution, in return for continued use of the lab; this would allow me to graduate and still have access to the expensive equipment for the additional research needed for KS Biotech's development of its first product.

I finally gave in to Sam's idea of having my parents over for Thanksgiving dinner; and he gave in to having a small party for my friends over Christmas, rather than visiting Robert and Jessica – and Sam's new grandson. Assuming I actually graduated by the end of the year, we would visit them early in the new year.

I'd only seen Julie, Linda and Kathy once since we'd returned from Kauai, and much of that had been Kathy fawning over Christian. She had spent a week there during her birthday, and the relationship seemed to be heating up – not that it could get much hotter than when we'd been on Kauai. I'd never seen Kathy so happy.

As we were walking out of the shopping center, Julie had quipped, "I wonder who will be married first: You or Kathy?" It was true – at this point, I would have put my money on Kathy; if I didn't pass my doctoral defense, or publish my dissertation in the next four weeks, it would be summer, before Sam and I would even set a date.

I could imagine that it would be delayed further, if we concentrated on our startup business. And, assuming I *did* graduate in a month, I would still want to take the domme course from Elena; most appropriately, while I was still single.

Although, I guess it didn't matter, as long as Sam was OK with it; or, at least, would give me the freedom to pursue my interests ... which I knew he would. And, I knew that Sam would also gain by having me go through the challenging experience.

Over the past year, I had done some research into BDSM ... and realized that there were many interpretations of these letters. Bondage, Discipline, Sadism, and Masochism; and Dominance and Submission (D/s); and Master and Slave (M/s). Sam and I didn't really seem to fit any of these categories, although 'discipline' and D/s came the closest.

But neither of us wanted to hurt the other, nor did we crave pain, for its own sake. We enjoyed 'power transfer', the giving over of control to the other person. And submitting to their will, trusting them, even if there was some pain involved.

Sam was a sweet person, and we had learned early in our relationship that Sam wasn't a sadist; he didn't want to see someone in pain, just in submission. And he wasn't really willing to cause more pain, such as during a spanking, than we had already given and received.

When Elena had asked me to give Sam a long and hard spanking, I didn't hesitate to use my strength and stamina: I knew that it wouldn't damage Sam, and the pain would be only temporary.

I squeezed my legs together, as I imagined Sam giving me a severe beating. He would object to that term, and use 'spanking', as the pain was mainly directed to our bums. Then, I imagined a scene with Sam and my friends, being tied up and abused by all of them.

This line of thinking surprised me: We had all spanked each other and submitted in many ways; but my fantasy involved all of them dominating me. Now that I realized that I wanted this, I would let Sam know. I had no doubt that he would be delighted to please me; but I *did* have some doubts as to whether the reality could ever match the intensity of what I had just envisioned.

I had invited my friends for a get-together over the long Christmas weekend, starting on Thursday afternoon for Christmas eve. Sam was planning everything, but it would be great to spend time with my three friends during the holidays. Especially, if I had graduated, and could start to relax for a while.

Kelly's parents came over for a traditional Thanksgiving dinner, but she was preoccupied. She had submitted her dissertation, and had to defend it before a panel of professors next week. She had 'lived' her research so long, and had put such intensity into it, that I knew she would pass. I was still amazed that she could have finished this quickly.

Kelly poured the wine, a nice California cabernet, as I put the various dishes on the buffet counter. The turkey had come out great – a golden brown, and I'd sliced the breast and laid out the drumsticks and wings on a large platter, decorated with sprigs of parsley.

My specialty was the gravy: I made a roux that I cooked to a dark brown, then stirred in the turkey drippings and turkey stock that I'd previously made and frozen, with enough pepper to give it a little bite. The thick, smooth, mocha-colored liquid filled the gravy boat, and I poured the rest into a large measuring cup.

The stuffing – my own recipe that included a large amount of sautéed onions and a gigantic amount of mushrooms, cooked in butter – had been baked inside the turkey. I'd also made fresh string beans with fried onion topping, and sweet potato casserole with marshmallows.

This last dish brought back memories of our cookout in Kalalau, roasting marshmallows and making s'mores under the sea of stars. That really *had* been an epic trip; except it was over too quickly. I had already made a slide and video show from the trip, which I planned to debut for Kelly's friends during the Christmas party.

I put out the silver spoons and meat fork, and then announced that it would be a casual 'serve yourself' dinner. Dave headed into the kitchen, Darlene following and smiling sweetly. They seemed more than cordial, tonight, Dave more reserved than I'd ever seen him. I looked at Kelly, and she shrugged.

During dinner, Kelly tried to explain her dissertation, but I could see that her parents didn't understand most of what she'd told them. They were pleased that she would be graduating, but weren't sure what she would do with her degree. We told them about KS Biotech again, but they didn't 'get' that it could be hugely important for society – and profitable for us.

After dinner, Kelly suggested that I show the images and video from our Kauai trip. I coughed, "Umm, it's going to take a few minutes to get ready." She gave me a funny look; I couldn't explain – in front of her parents – that I had *one* version of the show finished ... but that was for Kelly and her friends.

I couldn't even imagine what her parents would think, if they saw some of the images; for example, the girls lined up, their bottoms bare, bending over the back of the couch. I chuckled, as I went down to the playroom to edit the show and get the projector fired up.

Darlene 'Oooh'ed' and 'Aaah'ed', as we showed images of beautiful beaches, some underwater shots, and the trail. Of course, there was no way that we could communicate the difficulty and adventure of hiking to Kalalau.

Dave's only question was whether we played golf. I had learned to play in junior high and high school, and I knew that Dave had taught Kelly to play. But we'd never played a round of golf together, and I didn't think either of us had hit a ball in a long time. Perhaps we could start going to the driving range, now that Kelly was going to graduate?

Then, an image flashed on the screen that I had not intended Kelly's parents to see; in my quick editing, I hadn't noticed this one. It really didn't show anything — just Kelly, Julie and Linda, smiling at the camera, their heads just above the back of the couch.

Of course, Kelly and I knew instantly that it was when the three girls had 'humored' me the last morning at the house. But you couldn't see from the picture that all three girls were bare from the waist down, and that each of them had a butt plug in her rear.

Dave laughed, "I don't know about you going to a tropical island with so many beautiful, young girls, Sam." It was an offhand comment, not really requiring an explanation; Dave knew that Julie and Linda were Kelly's friends. But Darlene's smile disappeared, and she was suddenly upset.

She screamed at Dave, "Of *course* you 'know' about it! You're screwing a girl not much older than Kelly, yourself!"

We were in shock; I thought Kelly was about to pass out. I waited for her to say 'What!?!?' ... but only saw her mouth drop open; and gears turning in her head. She looked at Dave, then back to Darlene, and her eyes were suddenly wet.

Her mother nodded, "Yes, dear, it's true. Your father has taken up more than poker or pool in his new 'man cave'." She glanced at Dave, "Not that he never fooled around, before."

Dave shook his head, "I never had sexual relations with another woman ..." Somehow, that sounded familiar. Dave looked down, and mumbled, "A man needs some release, every once in a while."

Darlene held Kelly's hand, "Don't worry about it, Kelly, it doesn't bother me. Your father and I haven't had sex for some time, now." She was shaking her head, then looked at Kelly and smiled weakly, "But I think he understands how Sam could be so happy being with you."

I started to say, 'It's not – just – about sex!', but Dave exploded, "Yeah, I can understand what's in it for *him*; but I still would like to see my daughter marry someone her own age, someone who will grow old with her."

Kelly drew her hand away from her mother's, "It's *my* choice! Sam is the man I love ... I will always love him."

Dave harrumphed, and I went to the bar, where I poured a Scotch for him, then offered Darlene and Kelly something to drink. Kelly said, "Whatever," and Darlene said, "Me too." I poured a small glass of port for each of us, and brought a bar of 70% dark chocolate to the coffee table, breaking it into small squares.

As Darlene tasted the port, I glanced at Kelly, and she gave a nearly imperceptible shake of her head. It still made sense to make sure she graduated, and a date was set, before informing her parents. But, Dave's sexual escapades with a younger woman weakened his argument against Kelly and I. Somewhat.

My dissertation committee asked some incredibly astute questions, but I evidently addressed them well enough, because Raj accepted my dissertation, and I ended the year with my degree: *Doctor* Kelly Walsh!

Sam and I agreed that we would not discuss my research or KS Biotech until the first of the year; we deserved to take the next ten days off. We also agreed not to talk about marriage; I wanted – *needed* – a few days without added pressures.

Although my father had softened regarding the relationship that Sam and I had, he would still undoubtedly go ballistic, when we told him we were going to be married.

Sam was still suggesting that he formally ask permission from my father, but I told him to forget about it, and focus on my desires. After more thought, I realized that this was another manifestation of my sensitivity when it was implied that I was young or immature.

As school was now finished – *really* finished – I helped Sam prepare for the small party with my friends. I'd found out that Kathy was on her way to Kauai again, paid-for by Christian, and would be gone over the holidays; so our small party would now be even smaller.

But then I received an e-mail from Fiona, letting me know that they would be coming our way – staying with Alex for a week, and going back to Toronto for their New Year's celebration. Sam thought it was a great idea, so I invited them to come over on Christmas day, and stay for dinner.

Sam spoke with Alex, and invited her to the party, but she equivocated, and told us that she would have to let us know. That was fine; it would be a fun party with or without Alex … but it would undoubtedly also be a very different experience.

On Thursday, the 24th, Julie and Linda arrived in the early afternoon. They rolled their cases through the front door, then hugged me, "Congratulations, Kelly! Or, should we say 'Doctor Walsh'?"

I laughed, "'Kelly' is fine ... unless you need some of the doctor's attention down in the exam room ..." My friends were surprised when I looked at them seriously, and they shook their heads, moments before I cracked up laughing.

Linda said, "We'll probably get enough of that kind of attention from Sam." Now, we were all laughing.

Sam came in and hugged Julie and Linda, "What's so funny?"

I replied, "I think Linda wants some of your attention in the exam room."

She screamed, "Kelly!" But she was still laughing, until Sam gave her a serious look, then she shook her head, and Julie and I laughed even louder.

It was too cold to sit outside and talk, but Sam had heated the jacuzzi and sauna, figuring they would probably get some use today or tomorrow.

We sat around the kitchen table, as Sam made 'mulled wine' – mixing two bottles of Bordeaux wine with some apple cider and a splash of port in a small pot, then adding a bunch of spices (Sam called them off to us – cinnamon, cloves, allspice, nutmeg and cardamom), a small box of raisins, and strips of fresh orange peel.

After adjusting the heat, he sat down with us. Looking at Julie and Linda, he said, "Now, I not only have to contend with Kelly as a domme, but also she's the smartest one in the house."

Julie laughed, "She always *was* the smartest one in the house, Sam. The Ph.D. just validated it." Sam was shaking his head slowly, then smiled, and started nodding.

Linda asked whether we had set a date for the wedding, I told her that we weren't talking about it until next year. That sounded far off, but it was only a week.

That got us onto the subject of Kathy. Julie had spent a day with Kathy before she left for Kauai the third time in four months. "I think she's really in love." Then, Julie chuckled, "At least, *she* thinks she's really in love." Julie looked at Sam, "And she's really fallen in love with Kauai, too. I wouldn't be surprised if she moved there."

Sam smiled, "It would be great having someone to visit, there." I didn't comment; Sam obviously already had several friends there. But it *would* give us a nice excuse to go back; and right about now, in this cold weather, Kauai sounded pretty good.

Sam strained the wine mixture through cheesecloth into a one quart Pyrex measuring cup. Then, he poured us each a portion in a glass cup that sat in a metal holder. Sangria in the summer, mulled wine in the winter. It warmed us nicely.

Julie and Linda brought their stuff upstairs, each taking a guest room, then brought their iPads down to the playroom, and Sam set-up wireless connections so they could display their pictures and video from Kauai. We had decided to leave Sam's show for tomorrow, so that we could share the experience with Fiona and Justin.

The waterproof cameras had worked well, taking great pictures both above and below the water. It had been more than three months since returning, and I hadn't even made the time to see all the pictures Sam and I had taken.

We re-lived the trip, as Julie flipped through images – our north shore tour, the little beach, the helicopter tour, hiking to the waterfall, the crazy Zodiac ride down the coast, Sam and Kathy nude mud wrestling in the swamp, Julie's birthday party and, of course, the Kalalau trail, campsite, and ginger pools. Then there was Honopu beach and waterfall, the stream and the rock arch.

Julie had taken plenty of pictures of Sam, wearing his skimpy bathing suit and nude, along with the rest of us – in our own skimpy thongs and bikinis, and nude. At the end of her show, Sam groaned as he saw pictures of himself – in a knee chest position on the coffee table, and lying there, having dozens of needles inserted into his bum.

Then, we watched Linda's rendition of the trip, which included many of the same things. Both my friends took some good underwater shots, which captured fish and sea turtles, and the sea cave where Sam had proposed to me. We all agreed that – for many reasons – it had been a very special trip.

We went upstairs to the kitchen to get sodas, and decided to test the temperature of the jacuzzi. We dipped our toes in the swirling water, but it wasn't hot enough to offset the cold weather. The backyard no longer looked green, no flowers in the beds, and no leaves on the trees.

Linda announced, "I'm getting chilled again. Let's go in the sauna." That sounded good to all of us, so I gave everyone a robe, and we all went to our rooms to undress. Less than ten minutes later, we were sitting in the dark red illumination of the sauna, the warmth now seeping into our bodies.

Sam went out to turn up the heat, then came back in, and lay down on the top bench. Linda sat up there on the other end, while Julie and I took the lower bench. I couldn't get over Linda's new 'look', her body now curvy but trim.

Before I could compliment her, Linda said, quietly, "I've been on a couple of dates, recently." We were all ears, and she continued, "And *not* with the shlub!" We laughed. "Actually, I've gone out with three guys, in the three months we've been back."

Under her breath, we heard a quiet, "That's a record!"

Linda told us about the guys, and they all sounded interesting. It seemed that our love lives were picking up – for all of us, except Julie. And, we would have expected that she would have been more sought by guys than the rest of us.

Sam asked us if Chinese take-out would be OK tonight, as he was cooking a big dinner tomorrow. After we'd cooled down in the shower, Sam brought the menu into the shower room, and we sat on the chaises, selecting the dishes.

As usual, we ended-up with way too much, Sam insisting that we get a few appetizers, and soup, as well as the obligatory beef, pork, shrimp and duck dishes; and the vegetable fried rice ... and pan-fried noodles. Sam smiled, "You guys can probably dress pretty casual for dinner."

Then, Sam took a quick shower, and went upstairs to dress. We stayed in for another two cycles, casually bathing each other in-between. I suspected that Sam had something planned for this evening, and that he was hinting that the 'casual' attire be *really* casual.

So my friends and I decided to wear the t-shirts we had brought back from Europe – Julie and Linda both having brought those for the weekend stay. And, we decided that black thongs might also be appropriate.

When Sam returned with an armful of bags, the aroma of Chinese cooking pervaded the kitchen. He asked what we all wanted to drink, and Julie pointed at the pineapple on the counter, and suggested Mai Tai's; so Sam made a pitcher, as we unpacked the boxes of food and set the kitchen table.

I had already begun setting the dining room table for our big Christmas dinner tomorrow, and the kitchen was a cozy setting for the four of us. It seemed strange to have a get-together without Kathy, and I wondered how she was doing in the nice warm Kauai weather.

After dinner, we retreated to the playroom, and sat around the coffee table with Diet Cokes. Sam was smiling, and I could see that he was excited to introduce whatever 'game' he had planned for this evening.

Sam began, "You must be wondering why I invited you here, today ..."

Linda broke in, "To challenge us, again?"

Then, Julie laughed, "To give us Christmas presents?"

Sam shouted, "Ha! You're *both* right!" We had bought some small presents for Julie, Linda, Fiona, Justin, and Alex, but I didn't think that was all that Sam would be giving us.

He pointed to the Christmas tree in the corner of the playroom that we'd decorated, "You'll notice that there are some 'presents' under the tree." I turned around and looked; I hadn't seen those there before.

Sam looked at each of us, then continued, "We'll take turns, each taking a box, and opening it. You can either use what's inside on someone you choose ... or have that person use it on you." Now, we had a good idea of what we would be doing this evening.

"And, maybe we should have Kelly warm us all up?" Julie and Linda looked at me, and shrugged. It was true that my arm hadn't gotten much exercise, lately.

Now, my friends were looking at Sam, and I made an executive decision, "OK, Sam. You're first." I sat in the middle of the couch, and Sam draped himself over my lap. I chuckled, "I think 100 hard and fast spanks should be sufficient, don't you?"

Sam nodded and, now being 'in the role', replied, "Yes, Miss." I lifted his tee onto his back, looked down at Sam's thonged rear, and rubbed his bum a little.

Then, I gave Sam a spanking like I'd done in London for Elena: His grunts and squeals indicated that he was shocked, and – glancing at Julie and Linda – my friends appeared shocked, also. But I had to 'practice' for my upcoming domme course, and didn't want to disappoint Sam ... or my friends.

Sam bounced around on my lap as I spanked him, but quieted down nicely, as his bum reddened. I was done in less than two minutes. As Sam got off my lap, I called, "Julie!" Sam rubbed his bum and took the chair, as Julie took his place across my lap. I decided to be consistent, and give Julie '100 of the best' with my hand.

As Sam had done, Julie squealed a couple of times, and was panting by the time her spanking was finished.

"Linda!" Now, Linda was over my lap, and she took her spanking without making a sound, although she appeared to be grinding on my leg by the time I gave her the last spank.

Sam asked, "So who wants to give Kelly *her* spanking?"

I was surprised that Linda volunteered, and even more surprised at the hard spanking she gave me.

When she sat down next to me, Sam further explained the rules of his little game. "There are only two boxes for each of us, so you may want to take the simple things for yourself, if you want to avoid the more serious implements."

He continued, "And, if you pick two of the same type of thing – like butt plugs or tawses – you'll need to take one yourself and give the other to someone else."

Then, Sam laughed, and said, "And I do plan to offer you a real 'present': I'll give you myself, to satisfy you or cooperate with whatever you ask of me ... or do to me. I was planning to offer you that in the morning ... an early Christmas morning present."

With that, Sam suggested that Julie take the first 'present'. She got up and walked to the tree, then brought back a small square box; it was too small for a paddle or cane, and even looked too short to fit a butt plug. When she opened the box, she groaned: It was a belt, coiled up. And, underneath the belt was a small slip of paper that read, '12 strokes'.

"I guess I'll give this to Linda." Linda shrugged, then got on her knees on the couch, and put her head down on her folded arms on the back of the couch. Julie stood, folded the belt over, and gave Linda twelve medium strokes.

We could see the red stripes on Linda's butt, but once again she had taken the spanking without moving or making a sound. It was now her turn, so she went to the tree and picked a box that was a foot square, and two inches thick – most likely the Ping-Pong paddle.

But when she opened the box, and removed the wrapping paper, Linda found the large, bumpy butt plug. She held it up, and pondered it for a moment, then said, resignedly, "I'll take this ... and Sam can insert it."

Sam smiled, and got out of the chair, then pointed to it, and Linda took off her thong, then got into position, her knees against the sides of the chair, and her butt high in the air, anus relaxed.

Sam went to his desk, and got a small tube of KY, then lubed the plug, and slowly inserted it into Linda's rear, playing with it for a couple of minutes before shoving it all the way in.

Then, Sam went to the tree and picked a box. As he walked back, he informed us, "I don't remember what's in every box ..." We trusted him, and he opened the box to find the metal anal beads. Under the beads, it said, 'And 25 jumping jacks'.

He smiled, then said, "I pick Julie ... and I'll let her decide who will get the beads." Julie decided to take them – probably a good idea, since they were likely one of the easiest 'challenges'. She took off her thong, and stepped over to the chair.

Linda was still in position the couch, and asked, "Can you take this thing out of me, now?" Sam looked at me, and I nodded; then he pulled the plug out of Linda, and she took it to the bathroom for cleaning.

Julie got into the chair position, and Sam lubricated her with a finger, then popped each of the heavy balls into her rectum. Julie stood, walked to the center of the room, and did twenty five nice jumping jacks – the beads clicking a rapid rhythm from within her rear.

Julie sat down, the beads still inside her, and I walked to the tree to select a box. There was only one long, thin tube in the pile, and I assumed it was the cane. Nobody deserved to be caned on Christmas eve ... except possibly Sam. I decided to pick this, and considered whether I should take it, maybe letting Julie cane me.

But when I opened the tube, and slid out the contents, it was two syringes, with needles attached, already pre-loaded with 3cc of saline each, and a note saying 'Simultaneously'.

Sam had promised my friends that they wouldn't have to take any more shots, so I decided to take the shots, and let Linda give them to me, denying Sam the chance to stick anyone with needles. I took off my thong, then lay across her lap, and Linda swabbed me, then inserted one needle and the other.

I turned my head toward Sam, and smiled, as I watched him stare at my butt as Linda injected me. It really wasn't a big deal, and I wondered why so many people were afraid of getting shots in the butt. It was over quickly, although I knew that Linda had left the needles in me for a while after the injections were finished.

Julie took another box – this one the biggest under the tree – a 12-inch cube. When she opened it, she howled, "Perfect!"

Then, she looked up, "This is for Sam," and pulled out the harness and dildo of the strap-on. She put it on, and lubed it, while Sam got into the chair, *his* butt now high in the air, awaiting Julie's rude intrusion. Or, perhaps not so rude, as Julie asked Sam if he would like to wear a condom.

I went into the downstairs bathroom, and brought Julie a condom, Sam now already hard from her stroking. She put it on Sam, then maneuvered the strap-on and entered him slowly with the large dildo. When I saw the string hanging out of her butt, I realized that Julie still had the anal beads inside her.

Julie reached under Sam and stroked him, as she moved the dildo in and out of his rear, which also had the effect of stimulating her. It took a few minutes, but Julie shrieked as she came, then made a series of short cries, as she continued thrusting against Sam until he came.

When Julie and Sam returned from their cleanup in the bathroom, Linda brought a box from under the tree – about a six-inch cube. I visualized a butt plug inside, but it turned out to be the tawse, folded around inside the box.

She put her hand between her legs, finally deciding, "I'll let Sam tawse me. It says three hard strokes." Linda stared at the tawse for what seemed a long time.

Linda looked at Sam, and then to me, "I'm not sure how to ask this … but we're supposed to be honest with each other. Could I please ask Sam for my 'real' present after he tawses me?" We laughed, and Sam – of course – readily agreed to whatever Linda had in mind.

Sam suggested that Linda take her tawsing over the end of the love seat, her legs on the cushion, and hands on the floor; she would be less likely to reach back with her hands.

Linda duly got into position, and Sam administered three of the hardest strokes I'd seen him deliver, the sound of leather impacting Linda's bottom resonating around the room. Both Julie and I jumped slightly off the couch each time a stroke was delivered.

Then, Sam led Linda to the bed, where she straddled the corner, and he entered her, as she brought both hands under herself. It didn't take long for Linda to climax, which was probably a good thing, as shortly after, Sam came explosively. Linda stood, facing Sam, and they hugged, as Sam rubbed Linda's bum.

Linda went to pee, and Sam accompanied her, so he could get cleaned up. When they returned, Linda hugged me, "Thank you for loaning me your fiancé."

It was Sam's turn, and he selected a box that contained twenty needles. I gave him a dirty look: I was certain that Sam knew exactly which box that had been. He looked around, and asked, "Will anybody volunteer?"

Sam was pushing again, and I decided to take the needles to save my friends. Then, I chuckled: Maybe Sam should insert all twenty needles in himself?

But, before I had said anything, Julie volunteered. "Are you sure, Julie? I'll take those, if you want." Julie shook her head, then smiled, "Well, I *would* take my present from *you* … if you feel like it."

Julie asked me to sit in the chair, and she put her legs over the arms of the chair, so that her clit was well-positioned within tongue-reach. I began my oral attention on her, as Sam swabbed her bum, and began inserting needles. Julie had already experienced getting nearly this many needles in Hawaii.

There was moaning and groaning, sounds of ecstasy and pain. Julie was also quick, her orgasm electric, as my tongue continued swirling around her clit, slower and slower, until it was not moving at all, just putting pressure under Julie's hood.

It was a lot of needles, but not as many as Sam had taken in Hawaii; or I had taken when Sam did 'needle art' on my backside. Now, Sam was pulling needles out, one after the other, as Julie pushed back toward him, and lowered her head to me. We kissed softly.

Julie sat on the couch, as I walked to the tree and eyed the last box. It was one of the larger, flatter boxes, and I found the clear Plexiglas school paddle inside, with a note that said 'twelve swats'. Looking at Sam, I smiled, "I think it's your turn for a little butt warming, now."

Sam frowned, but he had to expect that at least one of us would be spanking him; and it might as well be me. He got back into the chair, and I stepped behind him. The thick plastic paddle wasn't nearly as serious as the thicker wooden one, and I decided to see how well Sam would take these in front of my friends.

I swung the paddle hard, and it slapped against Sam's butt with a loud 'CRACK!', evoking a short yelp. This implement was much more of a stinger than a bruiser, so I continued the hard swats, Sam staying in position nicely, and only whimpering a bit near the end.

Sam hadn't bought a dessert for tonight, but insisted on opening a bottle of California sparkling wine. None of us objected. We toasted to Christmas, the New Year, and good friends; *really* good friends!

It was when Sam suggested that we all get into bed here in the playroom that the three of us decided that we were tired, and would rather get some real sleep. We walked up to our rooms, and Sam tucked in each of my friends, and kissed them goodnight.

Then, he tucked us in, and told me goodnight. As he spooned me, he whispered, "You'll get *your* present tomorrow morning." I hoped so. And, of course, Sam didn't disappoint me.

I spent Christmas morning making breakfast for the girls, and prepping the dinner: Prime rib, Dauphinoise potato gratin, and garlic-sautéed fresh spinach. I also made a salad with Green Goddess dressing, and baked my own cherry cobbler.

Then, for good measure, I made deviled eggs, cheese puffs, and a red pepper hummus with baked pita chips as appetizers. The girls were helping, and we were eating along the way.

Alex, Fiona and Justin arrived in the early afternoon, and we introduced Julie and Linda. We carried the appetizers down to the playroom, and I opened a nice bottle of wine.

Fiona and Justin updated us on their first six months of married life, and Alex was happy that her foundation now had several new benefactors.

We told (or re-told) Julie and Linda about our trip to Toronto, and Kelly suggested that I play the 'show' that I'd put together on the giant screen.

I realized that Julie and Linda had only seen the scene when Kelly spanked me during the wedding reception at Justin's club; they had not seen our pictures and videos from Niagra Falls, the jet boat trip, or indoor sky-diving with Justin and Fiona.

When we'd finished the show, we got onto the subject of our trip to Kauai. Kelly, Julie and Linda were a Gatling gun of experiences we'd had – from the snorkeling, to the Zodiac and helicopter rides, to the hiking and the camping.

By popular demand, we decided to continue with the Kauai show, which we'd been planning for after dinner. I looked at Kelly, "We could always share the compilation we showed in Kauai, for our after-dinner entertainment."

Kelly didn't think much of the idea – Julie and Linda having already seen it, and Alex probably not interested. I cued-up the Kauai show, and opened another bottle of wine. I went up to the kitchen, put the prime rib in the pre-heated oven, and set the timer.

In contrast to the show that Kelly's parents had seen, this one was the original – with uncut scenes, from the girls bent over the couch to our 'ritual' on the sand dune on Honopu Beach. Alex took it in stride, only shaking her head slowly a couple of times, and not commenting.

When the show ended, and most of the appetizers had been consumed, Kelly suggested we go in the jacuzzi. We'd been in the cave of the playroom more than two hours.

We provided robes for everyone (except me, as we had only six of them), and we undressed – Fiona and Justin in the playroom, Alex in the downstairs bathroom, and Julie, Linda, Kelly and I up in the pool room.

The jacuzzi was perfect in the cold weather, and the seven of us fit comfortably. The waterfall was turned off, and only Henk would be crazy enough to dive into the freezing pool.

The conversation continued with Justin telling some stories from the latest special events at his club – especially Halloween. And the girls telling Fiona and Alex about Kathy, and her recent love affair with Christian on Kauai.

Justin pointed, and we saw the full moon rising above the house. I moved over to Alex, and whispered an offer to give her a massage. She smiled, and whispered, "Not tonight, Sam. But I've decided to take you up on your offer of a massage with a happy ending, some other time."

We ate in the dining room, the dinner being simple, but satisfying. I opened two bottles of Margaux, which we finished, along with most of the food.

We never made it downstairs again, no more video shows. We ate the cobbler in the dining room, and exchanged small Christmas presents. Alex, Fiona and Justin took their leave before 9PM, and the girls and I went down to the playroom, undressed, and got under the covers of the big bed.

The idea had been to play around a little, but after a few hugs and kisses, we all faded. It was nearly midnight when I woke up, Julie and Linda snoring lightly next to me. Kelly turned onto her side, and raised her head, "Shall we put them to bed, or leave them here?"

We decided to tuck Julie and Linda in, and go upstairs to our own bed. Kelly and I had revived enough to make love, but were soon drifting off to sleep. Christmas was over, but sugar plums were still dancing in my head.

Kelly and I were awake early on Saturday, and we put on robes and went down to the playroom to say good morning to Julie and Linda. Amazingly, they were still in bed, still nude, and talking quietly. I whispered to Kelly, and she smiled and nodded.

We took off our robes, and climbed into bed, under the covers, Kelly going down on Julie, and me going down on Linda. Her friends giggled, but soon became sexually serious, as their legs fell apart, and the sound of heavy breathing filtered through the sheets into our claustrophobic space.

We all knew each other well, now, including sensual and sexual preferences, and both of Kelly's friends climaxed with high-pitched squeals. We all lay together for a while longer, savoring the mutual friendships we had developed.

I couldn't believe that it was already New Year's eve. We were celebrating at the French restaurant again, indulging in their special five-course wine-pairing dinner, but Sam insisted on starting with a half-bottle of an expensive French Champagne.

After we'd toasted, Sam put down his glass, and took mine out of my hand and put it down next to his. Then, he scooted out of the booth, and gently pulled me to the edge of the black tufted seat.

Glancing around, he got down on his knee, my hands in his. It was like a dream, and I couldn't imagine what Sam had in mind, as he'd already proposed to me in Kauai. This time, his eyes were not wet, but his gaze transfixed me with its seriousness.

"Kelly, if I had not proposed to you on Kauai, I would have done it now: You've graduated, it's New Year's eve, and we love each other more than ever." Tears were forming in *my* eyes.

"So I'm going to *re*-propose to you; give you another chance. But I can only tell you again: I'm deeply in love with you, and I want to spend the rest of my life with you." He squeezed my hand, and then reached up and pulled my head down to his.

Our kiss seemed electric – I flashed on our kiss at the top of the Eiffel Tower – and Sam held me tight as the heat of our mouths joined in an inferno of pure love.

Out of the corner of my eye, I noticed George walking toward us, then stopping suddenly; Sam didn't notice, or didn't care: He looked into my eyes, and asked, "Kelly, will you marry me ... again?"

It had come out funny, and I chuckled. Then, I held his head, gave him a peck on the lips, and answered, "Of course, Sam. I love you, too, and I want us to be together; always." We kissed again, then I pulled Sam back into the booth, and we picked up our Champagne flutes and toasted, once more.

After a respectable amount of time, George came to our table, and gave Sam a questioning look and smiled. Sam nodded, "Yes, George: I proposed to Kelly." Then, he chuckled, "Actually, I re-proposed to her ... in case she didn't believe me the first time."

"Congratulations, Mr. Johnson ... and Kelly!"

Sam shook his head, and corrected George, "This is *Doctor* Kelly Walsh. The future Doctor Kelly Johnson." Then, Sam frowned and looked at me, "Or, the future Doctor Kelly Walsh-Johnson." I hadn't even thought about the issue of changing my name.

George shook my hand, then leaned over and whispered something to Sam, before disappearing toward the kitchen.

The dinner was incredible – again – and it wasn't until we'd tasted several dishes that George came over and explained, "The chef wanted you to taste some of his other creations." Then, he winked, "And he's making a special dessert that takes time, so we need to slow your dinner."

That was fine with us, as we were already getting stuffed. Our wine tasting was special, also, as George left a bottle of each of the selections on our table, rather than pouring a small glass.

When the dessert was served, Sam and I made a resolution to continue running every day. It was a '*Bombe Alaska*', the chef's homemade ice cream, surrounded by cake, with a browned meringue making a large mound – it looked like a breast.

George splashed rum over the meringue and lit it, blue flames dancing up and around the mound. Then, George brought two brandy snifters and poured a dark liquid. "This is our best Cognac, sir ... and Madame."

We were already floating, in more ways than one. Now, memories of the past year flowed past my mind's eye: It had seemed to me that I'd been at school all the time; but we'd made time for quite a few special experiences.

There was our experience with Fiona and Justin, then their engagement party, and the wedding in Toronto, and our Niagra Falls experience; Sam's birthday party with my friends, and then their big submission challenge; our first anniversary, Linda's birthday, and Julie's birthday; and, of course the incredible trip to Kauai.

Then my mind drifted to the future, mostly unknown; I wondered where we'd be a year from now. But some of our future was becoming clearer: We would work hard on the business; I would take the domme course; we'd set a date for a wedding – whether or not it would actually happen next year.

And, there was the possibility that Kathy might get married; in fact, it was still possible that all my friends would get married before me. It didn't matter: Sam and I had made a commitment to each other through our actions a long time ago.

We'd also demonstrated, through our recent experiences, that we would continue our open lifestyle, and our fetish interests. I didn't know if Sam would become my 'slave' ... or I become his ... and, again, it didn't matter. We savored our time with each other, and every new experience we had together.

And, somehow, we continued to have new experiences – in love and in life, building a shared future together. The sharing of our bodies was nothing. The sharing of our friends was nothing. It was the sharing of our minds, our psyches, that had cemented our deep love for each other.

Sam and I went home and made love passionately and fully, utilizing all of our senses – tasting the sweetness, feeling the tenderness, looking into each other's eyes.

Gazing into the future ...

Thank you for reading Book 7 of the Experiences series. If you enjoyed it, please take a moment to leave a review at your favorite retailer. And, if you liked this story, you'll LOVE the continuation in Book 8: Domme Experience!

- Simone Freier

Discover other titles by Simone Freier

Experiences Series Book 1: Origins of a Fetish

Experiences Series Book 2: First Experience

Experiences Series Book 3: Weekend Experience

Experiences Series Book 4: Birthday Experience

Experiences Series Book 5: European Experience

Experiences Series Book 6: Friends' Experience

Experiences Series Book 7: Island Experience

Experiences Series Book 8: Domme Experience

Connect with the Author

Follow me on Twitter: http://twitter.com/SimoneFreier

Friend me on Facebook: http://facebook.com/SimoneFreierAuthor

Subscribe to my blog: http://SimoneFreier.com

Favorite me at Smashwords: http://smashwords.com/SimoneFreier